ALL DEBTS ARE NOW PAID

by

R.L. NAPOLITANO

ALL DEBTS ARE NOW PAID

R.L. NAPOLITANO

This is a work of fiction. Much of it is a product of the author's imagination and used fictitiously. Any resemblance to anyone living or dead is purely coincidental.

FIRST EDITION

MARCH 2026

Also by the author:

THE TWINS

GIRVAN

LEOPOLD CHRIST

THE SONS OF ABRAHAM

THE DISAPPOINTMENT OF ANNIE BROOKS

THE UNIVERSAL KILLER

THE LIGHTHOUSE KEEPER

Cover Design

CHRISTINA GEDICK

ISBN 979-8-9908044-4-9

ALL DEBTS ARE NOW PAID

To the friends of my youth who I shared wonderful times with on the fields, streets, and playgrounds of Everett. And special thanks to those who occupied the steps of the Horace Mann those years of endless Summer nights.
Ed, Charlie, Ernie, (3) Johns, (3) Steves, Tommy, Ralph, Richie, Mo, Sam, Peggy, Chickie, Roland, Chrissy, Linda, Ro, Mary, with apologies for those forgotten.

Table of Contents

PROLOGUE

I stand over him in the cold light of an overhead kitchen fixture, staring to see if the gun in his hand moves an inch. But it doesn't. My finger on the trigger relaxes, but the Adrenaline doesn't ebb. It's been my experience that dead men don't have the ability to continue a confrontation. This is my third experience.

"Call the police," I say, still not taking my eyes off the dead man.

I hear her slowly moving behind me, lifting the receiver beside the overhead cabinet off the wall and dialing 9-1-1. Nothing to do now but wait.

For my own peace of mind, I bend down and feel for a pulse at his neck. There is none, and I slump back onto a kitchen chair, laying my gun on the table. Then I look at Eileen, shivering as she stands there, leaning against the wall that leads to the dining room. She's wearing an off white nightgown that reaches mid thigh, mostly covering the more interesting parts of her anatomy. The sleeves aren't long enough to cover the ugly bruise on her right forearm. Her legs are bare, and the knee of the right one has a nasty scrape. Her long hair is messed up, partially obscuring the right side of her face, but I can see the marks on her neck, bruised and coloring. The shock and strain of the violence is evident in eyes that stare at the floor. Her lips, the first thing I had noticed when first seeing her at Harry's four months before, were pressed tightly together.

"Why don't you get some clothes on, baby," I say. "Cops will find it hard to concentrate on their job with you standing there like that."

Eileen looks over at me, then walks slowly through the dining room to the bedroom, coming back a minute later to silently sit across from me and wait for the police.

There's a silence in the kitchen now that's even more unsettling than the sound of gunfire. In that silence, I can't help but wonder how it all came to this. Why it came to this. Or was it simply inevitable.

I've noticed that things in life, important things, happen to you in two different ways. One way that things happen, is in an instant. You don't see it coming, and then, wham!, it happens. A car comes out of nowhere and slams into your car, and you spend months in rehab, your life never the same again. Your toe catches on something and you tumble down a flight of stairs, bones cracking with each step, and for the rest of your life your body aches and you know in advance when it's going to rain. In a split second, a weak hitting infielder hits a ball beyond the ivy covered wall in Pittsburgh, and the Pirates beat the Yankees in the series, and you're out five hundred bucks, the rent isn't paid, and what furniture you had is out on a sidewalk. A telephone rings, and a voice you've never heard before informs you your dad died. A doctor sits across from you and solemnly says he has bad news. One second familiar calm, the next, chaos and grief.

But things can come at you slowly, too. Like looking at a tidal wave in the distance that is approaching the dock where you stand. Or the lava from a volcanic eruption that flows red, devouring everything in its path, slowly making its way towards where you are watching. You are powerless to stop it. There is absolutely nothing you can do to alter the outcome. The destruction is inevitable. You aren't even a participant in the drama at the outset. Just a spectator caught up in the approaching chaos.

But, sometimes, the spectator becomes a participant, engulfed in the drama through circumstances beyond their control. Like an onrushing wall of water, propelled by forces that shook the ground beneath it, sending it hurtling towards disaster, sometimes, when that happens, that slow journey to the inevitable, death is the final result.

On a quiet street in Winthrop, Massachusetts, the body of a man lies crumbled on a kitchen floor, his life taken by a bullet, and it never should have come to this. But it did. And while the end came quickly, the reason for the bullet unfolded slowly. It began months ago. Perhaps, years before that. Events that began long before the ten seconds of violence that ended his life. Things that happened long before I became involved. Everyday occurrences, that once begun, took on a life of their own, and moved forward like a tidal wave. Gathering speed, power and urgency, until the final outcome.

So, now, I must deal with that outcome, and with the tsunami it will surely create. Another maelstrom may now be unleashed, with one event piled upon another. One action, creating a reaction, causing a reaction. No doubt this tsunami will also lead to another death. Probably mine.

Shit.

I need a drink.

A drink?

Isn't that what got me into this mess?

1

PAUL

"Quiet tonight," I said as I slid onto the padded stool.

It was always quiet on Thursday nights in Harry's Bar after Labor Day, and it was probably a dumb thing to say. But I figured, as a way of beginning a conversation for two men nearing fifty, it was more mature than asking how it was hanging. I'm fairly certain, in the future, I'll just nod a hello, and we'll see where that takes us. It won't be a problem. Harry Mills is a natural born talker. He can converse intelligently on almost any subject, and enjoys doing it. As a bartender, that comes in handy. But like any good bartender, he knows when to end a conversation. Just as he knows which patrons not to begin one with.

"That the best you got?" Harry said to me, frowning at my effort.

"Been a long day, and I napped through the news. Something happen today I should know about?"

"East Germany opened the gates. Looks like Reagan telling Gorbachev to tear down the wall a while back is finally happening." Harry filled a tall one from a tap and placed it in front of me.

I frowned. "Anything that concerns me directly?" There's something special about that first taste of cold beer after a tough day of aggravations. Second and third aren't bad either.

"It just has to be all about you, doesn't it?" Harry said. "Call your bookie. Bird's back and looking healthy. Might just be another banner hanging in the Garden next year. Remember, you heard it here first."

"Stick with hockey," I said, pleased with my phrasing. "What you know about basketball is what you read in the rags. Detroit or Chicago, and L A. Everyone else gets a long summer."

I looked around the near empty room.

"Sal been around?" I asked.

Harry shook his head. "Been two months. I'm telling you, Paul, something went down. Maybe this time he screwed with the wrong people. I'm hearing it's healthier not to ask about Sal."

"Sal can take care of himself," I said. "He'll show up one of these days." I said it, but not sure I believed it. Especially since Sal had a hard time taking care of himself.

Harry heard a lot of stuff. He didn't always share, and, if he did, it was prefaced with "maybe" or "I'm hearing", and never who he's hearing it from. Some of the clientele at Harry's Bar had a habit of running off at the mouth after a few drinks. It was never a good idea to repeat anything they said. But if you did, the names of those quoted were never shared.

As Harry went to the far end of the bar to mix a martini for a middle aged guy in a business suit, sitting with a younger guy, also in a business suit, I scanned the place again. It's the first thing I did when I walked in, but now I took my time.

Half way between me and the suits sat Rose, a half empty glass of red wine in front of her, an ashtray with three lip stained filters beside it. Sitting beside Rose was a regular named Mike, and the two were discussing something I would have no interest in. Rose was also a regular. She lived in a house within walking distance of the bar. Sometimes Rose needed a companion on the walk home, and Harry always made sure someone escorted her safely there. I'd been selected for the task several times in the distant past. Unlike some of the other mugs, I had no desire to enter the front door after it was opened, despite Rose's offers.

Rose had been one of Harry's first customers when he bought the place in 1971. That was eighteen years ago. It wasn't hard to imagine Rose had been an attractive woman at one time - she still looked good - and, while Harry never said it, I had the impression that the two had something going on back then. If you believed the rumors, over the years Harry has had something going on with a lot of women that came into his bar. He never talked about his love life, and I never inquired, nor did I care.

Along the far wall, beyond a dozen tables, there were six cozy booths. In the one in the far corner, a man and a woman sat leaning over the table towards each other in conversation. She was doing the talking, he did a lot of nodding in between sips of the drink in front of him. In the booth in the opposite corner, a woman sat by herself, smoke rising from a cigarette she held in one hand, a glass rising in the other hand to her lips. I couldn't help noticing they were fine looking lips. Painted red, like a Revere fire engine. Demanding attention, like a hook and ladder with the siren blaring.

Two tables in the middle of the room were each occupied by three guys I recognized as regulars, beers in front of them, eyes watching the Bruins playing the first game of the pre-season against Pittsburgh in what could end up being a Stanley Cup run. One thing you could count on in Harry's Bar, if the Bruins were playing, the game was on the TV. In fact, it was because of the Boston Bruins that Harold Mills ended up owning the bar.

It's a long story, and not a bad one, but the short version of one man's madness is pretty simple. Harold Mills worked for an investment firm in Southern California. San Diego to be exact. One early March day he flies into Logan to hear a pitch from a guy looking to build condos at the beginning of the one way boulevard that runs the stretch of Revere Beach, and needing investors to back him.

That night the guy treats Harry to dinner and tickets to a Bruins game, although, the guy says, he could get tickets for the Celtics the next night if Harry preferred.

In the telling of the story, Harry, who is a Black man, says he wasn't offended. Told the guy he loves hockey and has season tickets to the San Diego Gulls. That night he got to see the Big Bad Bruins in person, and Harry Mills was in hockey heaven.

The next day, Harry toured the proposed site for the hi-rise condo and walked the rest of the beach. It's March, so nothing is open, and it's chilly, but he gets a quick feel of the area; the pizza joints, amusements, arcades, the rides. Two thoughts went through his mind as he walked along the street that day. First, what a great place this must be in the summer, and second, what a shame it was all going to go away in a very short time. The property was just too valuable for roller-coasters and merry-go-rounds. And he was right.

All that stuff is gone now from the country's first public beach, and the high rise condos are going up one after the other.

Anyways, on his walk, after a roast beef sandwich at Kelly's, he saw an empty building with a for sale sign. Over the next two months, with two more trips across the country, and a few more Bruins games under his belt, Harold Mills left a career that was paying him six figures a year and buys the building, with the idea that the place will make a great bar. He was going to be a Black guy from California owning a bar in Revere, Massachusetts, and no one back then had the common courtesy to tell him he was crazy. I would have, had I known him.

Placing a martini in front of the older suit, Harry moved to his other customers, picking up empties and requests for refills. The martini drinker's suit was dark gray and definitely not off a rack in Sears. Expensive. Certainly beyond my modest means. His hair was mostly silver, fashionably long but neat. The hand that held the glass to his lips sported a gold bracelet on the attached wrist, and gold cufflinks below the tailored sleeve. As he lowered his glass, he smiled at something the younger guy said and, as his hand moved from the glass, it lightly grazed the younger guy's hand. I noticed the younger guy didn't seem to mind.

Whatever.

I'm noticing more and more people saying that now-a-days. 'Whatever.' Someone actually said it to me today. I wanted to smack her. I didn't. I mean you can't smack people for giving you attitude to a simple question. Well, you can't smack women, anyways. She was nineteen, wearing ripped jeans that her belly hung over and a well-worn V-neck sweater that barely contained massive breasts. On her feet were three hundred dollar Michael Jordan sneakers. I probably should have made an exception for her.

Harry was back and mixing a few drinks in front of me. “How's the investigation going?” he asked, tipping a bottle of vodka.

“About the same,” I replied. I've been hired to find a runaway daughter. I've had three conversations with the parents. One in my office when they hired me, the other two in their huge home in Lynnfield. When I find the kid, I may do her a favor and hand her a Greyhound ticket for Buffalo.

“She's still in the area, I'm sure of that, and still safe. Friends are watching out for her. Or so I believe. But that won't last forever, and it won't take long before the wolves start circling. It's not easy finding people who don't want to be found, Harry. Especially kids. They can sleep on a different couch every night and it doesn't bother them at all. And kids don't rat them out to a middle-aged guy.”

“It's an unkind world out there,” Harry said, like I needed reminding.

“I'll find her,” said I. And I will. “This is what's going to happen. I'm going to ask some kid where Dani is. He's going to tell me to go screw myself. Hasn't seen her in a year. Doesn't know anything. Then I'm going to give him one of my cards. Tell him to call me if he hears anything. Then the icing. I tell him there's a thousand dollar reward. The parents are really concerned.

"The kid won't care, or believe, that the parents are concerned. But when his supply of whatever drug he's on this month runs out, he'll remember the grand and he'll drop a dime. Loyalty and attitude aren't strong traits when the shakes begin."

Harry only nodded. He's a bar owner. He's seen it all.

I had spent the better part of the day in Charlestown chasing down a few leads that led nowhere. Sometimes you get lucky. A kid smart enough to know the girl's in over her head does the right thing and gives her up. Most of the time, the runaway isn't hanging with smart kids.

Dani Gallagher took off ten days ago. The second time she's done it. She's seventeen. Going to be eighteen in two months when she could legally do anything she wants. But she takes off now. Last year, a junior in high school, she's top of her class. Ten months later, the parents are worried she'll be Bonnie Parker if I don't find her quick.

The father is a broker in Boston in the family firm. Knows everyone. Plays golf with some of the Red Sox and Bruins. He's embarrassed by the whole situation. Would like it handled discreetly and quickly without calling in favors from his friends in law enforcement, whose job it is to find the under aged girl, and who should be notified.

The step-mom is disgusted with the kid. And angry. Six months ago when the kid took off the first time, mommy almost came apart at the seams, not knowing what had happened to the kid. She was a mess and hated what she called the 'fake empathy and concern from the country club crowd'. If word got out, she said to me while sitting in her home on a sofa the size of the Queen Mary, that her daughter had fled once again, the shame of it would probably force her to cancel her membership.

"Mr. Costa," she said to me two days ago, after draining a tall glass of liquid and escorting me to the door,"when you find Dani tell her to come home. Tell her I have a suitcase packed for her, with two thousand dollars in an envelope inside. On her eighteenth birthday,

I'll call the cab."

"Harry," I said, "it's times like this I don't regret not having kids. You know what I mean?"

"Sure," he said. "I never wanted any. Especially a daughter. Some guy looks cross eyed at her, and I'd have to kill him. Wife and kids were never in the plan."

"You had a plan?"

"Nah," he said running a draft and putting it in front of me. "But if I did, it would not have included a family."

"I don't want this," I said pushing the glass a few inches back towards him. "I'm ready to head out."

"Lady paid for it," he said, as he lifted a tray of beers for the hockey viewing tables.

"Lady?"

Harry lifted his chin towards the booth in the corner.

"Her name's Eileen," he said as he moved away from the bar, just as the two tables erupted in cheering a goal.

I turned on my stool to look at the woman, spending more time on the entire package than just the shade and shape of her lips. I was going to acknowledge her generosity. A tip of the head, a rise of the mug, but she wasn't looking at me. She sat quite still, staring at some unknown spot on the table, appearing to be a million miles away from a bar on the beach.

From the angle I had of her sitting in the booth, I couldn't get a feel for her age. But I'm a private eye, so I notice things, my brain does quick calculations, and opinions are formed. Her hair was dark, the length of it resting comfortably on the white turtleneck sweater she wore. Her slacks were black, casual, unlike her black spiked shoes. She was trim. Long, thin fingers of her left hand were curled about her martini glass. A rock the size of one of those balls Arnold Palmer swipes at for money occupied the ring finger of that hand. Without any thought at all, my brain calculated she was early to mid thirties, but could pass for thirty. A longer thought process, predicated by the rock, took more time to resolve. The argument raged for a full minute. Finally, the lips won out. I made my way to where she sat.

I stood beside her table. As if coming out of a trance, or a hypnotic spell performed at an upscale club by a famous hypnotist, after several seconds, she looked up at me. The eyes were green. Both of them. And they possessed a depth a man could have difficulty climbing out of, if he ever realized he had to.

"Thanks for the beer," I said. "I thought maybe, when I looked over, we knew one another, but I can see now we've never met. I'd remember if we had. My name's Paul."

She smiled. It was a sad smile.

"I've never done that before. Sent someone a drink. I saw you sitting there. You looked like you were deep in thought and rather lost. Pretty much like I'm feeling tonight. A kindred spirit, I thought. Perhaps an acknowledgment of his existence might lessen his burden."

She gave an almost imperceptible shrug and the smile became a little sadder.

"I don't know. It was just a spur of the moment thing."

Like I said, I'm a private eye, paid to notice things. I noticed she seemed like someone who, a while ago, wanted to be alone, but no longer did. So I stood by her table while a few awkward seconds of quiet passed. Her smile faded, but in her eyes I saw need.

"Would you like to join me, Paul?" she asked.

I looked down at her a second or two, noticed the diamond catching a reflection of the dim lighting in the corner. Despite that, I sat.

"I'm Eileen," she said and reached her hand across the table. "Eileen Landry."

I took those long, manicured, red tipped fingers in my paw and shook them gently. "Paul Costa. Pleased to meet you Eileen Landry. What brings you to Harry's Bar this evening?"

If she wanted to talk, I'd make it easy for her.

She gave a slight shake of her head, a tiny bit of a furrow creasing the middle of her forehead. Her face still held the shade of a summer tan, highlighting those bright emerald eyes, as they vied for my attention with those perfectly shaped lips.

"I was watching television at home," she said, "and suddenly decided I didn't want to. Didn't want to watch television. Didn't want to be home. I've passed this place a thousand times and never stopped in. I left the house and came here."

"Harry's is a good place to sit quietly, have a drink and think," said I. "Or don't think. During the week it's a good place to do either one. Friday and Saturday nights you can't hear yourself talk, let alone think."

"Just the kind of place I liked when I was younger," Eileen said, and she smiled. This smile showed some teeth. They were white and perfect. "I find I prefer quiet now."

She reached into her pocketbook, a big thing made of leather and some designers' name stitched onto it.

"Mind if I smoke?" she asked.

I shook my head. The white sleeve of the sweater rode up her arm a bit as she reached into the bag, revealing an expensive watch on her wrist and a bruise above the watchband. The watch was round, a solid rim of small diamonds circling the gold face where Geneve was tastefully printed. The watchband was yellow gold. The bruise was dark purple. Taking a book of matches from my suit coat pocket, I struck one for her. She cupped my hand as she leaned in for the light. Her hand was cool, with just a hint of a vibration. Before she pulled back, her eyes met mine. But only long enough for a heart to skip a beat.

"I should quit," she said, settling back against the cushion, a long stream of smoke escaping from the nostrils of an aquiline nose. "Filthy habit. Started when I was sixteen. Everyone smoked. You know that. It was just what we did. It was cool. Not so much anymore."

"I've quit nine or ten times myself," I said. "I'll probably ask a nurse for one while I'm lying in a hospital bed after they've taken out one of my lungs."

Another smile. More relaxed.

"So, Paul Costa, what is it you do for a living? Wait. Let me guess. I'm pretty good at this."

She stared at me then, taking her time, checking me out. My hands, face, clothes, haircut, which I was in need of.

"You sell real estate," she finally said and took a puff from the smoke. But she waved a hand as she released the smoke and said, "No. Forget that. No way. Insurance. Something to do with insurance. Not selling it. Maybe an adjuster. Insurance investigator. You look like a guy who could investigate fraud and could handle yourself if you had to. I almost said cop, but I don't think so. You're what? Forty-four, forty-five? Cops that age don't look like you."

"How do they look?"

"I don't know. More wary. Burnt out. Tired. Yeah, tired."

"Don't I look tired?" I asked, smiling. "I feel tired?"

"Yes, I see that," she said. "The reason I sent you a beer. But you're tired from a long day. Not from life. So, am I close?"

"Not bad. Actually, very good. Cop would have been close, too. I'm a private investigator."

"Really?" she said, her face lighting up. "Like Mannix? Or Magnum? Never met a PI before. You pulling my leg?"

"I can show you my license. I have business cards."

"You working a case tonight? Staking out someone in here?" Her eyes had brightened. She looked at the two tables with the hockey fans and lowered her voice. "Someone cheating on a wife?"

I noticed her smile faded a bit when she said that, as she snubbed out the smoke.

"I'm off tonight," I said. "Just having a beer before heading home."

"It must be dangerous what you do. I remember all the detective shows from the sixties and seventies. The good guys were always getting shot at at the end of the show, but never getting hit. But the bad guys always took a bullet. Funny thing, though, they hardly ever died. Do you remember that?"

"We avoid shooting people to death if we can. There are a lot of questions for the good guy from the cops if there's a dead body, because the bad guy isn't alive to answer any of them."

"You ever shoot anyone, Paul Costa?" she asked hesitantly, but not shyly.

"I think, Eileen, there should be more pleasant things to talk about. Don't you?"

"I'm sorry," she said. "Another bad habit. I'm a very curious person. My husband always said, 'Enough, Eileen. Remember what happened to the cat who got too curious.'"

She looked at her left hand, the diamond so big it was almost grotesque.

"We're separated. The divorce is almost finalized. Need to cross some t's and dot some i's and agree on a few more details. I'm hoping by Thanksgiving. You married, Paul Costa?"

"No," I said.

"Ever been?"

"Close once, but no."

"Were you two together a long time?"

"Long enough for her to realize she was making a mistake."

"I've had friends go through a divorce. No problems. A breeze. Not me. Benny's fought me every inch of the way. Nice payday for the lawyers, but the judge ruled that he picks up all attorney costs. Still, it's been an ordeal."

She smiled weakly. "But it's almost over."

"Benny?"

"Benjamin. He hates when people call him Benny. Hates it. So I do it."

"What does Benny do for a living?" I asked. I looked at the rock. "Lawyers aren't cheap."

Eileen drained her glass. "He's an accountant. And a shit."

She put the smokes back in her bag and slid her arm through the handles.

"Well, Mr. Paul Costa, this has been enjoyable. I'm glad you came over."

I stood up and offered my hand, helping her rise from the padded seat. With her heels, she was only a few inches shorter than my five ten.

"Nice meeting you, Mrs. Landry. Perhaps, should we meet again, you'll allow me to buy you a drink."

"I would like that," she said, still holding my hand. She smiled. "Good night."

I watched her until the door closed, then went back to the bar. Harry was waiting for me.

"You're the only guy I know who can strike out with a woman who bought him a drink," Harry said, his head slowly, sadly shaking.

"We can't all be as smooth as you," I said, laying a ten on the counter with one hand and reaching into a bowl for a handful of

nuts with the other.

"That's very true," said Harry as I walked towards the door.

2

I was leaning against the drivers side door of the '88 Mustang, thinking that all the designers at Ford must be Japanese, when he came down the steps of the triple-decker two streets below the Bunker Hill monument. He had a bounce to his steps despite his bulk, making me think he may have played some ball in high school. The body was no longer that of an athlete, however, unless Sumo wrestling was his sport.

He looked at me leaning against his car as he walked up to where I stood. "You mind?" he asked looking down at me from his six-two height.

I smiled, my hands folded in front of me. "Good morning, David. Mind if I ask you some questions?"

"You the police?"

"No."

"Then get off my car and get out of my way."

I stayed where I was, as did the smile.

"David, it has come to my attention that you may be harboring a runaway in your home. Danielle Gallagher."

"I told you to move" he said, taking a step closer. "I won't tell you again."

"Her parents are very concerned, David. They just want their little girl back."

David O'Brien must have gotten up on the wrong side of the bed. He took a swing at me. I ducked the punch, stepped away from the car, grabbed his arm by the wrist, spun it up behind his wide back without breaking it, swept his right leg out from under him dropping him to one knee. I put my other hand against the side of his head that was now level with my waist, pushed it hard against the door of the black Mustang and put my weight behind it. Angry spittle exploded from his mouth, along with a few expletives. When he tried to rise, I lifted his arm to the breaking point. He settled back down.

"Too early in the morning for this stuff, Davy boy," I said. "Perhaps cut back on your morning coffee. Now, I'm going to give you some advice. I suggest you take it. Are you listening, Dave?"

When he made no response except trying to rise a bit, I grabbed a handful of brown hair, pulled his head about a foot from the door and slammed it back into the shiny black paint.

"I didn't hear you, Dave."

He grunted as his knee touched the ground again.

"The girl is underage, big fella. Don't imagine she told you that. I know you graduated from Saugus High, so I know you're a smart guy, but let me make sure you understand. I'll use small words. She's been missing for two weeks. When I send the cops knocking on your door, you'll be looking at having improper relations with a child. Possibly charged with kidnapping, depending on what the girl might say. She might be in a playful mood, or you may have pissed her off, and that could cook your goose. Once the cops are in there, who knows what else they may find. Well, you know, don't you, Davy? Now, I'm going to release your arm and let you get up. You do anything that displeases me, I'm going to break your kneecap. We clear on that, Dave?"

He swore again.

"What was that?" I asked as I tightened the arm lock.

"Yeah," he cried.

I released his arm, tapped him hard twice on the top of his head and moved several feet away. He got to his feet quickly, but made no move towards me, just stood there massaging his arm.

"Now, I'm going to give you the benefit of the doubt, David. I'm going to believe that you had no idea she was seventeen. That she lied to you. It happens. Females never divulge their correct age. There is a thousand dollar reward for info on the girl. Now, is she still in there?"

I pointed toward his flat. He shook his head.

"I'm having a hard time believing that, Dave."

Still massaging his arm, he said, "She left Tuesday. Rather, I kicked her out Tuesday. The bitch is a psycho, man."

"Know where she went?"

He shook his head.

"I'm betting you can find out," I said as I laid my business card on the hood of the car. "Call me. I pick her up and you get the grand. If you don't, and something happens to the girl, you could be charged as an accessory. Do the smart thing, Davy boy, because up to now, you haven't. Don't wait too long to call," I said as I walked away, "because it only takes a bit of bad luck for all kinds of crazy shit to happen. I'm guessing you know that."

I WAS SITTING at my desk doing paperwork and eating a roast beef sub from Mel's on the Lynnway, when the phone rang.

"She's in Chelsea," the voice on the other end of the line said. The voice gave me an address. "When do I get the reward?"

"First things first, Davy boy," I said. "I get the girl, I know where you live." I hung up. In ten minutes I was driving down Route One towards the Revere Beach Parkway and then into Chelsea. Parking across from the address I had, I scoped out the area. Dave O'Brien wasn't the sharpest tool in the shed, so thoughts he may have set me up in an ambush with a few of his friends did occur to me.

The house was two floors with ten concrete steps up from the sidewalk to the front porch. It was painted brown, cream trim, and in good condition. The sounds from the two busy streets on both ends of this street was constant, but this street was quiet. Leaving my car, I crossed the street and walked up the steps, peeking into the hallway through the glass of the front door of the lower apartment. Nothing. I decided I'd peek in the backdoor, and at the same time see what the girl would have to deal with if she took a runner. Walking up the narrow empty driveway to the back of the house, I saw there was a five foot high chain link fence that ran along the back of the property. Sitting in a lawn chair on a patch of gravel, as leaves fell from a pear tree above her, sat Danielle Gallagher. She wore a white t-shirt and yellow shorts in the warmth of an early October day, a black and white cat lay in her lap. Dani was gently petting her. The cat noticed me first and jumped down. Dani turned towards me. I was fifteen feet from her.

"Who are you?" she asked, as she began rising.

"Don't run, Dani. It'll do you no good. Just sit. Let's talk a minute."

Settling back onto the chair, I noticed she wasn't afraid of me. Just pissed off. I had the distinct impression, that while her face and body showed anger at me being there, and boredom as to what that implied, her mind was calmly calculating an exit strategy and what she would have to do to implement it. Seventeen going on thirty. A kid with street smarts who grew up in an affluent community. Smart and manipulative was my first impression of her. I found myself curious as to how she was going to play this.

The picture I had of her, supplied by her parents, was from her freshman year of high school. She was dressed in a field hockey uniform. Her face was fresh and thin and smiling. Brown hair, curly and shoulder length. Eyes too big for the face. Legs too thin under a short uniform skirt, thin arms holding the stick. The kid who sat in front of me now bore a resemblance to that fourteen year old girl in the photo, but just barely. The hair was now cut short, hung straight and dyed navy blue. The arms were toned, the legs were long and shapely. The braless breasts beneath the t-shirt were proud C-cups demanding attention. The eyes that watched me noticing those breasts were those of someone much older than seventeen. Someone who knew the game, and knew how to play it

"My name is Paul Costa, Dani," I said as I moved to

stand in front of her at a distance of ten feet. "I'm a private investigator hired by your parents to find you." I left out the 'concerned parents' part. "You have to help me understand something here. You have a birthday coming up soon. Eighteen. Free to legally do anything you want. With anyone you want. Anywhere you want. Why take off now?"

"It doesn't matter," she said. "You wouldn't understand." She shifted slightly in the chair, her hands pulling the cotton fabric of the t-shirt a little tighter across her chest.

"Maybe not," I said. "But I am curious."

She looked at me then, coolly. I think she wanted to say something, wanted to see if she could get an adult to understand as easily as she got her young friends to agree with her actions. Instead, she frowned.

"You'd have to live in that house before you could understand," she finally said. "You going to take me back?" She said it like we might negotiate a different outcome. At some point in the next few years, real life may become a harsh reality for Danielle Gallagher. Maybe then, if she survives all the lessons she'll learn before then, perhaps, after, she'll make better choices going forward. I wouldn't bet the mortgage on it.

"Your mother wanted me to tell you she has a bag packed for you with money inside. The morning of your eighteenth birthday, you are free to go. There will be no demands. No theatrics." No need to mention the mother said she would call the cab.

This brought a small grin to Dani's face. "I could probably bribe her to buy me a car, she wants me out so bad. It's something to consider."

"Why does she want you out?"

"It doesn't matter. Certainly not to you. You're just the hired help."

I smiled. Can't allow kids to think they can get under your skin.

"Just curious," I said. "But you're right. It doesn't matter to me. I drop you off in the next hour, Mom makes out a check for expenses, hopefully, we never see each other again."

"Or?" she whispered and stood up. She smiled. It was easy to see how she kept finding places to stay after wearing out her welcome somewhere else.

I smiled again.

"Sit down, Dani."

I thought she was going to bolt then. I could see she was considering it. But after a few seconds she plopped back down, her arms crossing her chest. If looks could kill.

"I'm going to say something now," I said. "A bit of advice. Advice I don't expect you'll give a shit about, but I'd rather say it than be pissed tomorrow that I didn't. You, Danielle Gallagher, have everything going for you. I have no idea what you'll do with it. But I do know that a sharp woman like yourself can come up with a better plan than what you're doing now. Your choice. As it is with all of us."

"Easy for you to say," she snapped at me. "You don't have to live with Miranda and Jeffrey Gallagher."

"In a few weeks, neither do you. All I'm saying is, whatever decision you make, make it for the long run and not for the next day, week or month."

Over the years, I've tracked down over thirty Dani Gallaghers. Some two or three times. Always, there came the time when no one asked anymore where they were.

"Is the cat yours?"

"A stray," she said, frowning. "Just showed up this morning."

"Why don't you go get your stuff," I said. "You hungry? We could stop."

Dani shrugged. "I could eat. Their fridge is empty." She stood up.

"You got it," I said. "Just do me a favor, Dani. A little different wardrobe."

This time, the smile was genuine.

WE STOPPED ON Route One for pizza. She ate like

she hadn't eaten in a week. Conversation was non-existent. But as I took the exit for Lynnfield, Dani said, “Miranda isn't my mother. She's my stepmom.”

“I know,” I said as I navigated the crossover. They looked nothing alike.

“My mom died when I was nine. Miranda and I have never gotten along. Yeah, she's all motherly like when Dad is around, but it's an act.”

“Yeah, step parents can sometimes be in a tough situation. If you weren't an only child, it might have been easier on both of you.”

She fell quiet again as we drove down the main street into town. A few streets from her home she said, “She's having an affair. Dad doesn't know. He's clueless.” She looked at me. “I don't know what to do. I want to tell my dad, because he's a good guy and he doesn't deserve this crap. But he's crazy about her and it would kill him. I don't know what to do.”

When I stopped in her driveway, I took a business card from my pocket.

“Anytime,” I said as she looked at the card. “For any reason.”

I looked at the house. Miranda Gallagher stood in the front doorway, her arms crossed over her chest, her face expressionless.

3

I had spent the better part of Thursday afternoon at the Boston Public Library doing research. My new client, who I met that morning, was a rich guy who decided he preferred living in a big spread on the water than in a high rise in Boston. Several months ago, his house was broken into and, despite an elaborate alarm system, several valuable pieces of art were pilfered. The police arrived nine minutes after the first call from the security firm. They found no one on the premises. Two paintings and a small sculpture with a total value of six point three million were gone. Several other paintings worth more than lunch money were left behind. The burglar, or burglars, knew what they wanted and how much time they had to get away. The police and insurance investigators both believed it was a three man operation. Neither had a lead on who might have done it. Both claim they are still working the case, but the client feels not hard enough. Or fast enough.

The insurance company had yet to settle, but would do so soon, so they said. My client was impatient. He believed putting me on the case would prod them along. So I drove out to Marblehead, drove through the lovely town, crossed narrow Ocean Avenue to Marblehead Neck where the rich folks bask, and met him at his house, a massive place of stone on the outside and heavy wood on the inside. He's a bachelor who seems to enjoy having manly things around him. Suits of armor, game heads on the wall, a desk in his study the size of Old Ironsides .

From the very beginning of our chat, he made it very clear he wanted the paintings back. He wanted the paintings, and he wanted the thieves brought to justice. He owned a software start-up, he said, whatever the hell that is, and money was no object, he also said. I got that, when he gave me a fat retainer, and promised a lot more if I found the paintings. I told him the pieces had probably already been fenced, that after eight months the odds I'd find something the insurance investigators had missed, were low. He said I should do my best and signed the check. So I'll do my best. After leaving him, I went to the Library to do some research.

But on Thursday night, I was sitting at Harry's Bar on the beach and enjoying a cold one. Four stools away from me, Rose was sipping a rum and cola, while a young guy with a Prince Valiant hairdo was talking to her about life insurance. At the far end of the bar, Harry was chatting up a pretty, young blonde who was giggling at something he said. Harry looked up when the door opened, then he looked at me and gave me a chin lift. Turning, I saw Eileen Landry walking towards the booth she was in last week.

I've thought about Eileen Landry off and on, wondering if I'd ever see her again, wondering if anything could or should come of it if I did. As attractive as she is, she was going through what she alluded to as a difficult divorce. The last thing she probably needed was another guy requiring her attention. But that purple bruise on her arm that I had noticed suggested, at least to me, that that may be exactly what she did need. Perhaps I shouldn't have jumped to the conclusion that her soon to be ex caused the bruise. For all I knew, Eileen Landry could have been a jammer on a women's roller derby team.

After coming back from Eileen's booth, Harry mixed up a Manhattan. He placed it in front of me.

"Don't embarrass yourself again," he said.

"Does she know how old you are?" I asked him, as I looked over at the blonde.

"Tonight, she doesn't care," he grinned. I picked up the Manhattan and walked towards Eileen.

She looked up at me as I laid down a napkin and

placed the drink on top. She looked pleased to see me. I'd like to think she'd been sitting there, waiting for her drink, hoping I'd come sniffing around.

"Is the private detective business so slow that you have to moonlight as a waiter in a bar on the beach?"

"You'd be surprised at the things I've done to earn a buck, and I'd be embarrassed to tell you. May I join you?"

"Please."

She took a long sip of the drink as I settled in across from her. We both began to speak at the same time. I smiled. "Sorry. You first."

"I was just going to say it's nice seeing you again," she said. "And remind you that you promised to buy me a drink."

"You're sipping it now."

"Do you always do what you say you're going to do?" asked Eileen.

"I try." I shrugged. "I have two traits that can drive people crazy. Honesty and tenacity. It's a funny thing, people don't always want to hear the truth. They say they do, but they don't. And if I didn't have tenacity, I'd probably be selling riding mowers at Sears."

"You know a lot about riding mowers?"

"I didn't say I'd be selling a lot of them."

"What is it you were going to say?"

"What you said," I replied. "Normally, if I get into a conversation in here, and it's rare that I do, one of the Boston teams are in the play-offs and everyone strikes up conversations with complete strangers. It was nice to talk with someone with no reference to a game being mentioned once."

"I've been known to watch the Red Sox if nothing else is on," she said and smiled. "I like Larry Bird, too. We can talk sports if you like, although I'm not that knowledgeable. I was a cheerleader in high school, though."

I had no problem believing that. I might have played football if my high school had cheerleaders who looked like Eileen Landry.

"Maybe some other time," I said.

"What should we talk about then?"

"How about you," I said. "Where did you grow up?"

She looked at me. The index finger of her right hand traveled around the rim of the glass creating a musical sound. The finger came to a stop, as did the sound. Her eyes searched my face. They were sad eyes.

"Mr. Costa," she said.

"Paul," I said interrupting her.

"Paul. Last week, I shared that I was going through a nasty divorce. I don't make a habit of telling complete strangers my business. But I could see you found me....interesting, so I was letting you know I am not in a good place right now, and you would be wise not to waste your time on me."

"I'm forty-seven years old, Eileen, and while I didn't graduate top of my class, I consider myself fairly intelligent and, as stated before, tenacious. And patient.

"Why don't we do this? We talk. Have a drink or two and talk. Maybe laugh. Maybe next week, we do the same thing. Maybe some night we talk while we're in a restaurant having dinner. If we find conversation drying up, interest waning, we shake hands and wish each other good fortune."

"Ships in the night?" She asked without smiling.

"More 'Strangers in the Night' I think, as Sinatra so eloquently explained it. Look, anytime you say you want to be alone, I'll go sit at the bar. If you ever say you're not comfortable, or you prefer not to be in the situation I suggested, we shake hands and part. Should the time come when you don't come in Harry's, you will not find me at your door wondering why you haven't come in."

"So, if I'm hearing you right," Eileen said, leaning back against the cushion, a teasing smile on those incredible lips,"you don't find me attractive enough to pursue."

"Don't do that," I said. Not angrily, but firmly.

Frowning, she said, "I'm sorry. It was a lame attempt at humor."

She reached into her bag for the Winston's. This bag was black leather and just as big as the one last week. A different designer logo. The watch was the same. The bruise was bluish green and fading. I struck a match from a book of them I carried, just in case we sat together again, and just in case she reached for the smokes.

As she exhaled, she said, "I think I like what you're suggesting, Paul. It would be nice to have a conversation where no one raised their voice, no one made demands, no one was giving me legal advice. I think I need a bit of normalcy. I think I also need intimacy, but I don't feel I'm at a place right now where I can share. I think I will need to learn to trust again before I can be a giving partner."

"I did mention the patient part, correct?"

"You had me at tenacious. We'll see."

WHERE DID YOU find my little girl?" Jeffrey Gallagher asked.

It was seven thirty in the morning. He was sitting in my office. He had been standing by the entry door when I showed up. He was in luck. Usually, I don't show up for work until nine or ten. And some days I'm not even in town.

"In Chelsea," I said.

"Was she with a man?"

Gallagher was obviously worked up, but he was holding it together well. I saw no need to sugarcoat anything. His 'little girl' was no longer little. I told him there was no one in the house except Danielle when I got there. He asked how I knew where she was. I told him.

"And this man who called you, you said Dani was with him a while?"

"Yes."

"Do you think they were doing drugs? Having sex?"

"I don't know."

"I'm insisting she spends time in a clinic getting checked out. She absolutely refuses. Says it isn't necessary. Not necessary? With the stuff that's out there now? The argument last night was horrible. I stayed up all night, expecting her to try and leave the house again."

"In a few months," I said, "you'll have no legal right to keep her from leaving your house. Perhaps, it might be better to temper your demands now."

Jeffery Gallagher nodded his head a few times. "Do you have children, Mr. Costa?"

"No, none that I'm aware of." I shouldn't have been flip. A simple 'no' would have sufficed.

"Then perhaps you should refrain from dispensing parental advice." After several seconds of silence, he continued. "I'd like to know the name of the man who told you where my daughter was."

"You wish to speak with him?"

"Yes, I do."

"I don't think that's a good idea, Mr. Gallagher."

"I paid the man one thousand dollars," Gallagher said, his voice rising a bit. "You did deliver the money to him?"

"Oh, yes. He didn't thank me. Just took the envelope and closed the door in my face."

"But you don't think I should speak with him?"

"These last few pages of his life concerning your daughter, are not something he wants to talk about anymore. In fact, he wishes he never got involved. Were you to approach him, he might react in a hostile way."

"I can take care of myself, Mr. Costa, I assure you."

"No doubt," I said. "But he's half your age, outweighs you by seventy pounds, and you won't have the element of surprise. Let it go."

He stood then and glared down at me. After several seconds, he turned and left the office. I was surprised the glass in the door didn't shatter.

I was paid to do a job, paid fairly, and I did it. I had no obligation to keep a former client out of harms way. I have had clients in the past that I gladly would have sent to the big guy in Charlestown for a beating, but not Jeffrey Gallagher. He was a concerned dad. Maybe not a great parent, but definitely a concerned one. It was my hope, that Danielle and her dad would figure things out.

Taking the lid off my Dunkin's, I began reviewing the notes I had scribbled at the library yesterday. The paintings were by two artists I had never heard of. You would think a painting that is valued at a couple of million dollars, I would have at least heard of the artist. Perhaps the cocktail parties I attend aren't high brow enough. I had photostats of each in the folder. The paintings were from the early seventeenth century. Both paintings were of a well dressed man, not the same man, standing, looking dignified and important. Both portraits looking like a thousand others you see in art museums, if that's your thing to frequent art museums. One painting was twenty-four inches by thirty-four inches. The other was twenty-four by forty. The bronze sculpture was by Remington. Him I have heard of, though not at a cocktail party.

Like the famous burglary at the Gardner Museum in Boston, only the canvas was taken, the frames left behind. And like the Gardner, my client, Mr. Gladstone, has left the empty frames on his wall. I suppose seeing the wood paneling behind those elaborate frames everyday might make a fellow desperate for revenge. It would certainly leave a bad taste in my mouth.

Eight months since the robbery. The odds I'll find out who did it are slim. However, they're better odds than me recovering the stolen property. But I'm not without my contacts in the world of crime.

4

Packy is what some people might call a character. Others, a pain in the ass. He has idiosyncrasies that can sometimes leave you shaking your head, sometimes in confusion, sometimes in amazement. Often when he's talking, you have no idea what he's talking about. I don't know if he's autistic, a savant, or a certifiable genius. Or he's just having fun and he thinks he's funny. What I do know, Packy knows a lot about crime in the Northeast, and the folks who commit it.

Packy, that's what everyone calls him, I have no idea what his given name is, nor do I care, has a residence in Lynn, and I drove over there to try and find him. He rarely stays in his apartment. He has no phone. If you want to talk with Packy, you need to frequent the dives he frequents, ask questions of the clientele, and eventually you'll find him. You can easily burn a Franklin, one Hamilton at a time, asking questions of the questionable people who might know where Packy is.

Usually, when a stranger starts asking about a local, no one knows the guy and no one has seen him if they do know the guy. That goes without saying. Maybe a Jackson might loosen a tongue if the guy is tapped out, or of low integrity, but trying to get information on the street is like trying to milk a bull. But when it comes to Packy, everyone knows him, and everyone knows that he wants them to pass on any information they have to anyone who asks. It'll still cost you the twenty, though. Packy will talk to anyone, even the cops, but that doesn't mean he'll tell you anything that you can use. There's even the chance you'll walk away from the conversation more confused than when you entered it. He's been roughed up a few times because of it. But for a good reason that goes way back, the muscle north of Boston has a soft spot for Packy, and people have been known to need medical attention if they give Packy a hard time.

'Lynn, Lynn, city of sin, you never come out like you went in.' And that's the truth. A hundred thousand people sandwiched in like sardines, with a hundred thousand stories, none of which are uplifting. Hopes and dreams can die here faster than Sham's chances at the Belmont. It took me three bars and a boxing gym, but I finally found Packy in a poolroom shooting pool by himself.

As I approached his table, he was lining up the five ball. Without looking up, he said, “Hey, hey, whadda ya say, the shamus from Saugus visits today.” The tip of the stick made contact with the white ball and the five disappeared in a side pocket. Packy moved to the other side of the table, never once looking at me.

“Packy, how have you been?”

“Never better, I gotta say. What brings you to Packy today?” The nine dropped in the other side pocket.

“I'd like to buy you a drink and catch up. Been a year or two.”

“Been three, but who's counting.” He lined up the thirteen. Took his time. When it dropped in the far pocket, the cue ball came to rest in perfect position to sink the last ball.

“Heard you brought a wayward angel home safe and sound, Private Dick. And heard you roughed up someone related to the Mick.”

He sank the last ball, the cue ball coming to rest in the middle of the table. He looked up at me.

“I'd stay on my toes if I were you. The kid in question is the man's nephew.”

“I didn't rough him up that bad, and I dropped a grand in his lap. O'Neil won't sweat the small stuff.”

“It's his sister's kid.”

“Not even worth a visit. Certainly not worth a reaction.”

“If you say so. You should know. You here about the

Picasso?"

I had to smile. "Why do you think that?"

"Been three years, shamus. Can't think of any other reason you'd come out here to see Packy."

He lifted the cap off his head, the one that had the Green Bay Packers logo on the front of it, and furiously scratched the mop of hair under it. He had the name long before he had the cap.

"I think Kenny's couch has bed bugs," said Packy, as he started looking around the empty room. I had no idea who Kenny was.

"What makes you think I know anything about some stolen paintings?" he asked, still looking around the room like he was looking for something he misplaced.

"Worth a shot."

"Didn't hear Saint Paul was on the case."

"Just hired. You got anything?"

"Got an empty stomach."

I WATCHED PACKY packing it in. He stood five foot five and probably weighed a hundred forty soaking wet, but the man could eat. And while he ate, there was no conversation. He barely paused long enough to breathe.

Packy was close to forty years old and had done time twice. The first time, he was barely out of his teens. Car jacking. Even before he was old enough to get a driver's license, Packy was stealing cars. Always fast cars, with a fondness for Mopar. He was nineteen years old when he boosted a '69 Road Runner from a side street in Revere. He was on the Parkway, bringing the car to a chop shop in Chelsea, when a green '69 Goat pulled up to the stop light and raced the engine. Now the smart thing would have been to not take the bait. But Packy, who was known as Packy even back then, left a long strip of rubber when the light turned green.

The Road Runner and the GTO were side by side when they blew through the next light where a cop was waiting to take a right. It took six cop cars from Everett, Medford and Somerville to corral the two cars, but eventually they did. Packy got two years for that.

The second time, Packy was late twenties. Still stealing cars. A lot more sophisticated this time. High end luxury. You would place your order, say an Eldorado, Lincoln, Porshe, and Packy, through a network he had helped build and which he ran, would find what you wanted, right down to the color of the interior and the sound system. He would then send out one of his crew to steal it. Most product came from Jersey or New York, most were shipped out of the country. Quite successful for a few years, until one of the crew fell asleep at the wheel one night coming back from north of Albany and crashed into the trees on Route 2. He ratted out Packy in a plea deal. Six years for that one with a year off for good behavior.

That operation was big and sophisticated, and more than one guy like Packy could have possibly created. Packy never ratted out his partners, but, I'm guessing, and the rumor was, those partners had muscle and connections, because now, you harm Packy and misfortune is in your immediate future. To the best of my knowledge, Packy was no longer in the car business.

Packy used the paper napkin, dabbing at his lips like we were at Anthony's Pier 4, and it was cloth.

"You want dessert?" I asked. Maybe a little facetiously, because he frowned.

"I ever steer you wrong?" he asked.

He never had. "Time is money, Packy. What do you know?"

"I know you might want to return the retainer."

"And we both know that isn't going to happen."

He shrugged. "It's your funeral, shamus."

I waited, sipping at my coffee. Packy can't be rushed.

"You been to Boston?" he asked. "Christmas decorations up already. Can you believe it? Met a guy in Chinatown. No Christmas decorations there."

"Packy?"

"Alright already, alright. Don't say I didn't warn you. I'm hearing local guys were approached. Don't know who."

"Do you know if the stuff is out of the country, and who fenced it?" If I could find the middleman I'd be halfway there.

"No middleman," said Packy, draining his beer. "The stuff is still on the Northshore. Private collector. His eyes only."

"You know who?"

Shaking his head, Packy said, "No. You may not believe this, because these folks are not your crowd, but the rich all like to collect stuff. Sometimes they covet what their peers have. I imagine usually it's a trophy wife, but art is pretty high up on the list, too. And, of course, when they steal from their peers, the stolen artifacts can never again see the light of day, because their rich friends would visit and right away know that it was stolen right off the wall of another of their rich friends. So, the sick bastards put the stolen art in a secret room, where they sometimes visit. Closing the door, putting on the light, admiring something that no one else can ever see again. My understanding, is that these paintings are not particularly famous, therefore it is my belief that they must have been seen by someone who visited the rich guys mansion and coveted. Who knows why?"

Packy could care less if I bring a rich guy down. Probably rejoice over the bums fate. So if he knew a name, he would have told me. But if he knew who actually pulled the heist, and they were connected, he wouldn't tell me, or anyone, who they were. Loyalty isn't a one way street.

"You ever notice how crazy people get around the holidays?" Packy said, staring out the diner's huge window. "I blame it on the automobile. Nobody rushed around crazy until cars gave them the opportunity to do it. I tell you, it's a sick world, all because of Henry Ford."

The rich. I hate dealing with rich people. Difficult to squeeze them. Even more difficult to get the truth from them. You can do it, but, Jesus, it isn't easy. Guys like me, we need to find leverage to force the rich to open up.

Other guys, less civilized than me, all they need is a crowbar. I hope it doesn't come to that.

ON THE WAY back to the office, I thought about what Packy had said, and what he hadn't said. If the talent that pulled the heist was out of town talent, he would have told me. So, they were local. If he knew who they were, and they weren't affiliated with the mob, he wouldn't have ratted them out, but he would have said something like, 'You might want to talk to so and so, see what he has for you.' This guy wouldn't be the talent, either, but he would know who the talent was. Packy would never take money to be a rat. Not everyone held such high morals. So I'm guessing the local mob has prints on this one. Well, it won't be the first time we've tangoed. But it's not something I look forward to.

Both the cops and the insurance investigators found no connection to the local mob. Maybe they need detailed maps to find their way home at night, too. If, in fact, the paintings that were taken were targeted, then that meant the burglars had prior knowledge of the layout in the house, were familiar with the alarms and knew how much time they had before the first cop car would arrive. Packy may be right. A supposed friend of my client may now have the paintings.

One of the paintings had hung halfway up a long staircase to the second level. The other painting had hung in a paneled room by large French doors that opened to the garden expanse. The Remington sculpture had occupied a spot beside the massive desk in the study. Three pieces separated by a lot of living space. To get in the house, take the paintings from the frames, and get back out in the time required, meant at least three people were involved.

I thought about why they took the canvas and left the frames. The obvious reason would be the bulk. Getting three people and two framed paintings into a car would not have been easy, and the possibility of damaging the paintings if they tried had to be a concern. A van would have solved that problem. But tire prints thought to be those of the get away vehicle pointed to a car, probably a late model sedan, mid-size, with Michelin tires.

Packy's suggestion that an acquaintance of my client may be behind the theft, has me thinking of another reason to leave the frames hanging there. The frames would be a not so gentle reminder. Something someone might do who seriously didn't like the person they were stealing from. Poor guys don't like someone they know, they just punch them in the nose, or flash the middle finger. The rich....Jesus, they are nasty human beings.

I had three messages on the machine when I got back to the office. The first one was from my rich client asking me if I had made any progress. I was hired four days ago. I counted to ten and pressed the button again. The second message offered me a free microwave if I just sat through a short presentation detailing a fantastic opportunity for vacationing in Costa Rica. I already own a microwave. The third was from Dani Gallagher asking if I could meet her at a Dunkin's not far from her high school at three. Checking my watch, I had twenty minutes to get there.

There were three tables set away from the customer ordering spot. Dani sat at the one closest to the window. She was the only person in the place except for the two employees behind the counter. She watched me as I got a medium coffee with cream and extra sugar. Carrying the cardboard cup to Dani's table, I made a quick assessment, judging by how hot the cup was, that it would be fifteen minutes before I could drink the coffee without scalding my tongue. The first thing I did when I sat down was to pop the lid off. That cut the waiting time in half.

There was a bookbag on the chair beside Dani. It was not jammed full. Dani was dressed in faded blue jeans and a navy blue button up sweater worn over a white blouse. Her finger nails were painted the same shade as the sweater, which was the same shade as her hair. There was a thin metal ring in her right nostril.

“Thanks for coming,” she said. “Wasn't sure you got

the message."

"I see your attendance at school has resumed," I said.

She shrugged. "I'm trying to keep everything low key. Eliminate the drama. Graduate and move on."

I nodded my approval to that plan of action.

"But my father isn't making it easy. He wanted to send me to a clinic for a week. Check to see if I was pregnant, or had AIDS, or some other shit. Keep me from taking drugs, he said. I don't do drugs. Never have. Drugs are for losers. I have plans. I told him that. The only time I've had intercourse I was fifteen. The kid was a senior. It was over before I even began enjoying it. He never called me again. Ignored me in the halls."

She shrugged. "Can I tell you something, Mr. Costa?"

"It's Paul, Dani, and yes you can tell me anything you like or ask me anything. I'll listen, or I'll give you a truthful answer if I know the answer."

Looking down at her coffee, Dani said, "I think I might be a Lesbian."

She looked up quickly to see if I had a reaction to that. Which, of course, I didn't. Kids. Always trying to shock you. I don't shock easy.

"Do you think there's something wrong with me?"

"Because you think you might be attracted to girls instead of guys?" I asked.

She was looking at me with big eyes, like my opinion on the subject mattered, which I suppose it did, because she asked.

"No. Love anyone you want to love, Dani. Just be honest about it. There are a lot of things that can cause a person pain in this life, but the only thing worse than having a loved one die, is having someone break your heart."

"I was staying with someone in Charlestown, a guy, a friend of a friend who had a sleep sofa, and after a few nights of sitting around having a few beers and talking, he starts to come on to me. He was a good looking guy. Young. But I felt nothing for him. I said no. He got mad. We ended up shouting at each other, and at one point I thought he was going to hit me. The next morning, before he left for work, he told me not to be there when he got home."

Her shoulders hunched together making her look like she was shrinking. She sipped her coffee. I tried mine. Tolerable.

"You said you had plans," I said.

There was a look of confusion on her face.

"For after graduation," I specified.

"Yeah," she said showing a spark of enthusiasm. "I want to be a photo-journalist."

This time I couldn't help myself. I re-acted. I think my eyes got really wide. Dani looked pleased.

"You like taking pictures? You have a knack for it?"

She shrugged. "I bought a camera last year and I've been taking a lot of pictures. I like doing it."

"Okay," I said. I mean, what can you say?

"I saw a movie last year. Nick Nolte – you know the actor – was in it. I really like him. He was a photo-journalist. He took pictures in places where there are wars."

"And you want to do that? Take pictures in very dangerous places?"

"Oh, yeah. Can you imagine it? Every second feeling alive and on edge."

I said nothing. I saw no need to discuss something that was probably never going to happen. We both drank a little more coffee.

"I want to hire you," Dani said after a minute or two of silence. So we got to the reason for the phone call.

"I'm not the most expensive private detective out there, but I'm not cheap. Why do you want to hire me?" I had an inkling.

"I want you to find out who Miranda is cheating on my dad with. I want you to confront that person and make them stop."

"Dani, I can find out who he is. I can remind him that he is fooling around with a married woman. I can even check him out, maybe come up with something that could be used as leverage to convince him to sail in different waters. Perhaps he's married, too. But I can't force him to stop seeing your step-mom."

"Do you know people who can?"

"That is not something you want to be involved in, Dani. Trust me on that."

"It's going to destroy my dad when he finds out. People always find out, don't they?"

"Not always. Sometimes the affair ends with the spouse unaware. Sometimes the spouse knows, or suspects, and they deny the truth. This is something I would advise you to not get involved in."

"My dad and I can have terrible arguments, but that's only because he wants me to be safe. I know that. There is no one in this world I love more than my dad. No one. I hate Miranda."

I thought she was about to cry. But she gave her head an angry shake and looked at me. There were tears in those brown eyes, but not one reached a cheek.

"Look, I'll see what I can find out," I said. "But you need to be patient. Sometimes, these things take a while."

"Thank you, Paul. Really, thank you." She took in a deep breath.

"But I will not tell you who it is," I said. "No way I'll do that, and you know why. I talk to him and it ends there. If the affair continues, you've done all you could. Agreed?"

I could see she wasn't happy, but she knew I wouldn't change my mind about that. She nodded.

"How much do you charge for something like this?" she asked. "I have money."

"Thirty dollars a day that I actually work on the case, which won't be every day, plus expenses."

A fourth of what I normally charge. But I don't normally take clients who are still in high school.

"Do you think it might take you longer than ten days?" she asked.

"If it does, you hired the wrong guy."

5

Thursday morning, a week before Columbus Day, I was sitting in a fancy lawn chair on an expanse of green lawn behind Peter Gladstone's sprawling house. Fifty feet from where I sat, a large rectangular pool was covered, with leaves beginning to accumulate on the tightly pulled bright red tarp. Both sides of the landscaped expanse had a solid fence of twelve foot high yews for privacy. The far end of the property was open, with views of a dock, boathouse and Marblehead Harbor beyond.

The sky was clear, the air with a nip in it, because it was, after all, October in New England. I sat alone sipping some of the best coffee I have ever sipped, Gladstone inside, summoned by the help to take a call. Except for the sound of birds, there was quiet.

I can sit on the lawn at my condo, also. It's a six foot wide mostly green strip between the building and the parking lot. But it's always mowed neat and usually free of beer cans. Not always free of dog shit. I had noticed no animals on this property.

Gladstone came through the open French doors carrying a portable phone. He wore cuffed light tan slacks and a black long-sleeved pullover. And open-toed sandals with socks. Jesus. A lot of things bother me. Men wearing sandals and socks is just one of them.

"I'll call you later," I heard him say as he walked down the stone steps towards me. "Just get it done."

"I have to do everything," he said as he quickly took the chair across from me, crossing his legs and tapping on an arm of the chair. He was trim and fit and moved with confidence. “You pay people a lot of money. Is it too much to expect they have the balls to make the important decisions?”

“Do you encourage them to make important decisions?”

He picked up his cup and smiled. He showed a lot of teeth when he smiled. They were white and straight.

“Of course not. My company, my money. My vision. Can't take the chance they would mess it up. Now, what have you got for me? Do you know where my paintings are?”

“No idea,” I said. “Not yet. But I do have some questions. A different tact from the cops, perhaps.”

“Shoot.”

“I assume you host parties here.” I had found out that he did just by asking around.

“Of course. I enjoy hosting my friends. Plus, I have several benefits a year for some local charities. Fundraisers. I see where you're going with this, Costa, and the cops did the same thing. Two weeks before the burglary, I hosted a large event. Maybe a hundred guests. The company I hired to run the thing brought in twenty-two people. Twenty-two strangers running around my house, seeing where everything is. The cops and investigators interviewed everyone who worked here that night. Nothing came of it.”

“Do you have any enemies?” I asked.

“You're not covering new ground here, Costa.” He peered at me, a frown deepening. “You did that investigation for John Corey two years ago. John told me about it. He was impressed. John doesn't impress easily. Right now, I'm not impressed. Wasn't the check big enough?”

“How about jealous friends?” I asked. I never get defensive when clients get peevish. They have no idea what the job entails. All they know is, they want results. Yesterday.

The question got him to look out towards the pool.

“You don't get where I am without ruffling some feathers,” he said, “but grand theft seems a bit extreme for the people I know."

"Would these jealous friends be on your guest list?"

"They have been. These are business competitors who may have been business associates at one time and may feel my patents infringed on their patents. Lawyers and the courts settle those spats. I've brought suit against others for the same reason. Business enemies, not mortal enemies."

"Just patents?"

He shrugged. "Perceived agreements made over a half empty bottle of good stuff without a signed contract to back them up. Happens all the time."

"Agreements you reneged on?"

"Goes both ways, Costa. Mine is a generation that recognizes the validity of a signature on the bottom line and discounts the handshake across the table. Even with a signature, we have lawyers who will argue us out of any deal. It's a pedigree dog eat pedigree dog world. But, again, I don't think I've screwed anyone bad enough for them to risk prison. We all know the game. We all play it."

I'm a member of Gladstone's generation, perhaps at the higher age limit, and I'd like to take umbrage with his assessment of us. But I can't. There may have been a time when a handshake was enough to close a deal, when integrity and honesty were more important than profit. Old timers will tell you there was. There was also a time when cars had running boards and actresses didn't have to show their breasts on a twenty foot high screen.

"Tell me about the Remington," I said.

"What do you mean?"

"You have several small statues throughout the house. Did the Remington have special meaning to you?"

"After the IPO, when the stock surged, I wanted to do something for my dad. He had given me thirty thousand dollars to get me started twelve years ago, even though he knew nothing about computers and software. But he believed in me. It was almost all the money he had. Anyway, I wanted to get something for him. In the Times,

I saw a picture of the statue in an ad for an auction that was coming up in New York. A bucking bronco with a cowboy trying to break him. My dad loved cowboy movies and cowboy television shows. *The Man Who Shot Liberty Valance* was his favorite movie, John Wayne his favorite actor. So I went to the auction and outbid three others for that piece of bronze."

Gladstone sat quietly for a second, looking out to the far end of his property.

"He actually wept when I gave it to him. First time I had seen tears in my dads' eyes. At the time, I thought it was because he was so happy to have it. Six months later he was gone, the cancer I didn't know then that he had, taking him. So, yeah, it means something to me."

"And the paintings? You have a dozen paintings. The two taken, do they have stories?"

Gladstone continued looking out at the covered pool as a slight breeze stirred the few leaves resting on it. I sipped my coffee waiting for him to speak. I could see he was adding two and two together and coming up with four.

"The painting from the stairway is the van Dyck. I purchased it at the same auction as the Remington. I don't even know why, didn't think it was anything great, but I may have still been caught up in the excitement of the bidding on the statue, and the painting was next on the agenda. Three bids and it was over. I had a painting I didn't particularly want.

"But when my folks came for a visit a month or two later, by then I knew dad was dying, my mother paused on the stairway to stare at the painting. 'Peter, where did you get this painting?' she asked. I told her. My mother, who is of English descent, then said, 'This man looks like your great-grandfather.' Of course he wasn't. The painting is of a noble in King Charles court back in the sixteen hundreds. But mother was very taken with that painting and always stopped to admire it whenever on the stairs. She is heartbroken that it was stolen."

"And the other one? The one by de Keyser?" I asked.

“That one is personal,” he said.

He stood and stretched. “Can I refresh your cup? Add a little something a little stronger?”

“A bit early for me,” I replied.

“Used to be for me, too. Not anymore.”

There was a fancy cabinet behind us on the patio. He took a bottle from inside it and poured two fingers into his cup. Sitting again, he said, “I had never heard of de Keyser. I was at a chateau in France four years ago visiting an old friend. Sitting in front of a roaring fire one evening, enjoying a Cognac and talking, he confided to me that he had fallen on hard financial times. His company was bleeding money faster than he could infuse it. Banks were refusing him loans, and calling in the loans he had. He was about to lose the chateau. It had been in his family for over two hundred years. Even before Napoleon.

“I offered to lend him money. He refused. Said he doubted he would ever be able to repay me. 'Then I will gift you a million dollars,' I said, probably a little drunk on the brandy, 'and we will speak no more of this.' He shook his head and said no. A very proud man, my friend. I doubt I would have been so proud were I in similar straits.

“I stood, went to my room, and came back with my checkbook. I wrote out a check for one million dollars, placed it on the table beside him and walked to where the de Keyser hung on the wall, the only painting in the room. Taking it down, I said, 'This painting has caught my eye. I will be quite upset if you refuse to sell it to me.'

“I had no idea of its' value. I only assumed it was an original. I didn't even like it. Paintings of standing men are not my taste. My friend came to me, tears in his eyes, and kissed me on both cheeks.

“The money bought him some time, but couldn't save him. In time, he lost the chateau to the bank and a month after committed suicide. So, yes, that painting does mean something to me.”

Taking a long pull from his cup, he turned to face me.

“So, you're suggesting that these pieces were stolen by someone I know, someone who I have told the same stories to, someone who did this as an act of revenge for some perceived slight, real or imagined?”

I said, “Grand theft of items valued at over six million dollars that will bring a stiff prison sentence, not to mention condemnation of one's character were that person to be indicted, suggests, at least to me, that the perceived slight is not so slight and certainly not imagined. At least to them.”

I'm sometimes amazed that some rich people are rich. They seem to be able to fabricate an alternate reality so easily, it's a wonder they weren't easy prey for every shyster they came across. Gladstone frowned, but made no comment. Just sipped his drink and watched leaves skitter across the tarp.

Finally, he said, “In and out in nine minutes. They were told what to take and where to find it. I always wondered why they didn't take the two paintings that are worth more on either side of the van Dyck. Easy pickings. Now I know. The thieves had no idea of value. Just grab what you were hired to grab. I'll tell you, the investigators were stumped on that one. Why take a de Keyser when a Manet was in the house? Now I know.”

He nodded a few times, then rallied.

“Shall I begin putting together a list of guests who may have a grudge? I don't know if I'll remember the ones I shared those stories with. I did like telling them after a few.”

“That would be helpful,” I said.

“Well, Costa, you've made more progress in a week than the so called professionals made in eight months.”

“And so far the same results,” I said. I'm not a big compliment guy. I've seen plenty of quarterbacks look great the first four games of a season, and they're watching the play-offs on television when the season ends.

“What made you think of that angle?”

“An acquaintance of mine mentioned that it's well

known some rich people have secret rooms in their large houses, where certain pieces of art reside and are admired by only one set of eyes. I don't imagine you know anything about that?"

Once again, the leaves were under harsh scrutiny by my client.

WE HAD DINNER at the Kowloon on Rte. 1. It was a Friday night and business was brisk. We had a booth not far from the kitchen doors. The smells that floated out over the room every time the waitstaff burst through them was not something that had to be described in words. The drool running over your chin told the story.

We had the Pu-Pu Platter for two, with sides of pork fried rice and lo mien. Eileen ate sparingly. I did not. It had probably been seven or eight years since I had eaten there, even though my office is only a few miles north, and I had forgotten how good the food was.

Eileen looked good. She had had her hair done and there were now light highlights in the dark color. The Kowloon is casual dining, and Eileen was dressed casually. But like everything else about her, her casual is several steps above every other woman's casual. She seemed more relaxed than she did at Harry's.

After asking about my day, and receiving only an abbreviated response, she said, "I had an interesting day."

"You had your hair done," said I, ever the observant P.I. Nothing escapes my all encompassing eye. Like Sauron, only without the pyrotechnics.

Eileen frowned theatrically. "I get my hair done regularly. Nothing interesting about that. But it's what happened at the salon that is interesting."

"And what was that?" I asked between nibbles on a pork spare rib, and not the boneless kind, either.

"A friend of mine owns the shop. In fact, I worked there as a hairdresser before marrying Benny. Well, she wants me to come back and work there. Three days a week. She's worked hard to make it upscale, and she's bringing in a younger clientele. She wants stylists with talent and imagination. And, she said this, class."

"Pencil me in," I said. "I'll be your first customer."

"I'd prefer a little more hair than you have to work with," Eileen said with a smile, "Although I'm sure I could do something to hide that receding hairline."

"Ouch!"

"It's okay," she smiled. "I like your forehead. Draws attention to your eyes. You have nice eyes, Paul. Kind eyes. It's the first thing I noticed about you."

Eileen's smile always takes me to places I haven't been in a while.

"So you're thinking of going back to work," I said.

"I'm afraid I'll have to after the divorce is final. I'll get the house, and the BMW, and some money. But without a child for child support... my lawyer isn't hopeful for a large monthly decision. There is a possibility I'll get nothing. Benny's lawyer is pushing for that. The judge will look at my situation, healthy, young and I have held jobs in the past."

"You can survive on three days a week?" I asked. I had no idea what stylists made, but to the best of my knowledge, most of them weren't driving Cadillac's and vacationing on the Riviera.

"For a while, I think. If I get half of the bank account, I won't be running yard sales."

Eileen twirled her fork in the lo mien pile on her plate, but didn't raise it.

"If I could only get half of what Benny has off shore, I'd never have to work another day in my life."

I raised my eyebrows rather than ask the question. She shook her head.

"Forget I said that, Paul. No one knows about that. Not my lawyer, not the judge. If Benny knew I knew...Well, he doesn't. Thank God."

"Didn't you say your husband was a CPA?"

"He is."

"Business must be very good if he has to hide stuff out of the country."

"He is very good."

"Where's his office?" I know most of the big firms. Can't do what I do without running into the money guys.

"He doesn't have an office. Let's drop it, Paul."

"No office?" Holding a rib about a foot from my mouth, I stared at Eileen, who was frowning again.

"Small, exclusive clientele?" I asked.

"Paul, please, drop it. I don't want to talk about it. Please." A hint of anger had crept into her voice, along with something else. Fear?

"Sure," I said. "Sorry. So where's this fancy salon located?"

We spoke no more about her husband and his business, but, obviously, it was time for a little sleuthing on my part concerning Ben Landry.

After dinner, and a pleasant drive up into Gloucester and Marblehead on a clear and cool evening, we stopped at Harry's for a nightcap on the way back home.

There was a three piece combo on the small stage in the corner playing songs from the fifties and early sixties. Just the kind of songs Harry's clientele enjoyed. The dance floor, small as it is, was full.

Eileen and I got lucky. Just as we entered, a couple was slipping into their coats and Harry hustled us to the table before anyone at the bar got ideas.

"Wow," said Eileen as she shed her wrap and sat. "A lot busier than Thursday nights."

"Harry does a hell of a business on the weekend," I said, raising my voice a bit to be heard above the singer.

"This is nice," she said.

And it was. I watched her watching the band, watching the dancers, tapping her foot to the music, sipping her Manhattan. She was enjoying herself. The few times we had been together, she had never looked relaxed. The divorce was taking a heavy toll on her and it was obvious in the lines on her face, the constant strain of keeping it together. We stayed for an hour, until 11:30, when the combo took their last break before the last set. She kissed me lightly on the lips at her door and apologized for not being ready to go further. I brushed a strand of brown hair away from her eyes and told her I'd be ready when she was.

6

It has been my experience that Tuesdays and Wednesdays are the more popular days of the week for cheating spouses. I have several theories as to why that is, but none are backed up by government funded studies or articles written by phony doctors who host afternoon television shows. While I wait for Peter Gladstone to compile a list of names for me, I am out earning my thirty dollars a day.

Monday, Miranda Gallagher left her large home in Lynnfield at 10:30 in the A.M. She drove her white BMW to the main shopping area, parked on the street and entered a hair salon. At 11:45, she picked up dry cleaning several stores down from the salon. From there she drove to a grocery store, exiting at 1:15 with a shopping cart full. She opened her garage door at 1:42. Dani Gallagher was dropped off at the house at 3:55 by a boy driving a two year old Mazda.

Most people are under the impression that the life of a Private Eye is an exciting one. What they see on television is not quite accurate. I hate to be the one to dispel that notion, but there it is.

Tuesday morning I was back at my post, parked on the main street through the development with line of sight of the Gallagher house. I spent the entire day there, drinking coffee from a thermos and doing crossword puzzles. The BMW never left the garage. Jeffrey Gallagher's blue Lincoln pulled into the driveway seconds before the Mazda dropped off Dani. Father and daughter spoke briefly in the drive, then entered the house together. I had worked up a hefty appetite, and stopped at a favorite restaurant on the way home and spent my day's pay.

Wednesday was beginning to feel a lot like Tuesday, but the garage door slowly opened and the BMW backed out at 11:15 with Miranda behind the wheel. She drove to Route 1, then headed north, taking the exit for Route 128 East. She took the exit off 128 for the Mall, parked in the lot and entered the sprawling shopping center. At 12:10 she walked back to her car carrying a shopping bag. The store name on the bag; Victoria's Secret.

The BMW then drove back to Route 1, taking the exit south. A mile later, Miranda pulled into a motel. She was in the office for ten minutes, then drove right past me to the door furthest from the office. She locked the car door and opened the room's door, disappearing behind it at a quarter to one, but not before I had taken eight photos.

The motel's parking lot was almost completely empty, as you would expect at that time, most of the cars there I assumed belonging to the cleaning staff that were entering and exiting rooms with their cleaning carts.

At exactly one P.M., a sporty red car drove into the lot and parked beside the Beamer. From the drivers side a man stepped onto the pavement, rolling his head as if he had a crick in his neck. He looked young and in shape. He wore a tight fitting black tee shirt over black denim jeans. I took four photos of him before he got to the door, and three more after Miranda opened it. Even from the distance I was at, I couldn't help but admire Miranda's body standing in the doorway. The only two pieces of cloth on her well-cared-for frame, were a red lacy bra that hardly contained her breasts, and a thin strip of red lace just below her flat stomach. The door closed and I settled in to wait.

Dani's suspicions were correct. Her step-mom was indeed having an affair. I would follow the man when he left, and have a talk with him as I had promised I would do. He looked to be in his early twenties, the short sleeves of the tee tight on his biceps. There was a good chance he might not react well to what I had to say, but I'd deal with that when and if he resented my advice. My guess is, with the memory of Miranda in that red outfit still fresh in his mind, along with whatever delights were going on behind the door, he would not be reasonable.

I poured a cup of coffee from my thermos, but before I could take a sip, a blue Continental came speeding into the lot and parked on the other side of the BMW. Jeffrey Gallagher, in suit and tie, stepped from the car and hurried to the door of the room where his wife was entertaining her lover. He knocked twice.

Several thoughts raced through my mind in those few seconds and I almost spilled the cup trying to put it on the dash. Should I go to the room and end the fight that was sure to start? If Jeffrey had a gun, could I get there before he used it? Should I lay on my horn and make a distraction that would get the attention of all three.

The door opened quicker than I could decide on a course of action, and Gallagher, with a quick look around the area, stepped in and the door closed behind him. The sound of the traffic on Route 1 reached the back of the parking lot, but it was muted. I was sure I'd be able to hear a gun shot if there was one. The seconds ticked by slower than a Ronald Reagan speech. I had the car door partially open, ready to move, but I heard no sounds coming from the room. Perhaps they were in there discussing the situation like reasonable, intelligent adults. I had been so shocked by the appearance of Jeffrey Gallagher that I hadn't taken one picture of him.

It was 3:35 when the door opened again. The young guy strolled to his car and drove out of the lot, but not before I got a few more pictures of him, plus the plate on the car. My plan had been to follow him, but I wasn't going anywhere until I saw the Gallaghers. Ten minutes later, Jeffrey and Miranda came out of the room together. They stood at the door a few seconds, Miranda was talking, then they kissed and went to their cars. First Miranda left, Jeffrey right behind her. I snapped another dozen shots of it all.

I have been a Private Detective for a third my life, entering the trade after three years as a cop, and it isn't often when things happen that I'm surprised at. But every once and a while.... Jeffrey Gallagher spent two and a half hours in that room with his attractive wife and a young man, either as a spectator or a participant. I'm not one to make judgments. Live and let live, I say. As for me, I'm fine sharing my booze, my time and my advice. Anything else, get your own.

I drove back to the office. There were three messages on the machine, all from Dani. The final one said she would call me from school during her lunch break tomorrow. I thought about how I would tell her what I had to tell her about her father. I decided a picture is worth a thousand words. Five or six photos would write a convincing short story.

After dinner at my condo, I entered the small second bedroom that serves as a home office and dark room, and processed the film. I chose the dozen that I would show Dani. Then I put on the Bruins and grabbed a beer.

WE MET AT the Dunkin's again. Dani sat staring out the big windows at the traffic going by. I had shown her the pictures without a preamble. After studying them, she looked up at me, a puzzled look on her face. That lasted about ten seconds. She'd been staring outside ever since.

"And he has the nerve to lecture me," she hissed, still not looking at me. "Did you find out who the guy is?"

"Does it matter?" I asked.

She didn't answer.

"Dani...," I began to say, but she waved me off.

"I know, I know," she said. "It's just a bit of a shock is all. I suppose I should be relieved Miranda's not having an affair that would destroy my dad, but I'll never be able to look at him the same way again."

"It's always a shock when the child finds out the parent isn't Mother Teresa or Pope John Paul. They aren't doing anything illegal, Dani. My advice to you is, you never mention it. Ever. Not even when your dad gets all dad on you. This part of their life has no impact on you and your life."

"You ever find things out about your parents?" she asked.

"Yes, I did. When I was old enough to notice. I discovered my father cheated at Monopoly and my mother consumed two glasses of wine every night after us kids were in bed."

"Not the same thing, Paul."

"You know, Dani, if you really think about it, it is."

We sat for a while longer. She paid me ninety dollars. I offered her a ride home, but she said she wanted to walk. When I stood, I held out my hand for the photos that she still had in front of her. She hesitated for a second, but handed them over.

"Call me anytime," I said. "I'm a good listener."

Oh, to be seventeen again. Yeah, right. No thanks.

THE WEDNESDAY CROWD in Harry's is much like the Thursday night crowd. Thin. Celtics on the tube instead of the Bruins. Eileen said she had something to do on Thursday, so we had agreed to meet at Harry's on Wednesday. We sat in OUR booth, as she had begun calling it. It was eight-thirty. Eileen was in good spirits.

"You had a good day?" I asked.

"I did," Eileen answered, a smile on that lovely face. "I heard from my lawyer. We go to court again on December eighth. It could all be settled before Christmas. I couldn't ask for a better present."

"Well, I'll drink to that," I said and lifted my beer. "We should celebrate this weekend. What's your favorite restaurant?"

Her smile waned as she slowly traced a finger along the rim of her glass. When she looked up at me her eyes were wary.

"I have a friend," Eileen said. "He lives in New York. Across from Central Park."

"Must be a rich friend," I said, not sure where she was going.

"He is. He likes to brag that he can get tickets to any show, any night, any time."

"And?"

"Can you get away this weekend, Paul? Take a train to the city? See a show? I mean, if you want."

"Are you sure?" I asked.

I received a nod with no hesitancy.

"Then, I want."

Her face lit up. "It's been so long since I've been to the theater. You have no idea. I'll call him tonight when I get home. Do you like musicals? I love musicals."

"A musical would be fine," I said. I think I've been to two live shows in my life, both at North Shore Music for theater in the round. Enjoyable, but really not my thing. I'm more of a *Terminator* kind of guy. But to have the chance to spend a weekend in New York with Eileen, I'd sit through two shows.

Eileen reached across the table and took my hands in hers. "I'll go shopping tomorrow, Paul. Pick up something nice to wear. Make you happy to be seen in public with me."

"You could be wearing a potato sack, and I'd walk into the Ritz with you and consider myself a lucky man."

"You're kind," she said, her smile fading a bit. "I look in the mirror, Paul. I see the age lines, the puffiness around the eyes. The sag to the cheeks. This divorce has aged me."

"You're a knock-out, Eileen," I said, and I meant it. "You might want to buy new mirrors."

She smiled at that and became quiet. We drank in silence for a bit.

An attractive woman came through the door. She was about three inches over five feet and full figured, with black hair, shoulder length and thick. Her dress was simple, yet stylish, and came demurely to the top of her knees. She wore a black fur wrap that covered her shoulders and a wide silver necklace that highlighted her dark Mediterranean skin. The woman walked to the bar and took the stool at the far end. Leaving a table he had been standing beside, Harry immediately went to the woman, took her offered hand in his, leaned across the bar and they kissed each other on both cheeks. Very European.

"An old friend of Harry's?" asked Eileen, who had watched the whole thing, as did everyone else in the bar.

I nodded. "She's the reason we're sitting here?"

"I don't understand," said Eileen, a puzzled look on her face. "Who is she?"

"Marie Glendali."

"Oh."

"You know who she is?" I asked.

Eileen nodded. "How does Harry know her?"

"Now there's a story," I said.

ALL DEBTS ARE NOW PAID

7

Harry Mills pulled the plastic trash bag from the receptacle under the bar. It was a Saturday night after closing and the bag was barely half full. Six months since opening the bar, since sinking all his money and some of the banks into the renovated space last April, and still, even during the busy beach traffic during the summer, he rarely covered expenses each week. And now, with the amusements closed for the winter, and traffic light on the boulevard, the bar was sinking into a pit of red ink.

As he tied the top of the bag into a knot, he questioned, and not for the first time, the wisdom of walking away from a good job in San Diego to come across the country to Revere, Massachusetts, to open a bar. He had no experience in owning a bar, which clearly was a handicap in the beginning, but he felt his biggest handicap was the color of his skin. The good folks of Revere were not particularly friendly to a black businessman. At least Harry didn't believe they were. But he knew the place was a bar before he bought it, it was owned by a white guy, and the bank repossessed the property. The location wasn't bad, ample parking and prices were cheap. Still, he was losing money. The regulars he had weren't going to keep him afloat.

Harry pushed out through the metal back door stepping into the back lot. The dumpster was to his right, but as he turned, he heard a muffled noise. He looked ahead of him to a row of trees, a chain link fence, and the backs of two houses beyond his lot, but saw nothing. Raccoons had been getting into his trash and he half expected to see one. The muffled sound came again. It sounded like a person attempting to cry out but unable to. Harry took a few more steps toward the middle of the lot and the rear of a car came into sight beyond the side of his building. The sound seemed to be coming from that direction. As he walked towards the vehicle, he could see there were people in the back seat. Again the muffled cry, and suddenly a sharp slap followed by a painful moan. Harry dropped the bag and rushed to the car.

The car was a green two-door Dodge. Reaching the car, Harry looked in the open back window. The front bucket seats were leaning forward. There were two men in the back. One guy was holding a woman down on the seat by her shoulders, while the other was attempting to rip her slacks off. He had them down to her knees. Her blouse was open and her bra was torn in half.

Harry ripped open the car door, reached in to the guy who was struggling with the slacks, grabbed him by the collar of his shirt and dragged him from the car. The guy was so stunned, he came out easily. But when his backside made contact with the dirt, he swore and came quickly to his feet.

"Big mistake, asshole," he said as he charged Harry.

Harry Mills, a Golden Glove boxer for a few years after high school, side stepped the charge and landed a mean right to the temple, the man going face down into the dirt and laying still. The other guy was struggling to get out of the car. He had one hand on the door frame and a switchblade in the other as he pulled himself out. Harry heard bone break as he smashed his fist into the nose of the man. The force of the blow sent the assailant's head back, his neck hitting the frame of the roof hard. As he fell to his knees, Harry used his size twelve boot to send him to dreamland.

Looking inside the car, the woman was conscious, but was dazed. She was attempting to scurry into the corner of the backseat, away from him.

"It's all right," Harry said. "They can't hurt you now. You should come inside with me. I have to call the cops."

The woman refused to leave her spot. She was hugging her knees to her body.

"I'll be right back. I'm just going in to call 9-1-1. Stay

right there. I swear to you, I'll be right back. You're safe. These boys will be out for a while."

Harry rushed in, called 9-1-1, said he needed police and an ambulance, then rushed back out. The woman was out of the car. She had pulled her slacks up and was hugging her tattered blouse to her body, as she slowly walked toward the front of the building, unsteady on her feet, toward a car parked in the far end of the front lot. Harry came up into her line of vision, a good ten feet from her.

"Miss," he said. "Please come inside. I've called the police. They'll be here any minute. Please come inside. You should sit. We can wait together for them to get here. You shouldn't be out here."

The dazed woman took a few more steps, then stopped. She stood still for several moments, then she began sobbing, her body shaking. Harry took a few steps closer to her and reached out a hand.

"Please, Miss. Come inside. It's cold out here. You're safe. I promise. Come inside."

The young woman stood sobbing and gave no resistance when Harry came up beside her and gently steered her towards the front doors. He had locked them before beginning to clean up, so he reached into his pocket for the keys. Just then, the first Revere cop car pulled into the lot and drove right up to him. Two police officers got out of the car.

Stepping away from the woman, Harry met the two cops. "Two men tried to rape this woman. In that car over there." He pointed to the Dodge. "They're on the ground now. One of them may need an ambulance."

"What about her?" asked the older cop as the younger guy drew his gun and ran over to the Dodge.

"I think she'll be all right," said Harry. "She needs to sit. A stiff drink will help." Harry looked towards the Dodge. "I got there before they got what they wanted. But they did rough her up."

"You know her?" asked the cop.

"Never saw her before tonight. She came in a half hour

before closing. Ordered a seven and seven during last call. She was one of the last to leave, along with the two dudes lying on the ground now."

"Okay. Get her settled. We'll take care of this out here and then we'll come in to talk with her."

As Harry was about to enter the bar with the woman, another police car sped into the lot and in the distance he saw the flashing lights of the approaching ambulance.

The two officers who showed up first entered the bar about ten minutes after Harry had gotten the woman to sit and he had placed a whiskey in front of her. He had also given her one of his shirts from out back so she could cover herself, and an ice bag to place on her lip to ease the swelling. Harry met the two cops halfway across the room, as a paramedic was checking on the woman.

"She may still be a little unraveled, but she's a tough cookie. She seems okay. Said her name was Marie."

"Okay," said the older cop. "I'm going to talk with her. Meanwhile, my partner, Officer Carlson, will talk to you. Then I'll talk to you later."

"Sure," said Harry.

"By the way, what did you hit those boys with?"

"My fist."

"The kid on the ground was still groggy when we put him in the back of the cruiser. The other guy, crumpled up like a rag doll, still hasn't come around. The ambulance is going to take him to the hospital. You got a punch like a mule kick."

"Only wish I had gotten to her sooner," said Harry.

The older cop went around the table where the woman sat and introduced himself. Then he sat down. The younger cop, Officer Carlson, steered Harry to another table. Before Carlson sat, he looked over at the woman, really noticing her for the first time. He swore under his breath.

"Officer Webster," he called to his partner, who looked perturbed to be interrupted. "Can I see you a minute?"

Webster excused himself and walked to Carlson, who now stood off to the side, giving him an inquiring look.

"You know who she is?" asked Carlson.

"You didn't give me a chance to find out," said Webster.

"That's Marie Glendali," whispered Carlson.

Webster looked back at the woman. "You sure?"

"Positive."

"Okay." Webster walked over to the phone and made a call.

"What's going on?" Harry asked as Carlson sat down in front of him.

"You know who she is?" Carlson asked.

"She told me her name is Marie. That's all I know."

"Yeah. It is. Marie Glendali."

"Glendali?" said Harry. "Like the Mafia guy?"

"Like THE Mafia guy," whispered Carlson. "One and the same. Those boys you punched out tonight? Dead men walking."

Ten minutes after Websters' call, two cars came speeding into the lot, four men in each. One man from each car got out and entered the bar. The other six stood outside.

"Officer Webster?" said a well dressed middle aged man, the younger man of the two, as he approached .

"I'm Webster."

"My name is Richard Baldwin, Officer Webster, an attorney for the Glendali family. This gentleman is a doctor for the family. Mr. Glendali has asked me to convey to you his gratitude for the phone call and asks that you allow the doctor to take a quick evaluation of his daughter before asking any more questions."

"Of course," said Webster. "We're pretty much done with the questions."

"Then it would be all right if we took her to a hospital now and did the evaluation there?" asked the lawyer.

"I don't need a hospital, Dick," Marie Glendali said in a way that left no room for argument.

"Then we will take you home, Ms. Glendali, and leave that up to your father. Doctor, take her home in your car if you would."

Marie Glendali stood and began walking toward the door, then stopped and walked to where Harry Mills sat watching. She bent down and whispered in his ear, then touched his cheek with the palm of her right hand, turned and walked away.

After Marie left, the lawyer came and stood beside Harry.

"What is your name, sir?" he asked.

"Harry Mills, Mr. Baldwin."

"And this is your establishment?"

"Yes, sir, this is my bar."

The lawyer sat. "Could you please tell me everything that happened, Mr. Mills. Everything. Leave nothing out."

Harry looked at the two cops. Webster shrugged and took a seat. Carlson did the same.

8

And that's how Harry knows Marie Glendali," I said, finishing up my telling of the tale. "Eighteen years later, Marie still stops in every now and then. There isn't anything Harry wouldn't do for Marie. Run through a wall, kill anyone who tried to hurt her."

"Shouldn't it be the other way around?" asked Eileen, still watching the two of them at the end of the bar, talking and smiling, occasionally laughing.

"Well, therein lies the rest of the story, as Paul Harvey likes to say. The following day, Sunday, Harry opens the bar at five. Sunday nights were dead, but he would come in and putter around, clean up whatever he missed from the night before. Not that there was ever much to clean up. At eight, three men walk into the bar. Two of them stand by the door, the other man, around fifty years old, wearing a heavy gray overcoat, walks up to the bar where Harry is moving some bottles around.

"'Mr. Mills,' the man said. Harry turned and said, 'Yes sir, can I help you?' The man put out his hand and said, 'You already have. A service I can never repay. I'm Joseph Glendali.'

"Now, I wasn't here. Didn't even know this place existed. And Harry will never talk about the conversation. But Rose was here..."

"Rose?" said Eileen.

I pointed to Rose, who was in her customary position at the bar.

"I've noticed her before. She's been here when I've come in."

"Rose is here every night. Comes in at 7:30 and you can set your watch. When she leaves, varies. Anyway, it was Rose who told me what she heard, although she admitted she didn't hear much. Harry shook the man's hand and inquired about Marie. Rose heard Mr. Glendali say that Marie was resting, and other than a few bruises, she was okay. Just shook up, which you would expect. Then, Glendali takes a fat envelope from his pocket and holds it out to Harry. Rose said Harry took a full step back, like he had been slapped. She heard him say, 'No, sir. I only did what any man would have done. Knowing your daughter is well, is enough for me.' Rose said Glendali held that envelope out over the bar for ten seconds. Then he put it back in his pocket. Glendali then said, and Rose swears this is true, 'Any man, Mr. Mills? Two of those any men wanted to rape my baby. And they would have if you hadn't stopped them.'

"Rose said Glendali then looked around the bar, telling Harry to pour two shot glasses of bourbon. While Harry was doing that, Glendali mentioned that it seemed to be a quiet night in the bar. Glendali pushed one glass towards Harry and picked up the other. They touched glasses and drank. Then Glendali motioned Harry to the end of the bar where the two men talked out of ear shot of the five people in the place. Fifteen minutes later, Joseph Glendali shook hands again and left."

"And that was the end of it?" asked Eileen.

"No," I said. "That was the beginning."

"The beginning?"

"All of a sudden, Harry's Bar was the place to be. Wise guys were coming in for drinks in the afternoon. Stopping in nights during the week. Packing the place on weekends. Bringing their wives. Their girlfriends. Their mistresses. Harry had to start bringing in entertainment three nights a week, because they demanded it."

I pointed to the stage. "You know who's been on that stage?

"Who?"

"You ever hear of Jerry Vale?"

"Get out," Eileen said. "I love Jerry Vale."

"How about Al Martino?"

"*Red Roses For A Blue Lady.* I danced to that with my

boyfriend at prom."

"Almost everyone except Sinatra. If they were playing a club, Blinstrub's, Beverly, the Frolic, wherever, they managed to make an appearance here. Sing a few songs as a favor to the big man in Providence, who was doing a favor for Glendali. Over the years it's calmed down, mainly because the entertainment business has changed, but you've seen the business Harry does on weekends. More than carries him through the week."

"So Mr. Glendali paid his debt," stated Eileen, and she frowned.

"I don't think so," I said, "but I don't know. Again, Harry doesn't talk about this, but I don't believe Harry has ever had a reason to ask a favor. Glendali putting out the word to help fill the bar, is a big do, but compared to what Harry did for his daughter? I don't imagine, in the big man's eyes, scales were even. Not by a long shot."

"Have you ever met Mr. Glendali?" asked Eileen.

I shook my head. "Never a reason to. He runs a tight ship. Managed to stay out of prison. Greases the palms that need to be greased. And he is a hard, old man. You know those boys who tried to rape his daughter? They went on trial. Got a lawyer. Argued Marie was flirting with them and she was all in. Consensual. Until the black guy butted in for no reason and roughed them up. Joe Glendali sat in the third row every day of the trial, told his lawyer not to press. The boys walked. After the verdict, one of the boys turned and smirked at Marie. Flashed her the finger. Three weeks after the trial, no one saw or heard from those boys ever again."

Eileen slowly nodded as she picked up her drink. She looked over at the bar. Marie Glendali reached out her right hand and placed it against Harry's cheek. Harry smiled. Marie turned and walked from the bar. A very large man who had been sitting quietly, stood suddenly and followed her out. Eileen looked at me when that happened, concern on her attractive face.

"He's with her," I said. "Probably another guy in the car. Bush should have such protection. Enough about

Marie. What show should we see in New York?"

Eileen's face lit up. She should smile more and frown less.

"I was thinking *Les Miz*. Or maybe *Phantom.* I would really like to see them."

"Then I want to see them, too. Whatever you want."

I WAS BACK in my office Monday morning. The weekend in New York with Eileen was perfect. I enjoyed the shows, the food, and Eileen. Especially Eileen.

There were messages on the machine. Two of them from Peter Gladstone. The first message informed me he had a list of names compiled. The second message from the rich man claimed he knew who was behind the heist, and he wanted me at his business office at one. One message was from Timothy O'Neil, the Irish hood who runs the rackets in Charlestown and part of Chelsea, demanding that I call him at the earliest to discuss a matter of importance. He left a number to dial. I assumed he made the call with his sister standing beside him, showing her he would be taking care of things that concerned the roughing up of her son. I'll keep O'Neil waiting a day or two, call and we'll talk things through. Nothing will come of it.

The last message came just an hour before I got in. It was short and sweet. 'This is Ben Landry. Stay away from my wife. This is your only warning.' End of call. He didn't sound like a CPA.

I called Eileen.

"Good morning."

"Mmmm. Good morning," she sighed. It sounded like I woke her.

"I'm sorry. I woke you," I said.

"You did," Eileen said. "I had a very busy weekend. Exhausting. But fun. Why are you calling? Are you missing me already?"

"I am."

"It's nice to be missed."

"Are you okay?" I asked.

"Never better. Why? Is everything okay with you?"

"It is. I have a busy day. Shall we get together for dinner?"

She hesitated. "Not tonight, Paul. How about Wednesday? The Ship and a nightcap at Harry's?"

"Sure. I'll call you tomorrow," I said. "Go back to sleep."

I decided it was time to dig into Ben Landry, his job and his past. I knew nothing about the guy, other than what I had learned from Eileen, who spoke rarely of him. I also knew he had the bad habit of physically abusing women. Well, at least one woman. I would check him out, track him down, and we would have a conversation. But before my meeting with Gladstone, and after my coffee and doughnuts, I had a favor to do for a friend.

Billy Shute was an old friend from the neighborhood. We grew up together on the streets of Everett, terrorizing the projects where he lived above Glendale Park. Billy's a good egg. After high school, I spent two years in Community College before the Police Academy, Billy got a job in the trades. He's a plumber. A few years ago, Billy took a bad fall off a ladder while on the job. Hurt his back. Ended up he couldn't work, and has been collecting disability since. The company paying the disability has demanded different doctors check him out over the past eighteen months. They think he's taking them for a ride. That he's healthy enough to work, despite the doctors agreeing that climbing, bending, and maybe even walking, could lead to permanent damage that could have him in a wheelchair for the rest of his life.

Billy went to a lawyer, claiming the insurance company was harassing him. That they have people following him, ready to take pictures of him lifting a grocery bag. Or bowling. Billy is not above playing the system. Hey, that's Billy. But I love the guy. He got me out of plenty of scraps back in the day.

The lawyer wants to go after the insurance company for harassment, but needs proof that they are harassing him. That's where I come in. I'll follow Billy around on days he leaves the house, and see if any Ansel Adams are tailing him. I'll use my photographic skills to capture theirs. This will all be done pro bono. If my mother ever found out I was billing Billy for my services, she'd dig out the wooden spatula and give me a good 'what for', reminding me I'm not too old for reprimands of perceived social sins. Ma regards Billy Shute as family, even though he isn't Italian, and you don't charge family for services rendered. Ma's law, which is pretty much THE law. Billy is leaving his house in Malden at nine to do a little shopping at the Mall. I'll stick with him until twelve thirty, then drive up to Gladstone's offices in Burlington.

But first, two honey-dipped doughnuts.

GLADSTONE HAS OFFICES in Burlington in one of the buildings that face 128, the highway that circles the greater Boston area. The building, in a complex of six such buildings, is six stories, and has the name of his software company boldly attached across the top floor. What I know about software, and computers, could be printed in large letters on a dime. I do understand that computers will soon be an important part of everyone's life, or so I've read, but, like having children of my own, I hope to avoid their intrusion into my life.

His company uses the top three floors, the bottom three empty so far, and I showed up promptly at one at his office on the top floor.

The woman who greeted me was in her twenties, attractive, neatly dressed and professional. She offered me coffee, or a soft drink, showed me a comfortable area where I could sit, and assured me Mr. Gladstone would be available in a few minutes. Thirty minutes later my client buzzed her that he was ready for me. I didn't mind the wait. He was, after all, paying me for my time, and his secretary was quite pleasant to look at. Unlike the art that hung on the walls, which were all painted lines and shapes. Like Picasso on steroids. Or LSD.

Gladstone's office was almost as large as the foyer, but the art that hung in there was very different. Paintings of boats in harbor with weathered wooden buildings on docks in the distance. Two with lighthouses being battered by the sea. One was a huge blowup of a photograph of a slender cruiser, all mahogany and chrome, with Gladstone at the wheel. That one was centered behind the desk. He ushered me toward a pair of low-backed chairs that had a thirty inch round smoked glass and chrome table between them. He placed his drink on the glass and sat. I had nothing to contribute to the dust free table, so I just took the other chair.

"Thanks for coming," he said. "How was your weekend?"

Small talk. From Peter Gladstone. Made me think he had something that he was going to tell me, some accusation he was going to make about someone, but he wasn't a hundred percent sure he was correct. Maybe not even fifty percent sure. I'd play along. It was his dime.

"Better than most," I replied. "Is that your boat?" I asked, gesturing to the blowup behind his desk. I can make small talk, too.

"She's a beauty, isn't she?" he said. "Thirty-eight foot Stephens Brothers from the forties. Triple cockpit Roundabout. I had her all refurbished two years ago. When she's in the water, I have her up on Winnipesaukee. I have a place on the water in Wolfeboro. There's a forty-foot cabin cruiser in the boat house in Marblehead. A party boat. The Roundabout is mostly just for me and whoever I happen to be seeing.

"All my peers are buying yachts. What the hell am I going to do with a yacht? I'm not going to pilot it. Need a captain for that. No, this baby is the way to be on the water." He cocked his head towards the picture. "She can do forty knots and not even break a sweat."

He reached over to his cup, that I assumed held coffee, and took a sip.

"I may know who has my paintings," he said.

"Did it come to you while you were making the list I asked for, or did a name just pop into your head?"

"Does it matter?"

"It might," I answered. "A name that jumps out at you from a well thought out list is better than a name that you come up with because you think that person would do this to you because of something that happened in the past."

"I'll disagree with that," he said. "I sat down last night to start a list, and it was like a lightning bolt struck. First name that came to me is the guy who did it."

"If, in fact, my theory is correct," I said. "Could very well be a theft with no connection to you."

"I've been thinking about that, too. The more I thought about it, the more I think your theory is spot on. The whole thing was too smooth."

"A good crew could run an operation that smoothly. Don't kid yourself. Okay, what's the name, and why would they do it?"

"Gunther Kolb."

"Okay. Why him?"

"You know anything about computers?"

"Yeah. I know I don't want one."

Gladstone smirked. "You will. Everyone will. And in a few years, as the price drops, everyone will have one in their home and not just in their office. If I told you where the technology will be in twenty years, you wouldn't believe me. My software will help it get there."

"Good for you," I said. "Don't hold it against me if I don't share your enthusiasm. I'm getting along just fine without a computer in my place, or in my office."

"Dinosaurs died out sixty-five million years ago, Costa. You'll have one. Probably before I sell my business."

"You're selling?"

"Of course. All us small players will be selling. The big boys, and they are yet to be decided, will buy up all the competition, or merge us under their banner. They'll own it all. And they will pay handsomely for it."

"You're already a rich man," I said. Like I always say, the rich are a greedy bunch.

"Yes, I am," said Gladstone. "Very rich. But there are levels of wealth coming that most people won't be able to get their heads around. That's the level I want to be at. When I sell, I will be."

"Tell me about Gunther Kolb," I said.

I didn't want to hear any more about money. Or his business. Tell me you're going to make a fortune from the widget you just manufactured, and I can look at that widget and understand it. Tell me you're making a fortune from something I can't see or understand, and I'm thinking you're a snake oil salesman. Life was simpler when I was banging my Dodgem car into other Dodgem cars back when you could ride the Dodgems' in the amusement park at Revere Beach. The park is gone now. The Dodgems are gone. The Cyclone, Himalaya, the Wild Mouse, all gone. Now kids play Atari in their living rooms, and soon, I guess, a computer will be eating up hours of their days. Progress? You can have it.

"Kolb was a business associate of mine," Gladstone was saying, bringing me back from my trip along Nostalgia Lane and Middle Age Rant Row. "We shared an apartment when we were at MIT, and I had shared a vision of what was to become my software."

"Your software," I interrupted. "Was it a shared vision?"

"No. He never saw the potential. Fought me every step of the way. Argued we should go in another direction. Then, when I put it all together, Gunther then saw the genius of it. He was like a drummer in most rock groups. The ones who don't have the talent to write the songs or sing them. If they weren't part of the group, someone else would have been. Beatles, perfect example."

"Don't let Charlie Watts hear you say that."

He frowned.

"Then, after no real contribution, other than negativity, he thought we should have a fifty-fifty partnership. I laughed in his face. Got all the patents in my name. He threatened me. When I didn't succumb to his threats, he got a lawyer. The guy wasn't too sharp. My lawyer ate him for lunch. Gunther lost in court, and in the appeal."

"And you invite him to your house now?"

"Gunther hooked up with a guy from Stanford. Between the two of them, they created software that Gunther really wanted to go with when we were living together. No IPO yet, but their company is doing fine. We've actually partnered on a few things and share three patents. I thought the past was in the past. This stuff goes on all the time.

"But the other night, it hit me. Gunther has always been thin skinned. Even at school. He always thought some students were against him. He was always plotting ways to get even with them for perceived slights. And to seal the deal, I remembered telling him the story of when I picked up the de Keyser.

"It's Gunther. He always was a son-of-a-bitch. He'd sue his mother if he thought there was profit in it."

"Where is Gunther Kolb now?"

"He's in a high rise on the Cambridge side of the Charles when he's around here, and owns a huge house outside of Hartford. His company has main offices in Hartford, where they are based, and offices in Boston, Houston and Palo Alto. His partner is on the West Coast. A fellow named Wes Woodward. The two of them came up with a program that will revolutionize the insurance business. Brilliant, really. They use some of my stuff in the process.

"I'm hearing rumors they'll be acquired even before there can be an IPO. I think that's a mistake. Take the company public. Let the stock explode. Then sell. Take the buyers stock as payment. Ride the wave that will rise with the acquisition, sell and you and your future generations are set for life."

"So, with all this money Kolb will be worth, why bother stealing six million dollars worth of art that he could probably fence for only a million and a half?"

"It's personal, Costa. Just like you thought. I'm sure of it. So, how do we go about proving it?"

It was a little before two. We had been talking about fifteen minutes. I had felt pretty good before entering

Gladstone's office, but that was over. I had one name. I wanted several, but, instead, got one name. A name that may require trips to Hartford. Not that that was a big deal. Two hour drive up the Pike if the traffic isn't bad and if the road isn't being worked on. If Kolb did finance the heist, then he may have used Connecticut talent. I'm not familiar with the mob down there. Hopefully, Packy might be.

"Give me all the details on Gunther Kolb," I said in answer to Gladstone's question. "Everything you know from college days until now. Anything on his partner, too."

"Woodward? I doubt Gunther would involve him."

"Include him. Did Kolb ever show an interest in art? Ever go to art museums? Ever mention paintings? Did he paint?"

"This has nothing to do with owning art, Costa. This is all about getting even with me. I'm telling you."

"So, if Kolb took them, he may have already fenced them. They may be gone."

"I'm betting he has them," said Gladstone. "Let me tell you what's going to happen some day. I can almost guarantee it, because I know how much of an S. O. B. Gunther Kolb is. I thought about this while I was shaving this morning. Some day in the future, maybe ten, fifteen years from now, I will receive an anonymous package in the mail. And in that package will be photographs and a note. The photographs will be of the two paintings hanging on a wall with the statue in front of them. The note, with letters and words cut from newspapers or magazines, will tell me how much the sender is enjoying having them in his house. No name, obviously. But I'll know who it is."

"You've seen too many movies, Mr. Gladstone," I said.

"Not that many," Peter Gladstone said, "but Gunther has. He loves movies. And he loves theatrics. He's always been jealous of me. Jealous that I got my IPO out first. Jealous of my success. He's a petty little man. I really have had nothing to do with him since our falling out, except to invite him to a few parties. I only do it to show him how successful I've been. Even our joint ventures I run through intermediary's so I don't have to sit in the same room as him. I want you to nail the bastard."

FROM BURLINGTON, I drove to Cambridge. Not to check on Kolb's digs, but to the offices of a former client, a Certified Public Accountant, Robert Klein. Not the comedian. The last time I saw Klein, three years before, he must have weighed three hundred and fifty pounds. The guy who greeted me with a smile and limp handshake was a slim one eighty. I hardly recognized him. The not so obvious toupee made him look years younger, too.

"Mr. Costa, wonderful to see you again," he said, greeting me as he came out of his small office. "If you need help with your taxes, it's pro bono." Then Klein chuckled.

CPA Klein had hired me three years before to find out who his wife was seeing on the side, and get pictures for the divorce that he would sue for as soon as he had those photos. Mrs. Klein wasn't a bad looking woman, in fact she was pretty hot, with breasts that could be in one time zone while her feet were in another, so I wasn't surprised she had a lover, just surprised she had married Klein. Considering her husband was hardly ever home as he labored to build his business, I could understand the infidelity. During tax season, Robert Klein often slept on a futon he set up in his office. They had no kids to occupy her time.

Within three days, I had enough candids with her and her lover that any lawyer would salivate over. In seven days, I had a portfolio that rivaled the cameramen who are fortunate enough to click away on the Sports Illustrated's swimsuit issues. Instead of top models in scanty bathing suits on exotic beaches, my pictures, many taken through partially opened curtains of drab rooms, starred the lovely Mrs. Klein, and three buff studs who she rotated with in cheap motels that had weeds growing up through cracks in the parking lot. Insatiable, she was, in my humble opinion. The Ivory soap girl definitely had a rival, both in looks and imagination. Thanks to my photos, Klein walked away from the marriage with no loss of property or financial hardship at all.

"If I find myself above water, you're the guy I'm going to call," I said in answer to his pro bono offer.

"No, no, Mr. Costa. I'm the guy you call when you want someone to drain the water."

"Well, let's put that on a side-burner for now," I said as he led me into his office, away from the prying ears of three associates sitting at their desks sweating over pages of numbers, I could only assume.

Getting right to the reason for my visit, as I sat I asked, "Do you know, or have you ever heard of, a tax guy name of Ben Landry?"

"I've heard the name," said Klein frowning. "Never met him, though. He doesn't attend any conferences as far as I know. None that I've been to. I wouldn't suggest you hire him, Mr. Costa, not that you could. I believe his clientele is exclusive."

"Meaning?"

"He's the accountant for the mob," said Klein, his head shaking a bit. "They are his only client. Or so I've been told. But, again, I don't know him."

"Do you know how long he's been doing that?"

"I believe since graduating college. Twenty or so years ago. His father took care of the books for years, back in the heyday of the forties and fifties. When he keeled over with a heart attack, Kennedy was still alive, Robert, not John, Ben stepped in."

"You do seem to know about him, Bob. Why is that?"

"Only what I've heard, and that was a while ago. When I was at Suffolk, one of my buddies had an uncle in the mob. The uncle had Landry talk to my friend, maybe give him some help in seeing what he would be up against. Give him some hints on the business and the school. Landry graduated from the school in '65, I think it was. My buddy raved about Landry. Said he was a cool guy. Hip. CPA's aren't usually thought of as cool. Or hip. Know what I mean?"

"Sure," I said."You seem to be doing well. Everything's good?"

"Never better. Getting married again. High school sweetheart. She's pregnant."

I looked at the brown couch against the side wall that could become flat with very little effort. Were I the type of guy who dispensed advice like silly looking plastic containers dispensed Pez candy, I would advise Robert Klein to bring the damn thing to Goodwill. But, hey, I have bills to pay, too.

9

Coffee and doughnuts. Breakfast of champions. Preferably honey-dipped doughnuts, or glazed if you don't know any better. Powdered, if you're feeling a bit docile and needing the aggravation of constant brushing at powder on your vest to get the body moving and the juices flowing. Or, if you're feeling just a bit whimsical, plain, so you can dunk them in the coffee.

Normally, I enjoy licking the residue of honey-dip off my fingers, but I reached for a napkin when I spotted a dark shape casting a shadow on my pebbled glass office door in the outer office. The door opened without a knock, and two men walked in. I was sitting at my desk in the inner office, an empty Dunkin's bag to my left, a large regular to my right, and a holstered Beretta, fully loaded, that was taped to an easily accessible spot under the middle drawer of the desk. The smaller of the two men, a thin guy with eyes that bounced around like those of a cornered rat, closed the door and stood in front of it, hands folded in front of him. The bigger guy, about my size, sauntered into the office and sat down without an invitation to do so. He wore black jeans, white sneakers, a black tee shirt under a green Celtics windbreaker. His face beneath a buzz cut was pock-marked. This was Timothy O'Neil.

"We need to talk," O'Neil said.

"Sure," I said. "No charge for that. What do you want to talk about?"

"Don't get cute. You know why I'm here."

"Actually, I don't," I said. "I rough a dumb kid up a little, who happens to be your nephew, and you take exception. Or so I'm hearing. You know I could have broken bones were I so inclined.

You also know the girl was under aged, and while you could have bought his way out of that mess, it would have cost you. And you also know, at least I assume you do, the kid picked up a grand for his trouble."

O'Neil's brow furrowed. Not much. But enough.

"The kid didn't mention the money," I said. "Yeah. Family. What can you do?"

O'Neil rallied and tried to gain some momentum.

"Before you come to Charlestown, Costa, and throw your weight around, maybe you should check with me first."

"If I thought you had the girl," I said, smiling just a bit, "you're the first guy I would have looked up. But seventeen year old girls aren't your thing, are they, Timmy? Not unless they're desperate enough to work the streets for you. This one wasn't."

O'Neil gave me the hard stare. Maybe he didn't like the remark about his teenage hookers, or, maybe he didn't like being called Timmy. Either way, the conversation wasn't going exactly as he had planned. He reached into the pocket of his windbreaker. My hand wrapped around the handle of the Beretta. The rat in the other office, where a secretary would sit typing away like a good little secretary, if I had a secretary, was staring at something on the wall to his left. I can't imagine what. There's nothing hanging on that wall. Maybe a spider. The building has spiders. O'Neil pulled a pack of smokes from his pocket and a lighter. Without asking if he could smoke, he lit one up. No manners. I've always said that about the Irish. Ill-mannered drunks. Except for my best friend, Billy Shute, who's half Irish. Billy can drink with the best of them, but he has good manners. My mother was very impressed with his manners, and often told me I should be more like my friend Billy, before the wooden spatula spanked the back of my head.

We sat silently for a minute, staring at each other, him smoking and flicking ashes on my floor, me fighting the urge to plug him and make the world a better place. If he grinds the cigarette out on my floor, I may have to act on that urge.

"I don't give second warnings, Costa," he finally said as he stood.

"That's a shame," I said. "I've enjoyed our time together so much, I was hoping we'd have a chance to chat again."

He grinned at that. More a sneer, actually. "I heard about you, Costa. You ain't as tough as you think." O'Neil turned and walked out of my office, the little guy snapping out of his daydream and opening the door for his boss. When they were gone, I released the grip on the gun. So now I had the Irish mob pissed at me, and, if Ben Landry, accountant for the Italians, ever complained to his bosses, they may have reasons to visit my campus, too. Suddenly, I was becoming a very popular guy.

THE TRAFFIC ON the Pike wasn't heavy, and I got to the exit for the Interstate into Hartford by ten. Hartford, Connecticut, is an easy city to maneuver around and I pulled into a parking garage in the center of town across the street from the office building where Gunther Kolb's software business rented three entire floors. I don't know what this software stuff is, but it must be very profitable. The front lobby for the company was glass and chrome, and thick piled carpet that had a swirling design that made me think of the yellow bricked road to OZ. I assumed it was to convey the path to the future. Or riches. Or maybe it was just a swirl and didn't mean a damn thing. I was greeted by a lovely young woman who flashed a megawatt smile.

"May I help you?" she asked from her seat beyond a glass counter.

"Yes," I replied, gracing her with a smile of my own, pale in comparison at forty watts. "I have an appointment with Mr. Kolb. The name is Costa."

Normally, I like to drop in on people without an appointment. Catches them off guard. But Hartford isn't a short drive down 93 or up Route 1.

"Won't you please take a seat while you wait," she

said pleasantly, the smile actually, impossibly, becoming more radiant. "I'll ring Mr. Kolb's secretary."

After ten pleasant minutes spent admiring the young, attractive people who moved about the space, another young, attractive woman approached me. This one didn't smile.

"Mr. Costa?" she asked as she approached. "Please follow me."

As we walked along the tiled perimeter of the room, her four inch high heels kept a perfect beat to *Staying Alive.* I was remembering the one CPR class I took when I was a cop, when she said, "I'm afraid something very important has come up. Mr. Kolb, knowing you have driven a distance to meet, pushed a meeting back fifteen minutes to make sure he had time to speak with you, but he can only give you a few moments. I hope you understand."

More than you know, sweetheart, more than you know, is what I thought.

"I certainly appreciate whatever time he can spare," is what I said.

Kolb met me at the door to his office with a firm handshake. I was offered a stylish chair to sit in, all chrome and leather, with curved legs that I thought defied the laws governing the physics of sitting. I was offered bottled water, with my choice of four different fruit flavors. I politely declined.

"I understand you have an important meeting, so let me get right to it," I said. "Were you ever interviewed concerning the theft of art from Peter Gladstone's mansion?" No sense wasting time.

"Interviewed?" Kolb asked as he settled in behind his desk. He was a tall, lean man. Wiry. Good looking, with longish blonde hair and deep blue eyes. Tennis player, probably. Or handball. He was very tanned, even though we were now well into October. Maybe he had just returned from a Caribbean vacation. Maybe he was a member of a health club that had tanning booths.

"By the police. Or insurance investigators," I said.

He opened two manicured hands in front of him that had probably never suffered a callous, and asked, "Why would any investigator interview me, Mr. Costa, about the theft? Is that why you're here?"

"It is, yes."

"I see. And what is it you think I might know about it?"

"Were you at the gathering at Mr. Gladstone's a few weeks before they were stolen?"

"Are you working for Peter, Mr. Costa?"

"I am."

"I see. Did Peter say I was there?"

"Mr. Gladstone is compiling a list for me of those who attended that particular event."

"I see," said Kolb, folding his hands in front of him. "I have not been to Peter's home in at least three years. Did he not mention to you that we had a falling out?"

"He did," I said. "Patent infringements, disagreements on product, stuff like that. I got the impression that those kinds of things happen in your, uh, your....What exactly is it your company does?"

"We have created software that other businesses can use in their computers that makes it easier for them to do business. Do you understand computers at all, Mr. Costa?"

"I do not."

"I see. Well, computers are the hardware. Software is what you put into them that makes them work. Without software, all you would have is a few pounds of plastic, metal and electronics."

"And there is money in this software stuff?"

"There will be. The future is bright."

"I got that impression when I was at Mr. Gladstone's home."

"Yes. Peter has always been a bit extravagant. He did very well with the IPO," Kolb said, leaning back in the big chair. "I'm afraid his stock holders may not be as fortunate in the next year or two."

"Why is that, Mr. Kolb?" I suddenly had the feeling

that the second participant in the cat fight was about to bare their claws.

"Do you understand the market, Mr. Costa?" He was frowning at me, like Mr. Zinno, my high school algebra teacher, did whenever I asked a question that he felt I should already know the answer to.

"The only market I've been in is Star. I know the aisles fairly well. But if you mean the stock market, I regard that the same way I regard Las Vegas and Atlantic City. I shun them all like the plague."

"Very wise," Kolb said. "No place for amateurs. Yet amateurs try their luck every day. For every stock that rockets into the heavens with a rising price, there are a dozen that spiral down. Peter's IPO opened at five. Rose thirty percent the first day. With a six and a quarter million float, the market valued his company at a little over thirty-one million. Not bad. It leveled off at six and an eighth after the first week. Currently trades between four and three quarters and five and a quarter. Not a lot of daily trading. Still, after two years it has held fairly steady. It is my belief, however, that by this time next year, it will be down to close to three. In two years, a penny stock."

"And why is that, Mr. Kolb?"

"Glitches showing up in the product that haven't been fixed. Not sure they can be. But it doesn't matter. There will soon be similar software that will be better. His company will lose half its client list and begin bleeding money. The sting of having an inferior product will linger, drying up future clients. Plus, he has nothing in the pipeline. If he's fortunate, one of the big boys will buy his patents just to get him out of the way and bury the stench. But at a fraction of what he could have gotten three years ago. I tried to council him, but he wouldn't listen. Peter has always believed he is always the smartest guy in the room. And that will be his downfall."

"I see," I said. I know, I can be a jerk when the mood strikes, but Kolb didn't seem to notice. Or he was too polite to react. "So, you believe his company will fail. Is this based on hard facts, or animosity towards him?"

Kolb smiled. "Technology stocks are about to explode, Mr. Costa. There is a new world out there. The horror of 'Black Monday' has faded. And in this technology world, any company with a good product, or a great idea, will be seeing an increase in their stock price. If you own shares in a company whose price is dropping, sell and move on. The professional money managers will be abandoning Peter's ship. The amateurs will ride it to the bottom of a cruel sea."

Gunther Kolb glanced at his Rolex. "Now, if there is nothing else, I do have a very important meeting to attend."

"Just one more thing," I said. "By any chance, are you an art aficionado?"

Kolb calmly stared across his desk at me. The man is probably a very good poker player.

"There was a time, Mr. Costa, when we were roommates at MIT, and even a few years later, when Peter and I were very good friends. But over time, when you are that close to another, you eventually see all sides to them. Sometimes, what you see is not pleasant. Peter Gladstone is not a pleasant person. He is vindictive. Petty. Can be quite cruel. And not trustworthy. Among his many flaws. Did I have his art stolen? I did not. He may have suggested to you that I did, as some sort of retribution towards him for our falling out, but I did not. Soon, Peter will be broken, and I will find no pleasure in that. Nor will I grieve for him. Success or failure for him, means nothing to me anymore."

10

I was sitting at the bar at Harry's, sipping a beer and dining on peanuts, waiting for Eileen to show up. When I had called her to settle on a time to pick her up for dinner, she had said something came up and she had to cancel, but she'd meet me at Harry's around eight. It was eight-fifteen and still no Eileen.

I had spent the morning shadowing Billy Shute with nothing to show for it, but it gave me plenty of time to think about my meeting with Gunther Kolb the day before, and everything he said about my client, Peter Gladstone.

I'm in a business where lies and embellishments litter my path forward. Truth is somewhere on the horizon, and I will get to it only after a difficult trek through a maze of garbage. I never believe anything anyone tells me until I verify it. But it wasn't difficult for me to believe that my client would never be in a Papal discussion for sainthood after departing this life. Peter Gladstone may be the biggest jerk on the planet, it doesn't matter. He's my client. I'll do the best I can for him. Doesn't mean I'll have a beer with him after I'm done, however.

"Still no word from Sal?" I asked as Harry stood before me pulling on a draft beer handle. He looked at me and frowned.

"Paul, I'm telling you," Harry said, "that boy, if he has any intelligence at all, will stay wherever he is. He pissed off Wachowski and the Lynn boys with that stunt, and they have long memories. You and me, we'd say it's just Sal being Sal. Wachowski has no sense of humor. You know that."

"I know. But Sal will figure out something. He'll make

amends. Get back in their good graces. Come on. It's Sal."

"You always had a soft spot for him, Paul. Your partners kid. I get it. But he's not six years old anymore and you haven't thrown him a ball in over ten years. He's a grown ass man and should have known better. He damned near started a war between Wachowski and O'Neil with that stunt, and no one is laughing it off. My advice, and I know you know, Sal calls you, tell him this is no time to be coming back."

Harry topped off the third tall one and said, "Eileen's here."

I turned just as the door closed. Eileen gave a quick wave, then headed for a booth. Our booth. Harry mixed a Manhattan and I carried it, and my beer, over to sit with her.

"Everything okay?" I asked as I slipped into the booth. Eileen smiled up at me, but it was forced.

"Just a long day. Better now." She took a long sip from the Manhattan.

"Want to share?"

"Not really. Let's talk about more pleasant things. How was your day?"

In my business, I have found that when people say they don't want to talk about something, that could mean two things. First, they don't, and won't, talk about something. Second, they do want to talk about something, just not at that particular moment. Eventually, if Eileen wanted, she'd share. In the meantime, I had stuff I wanted to share, questions I wanted to ask, things I wanted to know.

"I've had a few easy days," I said, "doing detective stuff."

Eileen smiled. "Detective stuff? What does that mean? You found Jimmy Hoffa? Your investigation solved the mystery of the Black Dahlia? Your intuitive digging answered the question of the chicken or the egg? You finished a New York Times Sunday crossword puzzle? I'd believe anything, except the crossword puzzle."

Eileen was cute when she was trying to be cute.

"Only two of those," I answered, playing along. "And I still found time to make inquiries about your soon to be ex."

Her smile faded. Funny how men can make women's moods change so quickly. It's a skill all men seem to possess.

"And what did you find out?" she asked, reaching into a designer bag for her smokes. She ignored my match and used her lighter.

"It appears Benjamin Landry has a very exclusive clientele," I said, blowing out the match. "You might have shared that with me."

"Maybe. Would it have made a difference?" Her eyes held mine.

"Not in the least," I said. "But I still should have known."

Eileen shrugged, which did nothing for my mood.

"In a few months," she said, "he won't be my husband. Just someone I'll wish I never met."

"Do his employers know that you're divorcing him?"

Eileen shrugged again. I didn't know if the shrug meant she didn't know or she didn't care.

"Benny doesn't discuss his business with me," she said after another sip of her drink. "Not ever."

"Yet you know about off shore accounts." I said that like I would have said it to someone I was interrogating, rather than someone I was intimately involved with. I needed to ratchet it down a bit.

Eileen stared at me for a second, then stubbed out the cigarette, put the pack in the bag and her arm into the handles of the bag.

I put my hands in the air. "Sorry. That came out wrong. I'm just concerned about you."

Her backside came to rest on the edge of the seat, one foot outside the booth, hand on the table. It was fifty-fifty if my apology would keep her from standing.

"Please," I said. "We should talk. I think we need to talk."

"I'm not going to sit here and be grilled, like I've done something wrong," she said, her angry eyes displaying a temper I had not witnessed before. "I know who he works for. I have nothing to do with it. He didn't confide in me, ever, and I never asked. One day, while cleaning his study, I saw paperwork on his desk. From a bank in the Cayman's. I read it. There's about a million dollars in that bank in Ben's name. You could have knocked me over with a feather. We live comfortably, but not like we're millionaires. We have sixteen thousand in the checking and eighty-five thousand in savings. That I know of. He may have other accounts I don't know about."

Eileen slid back to the middle of the booth. She lit up another cigarette and leaned towards me, lowering her voice.

"I've only told my lawyer about our joint accounts," she said. "Nothing about the Cayman's. I'm not stupid, Paul. I have a pretty good idea where that money came from. I don't want anyone to get the idea that I was part of anything Ben has done. I want out. I mention that money, and it becomes known that he has skimmed from the mob, and that I knew about it, and I'm as good as dead. Same as him."

"I don't want to frighten you," I said just before I said something that I knew should frighten her, "but you may well be in danger."

"Why? I don't know anything. I know as much as anyone else. Don't you think the cops and the feds know that Ben Landry is the accountant for the mob north of Boston? So what? Even mobsters need to pay taxes. Doesn't mean he's involved in their day to day practices, or, if he is, that I knew anything about them. Why should I be in danger?"

There was no easy way to say it. "A wife cannot be forced to testify against her husband. An ex-wife is a different story. You can swear on a stack of bibles as high as the Pru that you don't know anything about what Ben knows about organized crime, that he never told you anything, but that doesn't mean the mob bosses will believe you."

"What are you saying? They'll kill me just because I might know something, afraid I'll testify because I'll have to? Is that what you're saying?"

"Ben has been involved since graduating college. Before him, his father provided the same service going all the way back to the forties. You can believe Ben knows a lot. Maybe where the bodies are hidden, certainly where the money is. And an ex-wife, maybe she's vindictive, maybe she might volunteer information to the authorities. Maybe, she shouldn't have the opportunity."

"But I don't know anything," Eileen said and leaned back into the cushion.

"Look," I said, "a regular soldier, a guy on the streets, he gets divorced, so what. Plenty of layers between him and Glendali. There are no layers between the boss and Ben."

We sat in silence for a bit while she smoked and I finished my beer.

As she stubbed out the smoke she asked, "So what do I do? I'm not staying married to him." She pushed the sleeve of her blouse up to the elbow. Her forearm was purple from bruises.

"He barged into the house after I got home Sunday night. Very upset. Demanding to know where I had been all weekend. Who I had been with. I told him to get out. That made him even more angry."

"Why didn't you tell me when I called Monday morning?" I asked. My hand was trembling. If Landry was to walk in, I'd beat the shit out of him. If I knew where he was, I'd be heading there.

"Because I knew you'd go after him, Paul, and that would be a bad idea. He's never hit me in the face, or broken any bones. I can take it." She smiled. "I'm a tough broad. I had three brothers. But the question remains; what do I do?"

I WAS IN Cambridge taking a look at the plans for the high-rise condo building where Gunther Kolb lives on the fourteenth floor when he's in the area. Four spacious residences take up the entire floor. Kolb's was in the southwest corner overlooking the Charles with what must be a fantastic view of Boston.

The floor plan was basic luxury. Two bedrooms larger than Rhode Island, two palace sized bathrooms, a kitchen Julia Childs would die for, a massive living room with floor to ceiling windows, a smaller room between the two bedrooms that could be a study, or office. Or, behind a locked door, a place to hang pilfered art. Or any other secrets.

I didn't really believe Kolb had planned the heist, or had the art, but an investigators job is to investigate. I got a fax this morning from Gladstone with the list of names I had asked for. Kolb's name topped the list in all cap letters. I had been worried that, once started, the list would be long, but there were only fourteen names on it. Still, that is a lot of names that needed to be investigated. And it's been eight months since the theft. I had a better chance that Publisher's Clearing House would be knocking on my door, than I had recovering the paintings.

Of the fourteen names, half lived in Boston or the surrounding affluent areas, three in New Hampshire, one in Ogunquit, Maine, Kolb in Connecticut, two in New York City. I recognized none of the names on the list. Not that I expected I would. But I expected that all were wealthy, and wealth does bring notoriety of some sort. Notoriety makes research easier. Having someone helping you with the research makes it easier still.

There is a kid I had recently begun using to do research for me. Twenty years old, enrolled in Northeastern, and the son of a cop friend of mine from Saugus. The kid knew his way around computers and could cover more ground in fifteen minutes than I could in a week. Maybe a month. I left the list with his mother before coming to Cambridge. In two days, I'd know everything about those people on the list that was available for the public to know. Which would leave me plenty of time to golf, or whatever it was people got to do now that computers supposedly were making life easier.

I was thinking, instead of renting clubs and going golfing, I would spend any spare time trying to locate Ben Landry. It was time he and I had a serious talk. Eileen had absolutely refused to tell me where I might find him, demanding that I promise not to do anything about him. I had kissed her good night with 'if that's what you want', which is a far cry from a promise.

I know several guys in the rackets who don't treat me like an ex-cop, wise guys who have done all right for themselves and made a nice living skirting the law, but none I thought who were high enough up the hierarchy to be aware of Landry's current whereabouts. But this evening, after the workday, I'd make a few calls and see what they might dig up. Discreetly. One thing you need to understand, anytime you're dealing with these groups who make their living in the dim light of the underworld, you need to be careful. Doesn't matter who they are. The Italians, Irish, Poles, and now the crazy Russians, they are all paranoid. A simple question suddenly becomes a conspiracy to take down the organization. And these groups are like Masons in their paranoia.

Almost fifteen years as a Private Investigator, and I had been lucky enough to never have crossed the mob. Two or three times there were minor disagreements concerning low level soldiers who ended up doing time for their stupidity, but never a visit or a phone call from a higher up warning me to tread lightly. Maybe they knew it would do them no good. Maybe they were happy to have the fool in Walpole, where he could cool his heels for a while and maybe gain some intelligence. I was guessing, I rough up the accountant, that won't be ignored. But the abuse of Eileen had to stop. We'll see how reasonable a man Landry is. Of course, with the weight of the Glendali organization behind him, he might reject reason. Should that happen.....Well, we'll cross that heavily mined highway should we come to it.

Speaking of Eileen, we had plans for Saturday night. She wanted to get to Harry's early so she could enjoy the crowd and dance the night away. Playing that night, Harry had a group of four guys coming in who sang songs from the fifties and sixties in the style of the Four Freshman, Four Aces, four anybodies. They were favorites on the North Shore, Eileen knew of them, and Harry said they were fabulous. I like a little Country, but I can get into the oldies, too. Especially if Eileen is in my arms on the dance floor.

I swung by the tower to see if Gunther Kolb might be in residence, but the doorman said Mr. Kolb was not currently in. A twenty got the man to divulge that Mr. Kolb was scheduled to be spending the month of December at the residence. That's a month away. I'm fairly certain I'll still be working the case then, providing Peter Gladstone doesn't drive me too crazy.

On the way back to the office, I detoured into Everett and stopped at a sub shop on Broadway that I go to every once and a while for an American with everything on it. As kids, Billy and I would head to Angie's for a sub when we had two quarters in our pocket. Back then, the shop was across the street from where it is now, just a tiny hole in the wall place. Three regular sized humans could occupy the space in front of the counter, all others stood outside. People would stand in the cold and the snow, if it happened to be snowing, which I believe happened almost every day in the winters of my youth, rocking back and forth in the slush, patiently waiting their turn.

A half-dollar. Nowadays you might get a doughnut for a half-dollar. Back then, you got two long pieces of french loaf sliced in half and filled with meat and cheese, shredded lettuce and sliced tomato, thinly sliced onion and enough oil to float an aircraft carrier. Eat one of those at noon, and you were full until dinner at six, when your father came home from work demanding to know if you had done your chores.

Angie had aged, but was still making great subs. They were a little more expensive, however. He always greeted me like I had been in yesterday, remembering my name, and that meant something to me. No one in Star Market ever greeted me, and I'm in there every week.

There were messages on the machine when I sat down at my desk and unwrapped the wax paper around the sub, but they could wait until I was done eating. Greatness can't be rushed. I grabbed a beer from the small fridge in the corner, popped the tab and took my first bite. That was when the phone rang. I stared at it, giving it my best DeNiro disgusted look, but it kept ringing.

"This is Paul Costa," I said into the receiver without much enthusiasm.

"Paul. I've been leaving messages all morning."

"Some of us work for a living, kid."

I tried to keep my tone light. It was Sal. The son-of-a-bitch. I'd been worrying about him for two months.

"How you been?" he asked, like we had hung out last week.

"Where are you?" I asked, in no mood for small talk.

There were several seconds of silence before Sal said, "Needed a vaca. Soaking up some sun down south."

"You okay?"

"Never better, Paul. Planning on being home in a week or two."

"You might want to extend your holiday, kid. Harry thinks it might be better for your health."

Another stretch of silence.

"Paul, O'Neil set me up. He used me to try and get at Wachowski. I never saw it coming. Maybe I should have."

"They both want a piece of you, Sal. You stay put. Let me see if there is anything I can do on this end. You stay in touch, hear me?"

"Sure," said Sal. "Be careful with O'Neil. He's a real bastard."

The line went dead. I heard the fear in Sal's voice. I don't know what had gone down, why Sal had to flee, and why he couldn't come home. But I'd find out.

11

Saturday morning, I snapped a photo of a scrawny guy in a winter coat that was too big for him who was snapping a photo of Billy Shute picking up a thirty pack and putting it in his basket at the Malden Stop and Shop. I captured the guy, Billy, and the beer, in the lens. Thirty minutes later, I took several more snaps of the guy sitting in his car taking more pictures of Billy lifting grocery bags from the trunk of his Cadillac. Billy will have the pictures Sunday night and he can deliver them to his lawyer on Monday. My pro bono work will be over, the rest in the hands of the lawyer and the court.

Also on Monday, I could expect a report from my Northeastern research assistant, or so he had said when I called him last night. The kid promised to work on the list over the weekend. What is wrong with kids now-a-days? You would have never found me at his age at home on the weekend. I worry about this generation, and fearful for the next. I blame Atari. And the movies. Who wants to go to a theater? The crap Hollywood puts out now, they should be ashamed. You think Steve McQueen or Jim Morrison would have spent a Saturday night in the sixties at home? Fat chance.

I picked Eileen up at 8:30 at her comfortable Winthrop split-level, and we drove along the Boulevard to Harry's. The parking lot was near capacity when I pulled in, and I had to search for a spot. Harry had a table reserved for us near the dance floor, and within seconds of us sitting, Carla, the waitress, placed a cold beer and a Manhattan in front of us.

Carla was an attractive middle-aged woman with killer curves and spiked hair dyed blonde, except for the roots. Carla was not her real name. It was Cynthia. But she insisted everyone call her Carla, because, she said, there was a cool waitress on television who worked in a bar and Carla was her name. I had no idea if that was true or not.

The singers were four guys dressed in tuxedos, black pants, white jackets, who could have been brothers. They were all about the same height with similar features. Only one was overweight. One had gray hair. Not the same guy. Their harmony was terrific, and I noticed Eileen got right into it. With a smile on her face, and fingers tapping the table, she looked as if she wanted to join them on stage and be *UP ON THE ROOF.* I sipped my beer and smiled.

We danced to every other song, my knees needing the breaks in between. Eileen had several drinks, my limit was two beers. I was the designated driver. Also, I no longer got drunk. Or even buzzed. Not in years. Mainly because I am never not on alert. I always expect there to be trouble when I'm around others. Call it paranoia if you want, but that would just mean you don't read the newspapers or watch the eleven o'clock news. Don't let anyone ever tell you this isn't a crazy, sick world, populated by crazy, sick people.

It was during the singers second break that I noticed two guys at the bar who were talking to each other, with one of them, a handsome guy with thick wavy hair, nice threads, and heavy five o'clock shadow, occasionally glancing at my table. When Harry stopped by to ask how we were enjoying the group, I asked him if he knew the two men. 'Don't worry about them,' he said. 'They're Mr. Glendali's guys.' So I didn't worry about them, only about their interest in the woman I was sitting with.

We left Harry's a little before twelve, Eileen just a bit tipsy and silly. As I drove out of the parking lot, she slid in her seat up close to me and unzipped my fly. A minute later she demanded I pull up against the seawall and shut the engine down. Like a good little boy, I followed her instructions, which included pushing my seat all the way back. She hiked up her skirt and straddled me, her hands active, her breathing heavy. I lowered the window a bit for air and could hear the high tide waves pounding the sand. Not quite Burt and Deborah in *From Here To Eternity,* but it did cross my mind. From nowhere, a memory also crossed my mind. For only a fleeting second I was seventeen again, it was the summer of 1959, and I was in my father's '56 Chevy, parked in almost the exact same spot doing the exact same thing with an eighteen year old Goddess from the Woodlawn section of Everett. I suddenly felt very sorry for my Northeastern researcher who didn't know what he was missing.

MONDAY MORNING DURING my second honey-dipped, the fax chirped and the printing began. When silence returned, I had fourteen pages from my researcher waiting to be read, one for each name on Gladstone's list.

Along with the names Peter Gladstone had provided, Peter had also provided reasons why he believed they warranted being on the list. Perceived slights or business dealings that, in Gladstone's words, they may have taken offense with. Or just petty jealousies because they weren't as successful as he. So he wrote.

I took the new list and compiled one of my own, basing my rankings on what I was reading from my researcher. One through fourteen, with one being the first to be looked at and fourteen being a waste of time. I found number three to be the most intriguing, a man by the name of Casper Mansfield, a name I knew. No patent infringements or reneged agreements with Casper, just a destroyed marriage with allegations of impropriety by Mrs. Viola Mansfield with my client, Peter Gladstone. At last, something I could get my head around. Something I understood. Something right up my alley. I would have liked to put Mr. Mansfield in the top spot on my list, but there were two names that earned consideration ahead of him.

Brent Cabot and George Winslow. Both men earned their high rankings because, it appeared, they had lost a lot of money in a shady company Gladstone had championed as a sure bet, only to have it prove to be a house of cards that collapsed, losing investors their entire investments. Later, it became known that Gladstone, himself, had not lost a dime. He had never invested in the company, but had been paid handsomely as a shill for the men running the failed attempt. There were no charges ever brought against him, or anyone else in the failed enterprise. My researcher had dug into it, and found that the company had a get rich quick idea for software in the music industry, and when it failed to pan out, all was lost. A side note on the bottom of Cabot's page, written by my research student, told me that losing money in failed high-tech ideas was more common than making money. Hey, plenty of railroads and car makers had failed, too. Why should tech be any different?

Others on the list had lost money in the venture, too, but not to the extent of these two. Brent Cabot and George Winslow were the two on the list from New York City. Another reason to place them high up the list. I called both men, who worked for the same investment company, and asked if I could meet with them and talk, concerning Peter Gladstone. Neither was pleased with my request, but after some verbal maneuvering agreed to speak with me. I'd take Amtrak to the city on Wednesday. Trains don't fall out of the sky.

I wanted to talk with Mrs. Mansfield before speaking with her former husband, so I called Viola Mansfield, who lived on Commonwealth Avenue in Boston. She, too, didn't want to talk about Gladstone, but finally agreed to meet with me at her residence at four o'clock.

One of my greater assets, I believe, is I have the power of persuasion. I've often thought that I could make a fortune, a very large fortune, were I to be a television Evangelical Minister, begging for your hard earned money so I could defeat the Devil. I had no doubt my ratings, and my bank account, would be through the roof had I pursued that career. I could see me on Channel 27, 11:30 at night, the insomniacs hanging on every word. Letterman could only wish he had an audience as faithful as mine.

There was nothing on my calendar for the hours before my meeting with Viola Mansfield, so I decided to take a ride to Lynn and find Tomek Wachowski and try to smooth this problem he had with Sal. Guys like Wachowski, O'Neil, Glendali, guys on the wrong side of the law, they don't go looking for trouble. They don't shy away from it either. They have learned to deal with trouble fast and with finality. Don't let things fester, don't let things linger, take immediate action. And move on. If someone has to die to send the appropriate message, get it done. It's business. It's not personal. It's just business, said Sollozzo, explaining the facts to Tom Hagen, who then relayed them to Sonny Corleone, who wasn't listening. I didn't know if I could defuse this situation, especially since I wasn't privy to the exact reason Sal found himself in the cross-hairs, but I had to try.

Wachowski and I had some history. We didn't send each other Christmas cards, but we weren't enemies. We had crossed paths maybe eleven years before, when we were both looking for the same guy. I found him first, to his great luck. Because I had, he was doing twenty in a jail somewhere in the middle of the country instead of being fish food at the bottom of Flax Pond. I had no leverage on Wachowski or his gang, and even if I did I wasn't dumb enough to play that card. Not with him. I just hoped we could talk, find out how Sal could make amends, if he could, and move on. If there was a service I could provide to make that happen, I'd consider it.

Wachowski had a club on Union Street and I was shown to his office in the back. He waved the goon who escorted me away, poured two shots of whiskey, we toasted our health and he told me to sit.

"I was wondering when you'd show up here, Costa," Wachowski said, leaning back into the high padded swivel chair behind his desk. He was a big man, muscular, a full beard that covered the scar of the knife wound on his neck that almost killed him when he was an up and coming soldier in the Polish gang. Looking at him, you expected his voice would have a growl to it. Menacing and deep. Instead, it was high-pitched and soft. Menacing and deep would keep a person on edge. High-pitched and soft might lead to an easing of nerves. Being comfortable around Wachowski could be harmful to your health.

"I appreciate you seeing me, Tomek," I said. "I thought we should talk."

"You know what the kid did," he said. "You know I can't just let that pass."

"That's just it. I don't know. I heard from him a few days ago. First time in months. He wouldn't tell me what went down. Only that he would contact you and make things right." I shrugged. "He doesn't know you like I do. You feel like cluing me in on what happened?"

"Your boy set me up for a hit," Tomek Wachowski said, pouring himself another shot, but not one for me. "With the Charlestown boys. O'Neil and I have been in a dispute and I guess he got tired of the talking. I got a snitch in his outfit, so I found out what was going on just before I got in a car to drive to the meet. Otherwise, I'd probably be dead and there would be a war going on now."

"Sal would never do something like that," I said.

"He did it, Costa. He brought the news. I liked the kid. He was a useful conduit between the families. Had no ax to grind or money in the pot. He was just happy when he was included in a few things, made a little money on the side.

"But then, after I find out what O'Neil had planned, I find out Sal is in to O'Neil for fifteen G's in gambling debts. I have a tenth grade education, but I learned in the first grade one and one equals two."

"I was there when Sal was born," I said. "Known him all his life. He would never set anyone up. That's not him. Yeah, maybe O'Neil sent him to see you for a meet, but Sal would never have known what the Mick was planning. If he knew, he would have refused, debts or no."

“O'Neil may have threatened your boy.”

“What? And hurt him?”

“Not far fetched. Not for O'Neil.”

“And have me on a rampage?”

Wachowski frowned. “You ain't as tough as you think you are, Paul. Maybe never were. Yeah, I heard the stories. And, yeah, what you did ten years ago was impressive, but it's old news. These young guys today have never even heard your name.”

We stared across the desk at each other, Tomek sipping his drink. Sometimes, a stare is worth a thousand words.

“I'll tell you what,” Wachowski finally said, leaning forward. “You and Sal come here to see me. We'll talk. I'll hear him out. I'll give him a chance to convince me he was a dupe. Maybe he does convince me, maybe he doesn't. We're under a white flag while he's here. My word on that. He doesn't convince me, after you leave, I have a hit on him again. And we let the chips fall where they may. Then we find out how tough you are. Deal?”

I stood and we shook hands.

“By any chance, you know anything about some paintings that have gone missing?” I asked before leaving his office.

“I know it wasn't me who took 'em,” Tomek said. “My taste runs toward tasteful velour pictures of Elvis and Playboy centerfolds. I had no idea the Neck held such treasures. Now I know.”

12

The apartment in the brownstone that Viola Mansfield resided in on Commonwealth Ave was not just an apartment. She owned all three floors. The rooms were airy, well proportioned and tastefully appointed. The lady of the house was also well proportioned and tastefully appointed. Mid thirties, immaculately dressed at four in the afternoon, not a blond hair out of place, not an ounce of weight where it shouldn't be. She ushered me into a sitting room that had a pleasant view through large windows of the avenue and the tree-lined promenade that ran down the center of it. When she sat, her round tush barely caught the front edge of the cushion. Her lean legs, crossed at the ankles and sporting high heels, went left of her center, an arm, almost resting on the arm of the chair, right of center. The fingernails on the hand on the end of that arm were painted a bright red, the exact shade of her lips. The fabric of her skirt, black and tight, covered her knees by one inch. Grace Kelly came to mind. The Princess years in particular, although, even in the Hollywood years of her life, she was all class.

"I'm not sure how much you know, Mr. Costa, but I don't enjoy discussing Peter Gladstone. I'm not even sure why I agreed to speak with you."

"I understand, Mrs. Mans...."

"Ms., Mr Costa. Ms. Mansfield."

"Ms. Mansfield. I won't take much of your time. Mr. Gladstone has hired me to investigate the theft of several pieces of his art collection. Are you aware that there was a theft at his home?"

"Of course. I read about it in the newspapers when it happened. Some of my friends are also Peter's friends, and they have brought it up in my presence."

"You and Mr. Gladstone were close at one time," I said. I find it's best to get the unpleasantness out of the way early. Usually. Sometimes, I'm asked to leave before I can ask another question.

"I'm sure you know the whole sordid ordeal, Mr. Costa. Seems everyone does. Not very gallant of you to bring it up."

"I do apologize, Ms. Mansfield. I only mention it because you may be in a unique position to help me in my investigation."

"Me? I don't understand. What would I know about stolen art. The theft was a year ago and..."

"Nine months," I interrupted.

She frowned. "Nine months. I have not seen Peter in over a year. Nor do I care to ever see him again."

A blush colored her cheeks, but faded quickly. I didn't know if it was anger that caused the blush, or a memory.

"I still get mailed invitations to his fund-raisers, which I refuse," she said with a slight shake of her head, "along with the ones that are on my answering machine for the less public parties." She looked out the large window. "As if I ever would again."

Viola Mansfield's mouth turned downward as she looked at me. "Peter Gladstone is a son-of-a-bitch, Mr. Costa. I could use a thousand words to describe him, in the most vile way, but son-of-a-bitch fits him like a pair of Versace leather gloves."

I thought her assessment of my client was a prelude to a demand that I leave. Instead, she just sat there, motionless for several seconds. Then she looked up at me, prepared for the next question, almost as if she were determined not be cowed by anything from the past having to do with Peter Gladstone.

"I'd like to talk with you about friends of his. Get your impression of them. I have found that women often have a different take on the people a man considers friends, than he has."

"Really?"

"Yes. Women seem to have an ability to see through

the bullshit of male bantering, that men see as an attempt at camaraderie."

"Are you sure of that, Mr. Costa? We seem to be unable to recognize it when the banter is directed at us. We buy it all, hook, line and sinker."

"Even then," I said, "I believe women recognize the insincerity, the bullshit, but choose to ignore it. Perhaps they believe they can change the words into truths over time. Perhaps, they're just bored and want to play."

"The game ceases to be fun after a while, Mr. Costa. But for some inexplicable reason, even though we know what the outcome will be, we think this time will be different."

I shrugged. I'm a P. I., not a shrink. How do I know that? Shrinks charge by the hour the same rate I charge by the day.

"Were you ever with Mr. Gladstone when he was in the company of Brent Cabot or George Winslow?"

"Two or three times, I think," Viola Mansfield replied. "After a fund-raiser, or party, I don't remember which. George and Brent live in New York and would stay at Peter's after the party, flying out the next day. After all the others had left, Casper and I, along with Peter, George, Brent, and their significant others, would sit around for most of the night, drinking and talking. Eventually, the talk always turned to business and that was when I tuned it out."

"Significant others?"

"Yes. Let me think now." She pursed her lips. "Yes, they were fund-raisers."

"And you know this why?"

"Because George and Brent were with their wives. When Peter hosted a party instead of a fund-raiser, wives were optional and generally frowned upon. Girlfriends, the kind who didn't mind being shared, were encouraged."

"But you and your ex were there. I don't mean to be vulgar."

Viola Mansfield smiled for the first time. Well, her lips smiled. Her eyes did not.

"Yes, you do, Mr. Costa. Not that it should matter one bit in your investigation, but Casper would have killed anyone who even suggested being with me, and I would have left my hand print on their face."

"Casper is a jealous man?"

"Insanely."

"How did he react when he found out about you and Peter?"

"The sixty-four thousand dollar question that everyone who knows Casper always asks. Some less tactfully than others." Her eyes drifted to the window again.

"I told him. One night a few days before Christmas. We were getting dressed for a party at a friends house. We were in our bedroom. I was standing in front of a mirror fixing my hair. He came up behind me to zip me up, then placed his hands on my shoulders and looked at me in the mirror. I stared at him for several seconds, this man I had loved since I was eighteen years old, the man who had given me everything I ever wanted, who took so great care of me, and I said, 'I don't love you anymore'. There was no anger in his eyes. No surprise. No hurt, either. Just love. He said, 'I know'. He kissed my shoulder and went to put on his suit coat. He moved out after Christmas. Never contested the divorce. Even after I told him I'd been seeing Peter, he never spoke or treated me harshly. I deeply hurt the only man who has ever truly loved me, and I have to live with that."

"And you and Peter....?"

She stood and walked to a side table for a cigarette.

"I didn't divorce Casper for Peter," she said, smoke escaping her nostrils, like only Bette Davis could do it. "If it hadn't been Peter it would have been someone else. I had just fallen out of love with dear Casper. But Peter didn't have to be such a prick about everything."

Viola turned towards me, crossing her arms over her chest, the fingers of her right hand bringing the cigarette up to her red lips. Her perfectly plucked eyebrows lifted ever so slowly, a simple gesture of confession that she had no answer to why she had done the things she had. We've all been there.

I gave her a few seconds to compose herself, then asked, "Do you know Gunther Kolb?"

Viola lifted a crystal ashtray from the glass table, flicking ashes into it as she came back to sit in the chair.

"Yes, I've met Gunther. Peter introduced Casper and me to him at one of Peter's bashes. But then he stopped coming to the parties. Casper said they had a falling out over some business dealings. I thought Kolb to be a rather cold fish, that is my remembrance of him. Also, I remember I didn't like the way I would catch him looking at me across a room. Like he was thinking how nice my head would look mounted on a wall. His wall. The great white hunter triumphant again."

She frowned then, her eyes looking across the room. "I do remember the day Gunther showed up at Peter's mansion unannounced. It was a summer day. We were sunning by the pool. By then, I was spending weekends at Peter's. Saturday on his boat, Sunday by the pool, nights in whichever room Peter had decided he would have me."

She stubbed out the cigarette. "I'm sorry," she said. "That sounded like he was raping me, or playing with me. I was a willing participant. The freedom, the sex, it was like a drug. Much different than Casper."

Viola Mansfield suddenly became very still. Her eyes held mine. I couldn't read what thoughts were behind them.

"Do people often confess their sins to you, Mr. Costa?" she finally said. "I can't believe I just told you all that. I wouldn't tell my dearest friends what I just told you, a stranger."

"I think, Ms. Mansfield, it may be easier to reveal certain things to someone who you could care less what they think of you, than to feel embarrassment, or feel a friend is judging you. Of course, a good friend would never judge you. Neither would I. Let those without sin throw the first stone."

I smiled. The great philosopher.

She didn't.

I really didn't care if Gladstone had screwed her on the pool table, or the kitchen counter beside the toaster, or on the massive desk in the study, but I was interested in the visit by Kolb and if she knew what was said between them.

"Gunther was livid," Viola Mansfield told me when I asked. "Screaming obscenities as he approached the pool. Then he saw me lying on a chaise and stopped his tirade. I looked at Peter. He was unruffled. Smiling even."

"Do you remember what Gunther Kolb was upset about? Why he was angry?"

"Something about a business deal, I think. A shared investment in a company that had not panned out. That was my impression, anyway."

"And what happened?"

"Gunther insisted that Peter speak with him in private," she said, her face coloring a bit as she recounted.

"And did he?" I asked after a few seconds. Ms. Mansfield seemed lost in a memory, staring through the windows to the street below.

She brought her attention back to me.

"Peter calmly sipped at his drink, as Gunther stood barely ten feet away, his attention on me. I was sunning topless, without a towel nearby to cover up. I remember, I looked at Peter, and he seemed amused by my predicament. I was remembering how Gunther used to look at me at the parties, so I continued to lay on my back, allowing him to see what he would never have."

Viola Mansfield lit another cigarette.

"Did Peter eventually talk with Kolb?" I asked.

Viola Mansfield frowned. "After allowing Gunther to have a long look, Peter stood, walked to me, kissed a breast, suckled a nipple, and then excused himself. They walked up near the house, so I couldn't hear what they were arguing about, but Gunther was very loud and animated. Eventually, he stomped away, going around the house to the driveway. I really thought the argument would become physical. When Peter came back to his chaise, I asked what it was all about. He waved it all off. Said Gunther was just jealous of his success. Then he suggested we take a dip in the pool. Without our suits."

Awaiting the next question, Ms. Mansfield looked at me coolly, taking deep drags on a cigarette.

"Can I offer you a drink, Mr. Costa?" she asked.

People pay me their hard earned dollars and expect results when they do. Normally, I give them results because I am very good at what I do. I'm very good at what I do because I'm like a pack of hounds on the trail of a fox, sniffing out every scent that hangs in the air. I could ask one more question of Viola Mansfield, and then join the afternoon rush north out of the city, or I could accept the offer of a drink and have an easy commute home after midnight.

"One last question, Ms. Mansfield," I said. "Does your ex-husband hold any animosity towards Mr. Gladstone still?"

As I drove in rush hour traffic bumper to bumper out of Boston, I mentally crossed Casper Mansfield from the third spot on my list.

13

I met Brent Cabot and George Winslow at a hotel bar not far from the offices of the investment firm where they worked. Their job was to convince poor slobs to invest their hard-earned money in businesses that were ready to explode. Profits were just weeks away, they no doubt promised, and they would hate to see prospective clients lose out on the opportunity.

I, of course, knew nothing about such scams. I was just remembering what my twenty year old researcher had scribbled on the bottom of their bio's. Sitting across from the two well dressed men, both reeking from a cologne I found offensive, and both attacking their second martini with a vigor normally reserved for handball, while every other word they spoke was a profanity, I found myself hoping Gladstone had taken them for a heavy ride.

They both seemed a little hyper to me. Maybe they were on drugs, a little speed to liven up a slow day. Or maybe they were a bit worked up from the phone calls and could have used a downer. Either way, they got on my nerves.

Cabot did most of the talking, with Winslow interrupting every so often. When he did, Cabot nodded his head rapidly and kept saying, 'Yeah, yeah'. I think George Winslow was the smarter of the two, but that was like saying my Pit Bull is smarter than your Beagle.

Eventually, I got the story of why they were on Gladstone's list. During one long weekend at the Marblehead mansion, Gladstone had convinced them both to invest a quarter million each in a sure bet company that even the Wall Street boys didn't know about yet. Gladstone used their own scam against them, and with the help of booze, drugs and attractive escorts, took the boys for a ride. Before dumb and dumber got back to the city, they had transferred the funds.

By the time the two of them left my table half-cocked, I was crossing them off my list. These two couldn't steal a Bulova from Macy's without making a shambles of the men's jewelry department. Maybe they hired a crew to do it? That was a possibility, I supposed. There was certainly no shortage of talent in the City. But I was guessing any crew worth their reputation, who listened to the babble these two could unleash, would politely decline the job. The smart guys know that it only takes one moron in the stew to turn it rancid.

The train ride back to South Station from Penn gave me a little over four hours to do some serious thinking. And I had serious thinking to do about a lot of things. First, I may have been crossing names off the Gladstone list too quickly. Cabot and Winslow may have found a crew to do the job, they just wouldn't have had anything to do with the planning beyond providing an address and where the pieces were situated. Also, Casper Mansfield may have been quite noble in the amicable divorce with Viola, even going so far as leaving her the ritzy apartment on Commonwealth Avenue and a hefty bank account, but I found it difficult to believe he wouldn't be upset with Gladstone schlepping his beautiful ex, and be out for a little revenge, despite Viola assuring me Casper was understanding. I'd have to have a talk with Casper Mansfield in the next few days.

But mostly I thought about Gunther Kolb. Neither Kolb nor Gladstone had mentioned the verbal confrontation that Viola Mansfield had told me about. Both men had said it was at least three years since they had talked. Viola and Peter were doing the dirty a year and a half ago. I didn't know what it meant, that both men would have failed to mention the argument, if it meant anything, but it did pique my interest.

Viola had said she thought Kolb was upset about a business venture gone bad. A year and a half ago was when Cabot and Winslow had been scammed. Was it possible that Kolb, after his falling out with Gladstone almost two years before, had invested in the failed enterprise? Would I be surprised if he had? As I've said before, nothing the rich do surprises me. There is no honor among thieves. The most potent aphrodisiac in the world is money. It corrupts everything it touches. Isn't it an amazing thing that wealth leads to greed, and not the other way around?

I thought about all of this until the train got to Providence, and from there until Boston I thought about Sal, Ben Landry, and Eileen. Not in that order, but in no order at all. Just stuff entering and exiting my head.

I thought about how I could always work four cases at a time and keep everything compartmentalized without a problem, but how, when a dame entered the daily routine, I seemed to lose some focus. Eileen wasn't my first dance partner, so I have a history that I can look back on, and it was always the same. I am not at the top of my game when in a relationship. I'd like to think, eventually, with the passing of time in the relationship, I'd return to my normal sharp self. But in this there is no history, as my 'avventure amorose' have never lasted longer than the muddle. Except for Callie. But with her, I was young, a cop, and a cocky little shit, whose only thoughts were terrorizing punks on the street during the day and romping in bed with Callie at night. It was a damn simple life, and I didn't realize how good I had it until it was gone.

I HAD CALLED the offices of *Mansfield and Stein* and was told Mr. Mansfield was out of the office and not available, so I took a shot at where he might be available. And there he was.

Mansfield and Stein is a real estate development company. They own office space throughout Boston and, when the opportunity has presented itself in the last forty years, have built their own towers. Stein retired years ago and died maybe ten years back. Old man Mansfield is still Chairman of the Board, but his son, Casper, does the heavy lifting now. A few months ago, the Globe did a feature on the company, and there was a big picture of Casper Mansfield sticking a shovel in the ground for a new building that would be going up on Huntington Avenue. That was where I found him.

He stood at the far end of the busy site, as cranes lifted girders and iron workers put them in place. He was dressed in a navy blue pin-striped suit, with white shirt sans tie, and a bright white construction hard hat on his head with the *Mansfield and Stein* logo on the side. The Globe article had said he was a hands on guy. It appeared to me that he liked standing around so the guys who were actually doing the work knew they were on a deadline to get the building built.

I walked over to where he stood and introduced myself. He looked at me as if I were a homeless guy who had just crawled out of a refrigerator box and was about to ask him for a dollar.

"You're the guy who bothered Viola," he said. "She told me about you."

It had only been two days, but Boston isn't that big a city and news can travel fast.

"Why you bothering her about Peter Gladstone?"

Casper Mansfield stood several inches over six feet, wide at the shoulders and too thick at the waist. I could see that at one time he may well have been a hands on guy, but he was fifty-five now, twenty years older than his former wife, and he had the eyes of someone who liked his Johnnie Walker a little too often.

"I'm investigating the theft of art from Mr. Gladstone's home," I said. "I'd like to ask you a few questions."

"Why would you think I'd know anything about it? Or Viola?"

"You were friends with Mr. Gladstone," I said. "Attended his parties."

"We were never friends," Mansfield gruffly said. "I attended fund-raisers. I attend quite a few fund-raisers every year. His was one of them."

He failed to mention t he parties that weren't fund-raisers that Viola had mentioned. Maybe, I would mention them. Maybe, I wouldn't.

"It's possible the art theft was done by someone who attended his parties," I said. "Someone who had a reason to be angry with Mr. Gladstone. Someone looking for revenge."

Mansfield was tall enough that he could look down at me, and I guessed he fancied himself big enough that he could intimidate someone just by moving closer to them, which he did to me.

"Listen, Costa," he snarled, "if I wanted to get even with that shit for Viola, I'd have his bones broken, not steal his pathetic paintings. If I wanted to hurt him, he'd feel real pain. But Viola wouldn't have wanted that. The guilt of it. So, he should consider himself lucky. You can tell him that. Now be a good little messenger boy and run along and tell him that."

Which, of course, I wasn't about to do. The man's in a fifteen hundred dollar suit. And out of shape. He's not about to grapple.

"What can you tell me about Gunther Kolb? Or Brent Cabot and George Winslow?"

Mansfield glared down at me, his face coloring just a bit. "You stay away from Viola," he said. Then he turned and walked toward an office trailer, entered and closed the door behind him.

I believed him. He had too much to lose. Casper Mansfield wouldn't have risked the scandal and humiliation should a robbery get bungled and his name come up as the guy who set it all in motion. Which it might. Not all thieves have Packy's integrity. I also believed him when he said he would have preferred breaking Gladstone's bones. A guy comes in from Jersey, does the job, back home to kiss his kids off to school in the morning. Investigation dies out before the next full moon. Casts don't come off for months. Pain lingers for years.

So, once again, with more confidence this time, I pencil out the top names on the list.

I'm back at the office by one, with another of Angie's subs, when the phone squawks.

"Costa Investigation Agency," I said, liking the way it sounded. "This is Paul Costa."

"Costa Investigation Agency?" Sal said. "Next, some babe will be answering the phone."

"Hey, kid," I said. "I'm glad you called. I had a sit-down with Wachowski. He told me the story. Or at least his side of it. I want to hear yours. But not on the phone. He's promised a safe meet. When can you get up here?"

"Ten days. Two weeks."

"Why so long?"

"I've been staying with a woman I met. She's nice. A sweetheart. But her man gets out of prison in two weeks and she wants me gone before then. I didn't argue. But I don't want to leave before I have to."

"Make it ten days. Come to my place when you get in. Straight to my place. And wait for me. Don't go anywhere else, don't do anything else. Capiche? And don't tell anyone you're coming. And Sal?"

"Yeah?"

"Don't leave your wallet with your identification behind."

Sal laughed. "Come on, Paul. I'm not that dumb."

'Yeah, you are, kid,' I was thinking as I hung up.

I finished the sub and called Peter Gladstone at his office. He was just leaving for the weekend.

"We need to talk," I said.

"Sure."

"Tomorrow morning."

"Busy. Have a fund-raiser at my place tomorrow night, raising money for Christmas gifts for orphans or something crazy like that. I have an idea. You own a suit?"

I didn't answer.

"Of course you do. Party starts at eight. Come at seven, we'll chat, have a drink to loosen up, and you can stay for the festivities. Bring a date if you want. Sound good? See you then."

He hung up before I had a chance to respond. I drummed my fingers on the desk, and then called Eileen.

"You free tomorrow night?" I asked.

"I can be. Why?"

"I've been invited out to the Neck for a soiree. Want to join me?"

"Dress up?"

"Oh, yeah."

"I'm your girl. Haven't done this in a while. What time?"

14

It was a chilly night, but clear, with a half moon just rising above the water of the Atlantic as I drove over the thin patch of road onto Marblehead Neck, Eileen sitting close beside me, her hand on my thigh. She was in a black evening dress that hugged every delightful curve. It began two inches above her knees and ended with just a hint of cleavage thirty inches later, if your eyes were traveling up the landscape, as mine had done when she opened the door to her home. Neck and shoulders of flawless skin were bare, with only a thin gold chain around her neck that held an emerald gem that matched her eyes. Her nails were painted a shiny red. Lipstick matched the nails, a shade brighter than her usual color, making the lips seem fuller. Stud earrings sporting emeralds sparkled under hair that was piled high and off those bare shoulders.

I wore my best black suit over a new white Arrow, my Oxford's as black and shiny as a wet panther. I even got a haircut before lunch. I wanted to look good beside the lady I was with. The reality was, I could have been in my fishing gear. No one at this shindig was going to notice me, only the lady on my arm.

Because Gladstone had suggested we talk before the guests arrived, we came early to the big house. I flipped my keys to the valet, and Gladstone himself opened the front door as we walked up the long, flag-stoned walkway. He nodded at me and shook my hand, but the smile he graced Eileen with just about showed all thirty-two teeth. I knew he could be a little rough around the edges, and I was hoping I wasn't going to have to slug him for an indelicate comment, but he shook her hand with a warm hello and invited us into his home.

There was another couple in the huge living room when we entered. I didn't know them, but Gladstone had obviously had them come early in case I brought a date and we wouldn't have to leave her sitting by herself when we talked. Thoughtful.

He closed the door to the den behind us and immediately headed toward a well-stocked cabinet.

"What are we drinking?" he asked.

"Bourbon, two cubes," I said.

He made two drinks, handed me one, pointed to a set of comfortable looking high-backed chairs near a French door that led to the garden area, and we sat. A frame with no painting in it was on the wall.

"Okay, what have you got?"

I brought him up to speed on what I had been doing and who I had talked with. He raised eyebrows at the mention of Viola Mansfield.

"She's a knock-out, huh? That body. Casper was a fool to let her get away."

"But not you?"

"Best piece of ass I've ever had, but I like the bachelor life. Maybe if I didn't."

"She didn't speak fondly of you," I said.

Gladstone shrugged. "Not surprised." I didn't notice any remorse.

"We can cross her ex off the list," I said.

"You sure? Casper can't stand that I had a little fling with his wife. I could see him stealing my stuff."

"He was pretty emphatic that if he decided payback was an option, you'd be spending a great deal of time in rehab mending broken bones. He asked that I deliver that message. Said the only reason you're still able to walk, he didn't want Viola to feel any guilt."

"Casper Mansfield is a blowhard. Living high off the money his father made. If he was any kind of man at all, Viola wouldn't have left him."

Gladstone downed his drink. "Want another?" he asked

as he went back to the cabinet. I hadn't touched mine yet.

"The scam you ran on Cabot and Winslow," I said, "how many others on this list were taken?"

He came and sat down, sipping from the glass. "Easy, Costa. There was no scam. The company I was touting had a great game plan. I thought it was a solid idea and I urged my friends to invest. If it had clicked, they would have needed a wheelbarrow to carry the profits to the bank."

"Yet you didn't invest."

"Who told you that? My agreement with the guys in the start-up was a percentage of whatever I brought in. I took my payment fifty percent cash, fifty percent stock. If I brought in ten million, I got a five percent share of the company. So when the shit hit the fan, I lost out, too."

"Except for the fifty percent you pocketed," I said.

Gladstone shrugged again.

"Why did Gunther Kolb have money in the pot? I thought you guys were on the outs before that." I didn't know if the failed company was the reason for the blowout Viola witnessed, but I suspected it was. Gladstone removed all suspicion.

"You and Viola talked about a lot of stuff," Gladstone said, one knee uncrossing the other as he leaned forward. "I contacted Gunther about the deal. I thought it was a good way to maybe put the past behind us. You make some money for a guy, differences tend to smooth themselves out. Unfortunately, that didn't happen."

"Did he threaten anything when he showed up here?"

Gladstone waved a hand. "He was off the rails. Threatened to sue. Threatened to ruin my company. Threatened to destroy me. Said I set him up and he'd get even. I told you before, Gunther Kolb is an insecure little man. He thinks the world is against him and every little thing that happens, happens just to hurt him. Guy's crazy."

"You got Cabot and Wilson for a quarter mil each. How much did Kolb lose?"

"Doesn't matter. Look, Reaganomics got the market in

a bit of a mess. Bank money got tight. Capital dried up, and the guys I was backing failed because it did. This is how things work. Some times you hit a grand slam, most of the time it's an easy fly to left. It's all a game. You don't have the balls to play, sit in the stands."

He drained the drink.

"Anything else? I have guests arriving."

"Any others on your list lose heavy money?"

"A few. But you're wasting your time. And my money. It's Kolb. Find dirt on him. Maybe we can't get the stuff back, but I can hurt him other ways. Find out what I can use to get even."

Peter Gladstone stood. "Let's go have a good time. By the way, your date is a knockout. I'm impressed."

"Mind your manners," I said. "I'm not Casper Mansfield."

"Easy champ," he said, as he placed his hand on my back ushering me out of the room. "Tonight, I am on my best behavior."

I HADN'T PLANNED on Eileen spending the night at my place, but that's where we ended up, and she missed the ten A.M. mass at St. Michael's. Fortunately, I had cleaned up my spartan area before dressing for the party, just in case.

As for the party, the seventy or so people there weren't my crowd, but I did manage to find a couple of guys who were sports fans. They had actually played college ball in the Ivy League and seemed to be regular guys. So, while most of the talk in the room was about the stock market and companies I had never heard of, we stood off to the side sipping drinks and discussing the Bruins and Celtics and lamenting the Red Sox and Patriots.

Eileen had wandered in and out of our little circle throughout the night. There were two women that she knew at the party, and the three of them had moved around the house like it was their place. I kept noticing one of them looking my way. I had also kept noticing other men sneaking peeks at my girl whenever she entered or left the room. Or even if she was just standing still. Couldn't blame them. I could hardly keep my eyes off her, either.

When I carried a tray of bacon, eggs, toast and coffee into the bedroom. Eileen smiled up at me and stretched.

"I didn't know you could cook," she said as she propped herself up.

"Oh, yeah," I said. "Bacon, eggs, steak on the grill and pasta on the stove. Sauce from a bottle. All the essentials."

She took a bite of toast and a sip of coffee. Her hair was down now and it was messed up. Wild and thick.

"I had a wonderful time last night," she said with a smile. "During the party, and after. I can't remember the last time I was at such a fun party. Been ages."

"Who were the two women you were with?"

"The blonde was someone I knew. Chance Clinton. Chance Birch now."

"Chance?"

"Her mother is French," Eileen said, as if that explained the name. "We met a few years ago at a dinner Ben dragged me to. She was a date of some guy, but married now to a cute guy who owns a real estate business. She's really funny. Had me laughing all night. The other woman was Mary Hamilton. She told me what her husband does, but I forget. Did you get a good look at her?"

"I only had eyes for you," I said diplomatically.

"Thanks," Eileen said with a smile, "but when a woman has breasts that big, and most of them are out of the dress, every man notices. In her purse, she had more drugs than a Rite Aid. Oh, my God. She gave me this little blue one. Don't know what it was, but it was hours before I felt my feet on the ground again. And she told the raunchiest jokes. Oh, God, Paul, I just had the best time."

She looked at me then, the coffee cup near her lips.

"I can't tell you how much I needed last night," she said. "I've been so tense. It was wonderful to relax, and laugh, and be mischievous with co-conspirators again.

Thank you for bringing me."

"You're welcome," I said.

She leaned back against the headboard, the sheet slipping from her breasts.

"Why don't you put the tray on the dresser," she said, "and let me give you a proper thank you."

I had a vague memory that this is what Sunday mornings were for. Eileen reminded me twice so I wouldn't forget again.

15

I spent the week after the party visiting five more names on Peter Gladstone's list and asking questions. Four of them had invested money in the failed business and, while none were happy about the loss, no one told me they held any animosity against Gladstone. I came to find out that all of them got into the deal early on, and they all looked upon it as just another failed attempt by hopeful entrepreneurs. Like investing in a Broadway production that closes in the first week. What can you do? You backed a loser.

The fifth gentleman, a Michael Dean in Ogunquit, didn't lose money, just a wife, when he discovered she was having an affair with Gladstone. Yeah, my client was a real peach.

Late Thursday afternoon, after the drive back from Maine, I was sitting in my office with the fourteen sheets of paper from the researcher splayed upon my desk. I had notes written on the nine names that I had spoken with, and was going back and forth over all of it. I found myself wondering, if I had a computer in the office, and knew how to use it, would it be easier to keep track of it all. That was when my office door opened.

I looked up to see two men enter the outer space. The first guy in was about as wide as the door frame. Bald head, ill fitting suit, needed a shave. The guy who followed him was close to six foot, thin, sharp gray suit, neat haircut, thick eyeglasses. The first guy remained in the outer office staring in at me, hands folded in front of him. The second guy came and stood in front of me, staring down through thick lenses that made his eyes look like Don Knotts' in that fish movie.

"Can I help you?" I asked when the guy just stood

staring at me.

"I'm Ben Landry," he said.

"Mr. Landry," I said. "Care to sit?"

He remained standing.

"I warned you to stay away from my wife," he said. "I'm warning you a second time now. There won't be a third."

I stood. "Your marriage is over. The divorce is about to be final. The lady can do whatever she likes."

"We're separated and attempting to work things out," Landry said. "And that's none of your business. Stop seeing Eileen, or else."

He didn't sound like a man who was used to giving ultimatums. It didn't matter. I'm not a guy who responds well to ultimatums.

I smiled. He frowned. "Benny," I said, and the frown deepened, "that's not going to happen unless the lady tells me to stay away. But here is something that is going to happen, and you only get one warning on this, you lay your hands on her again, and I'll break you in half."

His brow furrowed deeply.

"You know who I work for?" he said.

"I do."

He drew himself up to his full height and stuck his chin out defiantly, and stared at me through the coke bottles.

"Either you're stupid or you're crazy," he said, his tone menacing, with just a hint of pity for me in it. "I don't care which. Watch your back, Costa."

Landry walked out of my office. The big guy with him opened the door and Landry walked through it into the hall, then the muscle turned to stare at me. I was thinking, if he came after me, we would probably destroy everything in my office in the scuffle. Also, I didn't have a lot of confidence I'd be the last guy standing. He looked like a guy who had lost a lot of fights, but had won more than he lost. The Beretta under my middle drawer suddenly held great appeal.

But he just stood there, in the doorway, expressionless,

staring at me, sending me a message. I replied by staring back at him. I didn't smile. Or wink. That would have been a mistake. That's the kind of stuff kids do when they think they're a smart-ass. Then they end up in the hospital trying to remember the color of the truck that must of hit them.

When he was sure I had gotten the message, he left, leaving the door open. I really hate it when people leave my door open.

Landry coming to see me saved me from tracking him down. I was seeing Eileen Friday night, dinner at the Continental, a movie at the Cineplex, drinks at Harry's to end the night. Op-la-de, op-la-da, life goes on. Next move after that will be up to Benny Landry.

FRIDAY, JUST AFTER noon, I was in Charlestown. It was time to speak with Timothy O'Neil. Sal would be here the following week, and I didn't want to waste any time getting the problem resolved. Accidents were known to happen because of dawdling.

O'Neil had a pretty good operation going in Charlestown and Chelsea. He started out as a two-bit hood, but, through some luck, balls and smarts, had built a nice business. Some of it legit, some not so much. He owned three bars, one in Sullivan Square, one in City Square, and another just off the Parkway near Chelsea stadium. His bars in Charlestown did a robust business, which all bars in Charlestown did. No surprise there. But in both spots there was a door off to the side of the bartender that only exclusive clientele were allowed to enter. Beyond those doors, your marker had to be good for five figures. Once in there, with the fancy walls, and the thick carpet, and, so I've heard, gaudy chandeliers, you could sit at tables where poker hands were dealt out with hundred dollar antes, or you could place your bets on anyone of fifty squares while the metal ball spun around before falling onto the spinning wheel. The most popular spot in those rooms, and the loudest, so I've been told, was the table where dice were thrown along felt covered table tops and dreams came true, or were dashed in a heartbeat by an unfortunate flip of a die.

O'Neil also owned a warehouse near the old Charlestown Navy Yard, where my dad had worked for thirty years as a welder after coming back from the war in 1945. The Navy Yard closed in the mid-seventies when Nixon paid Massachusetts back for being the only state he didn't carry in the '72 election. I've always said, Massachusetts people are the smartest people in the country. Condos and apartments now occupied the buildings where electricians, sheet-metal workers, welders, ship-fitters and a dozen other craftsmen buildings maintained the Atlantic fleet. Gone, too, are the cranes that slowly moved like giant leviathans on the tracks along the huge dry docks, slower, even, than Godzilla through Tokyo.

The ancient brick warehouse is where the Irish hood ran a legitimate business, supplying dozens of mom and pop corner grocery stores in the surrounding towns with everything they would need for their shelves, although that part of city living was rapidly disappearing. They just couldn't compete anymore with the huge grocery chains that were everywhere and multiplying. Not that O'Neil was that concerned about lost revenue. The operation was just a front. In the recesses of the warehouse, the grimy floors were stacked with microwaves, air conditioners, computers and VCR recorders that just happened to have fallen off trucks. The shelves along dirty walls were tight with Nintendo and Sega systems, and bootlegged games from China and Japan that could be played on them. They were also crammed with the hottest VHS tapes of movies still in theaters.

Yes, Tim O'Neil had a very good operation going and, like any other successful businessman, he was feeling some pressure from those who were envious. There were rumors the Somerville gang was looking to expand, and they only had to cross a few streets to be in the thick of it. Wachowski, in Lynn, deciding he didn't want to go to war with the Italians over Revere and the rest of the

Northshore, thought Chelsea, with their growing Latino population, looked ripe. That had led to his dispute with O'Neil. As far as I knew, things were at a standstill. But Sal had, somehow, gotten caught up in the mess.

I found O'Neil at the warehouse and sat down with him in his office in the front of the building. He offered me coffee from a pot on a warmer. It seemed I caught him in a good mood. In the spirit it was offered, I accepted.

"I'm glad you came to see me, Costa," he said as he settled in his chair behind the desk. I suddenly wondered if he had anything taped beneath his middle drawer. "You have business again in Charlestown? Another missing girl? Maybe I can help."

He smiled at me, like we were old friends, a gesture of Irish hospitality. The smile faded when I said, "I'm here about Sal Beradino."

"What's Sal to you?" he asked, his eyes narrowing, all pretense of bonhomie disappearing faster than Jets fans in the fourth quarter.

"I've known him since he was a kid. He seems to be caught in the middle of some problem between you and Tomek Wachowski. I want to clear that up."

"Don't know if you can."

"I believe reasonable men can always find reasonable solutions," I said, sounding like Henry Kissinger and not believing a word of it.

"The Polack ain't being reasonable," said O'Neil, his voice rising a bit. "He's being damn unreasonable, trying to move in on my turf, disrupting my operation. Threatening me."

"I talked with Wachowski," I said in a conversational tone. "He believes you used Sal to try and lure him to a meeting so you could assassinate him. He harbors the belief Sal knew."

"Assassinate him?" the Irishman was getting louder. I had to admit, he had some flair. Probably would have been a decent stage actor had he chosen a different path. A voice that could project to the cheap seats and beyond.

"Wachowski believes, had he attended the meeting

you sent Sal to inform him about, he would have been killed. That's between you and him. I have to believe Sal had no idea what you were planning, if you were planning anything. I want to set a meeting with you, Tomek, me and Sal, and clear this whole thing up."

Tim O'Neil leaned forward.

"You setting me up for the Polack, Costa?" He appeared angry, but his heart wasn't in it. He knew that was bullshit. I ignored the remark.

"I'll pick the neutral ground. We'll talk. We'll iron things out. Sal can come back home. You tell Tomek he has bad info, if you want. Tell him any damn thing you want. But tell him the truth about Sal, that the kid was only sent to bring the invite. That was it."

O'Neil leaned back and shook his head.

"The kid isn't my problem," he said. "I got no beef with him. But Wachowski and I are preparing for war. I don't see me sitting down with the enemy and talking nice. You convince him to stay out of Chelsea, then we'll talk."

I could see O'Neil wouldn't change his mind on this. I could also see he had intended on killing Wachowski.

"I understand Sal is in to you for fifteen thousand," I said. No use beating a dead horse.

"I'd have to check, but that sounds about right."

Yeah, he'd have to check. The Irishman knew the debt right down to the penny, including the interest accrued today.

"We'll make arrangements to pay it. Keep the interest light, and we'll clear it up in a few months."

"For you, no vig," O'Neil said, his arms opening in a gesture like we were old pals from the neighborhood.

I nodded a thanks. "In the meantime, no one touches Sal. Not a hair on his head. And he's told he's persona non grata at your clubs."

"He's a grown man, Costa. He's going to try his luck somewhere."

"Just not in Charlestown."

"You got some balls coming in here and making

demands in my town," O'Neil said, but he wasn't angry. At least if he was, he didn't show it. "I wouldn't suggest you make a habit of it."

Driving back over the hill to Sullivan Square and the short bridge into Everett over the Mystic, I wasn't happy the sit down with Tomek Wachowski would be minus O'Neil. But I could see the reason. O'Neil was going to make another run at Wachowski, and, I thought, soon. I half wished he'd do it before Sal got here in a few days.

I hustled home to get ready for my date with Eileen, but not before stopping at my favorite sub shop for an American sub with everything on it. Everything except onions, of course, with consideration of my plans for the evening.

16

I asked you not to get involved in my divorce," Eileen said as I got behind the wheel of my Chrysler 300. She had been waiting on the sidewalk when I pulled up in front of her house. I had hustled to open the door for her, but she had done it herself before I could reach her. By the time I got behind the wheel again, the temperature in the car seemed to have dipped twenty degrees.

"He came to see me," I explained. I saw no need to confess I had been asking about Ben Landry.

"You didn't tell me he called you before," she said, her arms crossed over her chest. She looked good. Her dark hair was pulled back and clipped. She had a pinkish shade of lipstick I hadn't seen before. Her cheeks had more color than usual. That may have been from the cold temps, or from her mood, which bordered on angry, which rose my temperature just a bit.

"He left a message on my machine," I said. "We didn't talk."

"But you talked yesterday."

"Yes. Ben came to my office. So, yes, we talked."

"And you threatened him."

"I threatened bodily harm if he ever hurt you again," I said, my volume up two decibels. "What did you expect me to say to him?"

"Nothing, Paul. Not a damn thing. I thought I was very clear about that."

"Eileen, he came to my office. I didn't go to him. Don't you think you're being just a bit unreasonable?"

I realized my mistake even as the words were coming out of my mouth. I took in a lot of air and let it out slowly, careful not to make a sound. I realized I was gripping the wheel much too hard, and allowed my fingers to loosen.

In control again, I said, "Eileen, he threatened me. That requires a forceful response."

"Benny would never threaten anyone," she said, still angry. "He abhors violence. I've never even seen him angry."

"The bruises I've seen on your arm say different."

"That was just him reaching for me and me pulling away. The divorce has really got him upset. And when he hears I'm dating another man, well, what would you expect?"

"He may abhor violence, Eileen, but the people he works for thrive on it. One word from him, and I'll have my hands full."

Her head snapped towards me, eyes angry. "You want to call this off?"

I smiled. I was going to reach for her hand, but one small step at a time. "I told you before, I can't be intimidated. I'll tell you what I told Benny. I'm with the lady until the lady tells me to get lost. And I'm hoping that never happens. Now, would you like to sit here longer and discuss this some more, or should we get something to eat and discuss plans for the weekend?"

Her eyes searched my face, and they softened a bit. "What plans for the weekend?" she asked.

"I thought we'd take a ride to the Berkshires. Should still be some nice color. Probably the last weekend for it. Find a nice bed and breakfast. Simple pleasures."

"We can talk about it over dinner," she said as she uncrossed her arms and moved an inch closer to me. "I'm starving."

THE WEEKEND PASSED too quickly. Friday, after our brief discussion in the car, we dined at the Continental on Route 1, one of my favorite restaurants. Big, delicious menu, comfortable, roomy booths and then they walk around offering you fried chicken wings, or stuffed mushrooms, popovers, or whatever. I still managed to finish the veal parm with spaghetti.

While we ate, we talked about where to go over the weekend. Ben Landry and the divorce was purposely not mentioned. But I knew it was only on the back burner. Eileen would get to it again, which she did on the ride back to her place late Sunday afternoon after a wonderful weekend. But I get ahead of myself.

After dinner we went to see *Rain Man,* making a return engagement after a successful run during last winter. Dustin Hoffman, and this young actor, Tom Cruise, star in the movie. It's a story about a young guy who finds out he has an older brother he didn't know about. The young guy, Cruise, is a bit of a hustler. The Hoffman character is a savant. Halfway through the movie, I'm starting to see my face on the Cruise character, and either Sal or Packy on the Hoffman guy. I don't know how the younger brother kept his sanity.

A nightcap at Harry's, and separate domiciles after, ended the night. Her choice. Not mine.

I picked Eileen up early Saturday and off we went to the Berkshires. Foliage, even at the end of October, was still alive with color. We found a lovely Bed and Breakfast in Cheshire. Overall, a calm and enjoyable two days, until the ride home. And then we talked of Ben Landry again.

"He screwed up, and he knows it, and he's sorry," Eileen said as I drove east along the Pike late Sunday afternoon .

"Was he seeing someone else?" I asked.

"Ben? Oh, God, no. I almost wished he were. Sex is not something that occupies his thoughts very often. If ever. That was the problem. I don't think I'm over-sexed, Paul, but I do have needs."

I'd swear in a court of law that that was a true statement. And the lady wasn't shy about telling me what she wanted during those needy periods.

"But Ben just wasn't interested," Eileen continued. "He was tired. Or stressed. Or had a headache."

She turned towards me. "A headache for Christ's sake.

I just couldn't take it anymore. Finally, neither could he. My complaining. My angry digs at his manhood. He moved out in June."

Eileen became quiet, staring out the window at Worcester.

"I should have seen it coming," she said after a while. "Even before we married, we didn't have sex that often, and back then I looked good."

"You still look good, babe," I said. "Better than good. The man's a damn fool."

"Thanks. But you should have seen me in my twenties. I could have had any man I wanted."

"So why choose a guy who didn't excite you?"

"Ben was charming. Took me to the best restaurants. Nice parties. He was smart. And funny. And when I found out what he did for a living, and who he did it for, I found that exciting."

"You found an accountant exciting?" I asked, smiling when I did, so as not to seem judgmental.

"Not the numbers part," she answered. "But the connected part. He was part of the mob. I found that exciting. Growing up in Brooklyn, I found the stories in the newspapers about the crime families fascinating. There were murders, and trials, and all these Italian guys, sharply dressed, talking about killing people like it was a sport. *The Godfather,* one and two, are still my favorite movies.

"Before we were married, and even after, we went to the Christmas parties the family threw. All these wise guys, and they're treating Ben like he's some kind of big shot. That attention wasn't lost on me."

"Yeah. The guy cooking the books, saving you money and keeping you out of jail, deserves a warm handshake. So you've met Joe Glendali?" I asked.

"Several times. He'd come. But he never stayed very long. The party would calm down while he was there, but pick up again after he left. Those guys could party."

"What did you think of Glendali?"

"He was a kind looking old man. Like everyone's

grandfather. He moved slowly. Spoke softly. Always shook my hand warmly, with a kiss on my cheek, and a smiling warning to Benny that he should never let me get away. I liked him."

Maybe the old man is warning Benny again that he shouldn't let her get away, I thought, but didn't say. We've discussed this before, the possible ramifications of a divorce. No need to do it again.

She was silent until we crossed the 495. With the Hopkinton Reservoir somewhere to our right, and the start of the Boston Marathon - the only Marathon that should ever matter, in my humble opinion - in the general vicinity, she said, "Ben's been calling a lot lately. He's stopped by the house three times in the last two weeks. He's begging me to reconsider. The last time, he got angry with me. Said he could change. He would change. Friday night, when you dropped me off, there was a diamond necklace on my kitchen table when I went in the house."

"You haven't changed the locks?" I asked, perhaps a bit harsher than was necessary.

"I never thought to. Like I've said, up till now, he was being agreeable to everything."

"Jesus, Eileen," was all I could say. Preaching to her wouldn't help, so I swallowed about a dozen reasons why the locks should have been changed.

"Please, don't get into it with Ben. I'll talk to him. Explain things. Make him understand that it's all over between us and I have a life to live. That we both have to move on. I'll make him understand."

"Sometimes," I said, "it's not that simple."

As we were to find out, truer words were never spoken.

17

Leaving my condo at 7:30 Monday morning, there was a quick movement behind me as a figure came rushing out of the bushes. I turned quickly, forced a body up against the brick of the building, sweeping my arm in case there was a gun in the guys hand, then bringing my fist up to smash into his face. I was about to lift my knee into his groin before hitting him, when the guy said, "Hey, cut it out." Salvatore Beradino was back in town.

"What did I tell you about sneaking up on people?" I said as I gave him a quick bear hug, then held him at arms length so I could check him out. He looked good. Maybe even gained a few pounds in the last two months.

"I expected you the end of the week," I said.

"Had to boogie quick," Sal said, his head bobbing and mouth frowning. "A brother-in-law was knocking at the front door while she was pushing me out the backdoor. Couldn't even finish my morning coffee, or grab extra clothes. I thumbed into town and grabbed a Greyhound. And here I am."

"You couldn't hook up with a single woman? Or at least a married woman whose husband was in for life?"

"None who looked like Holly. You should have seen her, Paul. You'd understand."

I ushered him into the house, taking a quick look to see if any eyes were watching my place. While he sat drinking coffee and eating eggs, I asked him what had happened between him, O'Neil and Wachowski. He swore he knew nothing about any hit. O'Neil had sent him to Wachowski with an invitation to meet so they could settle their differences. That was what O'Neil had said. Wachowski was agreeable to the meet and gave Sal a message for him to bring back to Charlestown. Two days later, Sal hears from a friend that there are people looking for him. Wachowski is pissed and Sal has no idea why. He seeks out O'Neil, who then accuses him of screwing up the meet with Wachowski and starts getting physical with him, punching him to the ground. Being smart enough to know he was no match for the angry Irishman, Sal ran. At his apartment, Sal spotted two guys sitting in a Pontiac at the corner of his street. He recognized them as guys from the Lynn mob. He took a cab to his mother's place in Malden, where she emptied her cookie jar of four hundred dollars, and Sal rode a Greyhound south. He had no idea why everyone was angry with him and he wasn't about to hang around to find out.

I told him to hang out in my place and get some rest. To call his mother and tell her he was doing fine, but not to say where he was. To call no one else. To not answer the phone or the door. I'd be back late afternoon and we'd put a plan in place. Tomek would see us, and we'd smooth it all out.

Then I was on 495 heading towards Lowell for a scheduled ten o'clock meeting with a gentleman named Thomas Madison. Madison, as far as I knew, had nothing to do with computers. According to my researcher, who called me last night with what he had found, The Madison Group remodeled old mill buildings into research and residential spaces. Lowell, Lawrence, Springfield, Manchester, Nashua, Dover and even as far north as Berlin, New Hampshire. Also according to my computer kid, Thomas Madison was, quietly, one of the wealthiest men in the Northeast. Wealth far exceeding most names on the Gladstone list. And I had never heard of the man.

Thomas Madison was not a name on the Gladstone list. It was Michael Dean, the Maine guy with the wandering wife, who brought him to my attention when I interviewed him a few days before. After going on a ten minute profanity laced rant about Peter Gladstone, Dean had looked at me and said, 'You don't believe me.' Then he spun through a Rolodex on his desk and quickly wrote down a name and phone number, handing it to me. 'Call this guy,' he said. 'He'll tell you.' Dean had then grabbed the paper from my hand and dialed the number himself. When he got Thomas Madison on the line, he said into the receiver, 'Tom, I have a guy here. A private investigator. I want you to talk to him. Doesn't matter what about. I want you to be surprised. Yeah, it's important. Monday at ten.' I nodded when he had looked at me. 'He'll be there. Name is Costa. Paul Costa. Good. How's Shirley? Good, good. We're heading to Fort Lauderdale after the holidays. Will we see you two down there? Good, good. Thanks, Tom. See you soon.'

I called the Northeastern kid that night and gave him the name Thomas Madison. Two days later, he gave me what I needed. The kid is worth every penny I'm paying him.

Traffic on the 495 was brutal, as it always is, and by the time I took the exit for the Madison offices, the coffee cup in the holder was empty and I was ten minutes late. Madison didn't seem to mind when we shook hands in his office ten minutes after that.

"What is it I can help you with, Mr. Costa?" he asked as he showed me where to sit and he settled in behind a cluttered desk.

He was a big guy. Over six feet and a solid one ninety, or there about. Pretty good for a man over fifty who sat behind a desk during the day. He had a crew cut that was still more straw color than gray, and pale blue eyes in a round, open, clean shaven face. I noticed an efficiency in his walk when he moved from the door to his desk, and a bearing that made me think military. A picture on the wall to the right of his desk showed four men in military garb standing beside a large helicopter. One of the guys looked like Madison, only twenty odd years younger.

"I'd like to ask you some questions about Peter Gladstone," I said.

"Peter?" Madison frowned. "You working for someone he screwed? Business associate, or husband of a seduced wife? Who is it this time?"

"Actually, it's Mr. Gladstone who's my client."

"No wonder Michael didn't tell me more on the phone. Mr. Costa, my advice to you is to make sure your advance was enough to cover your expenses, and don't work an hour beyond what he's paid you."

I smiled. "I'll remember that. You've attended parties at his place on the Neck?"

"I have."

"Often?"

"Often enough. The fund-raisers. Not the others. Do you know about the others, Mr. Costa?"

"Only what I've heard. Were you at the fund-raiser that he hosted before the break-in?"

"You mean the art theft?"

"Yes."

"Yes, I was. Mrs. Madison and I were there."

"Do you remember who the fund-raiser was for?"

Thomas Madison reached across his desk for a pack of Marlboro's, offered me one, which I refused, and lit one up. He stared across the desk at me, a look of amusement on his face.

"I have no idea who got my money that night, Mr. Costa. I really don't. Did you serve?"

I assumed he meant the military. I shook my head. "No, sir, I did not."

"I spent ten years of my youth in the army, finishing up in the very early years of Vietnam. I've commanded men. I've been in combat. Skirmishes that some nights still wake me from my sleep. I've fought even more battles in board rooms and bank offices with some very determined men who seemed hell-bent in keeping me from building a successful business. I earned a pace-maker for all that effort, but I faced it all and survived and thrived. And now I answer to no man."

He smiled. "But, when Mrs. Madison tells me we have to attend a dinner, I ask what time I have to be ready. When she tells me to sign a check, I do so immediately, without a glance at who it's made out to.

When she tells me it is time to leave the party, I find her coat and help her into it.

"Are you married, Mr. Costa?"

"No, sir."

"It's rather like the military. Your wants and desires don't always enter into your superiors' thought process. I'm a sergeant again. Mrs. Madison is the Captain. Seems to work quite well this way."

I had to smile at that.

"You mentioned I should be wary about being paid for my expenses. Care to elaborate?"

"I try not to be a crude man anymore, Mr. Costa. God knows, I was a hard drinking, foul mouthed man in my military career. That all changed when I met the woman who would become my wife. Mrs. Madison does not tolerate profanity or rude behavior. So I will put this as delicately as I can. Peter Gladstone has screwed more people out of money than Wilt the Stilt screwed women. Have you heard the rumors concerning Wilt's prowess with the opposite sex?"

I actually laughed. "Yes, sir, I have."

"And he still grabbed twenty rebounds a night. Where does a man find that kind of energy?" Madison was smiling, but when he looked at me the smile faded.

"Gladstone has been known to stiff laborers who work on his property. Two companies that built his offices in Burlington went bankrupt when he failed to pay them. These are men I know. Before the IPO, Peter borrowed money from people he knew with the promise that they would be in the front of the line when the stock went public. They weren't, and Peter paid them back with stock that was almost twice the price of the opening. And now the stock is down. He's a snake-oil salesman, Mr. Costa. A man of low moral fiber and absolutely no redeeming qualities. So, watch yourself."

I was about to ask, as delicately as possible, why he attended the fund-raisers if he found Peter Gladstone so offensive, but Madison, perhaps sensing the question, beat me to it.

"So why do Mrs. Madison and I go to his parties? Because the charities that they benefit are usually important ones. I don't drink the man's liquor. We rarely say anything to each other beyond a strained hello. And the Mrs. and I are out of there by ten. He's an offensive man. I find his house to be offensive. All those animals on the walls, the heavy wood, the stone exterior. It's all a prop for a man, who is less than a man, trying to show the world he is a man. He's a weasel.

"Did Michael Dean tell you the same thing?" Madison asked, eyebrows raised.

"Pretty much. Only with more colorful words."

"Yes, Michael can get carried away at times. Mrs. Madison has had to caution him several times when we're together. Did Michael mention he caught his ex and Gladstone having an affair?"

"He did not," I replied. "But I did know about it."

"Not surprising. Michael is a proud man. Just what is it you are investigating, Mr. Costa?"

"The art theft."

"What does he expect you to do after so much time? By now, the stuff has been fenced and probably out of the country."

"We're taking a different tact." I said, not elaborating.

Madison stared at me for several seconds. Then frowned. "Gladstone now thinks an acquaintance might have had the paintings stolen? In retribution for something Gladstone had done to them in the past? Well, Mr. Costa, I have to wish you luck. Trying to find out who that may be is a task I would not wish on my greatest enemy. The list is very long."

Even longer than I thought, is what I thought.

18

From the Madison offices, I drove back to my condo with a stop at Star Market to pick up groceries for my guest. Sal was easy to shop for. Peanut butter, grape jelly, a loaf of Wonder Bread and several 2-liter bottles of Pepsi, and Sal would be fine. He was sleeping on the couch when I walked in and never woke. I was in my office by 12:30 and on the phone with Tomek Wachowski five minutes after that. I said I wanted to talk, he said he'd be at his club at 3:30.

Something had been bothering me ever since the meeting with Thomas Madison earlier. I called my researcher. His mother informed me her son was attending classes, but was expected home by 4:30. I left a name with her and what I wanted him to find out about that name. He should call me when he had what I wanted. Then I checked the messages on the machine. There were four.

The first was from Eileen thanking me for a wonderful weekend. Near the end of the message, which included a brief outline of what she was going to do to me for planning such a nice weekend, was a short apology for her defense of Ben Landry during our drive back home. She reminded me that she was going through a difficult time and that I had to be understanding of her situation.

The second message was from an insurance company I often did investigative work for. I'd call them back in the morning and get the details. The third and fourth messages had no message at all, just silence until the connection was broken.

I was putting together an expense report for Peter Gladstone when the phone rang.

"Costa Investigating Agency. This is Paul Costa."

"Costa. Tim O'Neil here. I was thinking about our talk the other day. Maybe you're right."

"In what way?" I asked.

"Maybe we should all meet about the kid. Do you know where he is?"

"I know. Now you want to meet? What changed your mind?"

"Sal has no business being caught up in the disagreement I have with the Polack. We meet, clear that mess up, and maybe Wachowski and I come to some agreement on the other stuff. Use the kid as a chance to settle other differences. What do you think?"

"Tim, the only thing I care about is Sal. I'm not getting involved in anything else."

"Of course not," O'Neil said. "None of your business. But the kid gives Wachowski and I a reason to be in the same room. Maybe some good comes out of it. Can you set the meet?"

"I'll get back to you," I said, and hung up.

I ENTERED THE club in Lynn and was escorted to the back room. Tomek Wachowski sat at the desk counting money, stacks of bills in front of him in piles of ones, fives, tens and twenties.

"Give me a minute," he said as he indicated a place to sit. He finished counting one stack, placed a rubber band around it, wrote a figure onto a lined notepad, then put bands around the other stacks. The stacks then went into a bottom drawer.

"The economy sucks," he said, then poured himself some orange juice. "So, what have we got?"

"Heard from O'Neil after talking with you," I said, waving off an invitation to join him in the libation. "Says he wants to be part of the meet."

"Him? What for?"

"He'll explain that there was no evil intent in the suggestion to meet. That you were misinformed that there was a plan to harm you. That Sal was just a messenger."

"You asked him to do that?"

"I did."

"I know what I know," Wachowski said.

I held a hand up in front of me. "I'll tell you the same thing I told him, that's between you and him. My only concern is Sal. He gets taken out of the equation. Sal has told me what I already knew, he knew nothing about any bad intent when he brought the message. He was just doing what he does, which is to be the messenger between the different interests. The kid is innocent, Tomek, you have to know that."

"I want to hear it from Sal. I want to look in his eyes when he tells me. Then I'll know."

He brought a finger up to his lips and looked across the room. "I don't trust O'Neil."

"I don't either," I said. "The first time I spoke with him about this, he said no way to him being there. This afternoon he called and he had changed his mind."

"Did he say why?"

"Says he wants to see if you two can work something out."

"Has to be a public place. A quiet spot among people."

"There's a restaurant on One," I said. "It's busy, but at eight we should have a booth where we'll have some privacy."

After a few seconds of nodding, Wachowski said, "Set it up."

I started to get up when he said, "There's someone here wants to see you."

Normally, I don't feel the weight of the gun in the shoulder holster. After all these years, it's become part of the wardrobe. It would be like feeling the belt that holds up your pants. But when I encounter something that I wasn't expecting, the heft of the gun under my jacket suddenly becomes the central nerve in my body.

Wachowski pressed a button on his phone. "Send him in."

I looked at Wachowski. He was smirking. The door

opened slowly. Packy strolled in.

"Hey, hey, whadda ya say. Heard you'd be in Lynn today."

Packy plunked himself down in a chair next to mine. He wore the cap with the Green Bay logo on the front, a Red Sox jacket and sweat pants with the Bruins letters running down the sides. He was looking at the wall behind Wachowski when he said, "You find the Picasso's yet, Shamus?"

I relaxed.

"I'm working on it, Packy. You hear anything?"

"I'm hearing the Patriots might be for sale, if you have a hundred million under the mattress. I'm hearing Birdman is healthy once again and the parquet floor is where the magic will happen, and where the the Magic man will fail come May. I'm hearing T-bills are the place to put your money right now."

"I mean about the paintings," I said. Tomek Wachowski was chuckling.

Packy looked at me. He sadly shook his head. "The P.I. needs a better eye."

"Meaning?"

"What is the hardest thing to see?" Packy asked.

"A little late in the day for riddles, Packy," I said. I was trying to mask my impatience. For Packy to be sitting here, however, it could only mean he had something to share. He would share it when he was ready.

"The hardest thing of all, is to see a black cat in a dark room," he said.

"Sure," I said. "Meaning?"

"Especially if there is no cat." Packy nodded, like he had just solved the mystery of life on earth.

"Is that Shakespeare?" I asked.

"Confucius." He sadly shook his head again at my ignorance.

"Confucius?" I had to smile.

"In prison, some guys lifted weights," Packy said. "I lifted books."

I hardly heard that. The riddle had finally caught my

attention. It must have shown on my face, because Packy had a satisfied smile on his.

After a few seconds, Packy said, “When a wise man points at the moon, the imbecile examines the finger.”

“Confucius again?” I asked.

“Batting fifty percent, Shamus.”

“You sure about this, Packy?”

“The odds are a little better than your batting average,” he said. “And the source bats in the four spot.”

THE DRIVE BACK to my condo from Lynn was a dangerous one, especially for any car that was in my immediate vicinity. My mind was everywhere but the road. The morning, and Thomas Madison, had planted a seed of an idea in my head. The afternoon, and Packy, had the seed sprouting. I was more than a little interested in what my Northeastern talent would report. Was it possible the art had never left Peter Gladstone's stone home? But then, why hire me? He would soon have the money from the insurance company. He was home free. Why have me dig it all up again? By the time I pulled up in front of my place, I knew the answer. At least I thought I did. I needed the report to confirm it.

When I went inside, Sal was still on the couch, sitting up and watching one of the crazy afternoon shows where everyone yells at everyone else and the host plays mediator. What is this world coming to?

“Hey, kid,” I said.

“Paul. You got to see this. The girl in the pink blouse with the pink hair, is accusing the fat girl of trying to steal her boyfriend. The fat girl is pregnant with the guys kid. The guy hasn't said a word. He's just sitting there laughing. Security has already had to separate the two girls. It's a freaking riot.”

“Did you call your mom?” I asked, as I sat at the kitchen table putting the caps back on the peanut butter and jelly jars.

“Yeah, yeah,” Sal said never taking his eyes off the television. “She was really pissed. Said she was worried.

Said I should have called. I need to stop over there and see her."

"After the meet," I said, but Sal wasn't listening.

Until the meeting with the two hoods, Sal stayed here and out of sight. I'd get a call into O'Neil tomorrow and shoot for a meeting Wednesday night in Melrose.

As much as I wanted to trust Wachowski that we were under a white flag, I have learned to be very careful who I trust. High on the list of those I certainly do not trust, was Timmy O'Neil.

19

The meet was set for the next night, Thursday, O'Neil unavailable before then. I had rented a half dozen movies from my neighborhood video rental store, and those, along with afternoon television chaos, was keeping Sal occupied. I had to get away from him for a while to process what I had learned the last two days, so I had called Eileen and we met up at Harry's. Just being with her, even from across a table, was therapeutic, and put everything else out of my mind. I would deal with it all tomorrow.

Eileen seemed to be in good spirits. She certainly looked good. She wore tight fitting designer jeans, black, and so tight fitting that if there was a bill in a pocket I could have told you the founding father that was on it. Thankfully, she wore a loose fitting dark gray sweater. Had it been tight, also, my impure thoughts probably would have gotten the best of me. As it was, they were barely contained as I tried to make nice talk.

She had been to the salon she would be working in soon, and her and the owner had talked over ideas. She was looking forward to starting and expected she could now be in before Christmas. Eileen spoke of a phone call she had gotten Monday night from an old friend from Brooklyn who was getting married for the second time. Could I get away in January and go with her to the wedding? Halfway through her second Manhattan, she brought up a movie that was in the theaters that she wanted to see. It was then an older man in a long wool coat came into Harry's. Eileen didn't notice him, but I did. I had seen his photograph in the Globe once or twice over the years, although he looked much older now than in the photo.

Joseph Glendali walked right up to the bar, Harry hustling over from a table he had been standing beside to greet him.

The two men shook hands. Harry filled two shot glasses, they saluted each other and drank. The old man said something I couldn't hear, and Harry grinned and nodded his head. It was then another gentleman came through the front door and took a seat. He was dressed in a dark gray suit, maybe a little over five and a half feet tall, thin, with hooded eyes that seemed sleepy, but, I knew, were taking in everything, including me. Big muscles and wide backs weren't needed if you had the talent to shoot out the middle club from a three of clubs playing card at a distance of thirty feet with a hand gun. I've seen the look before in the eyes of guys who can do that. This guy had the look.

Eileen was still talking, although I had stopped listening. She noticed.

"Paul, are you listening to me?" she asked.

Bringing my attention back to her, I said, "A movie this weekend sounds wonderful."

Eileen frowned. She must have moved on to something else. And then Joe Glendali was standing beside our booth.

"Mrs. Landry," the old Italian said, smiling and extending a hand for hers.

Eileen paled when she looked at him, but recovered quickly.

"Mr. Glendali," she said, managing a smile and placing her hand in his. He covered her hand with his other hand and held it firmly, his eyes holding hers for several long seconds.

"May I join you?" he asked. He released Eileen's hand and looked at me. Then he took a step back.

I met his stare, my face impassive, even though I was surprised the Don himself had come to exert pressure on Eileen to reconsider the divorce, and on me to end the affair. He could have sent the guy sitting across the room, so I wasn't complaining. I stood and moved to sit beside

Eileen. Mr. Glendali took my seat. Harry came over with a martini, placing it in front of Glendali, quickly giving me a puzzling look. I hadn't told him who Eileen's husband was.

When Harry left, Glendali said, “Mrs. Landry, please, introduce me to your friend.”

I had no doubt the old man knew who I was. He wouldn't have come without checking me out first. I extended a hand across the table and said, “My name is Paul Costa, Mr. Glendali.”

He shook my hand. His hand was dry, the skin loose, the grasp firm. His eyes were almost steel gray and piercing. His hair was thin and combed straight back with no hint of gray in the dyed strands. His eyebrows were bushy over those intense eyes. There was just the slightest tint of yellow in the skin of his face, leaving me to believe he was dealing with some sickness. His voice, though soft, still had the sense of command.

“An Italian,” he said.

I nodded.

“And a private investigator,” he said. Just so I would know he had checked me out.

Again, I nodded.

“You know who I am?” he asked.

“Of course,” I said.

“May I share something with you, Mr. Costa, that you may not know?” Glendali asked. I assumed he was here to warn me away from Eileen. I prepared myself for the warning, thinking this would be it, veiled perhaps, but plain enough. I wasn't prepared for what the old man said next.

“I knew your father,” Glendali said. “Michael Costa. I didn't know him well. Met him two or three times.”

I'm sure my face didn't hide the surprise I felt. The old man saw it and nodded a few times.

“You didn't know,” he said. “I'm not surprised. You're wondering how a man in my profession would know a welder who worked in the Navy Yard? We had three men in the Navy Yard who picked up the number bets for the daily pool from those who worked there. You know the pool I'm talking about? The one with the name I despise? Makes us sound like ignorant baboons. Like the filth that calls us Italians by those crude names they like to use. Anyways, Michael Costa was one of those men who picked up the number chits. And the best of them. As a welder, he easily moved around the entire complex. For years, your father collected the most bets each day. After walking out of the gate after his shift, one of our men would meet him and collect the bets. Nickels, dimes, quarters, dollars, you'd be surprised at how much that amounted to each day. A few times, when the regular pick-up guy was sick, I picked up the bets, back in my younger days when responsibility didn't weigh so heavy. Let me tell you something, Mr. Costa, there was never a problem with your father. Never a shortage, or someone claiming a win we didn't have a chit for. Not all of our runners were that honest."

I had no idea my father ran numbers. Never once did he mention it, never once did I suspect. Obviously, not that big a deal, but I was a bit stunned.

Mr. Glendali sipped at his martini, then looked up at the two of us.

"So, what are we do about this problem you two have created?" he calmly asked.

"Mr. Glendali, please...," Eileen began to say.

"Eileen," the Don said, reaching across to cover her hand, "please, call me Joe. Think of me as an uncle. Someone who you can trust to speak honestly with and who has your best interests at heart. Someone who cares about you."

"Mr. Glendali.., Joe" Eileen said, and I was surprised at her composure, "please understand. I no longer love Ben. I loved him once, but no more."

The old man nodded his head several times, as if he understood her feelings.

"Every marriage has times of difficulty," he said, still covering her hand. "It is during those times when patience must be executed. When time must be given to allow reason to return."

Glendali looked at me. I met his stare. I would allow the man to have his say before I had mine.

Looking back at Eileen, Glendali said, "You are a young and beautiful woman." He shrugged. "And Ben, a few years older - and this is my fault - tired from the work I have placed on his shoulders, has, perhaps, neglected his duties as a husband."

"Mr Glendali...," Eileen began to say, but the old man raised a hand to silence her.

"None of my business. Please forgive me for mentioning such a delicate thing. But, who knows better than me the effects on the body the pressure of the job has on men as we age." He waved a hand in front of his face. "How those pressures lead to negligence of intimacy is something we don't even consider, until brought to our attention. So, it is understandable, especially the way things are in the world today, that a wife may feel unloved, may feel she is no longer desirable to her husband, may feel needs that he no longer satisfies." He looked at me again. "So she wanders.

"A sin in the eyes of God and the church," Glendali continued, his eyes on Eileen once again, "but, in the world of today, a sin that can be forgiven should it be renounced."

"Mr. Glendali," Eileen said, meeting his gaze and leaning towards him, "I don't regret my decision. I no longer love Ben. Have not loved him now for a long time. I think I deserve a chance to be happy."

"And this man," Joseph Glendali said, nodding at me," makes you happy?"

"Yes, he does," Eileen said, "but this is not about Paul. I met him only a few weeks ago. Ben and I separated months ago. I beg you, Joseph, to allow me to find happiness."

The old Mafia Don nodded a few times, sipped from his glass and then looked at me. Rising to the highest sitting position he could attain, I met his gaze with the respect it deserved. I don't think Eileen fully understood just how dangerous this conversation was to her. Maybe to the both of us. But I did. I would treat the man with respect, only because to not do so could escalate the problem to an ending that could cost us our lives. It may anyways. But I would support any decision Eileen determined.

"Tu capisci il perecolo in questo?" Glendali asked, his voice conversational, but his gray eyes conveying the gravity of the situation. He was asking me if I understood the danger in Eileen's decision.

I nodded. "Yes."

"Eppure sei con lei?" Glendali asked. And still I was with her?

I would try to reason with him, although I doubted it would make a difference.

"Lei non saniente. Lui non le ha detto segreti." I said, spreading my hands. I told him, in so many words, that Eileen didn't know anything about family business. Ben never told her a thing.

He frowned and gave me a look like I was the biggest fool in the world. Maybe he was right.

"Non e Italiano. Non essere sciocco. Le mie mani saranno legate," Glendali said sternly. He was telling me not to be stupid, although he said ignorant. Landry wasn't Italian. So, obviously, he couldn't be trusted not to say things to his wife.

"Don Glendali, con rispetto, la signora e libera di scegliere," I said. With respect, the lady was free to choose.

He gave a slight shake of his head and the frown deepened. With some force in his soft voice he said, "Non senza consequenze."

Not without consequences.

So, there it was.

"I know you two are talking about me," Eileen said in the pause that followed his statement. "I would like you to speak in English, please."

Glendali smiled and covered her hand again with his.

"Mrs. Landry," the old man said. "My dear Eileen.

Your husband loves you very much. He is very important to family business, and I regard him, and you, as family. So I pray that you will take more time in your decision. Do not rush into anything. Time has a way of healing. It also has a way of showing us what is best. Please, if you would like to speak with me again, do not hesitate to reach out. You are family, Eileen, and there is nothing I wouldn't do for family."

He turned his attention to me.

"Mr. Costa, I'm glad we had this opportunity to speak. Please, give my warmest regards to your father when you next see him."

"He passed away fifteen years ago, Mr. Glendali."

"I'm sorry to hear that. It seems every day I'm reminded of how many years I've lived, and that the clock never stops ticking."

Joseph Glendali stood, taking a slight step backwards to keep his balance. He buttoned up the expensive gray coat. Across the room, the bodyguard stood. Glendali went to the bar, shook Harry's hand, and walked out the door without another glance at us.

I looked at Harry, who was looking at me with a look that said, 'What the fuck?'

"What were you two saying in Italian?" Eileen asked. "Was it about me? He looked angry."

'Sonny,' Tom Hagen, the non-Italian consigliere, said, 'it's just business. It's not personal.'

The hell it's not.

20

I pulled my Chrysler off Route 1 and steered to a spot along the edge of the parking lot. It was ten of eight, so most of the dinner crowd was home getting ready to watch television, but the lot was still half full.

"Is everything going to be okay, Paul?" Sal asked before we got out of the car.

"Sure, kid," I said. "We're going to smooth it all out tonight. Don't worry."

I hoped I sounded convincing.

We began walking towards the entrance to the restaurant, when a dark four-door sedan sped in off the highway and stopped in the middle of the lot thirty feet from where we were. Instincts took over. My right hand reached in for the Beretta, my left grabbed Sal by the collar and started dragging him back towards parked cars. The two passenger side doors of the sedan flew open and two guys came out of the car firing at us with pistols. Sal was back-pedaling as I pulled him, and I felt him falter as he became a heavy weight.

"I'm shot, Paul," Sal cried. "Oh, God, they shot me. Paul, help me."

I took two quick shots at the car and the shooters, then pulled Sal hard the rest of the way behind the closest vehicle. I felt his body spasm as another bullet caught him. I ducked him down to safety and popped up to spray three more shots. One shooter hid behind the rear door, while it looked like the guy in front was going to sprint to the end of the lot where he could flank me. Then I heard two shots come from my left. I thought I was already flanked on the other side. They were about to have us in a crossfire with no hope of retreat.

Suddenly, the guy behind the rear door started crying out that he'd been shot. Then two shots followed, coming from my right, one of them taking out the window of the open front door. The shooter standing beside that door looked to the cars that were on my right. He began backing up and another bullet tore into the metal of the door right where he was standing.

"Get in the car, Jimmy," he screamed as he leapt onto the front seat. I fired two bullets at the legs of the guy who was desperately trying to claw his way into the backseat. One bullet must have caught him because he cried out again. The driver threw the car into reverse and swerved, the rear door closing from the maneuver, then threw the car into drive and bolted onto Route 1. A pick-up swerved to avoid it.

I looked up to see who was shooting at the car.

"Paul, I'm dying," Sal cried. He was tugging at the sleeve of the hand that held my gun. I tried shaking him off. Suddenly, Timothy O'Neil was standing behind me, a gun in his hand. From my left, Tomek Wachowski appeared, also holding a gun.

"Paul, Paul, help me," Sal cried. "I don't want to die."

A door opened on the side of the restaurant. Slowly, a head peeked around it.

I looked at the two hoods who were pointing their weapons at each other.

"Call an ambulance," I yelled to the guy in the doorway. "Hurry. Someone's shot."

From a distance I could hear sirens. Someone inside must have called the police. I took my belt off and used it as a tourniquet on Sal's leg, although the bleeding didn't seem bad. The other wound was to the stomach area and I used my handkerchief and pressure to try and stem the blood. When I looked up again, O'Neil and Wachowski hadn't moved, guns still trained on the other.

"We probably shouldn't be here when the cops come," O'Neil finally said.

"No, we shouldn't," said Wachowski.

The Irishman backed up a few steps, then went to his

car and drove out of the lot.

"You hit?" Wachowski asked.

"No," I said.

"Can you explain this?" he asked, the gun slipping into his coat pocket.

"Not now," I replied. "You better go."

Wachowski nodded.

Three Melrose police cars showed up a minute later, a Saugus ambulance close behind. I had laid my gun on the ground and pushed it away from me. My wallet was opened to my P.I. license and on the ground beside the gun. I was still applying pressure to Sal's wound when two cops came up to the car, weapons drawn.

"Over here," one of the cops yelled out as the ambulance came to a stop.

Two paramedics rushed over and looked down at me and Sal. One of them said to me, "You a doctor?"

I shook my head.

"Then get out of the way," he said.

"Leg and stomach wounds," I said as I stood.

"Paul, call my mom," Sal said, crying now. "Call mom, Paul. Tell her I need her."

"You're going to be okay, fella," said the paramedic kneeling beside him. "Just stay with us."

I took a few steps away to give the professionals room, then leaned against the back of a car. It is a well known fact that no matter how long it has been since a person has stopped smoking, there always comes a time when they wished they hadn't. I actually reached into my shirt pocket looking for the pack of Camel's that haven't been there for five years. A crowd had gathered in front of the restaurant as the diners emptied out to see what was going on.

"Can you tell me what happened here, Mr. Costa?" asked a cop as he handed me my wallet.

I shrugged. "Sal and I were just walking towards the restaurant, when a car pulled in from the highway and a couple of guys began shooting at us."

"Two guys?"

"Two shooters and a driver."

"What kind of car?"

"Four door. Dodge or Plymouth. Dark Green. Nothing fancy. One of the shooters got hit. Maybe pretty bad."

"So you shot one of them?"

"I believe so, yes."

The cops would eventually know I wasn't the only one returning fire.

"I hit him in the leg. Someone else got him, too."

"Someone else?" asked the cop. "Who?"

"I don't know," I said. "A good Samaritan, I guess. Actually, two good Samaritans."

"Two guys with guns? Are they still here?"

"They took off when they heard your sirens, I guess."

"Can you describe them? Or the car they were driving? Without guessing?"

"I'm afraid not," I said, and almost smiled, remembering having a similar conversation when I wore the badge "They weren't together. I didn't even get a chance to thank them. I was busy trying to keep Sal from bleeding out."

"So, two men begin shooting at you for no apparent reason," the cop said as Sal was being lifted onto a stretcher, "and two men you don't know, who happen to be in the parking lot at that time, and who happen to be packing guns for a meal at a restaurant, decide that they should place themselves in danger by joining in a gunfight, thereby saving you and your friend, Sal. Is that what you want me to believe?"

I thought another shrug might piss him off, so I turned my palms up and frowned. Two Saugus cruisers came into the lot, lights blinking, as Sal was wheeled to the ambulance. I went to Sal. He was still conscious.

"I'll see you at the hospital, Sal. I'll be there when you get out of surgery. You're going to be okay."

"Call mom, Paul," Sal said groggily. "Call my mom."

They lifted him into the back.

"Where you taking him? " I asked.

"Melrose-Wakefield," said the paramedic, then he

stepped in and closed the doors. They left the lot with sirens blaring.

The cop was behind me. “What's Sal's last name?”

“Salvatore Beradino,” I said as I watched the ambulance lights fade from view.

“Beradino? Any relation to Frank Beradino?”

“His son.”

“Really? No shit.”

“Did you know Frank?” I asked.

“No. Never met him. But I was new on the force when they had the funeral for him and, you know, we all went to pay our respects for a brother officer. Tragic how he died, but a real hero. So you knew him?”

“He was my partner for three years,” I said.

“You were a cop?”

“In another life. Listen, I'd like to get to the hospital. Can we continue this there? His mother has to be notified.”

“Sure. I'll drive you.”

I expected that. He wasn't about to let me out of his sight anytime soon.

“I need to reach his mother.”

“You know her address?”

“She's in Malden,” I said.

“I'll send a car to pick her up.”

He sat me in the back of his cruiser, then went to give directions to all the other cops. It was a crime scene and had to be treated as such. An APB went out on the car. As I sat there, finally alone, my mind was a muddled mess. When the first shot was fired, I thought O'Neil had set us up. Then he shows up and he's a savior. As was Wachowski. That left the Italians. Whatever Joseph Glendali had heard us not say the night before, it was enough for him to not wait on a hit. Of course, it was possible Ben Landry had sent the shooters out without going through the old man. If that was the situation, Landry was playing a dangerous game. Like I said. A muddled mess.

Officer Lenny Reed from the Saugus police was leaning

in the open front door asking me what had happened, when Officer Fuller, the Melrose cop, came back to his cruiser.

"That was Frank's kid they put in the ambulance?" Reed asked.

I nodded.

"I've been telling you, Paul, he's been walking too fine a line."

"We're going to the hospital," I said as Fuller got in the car. Lenny Reed was a good guy. And a good cop. But I wasn't in the mood for his reminders on Sal.

As we pulled onto Route 1, Officer Fuller said, "What did he mean by that? What he said about Sal?"

"Sal's a little wild," I said as matter-of-factly as I could. "And a little goofy. He's twenty-four with the maturity level of a sixteen year old. But he's not a bad kid."

"Let me ask you something?" said Fuller. "Were you the target or was it Sal? I've been thinking you pissed someone off during an investigation you're doing, and the kid was in the wrong place at the wrong time. Maybe that's wrong. Maybe Sal was the target?"

"Sal has been out of town for a few months. Just got back and I was taking him to dinner. If they were after anyone, it was me."

"If?" said Fuller, his eyes on me in the rearview. This time I shrugged.

"How long you been a P.I.," he suddenly asked.

"I was a cop for three years. Been doing this for sixteen."

"I've thought about doing it, too," he said. "Well, not so much detective work. More like security."

"Hey, whatever path you want to follow."

"Knowing what you know now, would you do it again? Quit the force. Go out on your own."

He was looking in the rearview again.

"Sometimes, guys in their twenties have a hard time seeing the bigger picture," I said.

"So you wouldn't?"

"Not what I said. But in another year or two, had I stayed a cop, I could retire with a very nice pension. Now, I have no pension. I'll be chasing down runaways when I'm seventy just to pay the bills. But to answer your question, yes, I would do it again."

21

Judy Beradino came into the waiting room displaying all the composure you would expect from a woman who was married to a cop for twenty years. But when I rose to meet her and gave her a hug, I felt her body shaking. She had three sons. Sal was the baby.

"He's in surgery, Judy," I said. "It looks like he's going to be okay."

I hadn't seen Judy Beradino in over six years, not since Sal graduated Malden High. She was fifty-seven years old and lived alone in the house where she raised three boys and shared twenty years of marriage with her husband, Frank. Judy had always fought a battle with her weight, spending much of her life on one diet or another. At fifty-seven, it appeared she had decided to call a truce. She carried the extra pounds well.

"What happened, Paul?" she asked.

I steered her to a corner of the room where we sat and I told her.

"I've been so worried," she said when I was done. "I knew something was up when he asked for money and he told me he'd be away for a while. He wouldn't tell me why. Maybe he should have stayed away longer. But you think these men might have been after you?"

I wasn't about to tell her about Eileen, but Judy knew what I did for a living and that pissing hard people off is sometimes part of the job.

We sat quietly for a while. I then asked about her other two sons, Bobby and Louis, both of whom lived out of state. She gave me a brief update, the birth of three grandchildren, and then fell silent again. Officer Fuller sat across the room reading a magazine and sipping vending machine coffee, and did his best to appear as if he wasn't trying to listen to our conversation. In the silence that followed, I thought back to everything that had happened since Monday, everything that I had learned, and all the problems now on my plate.

The biggest problem, obviously, was that someone had ordered a hit on me. At least I assumed I was the target. The only two men that I knew of who had a beef with Sal, were the two men who probably saved his life. And mine. The only people who would target me now, that I knew of, were the Italians. Using a phone in the hospital lobby, I had called Eileen a half hour before Judy arrived. She had been home all night, comfortably resting and watching television.

If Glendali was going to follow through with his threat, then Eileen would be killed if she signed the divorce papers. Should that happen, the old Don was smart enough to know I needed to be eliminated, too. But, and this made the most sense, eliminate me now and Eileen would certainly understand the consequences of her actions. Perhaps, change her mind. Should she still go through with the divorce, she could disappear after the papers were signed. Eliminating me didn't guarantee she would change her mind, but Glendali might have considered it an option.

There was also an argument to be made that Glendali didn't send the goons. Murder is a messy solution. Before authorizing it, I believe he would have waited to see if his warning at Harry's was enough to keep Eileen in her marriage.

Then there was Ben Landry.

Desperate men do desperate things. And what am I to do about him if it was him who put out the hit? If I harm the accountant, I'm in trouble with the Glendali family. If I kill him, it's probably my death sentence.

That's the Porterhouse on my full plate. The baked potato is Peter Gladstone.

After my eye-opening discussion with Thomas Madison, and later on Monday with Packy, I had my researcher check on the financial condition of Gladstone and his company, now a publicly traded entity on the American Stock Exchange. This morning there was a fax waiting for me at my office from my young assistant. I spent the morning reading through all the stuff in it several times so I understood it all, and then spent several hours playing out what it all could mean. Where it led me left me confused, but not for very long. The phone call I received at one o'clock became the vegetables on my plate. Broccoli. Steamed. A generous helping.

Earlier in the week, a message had been left by a mid-sized insurance company that I have done work for in the past. Nothing major, but they pay good and the checks don't bounce. With all my attention focused on Sal, I had forgotten to call them back. The one o'clock call was from them.

The guy on the line was a gentleman named Porter Tufts. Porter was from Nashville, Tennessee, although he lived in Quincy now, and he managed the Boston office of a top ten insurance company. He often joked he couldn't understand me because of my Boston accent. I said the same thing about his southern drawl, only I wasn't joking. Our chat was short. He heard I was investigating the Peter Gladstone art theft for Gladstone. We set a meeting for Friday morning at ten to discuss it. His company was one of the Underwriter's on the Gladstone property, sharing the policy with two other companies, and they had questions.

These were all the things going through my tired mind, when at one in the morning a doctor came in to tell us Sal was out of danger and sleeping, and would probably be out cold until mid-morning. The bullet in the leg had missed the artery, the other bullet had nicked the liver and was a concern, but he should have a full recovery. We could see him after nine in the morning.

I had promised Officer Fuller before he left at twelve-thirty that I would see him at the Melrose Police Station at three-thirty tomorrow afternoon to answer any questions he had. So after the doctor left, Judy and I were the only two in the waiting room.

She asked if I could bring her home, which I did.

THE PHONE RANG at seven just as I was stepping from the shower. I hustled to get it, hoping a nurse would not be on the line telling me Sal had taken a turn for the worse.

"This is Paul Costa," I said.

"How's the kid?"

It was Tomek Wachowski.

"Looks like he'll be okay," I said.

"You want to tell me how I got dragged into a gun fight last night?"

"I think it was the Italians," I said.

"So you pissed off Glendali?" Tomek said. I could hear him chuckling to himself. "Is there anyone, Costa, you haven't pissed off? You don't want to mess with those boys. I told you, you ain't that tough."

"Believe me, I don't want to," I said, toweling off. "Sometimes, life throws you curves."

"Listen," said Wachowski, "Sal won't have a problem with me. All in the past. But he stays out of Lynn. Out of sight, out of mind."

"Okay," I said.

"You know, when O'Neil and I stood there facing each other, I almost pulled the trigger. Probably should have."

"Under a white flag," I said, tossing the towel on the bed. "It's a bad look. Stuff like that gets around."

"Yeah. I was thinking about it last night. Our differences can't be settled over a dinner. You know what I mean?"

"Doesn't concern me, Tomek."

He grunted. "Good luck with the Italians, Costa. You'll need it." He broke the connection.

I made some scrambled eggs and toast, enjoying them while reading the morning papers. The shootout was page four in the Globe, two in the Herald. Diners were quoted as being horrified at the sound of gunshots being fired while they dined. Cops were quoted with the standard, "No comment." Thankfully, my name was not mentioned.

Neither was Sal Beradino's. But the story said someone was shot and transported to Melrose-Wakefield. A reporter would learn the name soon enough. Probably already had. Not a big deal. By the time Sal healed, the story would be old news. But not for me. People were shooting at me with deadly intent. Their failure only meant there would be another attempt. Eileen and I had plans for Saturday night. I would call her later and cancel. Until this was settled, I wouldn't risk her being collateral damage like poor Sal had been.

I PARKED IN the garage at the Prudential Center and took the elevator up to where Porter Tufts had his office with a grand view of the Hancock tower. Banks and insurance companies building towers into the sky all across this great country with other people's money. Not a bad racket.

We sat in Tufts' modest office talking basketball and drinking coffee, the sun pouring in from a clear sky through windows as tall as Kevin McHale. Porter was a tall, thin guy, neatly groomed, who dressed well and smiled a lot, and, thankfully, did not wear string ties. Even though, if you had only heard him speak and not seen him, you would have thought a string tie is what he would have on. If he were sitting across a kitchen table from you, showing you the various policies that you should consider purchasing to keep your family secure if, God forbid, something unforeseen should happen to you, you would find yourself happily signing on a dotted line for a term policy that you would statistically outlive.

After fifteen minutes of Porter touting the prowess of Michael Jordan, he got down to business.

"You're investigating the theft of art from Peter Gladstone," he stated. "Anything you can share?"

"How much are you in for?" I asked.

"A third," Tufts admitted, and then mentioned two other companies who shared the policy.

"You investigated and came up with nothing?" I asked.

"Nothing. Police came up with nothing. The other two companies investigated. Nothing. I wanted to get you in on this, but corporate insisted on a big firm from New York. Nothing. It's like the art just disappeared."

"Any reason Gladstone hasn't been paid yet?" I asked.

"The other two partners are ready to write checks," he said. "I'm not, although I can't wait much longer. Why did he hire you?"

"He told me he thought you guys did a lousy job investigating. Wanted me to look into it. I suspect he was tired of you dragging your feet in paying him, and may have thought if I came up empty, too, you might finally write it off and settle."

"He knew you have done work for us?"

"He knew John Corey. Knew I worked that. May have known I was working for you on that."

I had to be careful. Gladstone was my client. And, while I have done work for Tufts' firm in the past, I was not working for them on the art theft. I couldn't divulge stuff to Porter, but it didn't mean I couldn't ask questions.

"Why are you dragging your feet?" I asked. "What's bothering you?"

"We did a thorough investigation into Peter Gladstone's finances. He is seriously over-leveraged. Deep in debt."

Porter was confirming what my researcher had just supplied me. Other than the value of the shares of stock he owns in his company, the value of which is several million dollars, Gladstone was in a financial crisis.

"Question for you," I said. "Did it surprise you that the paintings by more famous masters, like the Manet, were left behind?"

Porter Tufts shook his head. "The three pieces that were taken are the most valuable. Everything else are phonies."

"They are?" I was stunned.

"We don't insure anything without verification first."

"Does Gladstone know they're copies?"

"Of course. Well, he knows now.

"Look," he said. "Gladstone is your client, so I know

there are things you may have discovered that you can't share. I get it. And I respect it. Is there anything you feel comfortable sharing?"

"I took a different approach than you and the cops," I said. "Knowing that your investigation would have been thorough, I have been looking into acquaintances and friends of Gladstone who may have had reason to steal from him."

"For financial gain? From what we gathered, his friends and acquaintances are wealthy people. And respected. Why risk prison and humiliation if we caught the burglars and they talked? We ruled them out quickly."

I peered at him over my coffee cup.

"But you found something," he said frowning. "Shit. The man has fundraisers for hungry kids and homeless shelters. We never considered he might be screwing his friends so bad that they would steal from him? Any names you feel comfortable sharing?"

"I've spoken to over a dozen of them from a list Gladstone supplied," I said. "I don't think there is anything there. Don't get me wrong, a few of them certainly have cause to want to cause Gladstone harm, but they would rather he suffer physically more than financially."

"So you have nothing more than we do?" Porter Tufts said.

I shrugged. "Have you ever read Confucius?"

AT ONE-THIRTY, I was in the parking lot of the building on Route 1 where I rent space on the second floor. I wanted to call the hospital to see how Sal was doing, and call his mother, although I suspected she would be at the hospital. I still had a three-thirty meeting with the Melrose police. From there I would go to the hospital. As I stepped from the 300, a man stepped from the front of a black Cadillac parked a few cars away. He was the shooter who was with Joseph Glendali a few nights ago in Harry's place. My hand went inside my coat, fingers wrapped around the Beretta. He placed both of his empty hands in front of him and walked several steps towards me.

"Mr. Glendali would like a word," he said.

Another guy got out from behind the wheel of the Caddy and opened a rear door. I recognized him from Harry's place. He was the good looking guy with the wavy hair who was sitting at the bar and spending a lot of time watching me and Eileen enjoying our evening. I could see the old man sitting in the backseat. He had a blanket over his legs. Maybe he had a gun under the blanket. Maybe he just wanted to know if I knew of any good restaurants in the area. Maybe I should have become a welder, like my old man.

Deciding that if they wanted to shoot me they would not do it in an open parking lot in broad daylight, or they already would have done it, I slowly walked towards the Cadillac, never taking my eyes off the shooter. He stepped in front of me as I neared the car, patiently waiting for me to relinquish my weapon, which I was debating refusing to do.

"Vincent," came the tired voice from inside the car, "it's okay."

Without a change of expression, Vincent stepped aside and I took a seat beside the old Don. He stared at me for several seconds. I saw fatigue in his eyes.

"Mr. Costa," Glendali said, "I wanted to personally assure you that the trouble you encountered last evening was not from me."

When I made no response to that, he nodded a few times, then continued.

"I had said to you and Mrs. Landry that there was time for her to change her mind, and time there is. I also know that the problem is not you. If she wasn't seeing you, it would probably be someone else. Correct?"

Again, no response from me. Another nod from him.

"You do understand the problem I have?" Joseph Glendali asked.

At last, something I could respond to.

"I do," I said. "I have spoken about your problem to

Eileen several times in the past month."

"And?"

"She claims to know nothing of her husbands affairs in his business with you. She knows what he does for you. She knows what your business is. Beyond that, she knows nothing. I believe her."

"And you know that I can't afford to."

The old man sighed and looked out the side window. "You have known the woman less than two months," he said as he turned towards me, "is she worth this danger in your life?"

"It's not about Eileen."

His eyes softened. "Yes. Yes, I have heard that about you. So, how do we resolve our problem, Mr. Costa? Is it your intention to marry the lady?"

"We've only just met."

"Let me propose a solution," Glendali said. "Benjamin has moved out of the house. That doesn't change. Eileen drops the divorce petition, but lives her life as she chooses, sees who she chooses. In every way imaginable she is a free woman, except in the eyes of the law. There, she is still a married woman."

"Mr. Glendali, with respect, I am not the person to make that decision. Mr. and Mrs. Landry are the two people you need to speak with."

He nodded again and pulled the blanket a little higher.

"Do you know who was shooting at you last night?"

"If it wasn't you, then it may have been Ben Landry who put the contract out," I said. "He's threatened me several times. But I don't know."

"I'll make inquiries," said the old man. "Benjamin would not do such a thing without my blessings. He is not a violent man."

"Perhaps he hasn't gone through a divorce before," I said. "It's been known to change a man's attitude toward violence."

"Good day, Mr. Costa," Glendali said.

I watched as the Cadillac pulled onto the highway. Someone had ordered a hit on me last night and all three of the prime candidates were no longer in the running. That left Benny Landry. Or so I reasoned.

I SAT WITH Officer Fuller at a narrow table in a room off of the main floor of the Melrose Police Station. The cup of police station coffee in front of me tasted just as horrible as I remembered Saugus Police Station coffee tasting sixteen years before. I harbor the belief that all police stations put something rancid in their coffee so that the officers head out to the streets in a surly mood. Keeps them on their toes, I imagine is the reason.

"We found the car, or what we believe is the car," Fuller said. "It had been reported stolen from a Malden residence at four that afternoon." He slid a photo in front of me of a car with a shattered side window, bullet hole in the door, dark green color.

I nodded.

"There was a ton of blood soaked into the fabric and rug in the back," he said. "Experts who know about such things, claim the bleeder probably succumbed to loss of blood. No body. We found the car in the back of a boatyard off the Lynnway. The body is probably somewhere under water out there. Maybe someday it will float to the surface."

Fuller picked up his cup, looked inside it, then put it down.

"After having a chance to sleep on it, you come up with any ideas?"

I shook my head. "No idea," I said. "All I'm sure of is, they wanted me, not Sal."

"Yet he was the one shot."

I had no response to that.

"I talked with Sal this morning," Fuller said.

That caught me by surprise, although it shouldn't have. I should have gone to the hospital before going into Boston. Should have coached Sal on answers to give the cops. Probably should have done a lot of things differently.

Fuller was staring at me with that look a cop has who

is about to ask a question he does not expect an honest answer to. "He said it might have been Tomek Wachowski or Timmy O'Neil who was shooting at you. Does it surprise you that I know who those gentlemen are?"

"It wasn't them," I said. "I know them, too. They weren't the shooters."

Fuller slid a picture of Wachowski in front of me. It was a police photo taken when Wachowski was much younger, arrested for some crime. Wachowski had never done prison time.

"The cook who stepped from the door last night to see what all the commotion was about, identified Wachowski as someone who was there and who was holding a gun," said Fuller. "He said he saw another man who was over by you, also holding a gun, but it was too dark for him to give us much of a description of what he looked like."

Officer Fuller leaned back in the chair, folded his arms across his chest, and frowned at me. "You want to help me out here, Mr. Costa, as to just what was going on in that parking lot last night?"

"My concern was for Sal," I said. "I was returning fire and attempting to stop Sal's bleeding. I didn't see who the Samaritans were. You should speak with Wachowski. See if he was there."

Officer Fuller, with a deepening frown, said, "I'm sure he could dig up twenty people who would swear they saw him in church last night at the time of the shooting. Why would Sal have a reason to worry about two hoods like Wachowski and O'Neil? Are they the reason he's been traveling the past few months?"

"I'm going to assume Sal was so full of painkilling drugs when you spoke with him that he probably doesn't even remember the conversation," I said. The same thing a lawyer would say in a court of law, if it ever came to that, which I didn't say, and didn't need to say. Fuller knew better. "But let me tell you that the differences Wachowski and O'Neil had at one time with Sal Beradino, are all in the past. A simple misunderstanding."

"Why would the son of a cop be in a situation with two gang bosses where there might be a misunderstanding?" asked Fuller.

I had to give him something. "Sal lives in Charlestown. O'Neil knows the kid. Asked him to deliver a message to Wachowski. Which Sal did. Wachowski didn't like the message. O'Neil blamed Sal for screwing up the message. Wachowski took a 'shoot the messenger' attitude. It's all cleared up now. The shooters last night were after me."

"The second good Samaritan," said Fuller, "was that O'Neil?"

"I didn't see who it was."

"You think he may have been at his club last night at eight o'clock surrounded by thirty people?" Officer Fuller asked, frowning again.

"I have no idea," I said.

"Do you think whoever wants you dead will take another shot at you?"

I shrugged. "Some people can be quite determined."

"Maybe you should think about getting away for a while, like Sal did," said Officer Fuller. I didn't detect any real concern in his voice. I guessed he wasn't very happy with the answers I gave to his questions.

After my meeting with Officer Fuller, I went to the hospital. Sal was resting comfortably. Judy sat in a chair by his bed reading a paperback book. She got up and took me out beyond the doorway.

"Sal was awake for a while this morning, and again this afternoon. The nurse gave him something she said would probably keep him out until late tonight, when they would give him something else to put him out until morning. He asked for you. I told him you were stopping by tonight."

I asked if she had talked with a doctor. She had. They were happy with his progress, but it was still early. The next forty-eight hours would be important. But he was young and fit, and the doctor expected no problems. I told her I would come in the morning. Then I grabbed a pizza on Main St. and headed home. Two cold ones, and I was asleep in my recliner by the end of the first half of the Celtics game.

22

After an hour visit with Sal, I took a chance and drove out to Marblehead Neck. In a driveway of swirling leaves from a stiff November wind, Peter Gladstone's ridiculous ride occupied its usual spot, instead of being in the garage. The vehicle is a military green colored Jeep Gladiator Pick-up with massive tires. He probably uses it to pull a trailer carrying a boat. I'm guessing it would have no problem pulling Ari Onasis' yacht.

Gladstone answered the doorbell and escorted me into the kitchen where he was slicing interesting fruits and vegetables into small pieces and depositing them into a blender. I guess he has never heard of V8, which was one of the food groups in my mother's humble kitchen. She said V8 helped keep you regular. My mother has been known to say many things, none of which I argue. Little of which I believe.

"I was going to call you later today," he said. "You know what happened to my stuff?"

"I'm working on a theory," I said.

He frowned at me. "A theory? But you don't know who took them. I gave you a list. Told you it was Gunther. The best you have is a theory."

I shrugged.

"You were supposed to find something that would put this all to rest. Either get my stuff back, or get the insurance companies to finally settle. You've done neither."

Gladstone hit a blender button. The kitchen suddenly sounded like the Garden when Havlicek stole the ball. He glared across the room at me as the blades pureed the veggies into a drinkable liquid.

I'm certain the noise went on longer than was necessary. Finally, he hit stop.

"What is this theory you have?" he asked, as he took off the lid and poured the greenish hued concoction into a large glass.

"That the paintings never left this house," I said.

He smirked at me, then took a long drink.

"Why the hell would I hire a detective to find my stuff, if the stuff was still here?"

"Things were moving too slow for you," I said. "The insurance companies were dragging their feet, especially the one I have done work for. So you hired me, knowing I'd find nothing, and maybe that would get you a check. A check you need. And as a bonus, just for your amusement, you suggested I harass Gunther Kolb."

"Do I look like a man who needs money?" Gladstone asked, the smirk becoming a sneer.

This is what I knew, from the extensive report supplied to me from my Northeast wonder; Gladstone had purchased the house we stood in five years before, and the house in Wolfboro, on Winnipausaukee, four years before, when real estate was hot. The market had cooled faster than a woman who receives a vacuum cleaner for Christmas, both properties now heavily mortgaged and worth quite a bit less. He was three months behind on mortgage payments on the house on the lake, and two years in arrears in taxes. He still hadn't paid 1988 taxes on the Marblehead property. He owed several million to contractors on the property in Burlington that was being argued in court, and it appeared he would soon lose that lawsuit. There was also a lawsuit pending filed by a local charitable group, who felt their cut in one of Gladstone's fundraisers was shy quite a bit of what they believed was actually donated by the wealthy crowd who attended. On top of that, the lower three floors of his building had yet to be rented out and his companies bottom line was suffering because of it. As Gunther Kolb had told me, the software companies' client list was dwindling, and lawsuits from angry customers, upset with the software, were beginning to be filed. His stock was now below the IPO filing, and he risked losing controlling interest in the company if he divested any more shares of it.

The kid also made me aware of something I didn't know. There is a lock-up period, usually 90-180 days after the IPO, where the major shareholders of the company cannot sell stock. It appears Peter Gladstone agreed not to sell any of his stock for a period of two years. That condition, along with the problems in the software, had left him in a financial mess. A mess that six million dollars would help alleviate.

I hadn't driven out to his home to tear the place apart and find the paintings. I hadn't gone out there to lay bare what I knew of his financial problems. I was there to tell him, in person, that I was no longer working the case, and why.

I have no proof that he set the whole thing up. Just a belief. I am not a cop, or a legal representative of the law. If he has the art, and gets a check from the insurance company, no sweat off my back. It's not my job to bring him to justice. I was hired to do a job, and I did it to the best of my ability. I was paid for it. Case closed, as far as I was concerned, when I tell Peter Gladstone I'm done.

"I think you are a man who needs money," I said in answer to his question. "A lot of money. Not my concern. As of right now, I'm off the case. Your retainer has covered my time and expenses."

As I turned to leave, Gladstone said, "Some hotshot you are, Costa. I paid you good money to do a job. And when you failed miserably, you concoct this ridiculous accusation that I staged the theft. I should take you to court, sue you and and get my money back."

I turned to face him, almost telling him if he said another word two things were going to happen. I would tear the place apart until I found the art, but first I'd tear him apart. Instead, I headed for the door.

"You spread that lie, Costa," Gladstone yelled to my back, "and I'll sue you for slander. I'll have your license. You'll never work again. You hear me, Costa!"

The drive back to Saugus was a quiet one, WOKQ spinning some country platters that were playing low on the car radio speakers.

I HAD A planned date with Eileen that night. Dinner at a place in Beverly and tickets to the Christmas show at North Shore. When I called her to say I would have to cancel, not telling her the reason why, she told me she wasn't feeling well and was about to call me to cancel. She asked if I would mind picking up a pizza and watching a movie at her place? No, I would not mind. So there we were, sitting on the sofa in her Winthrop home, watching a DVD of *When Harry Met Sally*, sipping from our drinks, the remnants of pizza crust the only thing left in the pizza box.

Eileen didn't have a fever. I checked. But she seemed stiff and sore and, while we held hands, she shied away from any hugs. By the end of the movie she was yawning. She declared she was ready for bed, and asked if I wanted to stay. Just cuddling, she said. She wasn't feeling up for anything more than that. Maybe in the morning she would. Cuddling was fine with me.

We spooned in bed, me in my boxers, Eileen in a powder blue nightgown. She fell asleep rather quickly, her breathing a bit labored. I followed soon after.

The face of the digital alarm clock showed 3:13 when I opened my eyes. Eileen was kneeling on the bed beside me, her right hand struggling to lower my boxers, her left hand inside them with a firm grasp on me.

"Look what I found standing at attention," she whispered. "Were you dreaming of me?"

She got the underwear down to my knees, and in the faint light from outside I could see her lifting her nightgown up to her waist as she straddled me. It all went in slow motion, her movements up and down done slowly, more grinding than anything else. I let her control it all. There was an occasional moan from her that I thought might be from pain, but she took me easy enough so I thought it was for my benefit.

Eileen took me to the edge several times, stopping for a bit then beginning again. When I could take no more, I grabbed her by the waist, twisted so she was under me and I was on top. She screamed out in pain.

"What is it?" I asked, stopping immediately.

"It's nothing," she said, holding me tightly to her. "Don't stop." There was a trembling in her voice.

I tried lifting off of her. She held on to me.

"It's okay," she said.

I took her arms from my back and moved to the side of the bed.

"Paul, no, please," she cried. "It's okay. Let's finish."

I was off the bed and putting on the overhead light. Eileen was trying to get her nightgown below her waist, but not before I saw the ugly bruising that was on her left side. It began mid thigh and was visible until the blue of the nightgown. I lifted the nightgown up. The bruising went as far as her ribcage. It was a purple and yellow horrible stain on her beautiful body, and it appeared to have been done recently.

"I took a tumble down the steps, Paul," she said. There was a trembling in her voice and tears in her eyes. "That's all, darling. Just a tumble, Clumsy of me, really. But I'm okay. Nothing broken."

"When was he here?" I demanded.

"No, darling, no," she cried, and I could see the fear in her eyes. "It wasn't Ben. I just slipped on the stairs going to answer the door and took a tumble. Really, Paul, that's all it was."

The house is a large split entry. Could Eileen have slipped on the steps? Sure. Did I believe she did? No, I did not.

I sat on the bed beside her and took her hand in mine. There were tears in her eyes and she was trembling.

In a controlled voice, I said, "It's okay, baby. Let's just talk. Don't be upset. Just tell me what happened. Okay? Just tell me what happened."

Her head was slowly shaking back and forth on the pillow, fear in those incredible green eyes, and she was fighting to keep from bawling.

"It's okay, baby," I whispered again. "It's okay. I'm calm. Just tell me the truth."

I reached over and took some tissues from a box on the nightstand and used them to dry her tears. She was still slowly shaking her head when she said, "He was here yesterday."

"Ben was here?"

She nodded.

"He was calm. Said he just wanted to talk. Brought a bottle of wine and some flowers. I told him I didn't want to talk. That there was nothing more to say. He didn't get mad at that, didn't get defensive. He just took a seat at the kitchen table and smiled at me. I was leaning against the counter. I asked him to leave. He said until the judge declared us divorced, this was still his house. He just wanted to talk. He asked if I wanted a glass of wine."

She took the tissues from me and dabbed at her eyes.

"I've never been afraid of Benny. But yesterday, he was so calm, he was trying so hard to be in control of his temper, but there was this look on his face the whole time that I had never seen before. Like he had had enough and he wasn't going to take anymore. I mean, he was smiling, but the smile was more of a warning than it was of understanding or acceptance. Suddenly, Paul, I was afraid of him."

Eileen squeezed my hand.

"He was talking. Saying we could work things out. He'd be a better husband. We'd take a vacation over Christmas. Miami. Bahamas. Wherever I wanted to go. I kept telling him he had to leave. I didn't want to go anywhere with him. The marriage was over. He started talking louder. Started pacing the floor. Said I was making a mistake seeing you. I was getting more nervous, Paul. He was almost ranting. I moved towards the knife holder. I lost my composure and screamed at him that he better leave. Suddenly, he spun towards me, grabbing me by my shoulders, shoving me hard against the counter. Then he flung me onto the floor and I slammed into the lower cabinets. I thought I was going to pass out, the pain was so bad."

Eileen was crying again as she dabbed at eyes that were showing the horror of the attack.

"He grabbed a handful of my hair and began lifting me. I told him to stop. He had to leave. I'd call the police. I'd tell Mr. Glendali. He laughed at that and pushed me against the refrigerator, leaning his face close to mine, his body hard against me. His face was so contorted in anger I could hardly recognize him. He roughly grabbed my breast and squeezed, said it belonged to him, and told me to drop the divorce or I'd be sorry. I'd be very sorry. We stood like that for several seconds, his breathing heavy. I was dazed and in pain, feebly trying to remove his hand from me. He squeezed harder. Hurting me, and he knew it. He sneered at me, then kissed me hard. I bit his lip and he slapped me, throwing me onto the floor again. I thought he was going to kick me. He stood over me as I curled up, and warned me again. Said it didn't have to be like this. That we could be happy again. Then he left."

Eileen stopped crying, but her head was still slowly shaking back and forth on the pillow.

I fixed her nightgown so that she was covered, and pulled the blankets over her. Her hand reached out to me and pulled me into the bed beside her. Eileen rolled onto her side, the one not damaged, and pressed herself hard against me. She brought my hand up to her lips and kissed it, then placed it on her right breast.

"Can we stay like this until morning?" she asked. "Can we stay like this forever?"

I kissed her shoulder and held her, and felt the vibrations of her body slowly ease as she fell back asleep. There would be no sleep for me. I lay awake, unable to sleep, my only thought being what I would do when I found Ben Landry.

HARRY WAS PUTTERING around, changing a few bulbs in the ceiling, when I entered the bar early Sunday afternoon. The Patriots were playing at four and there would be a decent crowd watching the game and drinking beer.

Eileen and I had shared breakfast in her place, with me doing the pancakes from an old recipe my grandmother taught me. We spoke of Ben Landry, and she again insisted I do nothing. In a few days, she had said, she would heal, and in a month or so she'd be free of him. Me doing anything to him would only create problems, she said over and over. I nodded a lot, made her comfortable at the table, poured her two cups of coffee, helped her back to bed, tucked her in, and told her I needed to see Harry and that I'd be back to make her a light lunch. She suggested we fool around. I insisted she rest. I kissed her forehead and let myself out.

If I knew where Ben Landry was, I would have driven there. I didn't. Maybe Harry would know. That's why I was at his place.

"What brings you to my fine establishment while the sun still shines?" Harry asked, looking down at me from the height of the ladder.

"Got a problem," I said, taking a seat at one of the tables. "Maybe you can help me."

"If I can," Harry said, climbing down. "You want a beer? Coffee? Soda?"

I waved my hand no. Nineteen years living among the civilized, and Harry still couldn't bring himself to say tonic.

"Well, I need a coffee," he said.

He came to sit across from me carrying a huge mug of Joe.

"What can I do for you?" he asked.

I looked at him. He had bags under his eyes. "You look like shit," I said. "You getting enough sleep?"

Harry took a long sip, then frowned at me. "No, I am not. I definitely am not. Is it that obvious?"

"Yeah. It is. What's wrong? IRS after you for under reporting?"

"I wish. Remember the young woman I was talking to last week?"

"The blonde?"

"Yeah."

"Then you mean the girl."

"She's twenty-two."

"In a few years," I said. "What about her?"

"She's the reason I'm not sleeping," Harry said.

I had to laugh. "I can only imagine how difficult it must be to always have to prove the stories are true. To keep the legend alive. Must be what Billie the Kid faced every day. Always having to prove himself."

"Not funny, Paul,".

"Don't worry, grandpa. Eventually, she'll want to talk, and then what will you do? Hang in there and enjoy it as long as you can, is my advice. She'll be gone soon enough."

"If I don't have a heart attack first," Harry said with a chuckle. "Now, what can I do for you?"

"You know Benjamin Landry?"

"You want to tell me what's going on?" Harry asked, placing the mug on the table.

"You know him?"

"I know of him," said Harry. "I've heard the name. Have an idea what he does for the Glendali family. Wouldn't know him if he walked in my door. Why?"

"I'd like to have a discussion with him."

"A discussion?" said Harry, and he shook his head. "Now let me give you some advice. Landry is not a guy you want to talk with. His connections run deep."

"Deeper than you know," I said. "Eileen is Mrs. Ben Landry."

Harry leaned back and looked down his nose at me. "I've known you fifteen years, Paul. You saved my ass once. I know you to be an intelligent man, if not somewhat volatile at times, but always with good reason. I've never thought you to be suicidal. Is this why the old man sat with you the other night?"

I shrugged.

"I was wondering why. Couldn't imagine why or how you two would have known each other. Did you know who her husband was before getting involved with her?"

"After a few weeks, I did."

"Married woman. Should have walked right away. Then you find out who her husband is? Should have done a Bob Hayes. Christ, what were you thinking?"

"They're getting divorced," I said. "He moved out in June."

"Sure," said Harry. "Wait a second. I read where Sal was shot. The report said he was walking into the restaurant with someone. Was that you?"

I shrugged again.

"Were the shooters after you or Sal?"

"Probably me," I said.

Harry vigorously rubbed the back of his close cropped head and frowned. "You can't touch the guy. You know that, right?"

"That's what Eileen says, too."

"And she's right. Listen to her."

"He paid Eileen a visit Friday night. Left his calling card all over her left side."

Harry leaned back again and stared out the front windows. He whispered a curse word.

"As hard as it may be, Paul, and I know it's hard, you have to let it go."

"I can't do that."

He nodded. Then sipped his coffee.

"You don't want to mess with these people, Paul."

"He's left me no choice."

Harry Mills frowned and nodded again.

I STAYED AT Eileen's Sunday night, and we shared breakfast Monday morning. I was in a hardware store by 9:30 and had the locks on her front and back doors changed by noon. By one I was sitting beside Sal's bed at the hospital. He was sitting up after eating all his lunch, including the green jello, and he seemed in fine spirits. By Thursday it was expected he would be released and he'd be spending the foreseeable future at his mother's place. I filled him in on what happened after he was wounded.

"So this wasn't Tim or Wachowski trying to kill me?" Sal had asked. He seemed relieved when I told him I was probably the target.

After the visit with Sal, I drove the long, narrow, mile long road that connects Nahant to the rest of the world. With Lynn Harbor on the right of the two lanes in, and two more lanes on the road out between my car and Nahant Beach and Bay, this was the only way onto Nahant for vehicles that couldn't float or fly.

Several streets wound around and up the geography of the hilly land mass, and many gated homes hid behind thick vegetation. No wonder the mob found Nahant to be a desirable place to hang their hat.

On the far end of the terrain, I pulled up to an iron gate that blocked a driveway. Through high bushes, I could see the ranch styled home built with white brick. There was no intercom or button to push to signal my presence. It wasn't needed. Within seconds, a very large gentleman approached the gate. I could see another man forty feet behind him standing at the side of the house. When the big guy reached the gate, I rolled down my window and stuck my head out.

"I'd like to speak with Mr. Glendali," I said. "The name is Paul Costa."

The guy looked at me like I may have had a serious head injury and was talking gibberish.

"Is Mr. Glendali expecting you?"

"No," I said. "Check with him. He'll want to see me. I'll wait."

The guy stood staring at my car for almost a minute. I didn't say anything. There was no need. When he finally saw that I wasn't leaving, he'd contact the house. Which he finally did by walkie-talkie. With a nod to whatever was said to him, he pressed a button and the tall iron gate slowly rolled open. He pointed to a spot under a leafless oak tree, behind the late model black Cadillac. The tall, well built guy who was driving when Glendali and I spoke in my parking lot, was wiping down the interior of the car and he stared out of it at me when I pulled up. As I stepped from the car, Vincent, the shooter, walked up to me. He patted me down quite thoroughly. The Beretta was in the glove box. Without him saying a word, I followed him into the house.

Joseph Glendali was sitting in a stuffed chair in the back of the house, in an enclosed patio room with large windows that allowed the sun to shine in and gave a magnificent view of the dark waters of the Atlantic. A space heater in the corner made the room feel like a sauna. Glendali had a blanket over his legs. The morning Globe lay on the floor at his feet. The remnants of a sandwich was on a plate on the end table beside him. He pointed at a chair for me to sit, and then waved Vincent away.

"People don't usually come to my home uninvited, Mr. Costa. It shows poor manners."

"With respect, my apologies. I have a problem that you may want to help me with."

"And why would I want to concern myself with your problem?"

"It concerns Ben Landry and Eileen."

"We discussed Mr. and Mrs. Landry just the other day, Mr. Costa. I made some suggestions that I thought would help settle that problem. I don't believe I can do more than that."

"Friday night Ben Landry beat Eileen in her kitchen. Beat her badly."

The old man looked away from me, looked out through those spotless windows to the roiling water beyond his property. After several seconds he said, "A man should never place himself between a husband and a wife and what goes on within the walls of their home. He may disagree with violence, and the use of a man's hands against a woman, but it is not his business."

"In my line of work, I have seen first hand the damage a man can do to a woman," I said. "Which is why I have come to see you. Married or not, when given the opportunity to prevent such violence, I have inflicted violence of my own, without hesitation. Ben Landry is an employee of yours, a valuable employee you have led me to believe. Out of courtesy, and respect, I offer you the opportunity to speak with your employee. If it is left to me to have this conversation with him, our relationship, yours and mine, already on shaky ground, will take a turn for the worse."

The old Italian looked at me, his left eye, in the brightness of the room, was clouded over and gray. I noticed the slightest tremor in his left hand that rested on his leg over the blanket.

"You are aware of the consequences of such an action?" he said, his voice steady.

"I'm aware, Mr. Glendali. But it should never come to that. If Landry is that important to your family, affairs should never be allowed to progress where he is unable to perform his job. Despite what penalties you may try to inflict on me, what good does it do you after the fact?"

"You show me your cards, Mr. Costa, and still expect to win the hand? Are you a fool?"

I stared at him with my best poker face.

"You have an ace up your sleeve," he said at last, "don't you? I can't imagine what that is." He frowned. "Or, you are bluffing. You play a very dangerous game. You know that."

His right hand smoothed the hair that was left on the back of his head.

"There is a much easier solution," he said.

I shrugged. "Not as easy as you may think," I said.

"So I've been told," said Glendali. He waved a hand. "The last resort of desperation. Have we reached that point, Mr. Costa?"

"I hope not, Mr. Glendali," I said.

"Papa, are you out there?" came a voice from the interior of the house. A few seconds later, Marie Glendali came through the open sliders. She wore black stretch pants and a white blouse. Her black hair was pulled back and clipped. Forty-one years old and she looked thirty. A very attractive woman without a diamond on her left hand.

"I'm sorry," Marie said, eyeing me with curiosity. "I didn't realize we had a guest." She held her hand out as I stood. "I'm Marie Glendali."

"Paul Costa," I said, taking her hand.

"Am I interrupting anything, Papa?" she asked as she pulled the blanket a little higher up and picked up the plate with the sandwich remnants.

"My daughter, Mr. Costa," said Glendali looking up at her. "She dotes on me as if I were an invalid. Do you have children?"

"No, sir, I do not. I am not as blessed as you."

"Yes," he said with a frown. "Well, my blessing has come to make sure I'm going to my room for my afternoon nap. More mother than daughter."

She kissed the top of his head. "I have always been what you need," Marie said. "And now, you need to be mothered. The nap can wait a few minutes if you have business to conclude." Again Marie looked at me with curiosity.

"Mr. Costa and I have concluded our business," said the old man. He stood then, a bit unsteady, and reached out his hand. I shook it.

"You've given me several things to consider, Mr. Costa. Good day."

Joseph Glendali walked unassisted from the sun room, his daughter Marie by his side. She took a backward glance towards me as Vincent came to the door and escorted me through the house and to my car. As I entered the car, he stood by the open door.

"Next time," Vincent warned, "don't come here without an appointment." He closed the car door for me and signaled the gate to be opened.

I wasn't sure if anything had been settled. Would the old man speak with Landry? I had no idea. I had the sense that things were going from bad to worse, and that Glendali may have been backed into a corner with only one way out.

23

It was two weeks after Thanksgiving, a time when things usually calm just a bit after one holiday and before the explosion of the next. Yeah. Explosion.

My sister, Donna, married to a house builder and living in Dracut, enjoys hosting Thanksgiving and Christmas. And I enjoy going there for the dinners. Her husband, Roger, is a regular guy, low key and can talk sports with intelligence. Politics, too, if he's pressed. We get along. I love my younger sis and we get along, too, since she stopped asking when I was going to get married and give her nieces and nephews. Fair question, since she has given me two of each, but she finally tired of asking a few years ago.

We have an older brother. He hasn't seen our mother in twenty years. Jimmy was always a little volatile as a kid, and one day he and dad had an argument. I didn't witness it, but Donna did, she was still living at home then, and she told me she thought they would come to blows. Jimmy stormed out of the house. A few days later, a friend of his stopped by and picked up Jimmy's clothes. Ma was very upset. Dad told the guy to make sure he got everything.

I asked Dad once what had caused the argument. He just said that after twenty years of bullshit from my brother, he had finally had enough. I tracked Jimmy down a few years ago, after Dad had passed. He was living by himself in a mobile home in central Vermont on the side of a mountain with a lovely view of a valley. He's a writer of stories that he sells to magazines. He sells enough to survive, I guess.

When I knocked on his door, I hardly recognized the man who answered. Jimmy was forty-four at the time and looked over sixty. He had deep crevices in the flesh of his face, and he was spaghetti thin. His hair was gray, thin, and long. And unkempt. He reluctantly invited me in after an uncomfortable time at the front door. He was edgy, unable, it seemed, to be still or to focus. The house was an absolute mess, with stacks of books, magazines and newspapers covering a large area of the floor space. After twenty minutes, it was obvious he wished I wasn't there. In those twenty minutes, he never asked about family. I asked a few questions about him, his answers always coming back to some conspiracy the government was inflicting on the population. When I left, I tried to give my older brother a hug. He moved away quickly, as if human contact was a death warrant. I haven't seen him since.

Anyways, for this Thanksgiving, as with others, I had picked up my mother from the senior housing where she lives in Malden, and spent the day with family. Christmas would be the same.

Eileen had flown into LaGuardia to spend the holiday and the weekend with her family in Brooklyn. Her mother and stepdad, dad, and two sisters, all still living close together. We had discussed spending Thanksgiving together, either at her mom's, or at my sister's, but in the end thought it may be too early in our relationship to be doing that. We would see about Christmas. It wasn't lost on me that I might get killed because of our relationship, yet it wasn't steady enough to meet family.

Eileen and I had been together a few times since she got back from Brooklyn, including an enjoyable overnight in each of our homes. If Ben Landry had been to see her again, she hadn't mentioned it. During our two sleepovers, I discreetly checked out every inch of her body and found no new damage. In a few days, Eileen would be back in court again before a judge. She had made no mention that she would postpone her desire for divorce. In fact, we hadn't discussed it. She would do what she would do. And then we would see.

There was never a minute since my meeting in the home of Joseph Glendali that I wasn't vigilant more than usual. I expected something to happen, even though I thought the arguments before the judge would happen first.

As for Sal, he was healing at his mother's house and I made the effort to visit every two days. Judy seemed happy to have him back in the house, even if the circumstances of him being there had terribly rattled her. The doctors assured us Sal would make a complete recovery.

But then, two weeks after Thanksgiving, the calm before the storm ended. My first clue that the calm was over began with a picture in the Herald. And then, like when you begin building a snowman with a snowball, rolling it around in wet snow - powder snow is useless - and it becomes bigger and bigger until it is big enough to be a base for Frosty, the chaos grew. Actually, thinking about it, a freight train traveling down a steep incline without the engineer at the controls, would probably be a better analogy.

The Tuesday morning Herald photo on the front page, was of an inferno in a Charlestown warehouse across from the Navy Yard. The flames were dramatically licking the night sky. It was a terrific photo. I recognized the building that was being destroyed. It was O'Neil's place. Several people interviewed recounted hearing several loud explosions, but they couldn't be certain if the explosions caused the fire, or the fire caused things to blow up. There was no mention of casualties, the building still too dangerous to enter by press time.

My first thought, of course, after reading the article, was that the Wachowski/O'Neil war had intensified. I knew nothing of what either gang was doing, nor was there any reason I should. Wachowski had sworn to leave Sal alone and O'Neil, as far as I knew, had no reason to want harm to come to Sal now that we had negotiated payment of the gambling debt. With Sal out of the equation concerning the two gangs, I no longer concerned myself with their operations. And there was no reason that the fire should concern me.

Until there was.

Sitting at my office desk that Tuesday morning, taking the second honey dipped from the bag and beginning my second reading of the story on the fire, the phone rang.

"Costa Detective Agency," I said with some enthusiasm into the receiver, as I am inclined to do when my dance card is empty. "This is Paul Costa."

"Mr. Costa," said the female voice on the other end of the line, "this is Marie Glendali. Are you available some time today to meet with my father?"

"Yes, Miss Glendali, I am," I replied, surprised it was her calling.

"Does ten o'clock fit into your schedule?" she asked. It was a question, but I didn't feel like it was negotiable. I suppose when you are used to never being refused, the idea of providing options never enters your mind.

"It does," I said.

"Can you come to the house?" she asked.

"I can."

"Then we will see you at ten, Mr. Costa. Thank you." The line went dead.

I was good with it being at the house. The old man wouldn't kill me there after having his daughter call me.

A thought suddenly ran through my head and I called Eileen. It was eight-thirty and the ringing wasn't answered. Maybe she was in the shower. My thought was Glendali had met with her and they had come to some agreement, although I would have expected her to call and tell me that, if that was the case. Eileen and I weren't seeing each other until Wednesday night at Harry's for a drink, but something as important as a truce would have demanded a phone call. I'd try her again before driving to Nahant. But a discussion between the two of them was simply conjecture on my part. Or maybe wishful thinking and hoping. There could be other reasons why the Don wanted to see me, although, off the top of my head, I couldn't think of one.

But then the morning got even more interesting.

There was a knock on the pebbled glass, and before I could say enter, the wide shoulders of Tomek Wachowski came through and took a seat in front of me, but not before glancing down at the Herald on the desk. He was alone.

"How was your weekend?" Tomek asked.

"Quiet," I said. "How about yours?"

"Can't complain," he said.

He looked around my office.

"You got bugs in here?" he asked.

I shrugged. "The place is loaded with spiders. Just spiders."

"I thought you should know something," Wachowski said.

"Only if it concerns me."

"Oh, it does," he said leveling his eyes on me. "It does."

I waited.

"It was our friend who planned that little party we attended a few weeks ago."

"You sure?" I asked. That caught me by surprise. O'Neil had been there in the parking lot with us. He had returned fire.

"Hundred percent. Got it on good authority. You, me, and the kid were the guests of honor. But, like everything else our dearly departed friend planned, it didn't go like he thought."

"You want to explain?" I said.

Wachowski chuckled. "You know, Costa, you are not a fun guy. We had this little dialogue going just now like it was a forties movie, and you had to ruin it."

I frowned.

"You know I didn't trust the Irishman," he said. "So I got to the restaurant an hour before the meet. Parked off to the side after checking to make sure there was nobody sitting in any car. And I waited. I see O'Neil pull in about seven-thirty. He makes no move to go inside. I figure he's waiting for you. Then you show up just before eight. You and the kid start walking toward the place like a dad and his kid walking into Fenway. Not a care in the world. Still, O'Neil ain't moving. Just watching. Then the car pulls in and the two guys jump out, guns blazing. You get to safety and return fire. I jump out of my car and plug the guy from the back seat. From the corner of my eye, I see O'Neil get out of his car. He hesitates. Then the guy who was shot starts yelling he's shot and the other guy takes a few steps back. You pop up and hit the wounded guy. Time for a retreat. O'Neil takes two shots. One kills a window, the other wounds a door. Both miss a guy twenty feet away from him. But, like you, O'Neil is shooting at the shooters, so I figure he's with us, just a bad shot.

"But like I told you before, I have someone in his organization on my payroll. He later finds out that when O'Neil got back to his Sullivan Square club later that night, he was on the warpath. Screaming at everyone. In a few days, the scuttlebutt among the gang is that a couple of guys, who no one has seen in a few days, did something to piss the boss off."

"And you think that was us?"

He shrugged. "Two ways to look at it. If I was planning it, this is what I would have done. The shooters drive into the lot. They see three guys, they pull up and fire away from twenty feet. They don't see three guys, they simply park and wait. We don't go in together, certainly a possibility. But we probably walk out of the place together. That's when they hit us, taking care not to hit O'Neil, if O'Neil hadn't said he needed to use the can. But then the guys screw up. Probably Irish. It's to be expected. One gets wounded bad. All three, including the driver, have to go."

"So the fire was you?" Not that I had harbored any doubt.

Wachowski shrugged again.

"You sure O'Neil was in the building?"

"No Irish in my crew," he said.

"And why was there a need for me to know?" I asked.

"Someone took a run at you," said Wachowski. "You may be wondering who. No need to wonder anymore."

"You expecting a war?"

"With Charlestown? A skirmish. The real problem will be with Somerville. Those boys are smarter. That's where negotiations will be important."

"They get Charlestown, you get Chelsea," I said, shaking my head. "Which is all you wanted to begin with."

He shrugged again. I nodded my respect.

"This doesn't change our agreement concerning Sal," I said.

Wachowski shook his head. "No. If you're lucky, anything on paper concerning a gambling debt was in the warehouse and burned like everything else. Should that be the case, you can thank me later."

We shook hands before he left the office.

I tried Eileen again. Still no answer. It was time to drive to Nahant to see why Joe Glendali was asking to see me.

I PULLED UP to the iron gate a few minutes before ten. The big guy from before took one look at me, and the car, and rolled the gate back. I parked under the same oak tree. Marie Glendali, wrapping a heavy sweater around her body and hugging it, walked up to greet me as I exited the 300.

"Thank you for coming, Mr. Costa," Marie said, extending her hand. I shook it. "My father is out back." She led me into the house. Vincent stood in the foyer. The young guy with the wavy hair sat in a chair in the living room reading a newspaper. He looked up as I entered.

"It's okay, Vincent," Marie said, as Vincent moved in front of me. "I'm sure Mr. Costa has not come into my home carrying a weapon."

She looked at me.

"My mother would be upset," I said, smiling, "to think someone would t hink she hadn't taught me better manners, Miss Glendali."

I could see Vincent wasn't happy, but he stepped aside. I followed Marie to the back of the house. As before, her father sat under a blanket in the stuffed chair, a Boston Globe folded and lying on the small table beside an empty coffee cup and a half full glass of what looked like orange juice. Joseph Glendali looked as if he had aged ten years in the last few weeks. He held a hand out to me, which I shook with minimum pressure. It was cool and dry. Marie left us alone.

"Thank you for coming on such short notice," the old man said, pointing to where he wanted me to sit.

"Let me be frank with you, Mr. Costa," said Glendali. "I had asked Mrs. Landry to come here on Sunday. She agreed. I had a car pick her up. Her husband was here when she arrived. No drama. We sat in the living room and discussed things calmly."

Glendali paused, waiting to see if I had a reaction to that. I didn't. I sat with my legs crossed and my hands folded in my lap. Eileen had not told me about any meeting when I spoke with her Sunday night, but it's not like she's obligated to report her calendar to me. But it would have been nice.

Seeing I had nothing to say to his statement, the Don continued.

"I again made clear my concerns about the divorce. Benjamin, very calmly, told me he now had no desire to go ahead with the divorce. During the summer, he was angry with his wife for saying she no longer loved him and because of that he wanted the divorce. But in recent months, he has had a change of heart and wants to see if they can work things out."

Again, I had nothing to say.

Marie Glendali came into the room with a cup of coffee for me. I hadn't asked for coffee, but I thanked her and set the cup on the table. She asked her father if he wanted anything. He smiled a no.

When we were alone again, the old man asked, "Has Mrs. Landry mentioned any of this to you?"

I told him she had not.

"I then asked Mrs. Landry her feelings. She, also very calmly, said she no longer loved Benjamin and just wanted a divorce so she could find a happier life. I told her I understood. That marriage can be difficult at times. That the seven year itch, as it is known, is real. But, I said, it is when difficulty comes that the husband and wife must take a step back and not rush into anything.

"We spoke of some things, then I asked them if, perhaps, the court proceedings could be put on hold for a bit. Give Eileen more time to think about what a divorce would mean. The finality of it. Was there really a need to rush into anything? Could we, perhaps, work something out?"

The old man paused and sipped at his orange juice. I sipped at the coffee.

"Would you like some pastry, Mr. Costa?" Glendali asked. "We have some delicious cannoli from a bakery in Revere. Cookies from a bakery in Everett, not far from where you grew up."

"No thank you, sir," I said.

"Right away, I saw there was hope in Benjamin's eyes, but I could also see that Mrs. Landry was prepared to firmly refuse. Then I said, perhaps a period of time where they remained married, but separated, and lived as if there was no union, might be the way to proceed. As I had once mentioned to you. Benjamin asked what that meant. Just what it sounds like, I told him. There is no divorce, but you both live as if you have no marriage.

"Ben sat quietly for several seconds while he digested that thought, then he said, and I quote him, 'Don Glendali. You want me to go on with my life as if everything is okay, while my wife is fucking other men?' And I said, yes, yes I do."

Joe Glendali lowered his eyes and brushed the fabric of the blanket with his right hand. "Mrs. Landry made no comment, but I could see that Benjamin was struggling to keep in control. I have never witnessed him losing his composure. Not in twenty years. You told me he raised his hands against his wife. I find that very difficult to believe, Mr. Costa. Very difficult. But who's to know what a man might do in certain circumstances? After many seconds of silence, Benjamin looked at me and asked how I expected him, a man, to be okay with what I suggested. How could any man be okay with it, he asked."

Glendali sipped at his juice again, and took in several breaths. "And this is what I said to him, Mr. Costa. I know of no other way. I then asked Mrs. Landry if she was agreeable to this compromise. She thought about it, and finally said she could try it. As long as there was no more contact between Ben and her. No phone calls. No visits. She was free to live her life. She said she didn't want to hurt Ben. That she didn't want to cause me any concerns should they divorce. So, if this was something I thought was a good thing, she would try it. She has no thoughts right now of marrying again, is what she said."

The old man looked at me through tired eyes that were clouding over. "We have talked about this solution before, Mr. Costa. Is it something you can live with?"

I had to smile. He could have Eileen and me killed and probably not lose a minute of sleep over it. That he is even worrying about this, I find interesting. I understand he doesn't want to upset his accountant by having his wife disappear, but Ben would know his boss was backed into a corner. I suppose he saw no need to take me out until there is a divorce, and even then it would only be done to keep me from possibly being in the way should it become necessary for Eileen to be silenced.

"Mr. Glendali, as I have mentioned before, if Eileen is free to see others, and she wants to see me, I enjoy her company. If she suddenly decides she no longer wants my company, I'm out of her life. And she knows this. We have been seeing each other only three months. We aren't kids. Given more time, who knows what will happen. If she is agreeable to what you proposed, so be it. I will not try to sway her one way or the other. All decisions are hers."

Glendali nodded several times and finished the juice. I sipped at my coffee that was cooling. I thought our meeting was ending. I was wrong.

"My good friend, Harry Mills, shared something with me a few days ago," said Glendali with a slight smile. "He mentioned you may have saved his life ten years ago. Had you not been there, he may not have survived those pigs. I remember the story. Harry and I had talked about it soon after it happened, and why those men were there. I forgot the name of the man who saved the day, until Harry reminded me it was you. I think you will agree, Harry Mills is a man worth saving, Mr. Costa, so I thank you for saving my dear friend. Are you aware of why Mr. Mills and I have a friendship?"

"I am," I said, "but not from Harry. He never speaks of that night to anyone."

"A debt I can never pay is what I owe that man, Mr. Costa. I know men who lose sleep when they are in someone's debt until they have the opportunity to repay it. In almost twenty years, I have lost not one moment of sleep to the debt I owe him, beyond the seconds lost in prayer thanking God for placing Mr. Harry Mills in that parking lot at that exact time."

Joseph Glendali became quiet then. I noticed his lips moving, but no words. Perhaps he was saying a silent prayer.

I looked into the house, and Marie was walking towards us with a plate in her hands. She looked at her father as she stepped into the room.

"Some pastry, Mr. Costa?" she asked. She was looking to see if her father was okay. He looked up at her and smiled.

"Freshen his coffee, Marie," he said. "And half a cannoli for me, bella mia."

"You already had one, Papa," Marie said disapprovingly. "You know what the doctor said."

"Bah! Il dottore e pazzo. Half a cannoli never killed anyone."

The old Don looked at me as Marie cut the pastry in

half. "This is what you can look forward to," he said. "You live long enough, and your children, and some quack doctor, will make you regret it."

Marie, the loving daughter, rolled her eyes, laid the half cannoli on the plate beside him, pulled his blanket up a bit and kissed his forehead.

"Almost time for your nap, Papa," she said as she walked away.

Joseph Glendali was eyeing the pastry, like a starving lion might eye an exhausted zebra, when he said to me, "So, what do you know about an explosion in Charlestown last night?"

"What makes you think I know anything about it?" I asked as I took my seat again. The old man was full of surprises.

"Actions such as this are unsavory," Glendali said, picking up the pastry. "They cast an unwanted light. Gang wars must become a thing of the past."

He took a small bite of the pastry and chewed it slowly. After swallowing, he said, "But I fear we may be in a time of violence, and the public won't tolerate it. The authorities will have to act. And why? A few hot heads get greedy. It casts a bad shadow. Bad for business."

I supposed I could have reminded him that in the sixties and seventies he had probably had more people killed as he consolidated his power than Al Capone had, but I was already on thin ice, so I nibbled at a cookie instead.

Looking at me, the old man said, "You have recently been seen in the company of the Irishman and the Polack. Am I wrong?"

I casually shrugged, but I was impressed. The old Italian had informers everywhere. "A misunderstanding I was attempting to clear up. Nothing to do with either of their operations."

"Involving the Beradino kid," said Glendali. "I know. I would like you to pass along a message to Mr. Wachowski. The violence stops now. With Mr. O'Neil dead, and yes he is dead. He was in the building. With him dead, opportunity arises for others. I want it known that I am available to host negotiations. That the pie is large enough to satisfy everyone. That solutions can be agreed to without blood in the streets. Can you bring that message to him for me, Mr. Costa?"

"I am a private investigator, Mr. Glendali," I said, "not a message boy. But, out of respect for you, I will do as you ask this one time. What comes from it, I have no interest in. I have my own problems and concerns."

Glendali took another small bite, chewing slowly. His brow furrowed when he said, "I am not a well man, Mr. Costa. Should I no longer be in charge of operations, who can say in which direction the new regime will head. Or how inherited problems will be handled. Do you understand?"

I understood.

Marie was coming towards us and I rose.

"Papa," she said. "I'm going to walk Mr. Costa to his car, then come back for you. Time for your nap."

Joseph Glendali waved us away as he attacked the last of the cannoli.

Marie led me to the front door, then took my arm as we walked to the car.

"Mr. Costa," she said, "I don't know why you have been to my home twice now, but my father seems to be worried. I don't wish for him to have worries at the moment. Do you understand?"

"I do, Miss Glendali. I would rather your father and I had never met. Hopefully, we shall never meet again, and our differences are in the past."

At my car she said, "Is there anything I can do?"

"I'm afraid not," I said, smiling. "The matter is now out of my hands. Others will decide what happens next."

She took my hand. "I noticed you in Harry's place the last time I was there. And once or twice before."

"Harry Mills is a good friend," I said.

"As he is mine. Good day, Mr. Costa." She slowly walked back to the house, where Vincent stood in the doorway watching.

24

The next night, Wednesday, the sixth of December, I met Eileen at Harry's Bar at eight. There was a Celtics game on the television and there were twenty guys at the various tables watching it, drinking beer, and cheering everything Bird was doing on the court. Larry was having one of those nights where it would have taken a team of Navy Seals, fully loaded, to keep him from scoring.

"I thought about calling you," Eileen said in answer to my question of why she hadn't called to tell me about her Sunday meeting with Joseph Glendali, "but I figured it could wait until tonight. So, he asked you out to the house yesterday? What did he want?"

"To tell me that you had been there and that an agreement was decided between you and Ben."

"I don't see where it's your business, Paul. It's my marriage and my life. You really don't have a say in what I do. You agree?"

"Sure," I said. "In most situations. But your husband doesn't work for Fidelity. Your decision could have an affect on me."

Eileen took out a cigarette and accepted the light I offered.

"I like you, Paul. I really like you. We have fun together, don't we?"

I smiled and nodded.

"But I want to be honest with you, Paul. I agreed to Mr. Glendali's proposal only because, right now, I'm not thinking about marrying anyone else. So staying married to Ben, with those stipulations, is fine with me. Of course, having him still giving me money each month helped me to decide. I probably wasn't going to get any alimony.

Right now, I don't want to see anyone else, except you. Just you. But it probably isn't fair to you, is it?"

"I happen to like our arrangement, babe," I said. "I've been living alone for fifteen years, and I'm comfortable. We've only been together three months. If we're still together in three years, I might be looking for something more."

"Three years!" she said, smiling. "Right after Christmas, half of your dresser drawers will be filled with my clothes. And I'll need some hangers in your closet. I've already emptied one of my drawers for your stuff. Three years, my darling? We may not sleep together every night, but I'm not letting you get away."

I told Eileen I didn't have much of a wardrobe, so I would only need half a drawer. We volleyed back and forth a few silly comments, then I asked, "Is your court date on Friday canceled?"

She frowned and shook her head.

"No. The plan is to keep it on the books, but to put the divorce on hold. I wanted that agreement. There is no way I want to drop the suit and then have to go through it all again if Ben breaks the deal. And I'm worried he might, Paul. He was not happy when the Don left him no wiggle room. Not happy at all."

We talked a little more, making plans for the weekend that might include a trip to New York to celebrate the end of court dates for the foreseeable future. A little after nine, Eileen said she was tired and was going home. She gave me a kiss good night and I watched through the window as she got into her car and drove away.

I leaned back into the cushions, closed my eyes and relaxed. It was still too early for bed, and the basketball game held little appeal. Celtics were up by eleven with less than two minutes left. I'd finish the beer in a minute or two and head home.

"Penny for your thoughts."

Rose was standing beside the booth.

"Hey, Rose, how are you tonight?"

"Mind if I sit, Paul?"

"Please," I said. "We haven't talked in a while. How have you been?"

"I'm good. I like this time of year. I can look out my windows at the water and there is a chill in the air. And not a lot of cars driving by. Not like the summer. Makes me think of all those great books I read when I was young. Lonely house, quiet, with just the sound of the sea disturbing the night."

"Sounds spooky," I said, smiling. Normally, by this time of the night, Rose is quite buzzed and ready for an escort home, but she seemed to not be there yet.

"Spooky, yes," she said. "With a touch of danger. But romantic, too. Speaking of romantic, you and your lady friend seem to have hit it off. What's her name again?"

"Her name is Eileen. We're taking things slow, but making progress."

"Yes, Eileen. I remember now. I've noticed how she looks at you. I'm guessing things aren't all that slow between the two of you. Lucky girl. I wish I had gotten that lucky."

"Jealousy doesn't become you, Rose. Besides," I smiled, "I think the last few years you've been luckier than me."

Her turn to smile. "Luck had nothing to do with it."

Rose took a sip from her drink. "You see the child Harry has been fooling around with?"

"She's twenty-two, Rose, and we aren't going to sit here and gossip. Was there something you wanted to talk about, or are we just visiting? I was just about to leave. I could take you home if you're ready."

"Only if you'll come in for a nightcap."

I frowned.

"Then never mind. Carl will take me home."

"Carl?"

Rose nodded towards the bar. I turned to look. There was a guy sitting beside Rose's usual seat, watching the post game chatter and sipping a beer.

She shrugged. "He's okay. Recently divorced and a bit lonely. But you know what they say about ships and storms."

There was only a small amount of liquid in the glass she had carried over, and Rose drained it then looked at me.

"You know," Rose said, "I remember wondering why your girl asked questions about you when we talked."

"I didn't realize you and Eileen had talked," I said. It must have been after I told Eileen the story about Marie Glendali, I thought, because I had to point Rose out to her that night.

"Oh, yeah. We had a long talk about you," said Rose, and there was a mischievous smile on her flushed face. "Maybe, too long. You should probably thank me for her being with you."

I was a bit confused about that. "What do you mean?"

"She didn't tell you?"

"Tell me what, Rose?"

"She was in here a few nights during the summer. July or August. I can't remember."

"And you were talking about me?"

"She asked about you. Asked if I knew you. Asked if you were seeing anyone."

"In July or August?"

"Yes. Yes, July or August. I have to be honest, Paul. I took one look at her body, at the competition, and I almost told her you're a rotten bastard. She should stay away from you. But you've been a good friend, Paul. A sweetheart. Always the gentleman. Even when I didn't want you to be. So I told her if she could hook you, she would never do better."

"How did she know about me?" I asked.

"Said she saw your picture in the newspaper one time, and then saw you in here one crowded Saturday night."

Eileen had never mentioned any of this, but it explained her buying me a beer that first night I saw her. Maybe her being in here that night wasn't coincidence. So much for karma.

I've only had my picture in the newspapers a few times. Usually it's a blowup taken from a group picture of

Saugas Police when I was a smooth faced pup. I was in the Herald a year ago. Someone had snapped a photo of me taking down a guy who had gone crazy at the Garden, threatening people with a knife. No big deal. The guy was just off his meds. He weighed one-fifty soaking wet and out of his mind, so it was easy subduing him. But the Herald reported it like I had just defeated the Ayatollah's army single handed, with a big picture of me on page five holding the guy until the cops came. Plus a short bio that included the gunfight here in Harry's place years before. That little business scored me free tickets for five games. And my office phone rang for the next five months. Free advertising. Can't beat it.

"You're sure it was summer when you two talked?" I asked.

Rose frowned. "There is nothing wrong with my memory, Paul. I remember everything. Except that night you were in my bed."

That got me to smile. "I've never been in your bed, Rose."

"That's why I don't have a memory of it," she said, her lips forming a dangerous smile. "But we could fix that anytime you want, Paul. All you have to do is whistle." Rose lowered her head and looked over at me. "You know how to whistle, Paul? Just put your lips together and blow."

Smiling, I shook my head. "Marie, in *To Have and Have Not.* Very good. You sounded like Bacall."

"I have the dvd," Rose said. "We could sit on my couch with a bowl of popcorn and watch it anytime you want. We'd have fun."

"I have no doubt," I said. "Let me take a rain check on that one, doll."

Rose frowned. "Sure. Listen, when you and the competition tie the knot, I should be invited to the wedding."

"Front row," I said.

"Good. That way everyone can see me stand when the priest asks if anyone has an objection to these two hooking up."

Rose looked over to the bar and then slid from the booth.

"My escort looks a little jealous," she said, then smiled. "Open invitation on that movie, Paul. You won't regret it."

In my best Bogart, I raised my near empty beer mug and said, "Here's looking at you, kid."

Rose frowned and said, "That was terrible." Then she smiled and went to sit beside her escort for the evening.

Sitting alone again, I supposed I should have been flattered Eileen had been asking about me, but the longer I sat the less flattered I felt. Something was niggling at me. I just didn't know what.

THURSDAY MORNING THE office phone rang while I was reading the Globe sports pages.

"You have a minute?" asked Porter Tufts.

"Things are slow," I answered. "I have all day."

"We obtained a search warrant for Peter Gladstone's property," Tufts said.

"Really?" I said. "On what basis?"

"Fraud on a grand scale. The judge was quite receptive to our request. She's a liberal."

"And?"

"We were out there yesterday. Gladstone followed us around with a smug look on his face and a glass in his hand, angrily accusing us of dereliction in our duty, demanding that we cover the insurance claim."

"Did you find anything? A secret room behind a revolving bookcase? The canvas rolled up and hidden in the air-conditioning duct ? The statue buried under rose bushes in the garden?"

"If only it had been that simple."

"But you did find something?"

"Tore the place apart and found nothing," said Porter Tufts. "But then, one of my guys said he read a book once where stolen art was not stolen but hidden behind other paintings. We took a few of them off the walls and out of the frames. And there they were. The Van Dyck and the de Keyser. Didn't find the Remington, but we'll be checking his office and his house in New Hampshire."

"You knew about his debts?" I asked.

"We knew when we investigated eight months ago, but they weren't as bad then. I thought you would want to know."

"I've been off the case for a few weeks now. Interestingly, I accused him of staging the theft before I quit. That he didn't even bother getting them out of the house after that tells us a lot about him, doesn't it? Gunther Kolb told me, Peter Gladstone always believed he was the smartest guy in the room."

"Well, whichever prison he ends up in, he probably will be the smartest guy in the place," said Porter. "How does your calendar look for the next few weeks?"

"Nothing stopping me from dressing up as Santa everyday and ringing a bell in front of Star Market for the Salvation Army."

"I may have something for you," Porter said. "Let you know in a few days. Thanks for this one."

After he hung up, I sat staring at the wall. It seemed to me, banks were quite zealous in giving mortgages and lines of credit to people who talked a good game. What did Peter Gladstone own beyond an idea? Yet that idea gave him the opportunity to purchase expensive property, which then gave him the means to secure lines of credit, which, in turn, allowed him to have the appearance of wealth. All because of the expected riches that would eventually come from that idea. Meanwhile, a hard working bum, busting his ass forty hours a week at his full time job, another twenty at a part time gig, showing up everyday, even when he wasn't feeling great, making sure he didn't go too crazy in his purchasing, had to jump through hoops just to get a bank to even look at his application for a loan.

People have always made money from their ideas. The titans of industry. But the idea was backed up with tangible assets. Factories, machinery, locomotives, printing presses, lathes, drilling equipment, trucks, looms, refineries. If he failed, or the business failed, there was always something solid that could be sold by the lender to recoup some of the money. I wonder how much ideas are worth on the resale market? Especially failed ones. All that's needed now for someone to make money is a floppy disc, or whatever they call that thing that holds the idea. And it appears the entire world is salivating for the next idea, happy to throw money at it, desperate to be a part of it. How easy it will be for the scammers to scam. And when the banks get taken for a ride and have to cover their losses, who do you think will be paying the piper? Same as always. The little guy. The guy who struggles and tries his best to do the right thing. The guy who can only afford to put art on his walls if it was bought at Sears. The poor smuck who busts his ass for three bedrooms and clothes for his kids. The guy who will be expected to bail out the jerk who lives in a penthouse across from Central Park. The poor slob who consistently has to pick up the check. Is it any wonder people are upset?

I DROVE OUT to Lynn after calling Wachowski and found him at his desk, again counting money and making stacks. Packy sat in a chair in front of him, chattering about something as I was shown in. He glanced up at me as I entered, then looked back at Wachowski.

"Tomek," Packy said, "what do you call a guy who runs around for a month looking for something missing, that ain't?"

Wachowski laughed.

"A Paul Costa," said Packy.

"Very funny," I said as I walked up to the desk. "Now, tell me why you thought they hadn't been stolen. What did you hear?"

"I didn't hear anything, Shamus," Packy said with a wide grin and raised eyebrows, waiting for light to dawn on marblehead. And it did.

"Because you heard nothing about art being fenced," I

said, frowning, "that meant there was nothing to sell. Which meant no theft."

"B sixteen. Bingo!" Packy said, pointing a finger at me.

"You're really that connected to what's happening out there, Packy?"

"I hear things, Shamus. And I see things. Sometimes, like now, I do things. So if you two will excuse me, Packy has gotta run."

He got up from his chair and, looking at the door, said to me, "I'll send you a bill for services rendered."

"You got a dinner," I said.

"That was a small retainer. I don't work cheap." And he was gone.

"You believe that guy?" I said to Tomek Wachowski, who was chuckling.

"One of a kind," he said. "If I had that much shit bouncing around inside of my head, I'd kill myself. Now, what's up? Why you in my neck of the woods again? I like you, Paul, but we are spending way too much time together."

I took the vacated seat.

"Any blow back from the other night?"

"None," said Tomek and waved a hand to signal any discussion on the explosion and fire at O'Neil's warehouse was off limits. Hey, I could have been wearing a wire. Can't be too careful.

"I had a meeting with the old man," I said.

"You two are getting chummy," Wachowski said. "Should I be concerned?"

"The main conversation did not concern you," I said. "But, before I left, he asked if I would deliver a message. I told him, and now you, one message is my limit. Anything else either of you want to convey to each other, you are on your own. Or pay my daily rate."

"What's the message?"

"He's concerned the territory in question may become volatile. He doesn't want that to happen. Bad for everyone. He is offering to be a negotiator."

Tomek laughed. "He just wants to make sure he still gets his percentage. The old dog."

Wachowski must have seen the look of confusion on my face. He said, "We all pay the Italians a percentage. He's got more judges, cops and politicians than the rest of us combined. Call it a tax if you want. Part of the cost of doing business and cheaper than a war we would probably lose. I'll think about it, but in the end, he'll be involved. Anything else?"

"That's all I have."

"How's the kid?" he asked, then poured two shots.

"Watching too much afternoon television."

We tapped glasses, wished each other a merry Christmas, and I was back in the 300 as snow flurries drifted down, melting as they hit the ground.

I THOUGHT ABOUT Packy, and his dig at me, as I drove back to my office, and it bothered me. I had been running around looking for clues on stuff that wasn't missing without once considering that there hadn't been a theft. Despite everyone I had interviewed during my investigation warning me that Peter Gladstone was not a man to be trusted, and despite my own conversations with Gladstone that showed me a man devoid of any dignity or remorse for those he had wronged, and, completely ignoring the failed investigations by competent investigators to find any clues in the theft, sirens had not gone off in my head that Gladstone may have faked the whole thing. Until Packy had quoted Confucius.

This wasn't the first time a client had tried to play me during my career. Using me in an effort to legitimize something they had done. When it had happened in the past, I picked up on it in a very short time. But not this time. Like I have said before, when I'm in the early stages of a relationship, I am not at the top of my game. I don't always see things clearly. It's a poor excuse for incompetence, I know, but there it is.

Eileen and I had discussed a trip to New York before Christmas to celebrate the divorce. Radio City,

Rockefeller Center, a Broadway show. But we hadn't firmed up the dates. If we were going to do it, it would have to be this weekend. Or I could take the train down there after Christmas when she was still staying with her mother in Brooklyn, meet up in the city and do some things before New Years. No way I wanted to do Times Square New Year's Eve, though. Been there, done that, never again.

I also thought about her court date that would be happening tomorrow. I was fine with her staying legally married, and, in fact, considered it the best possible solution to the situation. At forty-seven years old, marriage, like death, was not something I gave a lot of thought to. Living with someone, that I could consider. But for now, as Eileen suggested, sharing drawer space was fine.

If staying legally married satisfied the concerns of Joseph Glendali, then that was the way to go. That Ben Landry had agreed to continue helping Eileen with financial help, all the better. My concern, of course, was how long the accountant would continue with the charade. He could not possibly be happy with the old man's demands, no man would be, but he would be powerless to refuse them. What would happen to this agreement if the Don was no longer in charge, either through sickness or death, was something that would have to be dealt with should it happen.

Wouldn't it be nice, I thought, as I slid into a parking spot, if I had actual private investigating stuff to think about instead of my own personal crap. It would certainly help to get my mind off everything else, and help pay the bills, too.

25

How did it go?" I asked Eileen when she called at two-thirty on Friday afternoon. While she had been in court that morning, I had been in the office of Porter Tufts. Monday morning I would be doing some work for Porter's company. Or so I thought.

"Not good," Eileen said.

"Why? What happened?" Had Ben Landry changed his mind?

"We'll talk about it tonight," she said. She sounded tired. "What time are you picking me up?"

"Seven good? We'll grab a bite on the way." The plan was to drive almost into New York state, grab a motel for the night and then into the city in the morning.

"Yeah. I'll be ready."

"You okay?" I asked. She didn't sound okay.

"Sure. See you tonight." And she hung up.

The stress of the morning in court must have been difficult for her, at least she sounded as if it had been. A relaxing weekend in the city, good food, top show, comfortable room, was just what Eileen needed, is what I was thinking.

I was about to call Judy's number to see how Sal was and to tell him I'd be gone all weekend, when there came a knock on the door and Glendali's man, Vincent, entered. Without a thought, my hand grabbed at the Beretta under the middle drawer. Vincent entered alone, closed the door behind him and walked towards me, empty hands in full sight. I found some comfort in that, but I was sure he could be lightning quick when he wanted to be. Or needed to be. Vincent stopped in the doorway to my office and looked at me in that impassive way he had of looking at everything. No curiosity at all. No fear or hesitation either. What I found most disturbing, he never gave me the impression that he wanted me to know he knew he was a more superior man with a gun than I was. He assumed I would know, and that was enough for him. Like Roger Clemens on the mound facing the number nine hitter. The chances the guy would get on base against him were real slim, so he could be excused for being cocky. But he wasn't cocky, because Clemens had been around long enough to know that even a .150 hitter could get lucky. And Vincent knew I was no .150 hitter.

I said, "Does the Don want to see me?"

"He does not. He sent me to ask you a few questions he didn't want to ask over the phone."

"Shoot," I said. "Metaphorically speaking."

Vincent didn't smile.

"Are you aware of what happened in court this morning?"

"I wasn't there," I said.

"I know that," said Vincent. "I was."

"Is there something I should know?" I asked.

"Mrs. Landry reneged on the agreement she had with Mr. Glendali."

That caught me by surprise. My face must have shown my surprise, if only slightly, because I saw a look pass over the shooter's face. So that was why he was in my office asking the questions, instead of Glendali on the phone asking them. To catch my reaction, if there was one.

"May I ask what happened, Vincent?"

"Mrs. Landry's lawyer told the judge his client wanted to go through with the divorce."

"And?"

"Mr. Landry's lawyer immediately stood and asked if he could approach the bench. The two lawyers went and talked to the judge. It may have been a little heated up there. The judge did not look pleased. Neither did Mr. Landry's lawyer. Neither did Ben Landry. Mrs. Landry's lawyer looked a bit bewildered, too, like he was surprised by the attitude of the other lawyer."

"Your take on the whole thing?" I asked.

"Mr. Landry told his lawyer the divorce petition would be dropped. Mrs. Landry's lawyer was never told to drop it. The lady changed her mind. I have the feeling you didn't know she was going to do that. Or not do in this instance."

"So what happened?"

"The judge gave a continuance. Told the lawyers to get their shit together and to stop wasting the court's time. Needless to say, Mr. Glendali is upset. He has tried calling Mrs. Landry. She hasn't picked up. He told me to go see her. I suggested I see you instead. Maybe you could talk some sense into her. The boss was hot. He didn't like my idea, but, eventually, he said to come see you. Let me explain something to you, Costa. You've seen Mr. Glendali several times. Calm, old man. Dealing with a little sickness. Could be someone's caring grandfather. Right? Wrong. Mrs. Landry is playing a game she can't win. Her choice. Be smart. Do and say what you can, but in the end, should she stay down this path, you'd be wise to wave goodbye. Some people, Costa, you just can't reason with. The Don has no beef with you. So don't stick your nose where it don't belong."

We stared at each other for a few seconds, then Vincent left. I called Eileen. Her phone was busy. Or off the hook. I thought about driving to her house, but I'd be seeing her in a few hours, and she was probably napping before our trip. I had no idea what game she was playing at with her court room drama earlier in the day, but whatever it was, I'd like an explanation.

If Glendali decided she had to go, in reality there was little I could do about it, unless the attempt was made when we were together, at which point the attack would have to go through me. But I would not expect that to happen. More than likely, Eileen would be killed in her home, while she slept, made to look like a burglary gone wrong. Or an overdose of pills. Also, in reality, what was I supposed to do for retribution? What could I do?

Nothing.

Retribution against Ben Landry? Why? He wouldn't be the one making the call. Joseph Glendali? Ridiculous to even consider. I'm not a killer. I may carry a gun, and I may have taken the lives of others in defense of my own, but I am not a killer. Revenge was not something to waste time thinking about. Something to consider, however, was witness protection. I would council Eileen to drop the divorce proceedings, stay with the old man's deal she had agreed to, and go on with her life. If she refused, I would strongly suggest she approach the FBI and agree to give evidence against the Glendali family in exchange for protection in the witness program. It would mean she would be hidden away, eventually moved somewhere and our life together would be over. But at least her life would not.

I would pick her up a little before seven and we would have four hours in the car, and all weekend in New York, to talk about things. Or so I thought.

I BRAKED TO a hard stop in front of Eileen's house at ten to seven when I saw the light from the kitchen lights shining through the wide open front door. Eileen was not in the doorway. I took the Beretta from the glove box.

I hustled up the walkway to the open door, listening for any sounds from inside. At the door, I paused and noticed a movement in the kitchen, but couldn't see a person, the height of the stairs blocking my view. Suddenly, I heard glass shattering.

"Eileen?" I shouted, entering the house.

"No, Paul!" Eileen cried out.

Two shots erupted, the bullets taking out pieces of wood from the door frame just above my head. I fell prone against the stairs and started to crawl up towards the top so I could see into the kitchen, the Beretta in my hand.

"What are you doing?" I heard Eileen shout .

"Stop it!" someone growled at her, and then I heard someone being slapped, or punched, a cry of pain and a thud on the floor. A second later another two shots, these bullets embedding in the drywall just inches above my head. I crawled up another two steps, peeking above the top stair into the kitchen, and saw an arm reaching for the kitchen light switch. As the lights went out, I lifted off the steps. A bullet whizzed by my head, another shot rang out, and I fired twice, all in quick succession. There came a loud grunt in the dark, and then the sound of a body hitting the floor. Eileen screamed. A few seconds later, she was sobbing hysterically.

I took the last few steps quickly, throwing myself against the wall between the kitchen and the living room. I found the switch for the living room lights and flicked it. No shot came my way. Peeking around the wall, I saw a man sprawled on his stomach on the floor. I entered the kitchen, stood over him, reached out and flicked on the lights of the kitchen.

Ben Landry was under me.

26

And that is how I find myself sitting in the kitchen of a neat split-level in Winthrop on a chilly night in early December, the body of Ben Landry lying prone just feet away. His wife, a woman I have been seeing for the last three months, is sitting across from me as we wait for the police to come.

"He was crazy, Paul," Eileen finally says, coming out of her shock. "I've never seen him like that before. Angry, yeah. Cruel and mean. But tonight he was crazy."

"What happened?" I ask.

She shakes her head, like she's trying to get images, either to remember, or forget, out.

"He shows up tonight and starts knocking on the door. Demanding I let him in. I tell him to go away. I'll call the cops. He's yelling my name so loud, the neighbors must have heard him. I called you, but you must have already left. After hanging up, I start to dial the police. He's pounding at the door so hard, so before he breaks it, I went and unlocked it, then ran back up the stairs. He comes powering through the door. He's staring up the stairs at me, the phone is in my hand. I've never seen such hate in his eyes. He walks slowly up the stairs. Tells me to hang up the phone. I can tell by the sound of his voice he's been drinking. 'You better leave, Benny,' I say. 'I called the cops. They're on the way.'"

She picks up a pack of Winston's from the table and lights one with shaking fingers, drawing the smoke deep. It seems to calm her a bit, as she lays the lighter on the table.

"He didn't care. 'You'll be dead before they get here,' he said. I backed up against the counter as he entered the kitchen. I'm looking for a knife. Something to protect myself. All that's there is the can opener. I picked it up and threw it at him." She shakes her head. "Still plugged in. Hits the floor five feet in front of him. He rushed me then. Grabbed my arm. Twisted it. Hissed at me. Said I would regret going through with the divorce. Flung me to the floor. Grabbed me again, like a crazed man. I tried fighting him off, Paul. I punched at him as he was lifting me up by my hair. I must have hit him good, because he swore at me. He got me up and threw me onto a chair. Leaned over me. I could smell the liquor on his breath when he threatened me again. I tried pushing him away. He slapped at my arms. Then his hands went around my neck. I tried to pull them away, but I couldn't. 'I'm going to kill you, Eileen,' he said. His eyes. Oh, God, Paul, his eyes."

I wave a hand at her. "Okay. That's enough. I got it."

"Paul, he was crazy. He was going to kill me. I know he was. I've never been so scared."

I reach out and cover her hand with mine.

"He can't hurt you now, baby. Never again."

"If you hadn't come when you did, Paul, I'd be dead. When you yelled my name, you should have seen his face. The most horrible grin you can imagine. He took a gun out of his pocket. I thought he was going to shoot me. But he turned towards where you were coming up the steps and just shot at you. I couldn't believe it. I had to warn you. He punched me. I tumbled onto the floor. I think that punch beat some sense into me, Paul."

She looked at her hands.

"I was on the floor. Against the cabinets. Suddenly, I remembered Ben had put a gun in the drawer where we keep the place mats. I remember asking him when he put it in there why we needed a gun in the kitchen. He told me not to worry about it. You never know, is how he explained it. He was moving across the kitchen, keeping out of your sight, waiting for you to show yourself. Paul, he was going to kill you. I opened the drawer. The gun was there, under a dish towel. I didn't even know if it was loaded. I grabbed it. Suddenly, he shuts off the lights. But

I can see his shadow, and he's shooting at you. I pull the trigger. Two more shots shake the air, and I'm so scared I think I screamed. Did I scream, Paul? I don't know. I don't remember."

"Eileen, that's enough. Don't. You did what you had to do."

"Did I kill him, Paul, or did you?"

I hear a car brake to a stop out front and I push my gun to the far end of the table, away from me. I place my Private Investigator license beside it. The .38 that Eileen had used, I had taken from her hands and placed it on the counter near the sink. Two cops come through the still open door, weapons drawn. Half way up the stairs they stop for a second when they see us at the table and the body on the floor.

"Hands," one of them says. "Let me see your hands."

I raise my hands and signal Eileen to do the same. At the top of the stairs, the two officers take the widest path they can around the body so they can face us, their guns still trained on us. They notice the .38 by the sink and place themselves between us and it.

"Either one of you hurt, Paul?" asks one of the cops. We know each other. Professionally.

"She's bruised a bit, Glenn. I'm fine. My gun is on the table. Can we put our hands down now?"

Glenn's partner picks my gun up carefully and we lower our hands. He glances at the license, looks at me, and then calls it in.

"Is he dead?" asks Glenn.

"Yeah," I answer. "Ten, fifteen minutes.

"You shoot him."

"I did."

"Do you know who he is?"

"Her husband."

"Jesus, Paul."

I shrug. What else can I do? "Long story."

"With a bad ending," Glenn says, holstering his weapon.

Another shrug is my only assessment of his take on the

story. I look over at Eileen. She's looking down at the man she's been married to for seven years and separated from for the last six months. Judging by the look on her face, she's not going to grieve this permanent separation. Judging by the bruises on her neck, darkening by the minute, she may celebrate it. Me? I can't help wondering how I got caught up in this mess. Looking at Eileen, that face, those killer legs, everything in between, I have my answer. Women. Can't live with them, et cetera. But that really is a poor excuse.

Officer Glenn Foster leans against the marble counter top and pulls a small notebook from one shirt pocket and a pencil from the other.

"So, Paul, you have anything to say? Or should we start with Mrs.....?"

"Eileen Landry," I say. "The deceased is Benjamin Landry. Why don't we wait for the detective. It's been a long day, and I'd like to only go through this once."

"Sure, Paul, sure," Officer Foster says, folding the notebook up and returning it to his shirt pocket. He takes another look at the dead guy, the gun still clutched in his hand.

"Was his gun discharged?" Foster asks.

"Five times that I personally know of," I say, looking over at him, frowning. "Discharged with deadly intent, I might add."

Foster smiles at that. I fail to see the humor. I know someone else who will see no humor in this either.

A DETECTIVE HANCOCK enters the house, followed by several others. While the others take care of the crime scene, Hancock questions me and Eileen, me in the living room, Eileen in the dining room. Back and forth he goes between rooms, asking the same questions with different phrasing.

The obvious problem, the dead man is dead in the kitchen of the house he owns, shot by someone. Maybe it was me. I did, after all, discharge my weapon with deadly intent, also, even if I had no line of sight to the target.

Eileen shot once. Forensics will tell if I hit him, or if Eileen did, or if we both did. At first blush, to anyone who wasn't here, it could be argued Ben Landry was protecting his wife and property, that it was I who burst through the door. So it's no surprise that Hancock is somewhat hostile in his questions to me. I have no idea what he is asking and learning from Eileen, but each session with him after he returns from the dining room seems to be less hostile.

Finally, at 10:30, Hancock says to me, "Mr. Costa, I want to continue this at the station. Mrs. Landry is exhausted, still in some shock, and has asked if she can rest. You can ride with me."

"I'd like to speak with Eileen," I say. "Make sure she's all right."

"Her husband's dead. She's not all right."

"He got pretty physical with her," I say. "Maybe she should be brought to an emergency room."

"I had her checked out. She's okay. She'll be bruised for a while, but nothing too serious."

When I start to say something else, Hancock interrupts me. "You were a cop for three years. Never advanced further than the driver's seat of a squad car. I've been a detective for eight years. I'm good at it."

"She shouldn't be alone," I say, ignoring him. I'm not bothered by his insult, my only concern is Eileen's safety. For all I know, Joseph Glendali already knows his accountant is dead. That's all I'm worried about.

Hancock stares at me for several seconds. "And she won't be. I'll have a car parked out front all night. You okay with that? Now let's go."

On the drive to the station, Hancock says, "Mrs. Landry backs up your story. That she was separated from her husband and that the two of you have been seeing each other since September."

Hancock looks at me. "How much do you know about the late Ben Landry?"

"I know he's the accountant for the Glendali crime family."

"You're a private investigator," he says. "Ex-cop. You need me to tell you you're in deep shit?"

I have to chuckle at that, even though there's nothing funny.

At the police station, for my one call, I take a card from my wallet and dial the number of a lawyer I did some work for a few years ago. He tells me he can get to the station in forty-five minutes. Detective Hancock types up my statement, I read it and sign it. That won't make the lawyer happy, but the statement is exactly what happened. While I sit alone, drinking coffee and nibbling at some pound cake that's been hanging around the station all day, Hancock is on the phone. When my lawyer shows up, Attorney at law Mason West, we huddle together and I tell him the whole story. West listens without interrupting, and when I finish he tells me it's a clear case of self-defense, don't worry, it'll all turn out fine. Just leave everything up to him. A man is shot dead in his own kitchen. I'm not as confident as West.

Hancock enters the room where the lawyer and I are sitting. He nods at West, then sits across from us.

"Okay," says Hancock. "I spoke with Mrs. Judy Beradino. She confirms that you were at her house earlier today, leaving a little before five-thirty after visiting with her son who is recuperating from an injury. I spoke with your next door neighbor at your complex, Mr. Villa, who said he spoke with you around six, while he was hanging Christmas lights around his door and you were entering your condo, and vouches that you hurried out of the parking lot just before six-thirty as he was finishing up. Even with favorable traffic, you couldn't have gotten to Mrs. Landry's home much before quarter to seven. A neighbor of Mrs. Landry has testified to one of our officers that he saw a man matching your description entering the house at about ten minutes before seven. He has seen you there before. He will also testify that he saw Ben Landry enter the house fifteen minutes before you. How is he so sure of the time? He was in his kitchen with his wife, they were cleaning up after their supper, when he heard loud banging on his neighbors door. Knowing that the Landry's were separated, he was concerned that Mrs. Landry may have been in trouble. He peeked out the kitchen window and saw Ben Landry angrily pounding on the door. Then he saw him put his shoulder to the door several times until it finally opened. He said to his wife that he thought maybe he should go over there. She told him not to get involved. While they were going back and forth with that discussion, he said he saw your car pull up in front of the house. He recognized it as a car that had been there several times before. And then you entered. He said, even with the windows closed, he said to his wife that he thought he heard gun shots. They argued again if he should call the police. Once again she prevailed, that they should mind their own business."

With a look of disgust on his face that he made no effort to hide, Hancock lit a cigarette and continued. "There will have to be an autopsy, but the ME says there is evidence of only one entrance wound. A bullet entered the left side of Mr. Landry. The chest area. Exit wound in the back. We'll know more tomorrow. The bruises and scrapes on Mrs. Landry suggests they happened recently, which backs up her statement that Mr. Landry was violent with her. We dug five slugs out of the walls and woodwork around the stairwell, That backs up your account. We also retrieved two bullets from the kitchen wall that match the bullets in your gun, and one near the light switch that came from a .38. We can't prove who fired first. We can't disprove the testimony of you and Mrs. Landry, either, that the deceased started the shooting. We have no reports on file here, or from any surrounding towns, that there was any previous problems with you and Mr. Landry. But it is still early. You were involved recently in a shoot out at a restaurant on Route One. Does this have anything to do with that?"

I shrug.

"Is that an answer?" Hancock asks, not pleased with my response. I don't want to muddy the waters.

"I don't know who was shooting at me," I answer with

a version of the truth. "Ben Landry had warned me twice to stop seeing his wife, once in person, once on the phone. Maybe he was sending another message. I don't know."

"And if it was Mr. Landry, then a friend of yours, a Mr. Salvatore Beradino, got shot twice and almost died because of it. Certainly reason enough for retribution."

"I don't know who was shooting at us. They got away before I could ask them why they were shooting at us. I didn't go to Eileen's tonight for retribution, Detective. We had plans to get away for the weekend."

"And another gunfight ensued," Hancock says, frowning.

"Mr. Costa had every right to protect himself, Detective," lawyer West interjects. "Let's stick with what happened this evening."

"If Mr. Costa had been more concerned with threats received from Ben Landry, had reported them to the police, had taken them more seriously, perhaps we wouldn't be sitting here right now," says Hancock. "Ever think of that, Mr. Costa?"

"No." I reply. "My only concern is for Mrs. Landry. If the bullet that killed her husband came from the .38, I would want there to be dozens of photos in her file depicting the abuse she suffered in the minutes that he was in the house. Knowing she was being abused, I expect you to do an extensive investigation into their past for indications that this abuse has been going on for quite some time. A check by professionals to support previous abuse. You can start by asking me about it."

"There you go, again. Telling me how to do my job."

"You know the situation, Detective. You realize, or should realize, the danger Mrs. Landry may be in. She needs twenty-four hour protection."

"We don't have the resources for that," Hancock says, looking at me like I was crazy. "And this is still only the beginning of what is an ongoing investigation. I don't know how things worked in Saugus when you were a cop, but in Winthrop we don't short-change any investigation."

I lean forward, pointing a finger at him "Just do your job. Make sure she's safe."

Hancock stood, glaring down at me. "Don't leave the area, Mr. Costa. And do not contact Mrs. Landry until I have a chance to talk with her tomorrow. I'm serious." Then, looking at my lawyer, "I'd appreciate it, Mr. West, if you'd take your client out of here."

Detective Hancock spun and left the room.

Mason West was chuckling. "Do you enjoy pissing off the guy who's doing the investigating? Some detectives have been known to embellish. They've also been known to fabricate. Evidence mysteriously vanishes. None of which works to your benefit."

"Screw him," I say, standing.

27

I spoke with Eileen on the phone last night and she sounded exhausted. As I pull up in front of her home at ten o'clock, I nod at the cop who is parked across the street. If I had given it any thought, I would have brought him a Dunkin' treat. There are two reporters on the walk in front of her home. I ignore their questions as I walk past them.

Eileen is dressed in slacks and a heavy sweater, both in black. Even with her make-up on, she looks exhausted. As soon as the door closes behind me, she comes into my arms and I hold her, not easing the embrace until she does.

"I have coffee," she says as we climb the stairs. "Eggs if you'd like."

"Just coffee," I say, taking one of the chairs at the kitchen table. There's a Sunday Globe on the table. I read the paper before coming over. The shooting death of Ben Landry is on page five. The floor in front of my chair, the place where Ben Landry had died, has been cleaned of his blood.

Eileen places a steaming cup in front of me, along with milk and sugar.

"How long was Hancock here?"

She shrugs. "Long time. He came once in the morning and again in the afternoon. Asked me all kinds of questions about my marriage. My sister in Brooklyn called. I don't know how she found out about what happened, but she called and told me to get a lawyer. Do it right away, she said. Don't answer any questions, she said, without a lawyer. I don't know any lawyers. Then at noon, there's a knock on the door, and there's a guy standing there telling me he's a lawyer. That he was asked to come here by a Mr. Mason West, who, he said, was your lawyer. We talked, and he was here when Detective Hancock came back. Hancock seemed surprised to see a lawyer with me. I don't think he liked it. But the follow up questions he asked didn't seem to bother the lawyer. He only told me two or three times not to answer."

Eileen was frowning. "The lawyer, a Mr. Morris, said I may have to face a Grand Jury. He would fight it. That I was only protecting myself. That it was obvious, and he doubted the District Attorney would seek to bring charges. But he warned me that they might."

"It's possible," I say. "I spoke with Hancock before coming here. The bullet that killed Ben came from my gun. So there is nothing there for them. But the government may see it as a chance to get the widow of the accountant for the mob on the stand. It may be too big a temptation to pass up. Do you now understand why Glendali was concerned?"

"But I don't know anything, Paul. I've told you that."

"The D.A. doesn't know that and won't believe you when you tell him. Our concern right now, Eileen, has to be the old man."

"Mr. Glendali?"

I nod.

"Do you think I should go and see him?" she asks, her eyes imploring me.

Shaking my head, I say, "Not a good idea. He's not happy about what happened in court. I'll see if he'll see me. He probably won't. I want you to consider witness protection. Tell the feds everything you know. Let them protect you."

"I don't know anything, Paul," Eileen says, upset now. "How many times do I have to tell you?"

"Look," I say, "I'm going to see Hancock again tomorrow and see how long he can keep a cop car out front. I think it would be a good idea if I stayed here nights. At least until we can figure things out."

"Figure things out?"

I shrug.

"What are you going to do about Benny?" I ask.

"Mr. Morris is going to contact Benny's brother, who I hung up on when he called yesterday, and tell him I'm going to have Benny cremated as soon as the body is released. The brother, Matt, can do whatever he wants with the ashes. I don't care. It didn't have to be like this, Paul. He didn't have to come here to kill me."

There was another tact that must be considered. It, too, was fraught with danger, and was dependent on the word of Joseph Glendali being gospel.

"Think about this," I say. "You could tell Glendali that going through Benny's papers you had come across evidence that he had an account in a bank in the Cayman's. That there is a million dollars in that account. That it must be the Family's money, stolen by Ben. That you don't want the money. That you would give it back on the condition that you be left in peace."

Eileen stares into the bottom of her coffee cup for several seconds. Without looking at me, she says, "You think that's a good idea? It's a lot of money, Paul."

"If it can save your life, then I think it's a great idea, Eileen. Do you have the account number? Can you get the money?"

She shrugs. "I don't know. I haven't thought about the money at all. I'll have to dig through his stuff. Not that he left much here when he moved out. The information might not even be here."

"You do that. And think about what I've said."

I stand and go to her, hugging her head to my body.

"I'm going to drive out to Nahant. See if the old man will see me. You shouldn't go out today. I'll come back as soon as I can. Try not to worry, babe. We'll figure it out."

THE DAY IS overcast, traffic is light on the Lynnway, and I'm the only car on the road to Nahant. There is more traffic once I'm out here. Sunday Mass must have just emptied out. I'm behind a slow moving car as I weave through the narrow streets that lead to Glendali's home. I pull up to the iron gate, and wait patiently for someone to come out of the house to acknowledge me. A few minutes pass before Vincent walks up the drive. I step from the car and walk to the gate to meet him. He's wearing a heavy coat, his hands are in the pockets. Vincent stares at me with those humorless eyes.

After several very long seconds, Vincent says, "You got some balls coming here, Costa. I'll give you that."

My hands are not in any pockets, and obviously empty. "Mr. Glendali knows what happened, Vincent. He knows no one wanted this." I assume the old man has cops from every town north of Boston on his payroll, so he knows what really happened and not from something he read in the newspapers or heard on the six o'clock news.

"Will he see me?" I ask.

"He has no interest in anything you have to say. This has created a huge problem for him. He thought it was all taken care of. He thought he had solved the problem, and then Eileen pulled that stunt in the courtroom."

"She doesn't know anything," I say. "Nothing that can hurt the family."

"Not my call."

"Tell Mr. Glendali I would like to speak with him. Tell him, he calls and I'll meet with him anytime."

I didn't expect Glendali would see me, but I had to try. As I drive down the hill to the causeway, and approach the entrance to the beach parking, I decide to pull in through gates that are open. About half way along the paved lot, which always seems to have a layer of sand on it blown from the low dunes that rise above the parking area and hide the ocean from view, I pull the 300 to a stop. Leaving the car, I walk along a path through the low dunes until I can see water beyond the expanse of sand. A restless tide swells and ebbs. There's a wind, and the cold eats through my coat. The cold seems to bring things into a sharp focus.

Joseph Glendali, in an effort to keep a bad situation manageable, inserted himself into the marriage problems of his accountant. I believe he did so with only good intentions. But he also knew, if he could buy some time, things between the two might work out. And who knows, depending on just how ill he may be, he may have hoped to buy enough time that should the marriage dissolve at a future date, someone else would have to deal with the problem. But then Eileen reneged on the deal, Ben Landry went crazy, and Glendali must now know that he made a huge mistake showing his hand.

If he had never gotten involved, he simply could have waited to see how things played out. If the divorce went through, he could then decide what to do about Eileen. She could disappear, or he could simply wait to see if she was approached by the feds. I have little doubt, that were she to be subpoenaed, or even questioned by the feds, Glendali would know. At that point, Eileen could vanish, never getting the opportunity to sit in a witness chair. Or she could die in her bed, over-dosed on sleeping pills, caused by the distress of her divorce. Instead, he tried to keep her married, even if only in the eyes of the law, and he played his hand, alluding to the fact that a divorce could be hazardous to her health. Now, Eileen knows she may be in danger, and that knowledge may force her to do the one thing the old man was trying to avoid all along; her testimony to the feds.

Closing my eyes, I take cold air deep into my lungs and hold it in, allowing my body, and my mind, to relax. When I finally release the air, and open my eyes, I feel a sudden sense of calm. Alone, on a freezing cold expanse of sand and surf, I am well aware of what this calmness means, for I have, at times before, been held captive in its power.

Things may happen. I don't know what those things may be, so I will be powerless to prevent them from happening. Precautions can be taken, but they would probably prove to be inadequate. I am not in control. One may think that that feeling of being powerless would lead someone to be nervous, agitated, even angry. Understandable. But that's not me. I don't fear or worry about the unknown. It's a waste of time and energy.

Should something occur while I'm present, I will deal with it in the harshest way imaginable, to protect myself and those in my care. But I can't be everywhere all at once and all the time. And because I can't, I need to convince Eileen that she really only has one option. One action negates the unknown. Should she refuse to take it....?

This expanse of sand that I am standing on is Nahant Beach. I came here many times in my younger years, those teenage years when I was driving. Usually with a girl I was seeing at the time. Those times when laying on your towel tanning, a transistor radio tuned to WMEX beside you, the occasional dip in chilly water for a frolic, were a more relaxing way to spend the day, the beach less populated than Revere Beach, and no amusements to disturb the mood.

But in the years before I had my driver's license, the MTA bus would come down Chelsea Street to Ferry Street, bang a right onto Elm and take us all the way to Revere Beach. Once there, there was more to do beyond sand, sun and surf.

First, you would walk to your place on the beach, the place which your city called their section. Each city had their section. No visible borders, but everyone under twenty knew the boundaries. You could then leave the sand, maybe after a cool dip, and walk the Boulevard for hours. Dipping into arcades to try your skill at SkeeBall, or dozens of carnival games. Knock things over with a ball, fill things up with water pistols, try your luck at Ring Toss. A hundred different ways, a dime at a time, to spend the two dollars your mom had given you along with the large towel. Pizza slices, burgers, fried clams, ice cream cones, whatever you desired for lunch. Amusement rides in the afternoon for the very young, other rides lit up at night for the older crowd. Clubs with entertainment for adults.

Beyond the rides that spun around, like the Himalaya and the Tilt-a-Whirl and the Round-up, there were rides that dominated the landscape. The bumper cars, where you ignored all warnings not to crash head on into the other cars. The Ferris Wheel could be seen from anywhere on the beach. The Wild Mouse, a heart stopping ride in a car shaped like a mouse that sped along iron rails that seemed to suddenly end before the car snapped into a gut wrenching ninety degree turn, just as you thought you might plunge to the Boulevard far below. The double Ferris Wheel, rising high above the buildings below it, and providing thrills of its own. And terrors that never fade from memory.

I was nine years old. Billy Shute's mom had taken Billy, me, and his sister for a fun night at the beach. We rode the rides, finally coming to the double Ferris Wheel. Billy and his sister, Ann, got in one open car, Mrs. Shute and me in another, and off we went. Like a Ferris Wheel, each of the two wheels of the double spun slowly around. And the whole structure spun, also, so that you might be the top wheel, then the bottom wheel, then both wheels parallel fifty feet above the ground. Great fun. Until that night, when you're nine years old, and the ride stops so that people can get off, and your car, the one you are sitting in, the one that is at the very top of the top wheel, the one that looks out over the dark waters from a hundred feet off the ground, the one that just won't stop swinging, suddenly becomes the scariest place in the world, even though Mrs. Shute sits beside you. And the embarrassment you feel when you realize that she has realized you are scared out of your mind, and she begins telling you that everything is okay. That they are just letting the people from the lower wheel get off. That when they are done, the wheels will move and we'll be on the bottom. And the seconds become minutes, the minutes become years, and you can feel the bottom wheel turning, the clanging of metal as iron bars are lifted allowing the riders to depart, and still you are on the very top, noisily swaying above it all.

Almost forty years later, I still remember the terror I felt that night. Perhaps it was a good thing that it happened. Maybe, the memory of it has served me well over the years. I seem to always have a sense that what I am looking at, while it might not seem dangerous at first glance, a second glance may offer another perspective. Also, when recognizing there may be danger, I enter into it with a plan and an exit strategy. I don't scare so easily anymore, but that's not a reason to be foolish.

Another ride on the beach, the one that dominated the landscape, was the white wooden behemoth called Cyclone, a roller-coaster that may have been built in the Middle Ages and may have been spotted by the Pilgrims on their way to Plymouth. How it was still standing was a mystery to us all. From any spot on America's first public beach, you could hear the clanging of the cars speeding along the rails, feel the swaying of the cars from two hundred yards away, hear the screams of those fearing this was their final moments of life. Those with grit sat in the first car, bravely lifting their arms high into the air as the cars slowly were pulled up the first incline. Only the most foolish, those with suicidal tendencies, left their arms up as the cars crested the top and began hurtling down that first hill, gaining the speed necessary to propel the cars over more hills, around hairpin turns and dangerous dips. What a rush.

The Cyclone. Sometimes, life can feel like you're on a roller-coaster. Especially the sudden dips that leave your insides feeling out of place.

All the rides are gone now. As are the Arcades, most of the food places, the entertainment. Condo's rise high above the landscape, with more planned for the future. Even behind the Boulevard, still busy in the Summer with beach traffic, the dog track, Wonderland, seems to be on its last legs.

It's a December day in the Northeast, and the wind is chill, the sky is gray, the ocean lacks appeal. There is no mystery to it. Most December days are like this. There is no wonder to it. The wonder would be if the day was warm and sunny.

And in this moment, in the chill and the gray, comes clarity.

28

Hancock places a warm cup of station house coffee in front of me on his desk, then takes his chair, sipping from his cup. I'm feeling a lot less combative since our last sit-down, and would prefer this session to be more civil.

"I want to thank you for the presence out front, Detective," I say. "Mrs. Landry feels much safer having it out there."

"You know I can't have it there much longer," he says, "but I'll leave it as long as I can. I'll ask that we do a few more drive-byes during the day when that happens."

"I plan on being there nights," I say. "At least until the holidays."

Hancock lights a smoke. "You believe she's in danger?"

"You know how the Feds finally got Capone?"

Frowning, Hancock says, "Tax evasion."

"Tax evasion. So, yeah, I believe she may be in danger."

"Has she admitted her late husband told her things about Glendali's business?"

"Swears she knows nothing. They never talked about what he did for the Family. Obviously, she knew Ben Landry was the accountant, but he never discussed what he did."

"Shouldn't matter," says Hancock. "In a court of law, anything she says would be second, third hand, if she never personally witnessed her husband cooking the books."

"Which would be fine if Glendali believed it. Which he doesn't."

Sitting up a little straighter, Hancock asks, "You know this?"

"We've spoken several times."

Hancock frowns. "In the last few days, Mr. Costa, I've learned that you may have had dealings with an Irish hood, Timothy O'Neil, in Charlestown, before his charred body was recently found in what was left of a warehouse near the Navy Yard. And the police in Lynn told me you have been seen entering an establishment in that city belonging to Tomek Wachowski, the known leader of the rackets over there. Now you tell me that you and the head Mafia guy are on speaking terms. Interesting circles you inhabit. Also, you were recently involved in a shootout up on One, where a lot of blood was shed, not to mention you killed a man in a bar on the Boulevard a few years back, and left another fighting for his life in the OR. Should I even mention the two you shot up in Peabody six years ago? No one died, so maybe they don't warrant discussion."

"There were four of them," I said, shrugging. "I didn't shoot the other two while they were running away. And as for the other thing, up until September I had never met O'Neil or Glendali, and Wachowski and I had a misunderstanding a few years back that kept us from attending each other's birthday parties. I've never shot at anyone who wasn't threatening to shoot me first. But you can't do what I do, and not ruffle some feathers. I carry a license, Detective, not the protection of a badge. Makes me fair game for anyone with a hair across their ass."

Hancock crushed the cigarette out in an ashtray in desperate need of being emptied, then leaned back in the rolling chair.

"I got a call from the FBI this morning," he says.

Shit. "They're a lot quicker on the ball than I remember them being," I say. "And?"

"They were wondering where we stood on the investigation into the death of Ben Landry, as if they didn't know. Wondering what the wife's role was in the shooting. Wondering if I had reason to bring her down here for a talk."

"What did you tell them?"

"This department likes to keep good relations with the

Fed boys, Mr. Costa. Always helpful when we can be. Enjoy working with them when we have to, even when they are overbearing, making asses of themselves, and screwing everything up. I told them Mrs. Landry is not someone we are interested in talking with again unless we receive new information about the shooting. Which we are not anticipating."

I smiled.

"But, you know, maybe she should talk with them," he said. "Make a deal. Mrs. Landry may have no other options."

"Only if she had something to offer them," I say. "Which she has told me on many occasions, she does not."

Leaning forward again, Hancock frowns again. "I got a second call this morning. This one concerned you. I was told to close the case quickly. Obvious situation of self-defense. Not to waste tax-payers money. Plenty of other cases to take up my time. A man with obvious connections to the mob was dead. I was told that was a good thing. Button it up and move on. Among all this other stuff I've mentioned, it seems you have friends in high places, Mr. Costa?"

I do not, I think to myself. But I do know someone who may own some people in high places. May have them on the payroll. Immediately, I think back to the two punks who tried to rape Marie Glendali. During their trial, Joseph Glendali made sure those boys walked. Three weeks later, they were never heard from again. I find no comfort in being told the investigation is being filed away.

BY NOON MONDAY, I'm at the Pru taking the long elevator ride up to Porter Tufts rather bland office. There are two award plaques on the wall behind his desk from the insurance company he toils for, and beside them two pictures of his family. One shows him standing beside an attractive woman with a dazzling smile, the other is of Porter standing behind two sub-teen boys dressed in football outfits. This is the life of the other half. The luckier half.

"I want to thank you again for helping us with the Gladstone thing," he says as I take a seat in front of his desk.

"I didn't do anything," I say.

"You violated no ethics, Paul, but just being here, asking about Gladstone, aroused my curiosity. Now, Gladstone is facing years in prison and a hefty fine he can't pay. The lawsuits are piling up. He'll be tied up in court for years. How did you know?"

How does one even begin to tell another about Packy? So I won't.

"I heard enough bad things about Gladstone during my investigation that I had my researcher do a little digging into his finances. What he found out, planted the seed."

"You have a researcher?"

I shrug. I have a college kid who knows his way around a computer. I'm answering the office phone like I'm a high profile company with a dozen agents. A Winthrop detective believes I have friends in high places. Things appear so good, maybe I should check out digs in this fancy tower?

"Listen, Paul, I have something that I need your services for," Porter Tufts says. And he tells me what he'd like me to do. Porter believes he has a client who has been running a thing in his home that may eventually lead to a claim for loss. What he wants me to do will take time and be sporadic. Possibly take months. He offers me more than my daily rate, with a generous retainer. I can now pay my rent for the next few months and keep the lights on. He hands me a folder with all the pertinent things I'll need to know about what I'll be doing, then asks if I have an email account. I was hoping to retire before needing a computer, but I now see the world is moving faster than I anticipated. I tell Porter not yet, but I'm looking into it.

WHEN I PARK in front of Eileen's, I see Officer Glenn

Foster sitting in the squad car parked across the street. He rolls down the window as I approach.

"You staying?" he asks.

"Yeah. Thanks for being out here. Listen, you still seeing that redhead I saw you with a few years ago?"

"Married her, Paul. We have a two year old son. Glenn Junior."

"Congratulations," I say, smiling. Then I get serious. "You have what's important, Glenn. Don't get lost in the bushes."

Officer Foster says sternly, "I have a father, Paul." Then he smiles. "Who told me the same thing." Then he gets serious. "I hear things in the station. You better watch your back, my friend."

My turn to smile. "My father has passed on, Glen. But he would have told me the same thing."

Foster gives a little wave as the window rises, and I cross the street as he pulls away. Eileen is standing at the door as I climb the stairs.

"I took steaks out of the freezer," she says as she kisses me and leads me up to the kitchen. I head to the stove to heat up the kettle for instant coffee.

"The reporters are gone from out front," I say.

She nods. She still looks tired, but better than she did when I left this morning. She had a restless night of sleep. I had slept little. I tell her about my meeting with Hancock while I sip coffee and eat buttered Italian bread.

"So that's it?" she says. "Three days, and he's dropping the investigation?"

"Nothing really to investigate," I say. "Obvious case of self-defense. Why waste time and money?"

I didn't want to tell her what I really thought, but I could tell by the look on her face, she knew there was more to it than that.

Taking the seat across from me, Eileen says, "I had two phone calls this morning, Paul."

"Okay?"

"My sister wants me to come there early for Christmas. She says I need to be with family now. She's talked to dad and I can stay with him."

"I think that's a good idea," I say. And I do.

"The other call was from Mr. Glendali," Eileen says, staring across the table at me.

"And?"

"He asked how I was. If I was doing all right. Then he said, 'Eileen, I don't understand. I thought we had an arrangement. What went wrong?'"

"What did you tell him?" I asked.

"The truth. I told him the truth, Paul. Like I told you. The night before court, Benny had called me. Said there was no way he would be paying for things, giving me money, while I was with other men. He wasn't going to be the butt of everyone's jokes. I could go to hell. He told me to just smarten up and do the right thing."

"And what did Mr. Glendali say to that?"

"Nothing, Paul. He didn't say a thing. He was quiet for so long, I thought he had hung up. Then he says, and his voice was cold, he says that he would like Vincent to come over here. To go through any papers Ben may have in his study. He asked if I would have a problem with that."

"What did you tell him?"

"What do you think? If Vincent is coming, I want him coming through a door that is opened for him and not one he's breaking down. I told him any night this week would be fine. Then I tried telling him how crazy Ben was when he came here. That he was going to kill me. Then I told him, again, that I don't know anything about what Ben did for him. That we never discussed his business."

"And?"

"He never said a word. When I was done talking, all he said was, Vincent would be here tonight. At seven o'clock. Then he hung up."

Eileen is looking at me with obvious concern on her face. "Paul. I'm scared."

VINCENT ARRIVES PROMPTLY at seven, and when

I open the front door he doesn't look surprised that I'm standing there. He nods at me as I step aside for him to enter. Again, with Vincent, there is nothing in his face or movements that give you a clue at what he is thinking or contemplating, but for a quick second, when I opened the door, there was something in his eyes that caught my attention. Whatever it was meant to convey, it did nothing to ease my nerves. I'm wearing a suit coat, the Beretta in the shoulder holster.

Vincent climbs the stairs in front of me, apparently at ease showing me his back. Eileen stands in the entrance to the kitchen, her arms folded.

On the landing, he stops in front of her and says, "Mrs. Landry, I apologize for interrupting your evening, and for being in your home during this difficult time. I'm sure you understand the Don's concern."

"Of course. Whatever I can do, Vincent. I want Mr. Glendali to know that."

"Mr. Landry mentioned that he had a study in the house."

"Yes. The third bedroom. Small, but he had said it was adequate for his needs," Eileen says. I can see she is nervous, but her voice never wavers.

"Has anyone been in there in the last few days?" asks Vincent.

"No. Not even me," says Eileen. "I think Ben took what he needed when he left last June. You're welcomed to go through what's left, Vincent. I have no idea what's in there. Please, take whatever you want. I'm just going to toss everything else when I have time."

I'm standing off to the side, thinking that Vincent must have been in Ben Landry's apartment as soon as they heard he was dead.

Without another word, Vincent walks to the study, enters, closes the door behind him. Eileen looks at me. Her fear is evident. Fifteen minutes later, Vincent walks back down the hall. We're sitting in the kitchen. I stand when I hear him coming. In his hands are several filled plastic bags. It's not much.

"Mrs. Landry, again I apologize for the interruption. Mr. Glendali appreciates your cooperation. We won't bother you again."

"Vincent," Eileen says, standing. "Please tell the Don that Ben came here angry. He was going to kill me. I know he was. He was yelling at me that there was no way he would agree to a divorce and no way he would give me money as long as I was with another man. He said that to me on Thursday night, too. Which is why I changed my mind. Please, Vincent, tell Mr. Glendali that. I would never have reneged if Ben hadn't demanded that." Eileen tilted her head and pulled her hair away from her neck, the bruises purple and dark. "If Paul hadn't shown up when he did, I'd be dead. I'd be dead, Vincent."

The gunman looks at Eileen for a few seconds, then at me, then back to her. He says nothing. As he turns to leave, I cross in front of him and walk down the stairs, showing him my back. When I open the door, he's right behind me.

"Did you mention to the Don that I would like to speak with him?" I ask.

"Right now, he's not interested. Should that change, I'll be in touch."

Vincent stands there for several seconds looking at me. I expect he wants to say more, although I have no idea what that might be. But it appears to me he is thinking of saying more. He doesn't. He leaves, and I watch him walk down to his car and drive away. When I lock the door and turn, Eileen is staring down at me from the top of the stairs.

"My God, Paul, I was so afraid. That man gives me the chills."

I climb the stairs and take her in my arms. She's trembling.

"You should take me to bed and warm me up," Eileen says, rubbing her face against my chest, her cheek bumping against the holster several times. "You should take me to bed right now."

Who am I to argue with a grieving widow?

29

Tuesday and Wednesday I stayed with Eileen all day and night. The police protection was no longer out front, but I did notice several drive-byes during the day. I spent daylight hours reviewing the files Porter Tufts had given me concerning the job he wanted me to do, and planning a strategy on the best way to proceed. I called Sal each day at his mother's. He was feeling much better. He had even gotten out for a walk.

Eileen kept busy. She seemed preoccupied with something, but didn't share. A lingering heaviness to the violence is what I thought. I gave her space. She cleaned the entire house on Tuesday, and on Wednesday began preparing for her trip to see her family. She was leaving on Friday.

Tuesday, I dug the camera out of the trunk of the 300 and caught her as she was finishing vacuuming the downstairs.

She made a big deal of not wanting to be photographed without getting herself all dolled up first, but I told her I wanted candid shots and that they would be mostly head shots. 'At least let me comb my hair', she begged. I told her she was beautiful, and clicked away.

We watched television in the evenings, like an old married couple, and then coupled in the bedroom like teenage kids after. All in all, two quiet days.

But it's Thursday morning now, and I need to get a few things done. Eileen wants to do some shopping for her trip, so she'll be in public places. It is what it is, so what can I do? This is the new normal, and we are going to have to figure out how to navigate these waters. Like I've said, can't be everywhere all the time, so can't worry about it.

I kiss her on the sidewalk and watch her drive away. Then I'm in the 300 and beginning my day. I have a lot to do. First stop will be my place.

The morning sky is gray, as are my thoughts. I was hoping to meet with Joseph Glendali, but no offer came for a meeting. It's eleven days before Christmas, Eileen leaves for her dad's tomorrow. Maybe I'll hear from Glendali next week. Maybe it's healthier for me if I never hear from him again.

My mailbox has mostly junk mail, but there are two bills that I need to pay. Once inside, I head to the dark room with my camera and develop the shots I took of Eileen. The three close-ups I took of her face are stunning. They really are. They are black and whites. Some people, and I now know Eileen is one of them, photograph better in black and white, look more attractive in black and white, than they do in color. There is something about black and white film, I don't know what it is, that it loves some faces and not others. Think Ingrid Bergman. A very attractive lady. But in the movie Casablanca, has there ever been a more beautiful woman? These candid shots of Eileen are incredible. She's beautiful. Not just attractive. Stunningly beautiful.

There are three messages on my home answering machine. Billy Shute informs me his lawyer informs him that the insurance company that has been harassing him will no longer be harassing him. Thanks buddy, he says, and informs me the check is in the mail. That's followed by an audible laugh. Another call asks why I missed the monthly poker game last month, which I forgot all about, and that the one for December is Monday night. The third call is from my sister. Our mother will be spending a few days there, so I don't have to pick her up for Christmas dinner. She also reminded me what I could get my nephews and nieces for Christmas.

From the house I drive to my office. There are a few pieces of mail on the floor as I open the door and flick on the lights. Two office bills and one check. Taking a seat, I sip from my Dunkin's while I listen to the answering machine. There are a lot of messages, several from people I know who have read about the gunfight and want to know if I'm okay. Tomek Wachowski left a quick message. 'You're a piece of work, Paul, you really are'. Two callers, both women, left messages for me to call them. They have need of my services. So they claim. There is a rather nasty, expletive filled message from Peter Gladstone, saying he was going to sue me. Another from Gunther Kolb, reminding me he had told me Gladstone was a piece of shit. Two calls wanted me to attend a dinner, where I would be shown the tremendous benefits there are in owning a time share. I would leave the dinner with a Japanese kitchen knife set just for attending.

I quickly create a file for the job I'll be doing for Tufts, and place his files into it and put it all in my file cabinet. I call the two women who left messages. I reach one and make an appointment with her for early next week. The second one, I leave a message on her machine and we will now play phone tag.

I call my college researcher and wake him up. Christmas break, and it's late night video games and late morning sleep-ins. I give him a task to do and tell him I'll call back later. Out of the office and I'm off to see Sal.

The air smells like it's going to snow. When it snows in mid-December, and, yeah, while white Christmases are nice, it makes for a very long winter. The older I get, the less I want long winters. There is a hill in Everett, near where Billy lived above Glendale Park, a park Babe Ruth once smashed a ball far out of in his barnstorming days, that we used to sled down when we were kids. Fantastic hill. Back then, I wanted it to snow in November. Sometimes it did. But not now. Now, I can wait until January for snow. February, even better.

I have a quick visit with Sal. He's in good spirits. “So, listen,” I say to him. “You're square with Wachowski. Just stay out of Lynn. And I've heard nothing about gambling debts being owed, so maybe you skated past that mess.

Just in case, stay out of places in Charlestown. I'm serious, Sal."

"Scouts honor," he says, raising his right hand to God. Sal was never a scout.

"I have something I need you to do," I say. "You free in the morning."

"I like watching *The Price Is Right*," he says. "But for you I can miss it."

I give Sal a C-note and tell him what I need. Judy makes us salami and provolone sandwiches, and then I'm on my way again.

I knock on the red first floor door. Billy Shute answers. I'm at his apartment on a street in the hills of Malden.

"Hey," he says, "what the hell is going on with you? Two gun battles in a month? The same people, or is the whole world pissed off at you? Jesus, Paul, what the hell is going on?"

"Different problems," I say as I step into his house. "All taken care of now."

"You sure?" he says. "You need anything, need someone to ride shotgun, I'm available."

"That's why I'm here. Let's have a beer and we'll talk. There's something I need you to do."

By the time we empty the bottles, Sal knows what I may need from him, and he's all in. Excited even.

From Malden, I drive through Melrose into a ritzy development in Wakefield. I find the house I'm looking for. Big place. Three car garage. Manicured lot. This is where the husband and wife live that Porter Tufts has tasked me with discovering things about.

It seems to me, criminals are becoming more upper class. I'm thinking computers are the reason. But what do I know? Maybe there have always been upper class criminals and computers are now making it easier to identify them. Maybe everyone has a hustle going, and it's always been that way. Maybe I've procrastinated long enough. Time to go see Harry.

As I walk into the bar, Harry Mills is at the tap pouring a cold one for a guy who looks like he's been working outside in the cold all day. Late afternoon crowd of maybe ten men sitting in small groups. I walk to the extreme far end of the counter and take a seat. Harry hits the tap again and walks over with it, setting it in front of me.

"Don't say it," I say. Not that I expected him to. Harry had warned me about messing with Glendali's crew.

"Where does it go from here?" he asks seriously.

I shrug. "Up to the old man. I've asked for a sit down. He's not interested. Not yet, anyway."

"How's Eileen?"

"I've been staying with her. She leaves for her parents tomorrow. Stay there through the holidays."

"And the police?"

"Case closed, I've been told. Pressure from higher up. Who do you know who exerts that kind of pressure?"

Harry frowns. "The Don would not want a lot of discussion that leads to questions about his business. Still, the problem with Eileen."

"There is that."

"Any ideas?"

"The ball isn't in my court, Harry."

"Anything I can do?"

"Nah. I'm hoping Joe Glendali does nothing unless he hears Eileen is being approached by the Feds. If that happens, he'll know. Should that happen, this probably goes nuclear. If it doesn't happen, life goes on."

"He'll blame you for Landry's death."

"Five bullets to two, Harry. What was I supposed to do?"

"Yeah. Maybe Mr. Glendali will see it that way."

My turn to frown.

EARLY FRIDAY MORNING, after an energetic romp that Eileen promised would keep me from straying until she got back, and a light breakfast, I carry her bag down to a waiting cab. She wants to catch the shuttle to LaGuardia. She gives me a long kiss, then waves goodbye from the back seat as the cab pulls away.

Seconds later, another cab drives by.

Ten days before Christmas. After a shower, I'll lock her house up then head over to my office to make some calls, and await one.

I'm not sure how this will now play out. I have my suspicions. I hope I'm wrong.

30

EILEEN

Can you believe how hot it was today?" I said to the woman, as I took the stool beside her at the bar. It was eight-thirty on a Tuesday night, the place was half full and loud, most of the noise coming from a rowdy group sitting at tables near the small dance floor. They were a young group, all male, dressed like some kind of bicycle club in similar tight fitting outfits.

The woman glanced at me, smiled, but made no response, turning her attention once again to the drink in front of her.

"What can I get you?"

The bartender was standing in front of me. He was smiling.

"A White Russian," I said.

"Coming right up."

While he made the drink, I took a look around the place. I had been here two years before, when Benny and I had come for a birthday bash for the old man. The bar looked the same. It felt like a comfortable place to have a quiet drink, but it really lacked the feel of a modern club. More Dean Martin than Ozzy Osbourne, is what I thought.

"I've seen you in here before, haven't I?" the man asked as he placed the drink in front of me. "My name is Harry Mills. I'm the owner."

Which, of course, I remembered, having heard it at the party. Harry was a handsome Black man. Tall, in shape, late forties was my guess, hairline beginning to recede with just a touch of gray. His voice was deep and pleasant, smile friendly. It was his eyes that caught my attention. It looked like there could be some intelligence behind those eyes. Also, there was no mistaking the mischief in them. I reached for the glass with my left hand so he could see the diamond on my ring finger.

Smiling, I said, "Yes, Harry, I've been in before. A few years ago. You have a good memory." I didn't share my name, or why I had been there.

Looking up from the ring, Harry smiled and said, "Welcome back. Enjoy your drink." And he went to the rowdy boys who were waving at him.

"It's loud in here tonight," I said to the woman beside me.

"Canadians," she said. "On a bike trip. I think I heard them saying they were heading to the Cape."

"I'm Eileen," I said.

"Rose," she said.

"Do you come here often, Rose?" I asked.

"Occasionally," Rose replied. "I like it in here, and I don't live far away. How about you, Eileen? You live in the area, or just visiting?"

"Winthrop," I said. "I've driven past this place a million times, always saying I should stop in again for a drink. I just never do. It was so hot today, so uncomfortable in the house, I just had to get out. I drove along the Boulevard. The beach is still packed. Huge line at Kelly's. So much going on, I thought I had to be a part of it. Know what I mean? Not a night to be alone."

"You aren't married?" Rose asked. "Not many of us girls walking around with a ring like that."

"Separated."

"Seems to be a lot of that going on," Rose said.

"You, too?" I asked.

Rose shook her head after finishing her drink. "No. Widow. Husband died years ago."

"Sorry," I said. "Terrible. He must have been very young."

"Twenty-nine. I was twenty-five. Dump truck lost it on an icy road and slid into our lane. I had my seatbelt on. Marty never wore his. Marty died instantly." Rose gave a sad shake of her head. "The day before Christmas. I was pretty banged up. I was going to tell Marty about his Christmas present when we got home. Never got the chance."

"Oh, God, Rose, that is horrible. I'm so sorry."

She motioned to Harry for a refill.

"Long time ago, Eileen. Almost seventeen years now. Sometimes, when I close my eyes, I can still see those headlights coming right at us. It still startles me. It's why I don't drive anymore." Harry placed a drink in front of Rose, gave her a smile and a wink, then moved toward a balding guy at the end of the bar who was reading a newspaper. Picking up the glass, Rose looked at me and smiled. "Probably a good thing I don't."

Rose was petite, trim, almost to the point of being too slim, her bleached blonde hair cut short - too short in my opinion - her make-up done with some care. She wore a floral summer dress that did not flatter her figure. She reminded me of other women I've known in their forties who, when leaving the house in the evening, out of habit, make an effort to look as good as they can. But somewhere between start and finish abandon the effort, when the mirror makes it painfully obvious that what once was can never be again. There was a depth of sadness in her brown eyes, though her lips curled, making it seem she was content.

We sat quietly for a while, watching the Red Sox on the television and listening to the Canadians replaying some misadventure on a New Hampshire road. I waited until Rose finished her drink before getting to the reason I was sitting there.

"Rose, did you see that story in the newspapers almost a year ago? The one about the guy who disarmed a crazy nut with a knife at the Garden? I think the hero was someone named Peter, or, Pat Costa?"

"Paul Costa," Rose said looking at me. Her eyes were beginning to look a little heavy. "His name is Paul Costa."

"The newspaper said he had done something heroic right here in Harry's bar years before, but the story didn't go into much detail about it. You know anything about that?"

"I was sitting right here when it happened, Eileen. Scared me so bad I peed my undies."

"What happened?"

"The newspapers didn't get the story entirely right," said Rose. "But this is the way it happened. It was a cold night. A night you would be wearing a heavy coat, you know. There's only about ten of us in here. Game on the television. Three guys sitting together at a table watching the game. A guy comes in and I can feel the cold air blowing in on my legs. Big guy. Sits over at the end of the bar, over where Harry and Mike are now. Has the hood of his coat covering his head. Then another guy comes in a minute later and takes a seat at a table behind everyone else. The guy at the bar orders a beer. In a bottle."

Rose looked over at Harry who was reading a magazine. She knocked on the top of the bar to get his attention. Harry looked up, gave a slight shake of his head, and went back to reading the magazine.

Rose looked at me and smiled. "I've reached my limit," she said. "Harry looks out for me. He cares about me. It's important to have someone in your life that cares about you, Eileen. He's a good man."

She looked around the bar, as if unsure what to do next. She lit a cigarette and looked at herself in the mirror behind the bottles of liquor.

"What happened after the guy ordered the beer?" I asked.

"What?" said Rose.

"You were telling me about the night guys tried to rob the bar."

"Oh, yeah," Rose smiled. "That's right. Yeah, the big guy orders a beer. Then a minute later another guy comes in and sits at the other end of the bar. I mean, no one finds anything strange about any of that. It's a bar. Guys come and go all night. Except for Paul. I guess he found it strange, for whatever reason."

"He was already here?"

"Oh, yeah. We were lucky he was."

"So, what happened?"

"The guy who ordered the beer finishes it and puts a ten dollar bill on the bar. Harry gets a beer for the guy who came in last, then walks down to the other end to pick up the ten dollars. When he reaches for it, the big guy grabs his arm and tugs him into the bar and sticks a gun in his face. Then the other two guys stand and they have guns in their hands. They're yelling that no one moves or they'll start shooting."

"Where's Paul sitting?"

"He's in one of the booths. I think he was watching the game and nursing a beer. We had talked for a few minutes when he first came in. Before I even knew what was going on, the big guy hits Harry in the face with the gun, and yells at him to empty the register. Harry fell back, dazed, blood suddenly on his face. I must have screamed. The guy standing behind me yells for me to shut up. Someone told me later that he was moving towards me like he was going to hit me. That was when I heard the first gun shot."

"Who was shooting?" I asked.

"Paul. The guy in front of Harry was suddenly down, his hands trying to stop the blood coming out of his neck. I screamed again. I don't remember what happened after that. I guess I was in shock. But Harry did and he told me. Paul came out of the booth and shot the guy who was standing in the middle of the room. Shot him in the chest and the guy fell backwards onto a table, then the floor. The guy who was coming at me, turned and shot at Paul, who was charging at him. The bullet grazed Paul's arm as he barreled into the guy, and they crashed into the bar, Paul coming up on top of the guy and punching him until he was unconscious. Harry came out from behind the bar and stomped on the guy who was shot in the chest who was trying to get up and pick up his gun."

"Wow," I said.

"Later, I asked Paul why he didn't just let the guys take

the money. Someone could have gotten killed. We all could have gotten killed."

"What did he say?"

"Paul said he knew the guy was going to hit me. He couldn't allow that, he said."

"One of the guys died?" I asked, remembering the newspaper story.

"The big guy shot in the neck. The other two are now in prison. You know, Harry didn't think those guys were here just to rob the place. Tuesday night business would hardly pay for their gas. He said they were here to kill him, make it look like a robbery gone bad."

"Why would they want to kill Harry?"

"At first, Harry thought it was because of the color of his skin and that he owned a bar. But Paul did some digging and came up with something. Seems that the guy who was killed, he was friends with a couple of young guys Harry had caused trouble for years before, and then the friends disappeared. Harry doesn't talk about that."

Harry Mills came to stand in front of us. "Can I get you another?" he asked me.

"I'm good," I said.

"Rose," Harry said, "if you're ready, Mike said he'd walk you home."

Rose smiled and nodded, carefully sliding off the stool. Balding Mike was a stocky, middle aged man. He was dressed in a tee shirt and tan colored shorts. As he walked over, Rose smiled at him and put her arm in his.

"Nice talking to you, Rose?" I said.

"You, too," she answered as she walked away.

I paid for my drink. When Harry gave me the change, he said, "We all have our demons."

'Ain't that the truth', I thought as I walked out the door.

IT WAS MAYBE two weeks later, I walked in to Harry's Bar and sat beside Rose again. She remembered me. It was nine-thirty and Rose looked like she had already reached her limit. The ashtray held six cigarettes. She wore black slacks, white buttoned short sleeve blouse and a black beret. She looked very cute and seemed to be in good spirits.

"Eileen," she said as I sat down. "Where have you been?"

"Busy, Rose. Very busy. How are you?"

"I'm really good. This round is on me. Harry," she said to Harry Mills as he walked towards where we sat, "I'm going to buy my friend, Eileen, a drink." Rose looked at me. "What'll you have?"

Smiling at Harry, I said, "I think a Manhattan."

"Manhattan for my friend, and I think I'll have one of those, too."

Harry frowned.

Rose's smile was positively wicked. "One more, dear friend, and I shall sleep the sleep of the innocent. How can you deny me that? And Eileen should not have to drink alone."

Harry chuckled and made our drinks. Rose and I toasted each other.

We talked while we sipped at our drinks, chatting about nothing of importance, and I could tell that Rose enjoyed our conversation. She was quite animated, giggled when she thought something humorous had been said, either by me or her, and, despite the amount of alcohol she had probably consumed, kept the volume low and her manner ladylike. Which pleased me. I've been around enough alcoholics to know they can be loud, obnoxious, and their mood can turn ugly on a word.

Harry walked towards us when he saw the glasses were empty.

"Harry, I'll escort Rose home this evening," I said.

His eyebrows raised. Rose said, "Oh, you don't have to, Eileen."

"I want to," I said. "It's a beautiful night for a walk." And so I did. She lived about a quarter of a mile up the Boulevard in a lovely looking ranch styled home of brick.

"You want to come in for a nightcap?" Rose asked.

I declined, wished her a goodnight, and went back to my car. It would be a month before I went back to Harry's

Bar.

I NOTICED ROSE sitting at the bar and she was in a conversation with that guy Mike who had escorted her home my first night in Harry's, so I decided to take a booth. Within a minute, Harry came.

"Eileen", he said, smiling. "Nice to see you again. What can I get you?"

"Quiet night," I said.

"Summer's over."

"Maybe. Still hot during the day. I think a Manhattan, Harry."

I had a lot on my mind and barely noticed him when he came in. He sat at the bar and it seemed he and Harry had some silly dialogue going on, but I couldn't hear what it was. I didn't realize it was Paul Costa until he began looking around the room. He looked just like his picture in the newspaper.

I had been thinking about Paul Costa for a while. Even before my talk with Rose. I thought about approaching him at the bar and introducing myself, and I'm not beyond that kind of aggressiveness, but I had a sense that he would find that unbecoming. So, when Harry came to ask if I wanted another drink, I replied that I did, and that I wanted to buy the gentleman at the bar one, also. It was fifty-fifty he would come to my table to thank me. He did.

He stood beside my booth and said some ice breaking line that I don't remember, but I don't recall it being an eye-rolling one. I invited him to join me. Which he did.

I studied him closely while we got introductions out of the way. He was at least ten years older than me. He had that dark Italian complexion that I was used to. His hair was dark brown, thick and in need of cutting, with a hairline just beginning to recede. Having been a hairstylist, hair is always the first thing I notice about people. Then their eyes. Paul's eyes were brown, tired and kind looking. There was a slight scar in the eyebrow above his right eye. The nose was crooked and fit his face perfectly. I think if I had imagined his face, I would have imagined a crooked nose. It made him look rugged, as did his broad shoulders. A man who could take care of himself, is the impression I got. His lips were thick and curved, and when he wasn't talking they appeared to be the lips of a man who held a cynical view of life.

Obviously, I knew what he did for a living, but I didn't want him to know that. So, I inquired. We spoke a little about being a private eye, and I playfully asked if he was on a stakeout, watching someone who was in the bar. I made a serious mistake when I asked if he had ever shot anyone. Not cool. I think it almost ended our conversation. But we got past it. We moved on to talk about me and my separation. I noticed he was much more comfortable discussing me than he was discussing him. I also noticed, and wasn't surprised, that he seemed to notice everything. That's to be expected from a man in his profession. Nothing escaped him. Even my designer bag, and the bruise on my arm, when I reached into it for the cigarettes. This was a man a girl needed to be careful around. Very careful. He'd pick-up on everything. Before I left the booth, he promised to buy me a drink should we ever meet again. Which we did a week later in Harry's.

It was during this second meeting where we talked of more important things. He knew from our first conversation that I was going through a divorce. I made that very plain. But, even while talking about the emotional impact that was having on my life, I made sure Paul understood that I wasn't adverse to a relationship that moved along slowly.

Slowly, being a relative term.

31

Ben Landry, my husband of seven years, was sitting at my kitchen table when I came into the house carrying two bags of groceries.

"What are you doing here, Benny?" I said, laying the bags on the counter. He hates when I call him Benny, instead of Ben, and I do it when he pisses me off. "You're supposed to call before coming here. Judge told you that."

"I thought you'd be home," he said, as if that explained his disregarding the court order.

"What do you want?"

He took a sip from the can of cola he had taken from my fridge. Ben Landry has an infuriating way of taking a great deal of time before answering questions. And it's not like he's thinking of which answer to give, either. He just likes the attention he gets in anticipation of what he's going to say. Just one of the things he does that irks the shit out of me. Just one of many.

"Listen, Sweetheart, I've been thinking. My lawyer called today. Said we've got a court date on December eighth."

I turned from putting cans in the cabinet, to face him. "Yeah?"

"What's the rush? I've been thinking, Eileen. Maybe we should reconsider this. Maybe I was a little rash in getting angry over your always complaining."

"You mean this is my fault?" I said. Benny is never at fault for anything. Another thing that irks me.

"Can we forget about who's fault it is for a minute?" Ben said, frowning. "Can we just agree that maybe we might put the brakes on this thing for a little bit. Give us time to think. I mean, what's the rush? We're separated. I'm not living here. I've given you plenty of space,

Eileen. No pressure. You know that."

"You moved out," I said.

"You gave me no choice, Eileen. You were driving me crazy."

"You're the one who brought up divorce," I said.

"I know, I know. I was under a lot of pressure, Sweetheart. You know what it's like sometimes. I just had a lot on my mind. But I've had plenty of time to think about it now, and I don't want to get divorced."

"Well, I do."

Ben Landry looked surprised. "Oh, now you do. You serious?"

"I was thinking about it even before you brought it up," I said. "I'd like a little bit more out of life than an absent husband."

"What are you talking about, Eileen? I was home almost every night."

"Yeah, always with something on your mind, and it wasn't me."

"Is this the sex thing again? Jesus Christ, you're like a broken record."

"Listen, Ben, I'd like you to go now. Please. I'm not in the mood tonight. Please, just go."

He sat there, sipping away, looking at me with eyes, behind thick lenses, that always appeared bigger than they were. Finally, he stood, took an envelope from his coat pocket, tossed it on the table, and said, "Think about what I said, Eileen. You have a good life here. Don't blow it."

After I heard the door close, I thought that I should have told him to leave the key. He probably would have laughed at me, but I should have asked.

PAUL AND I had made plans for later that week for dinner at the Kowloon, I think it was. An actual date. A meeting away from the bar. Maybe a movie after, maybe not. It was a nice time. I told him what I was planning on doing after the divorce, that I was thinking of going back to being a hairdresser again. I also told him Benny was a

CPA, when he asked. But that was all I said about Ben Landry. I didn't want to tell him who he was an accountant for. After dinner, instead of a movie, we took a nice drive along the coast, then stopped at Harry's for a nightcap.

It was a Friday night, big crowd, and a band playing in the corner. We danced a few dances, then Paul drove me home. I kissed him at my door. I was thinking of inviting him in, but it was a little early in our relationship for that. But soon. I would need to do it soon.

So it was that the following week I brought up the idea of spending a weekend in New York City. Sharing a hotel room, and a queen size bed, was the surest way in taking the next step in our relationship. I told Paul it was to celebrate my court date in December for the divorce. I was very pleased when he quickly agreed. I was fairly certain he found me physically attractive, but I could see in his eyes that the idea of having me in an obvious romantic setting was something he very much wanted. The look in his eyes that night, the look of anticipation, was a look I had never seen in my husband's eyes.

That night Marie Glendali came into Harry's, and Paul told me what had happened to her years before. I had never heard that story. I had seen Marie only a few times before, always with her father and at some festive occasion. I had never been introduced to her, so she wouldn't know me from Eve. The few times I have seen her, I have always been impressed by her beauty. Her look. She is a short woman, an inch or two over five feet, with those Italian curves that I friggin' envy. Her black hair is always perfect. The style exactly what I would have chosen for her. Her make-up impeccable. Marie is a beautiful woman, no way around it, and I am jealous of such beauty. Don't get me wrong, I'm a great looking broad, but Marie Glendali has the kind of beauty the great masters would want to paint on canvas for the world to admire for eternity. Or a Hollywood director would want on a huge theater screen.

Anyways, I was touched by the intimacy I witnessed

between Marie and Harry that night. Her fondness for him was obvious. The way she touched his hand, the tilt of her head when he was speaking, the genuine smile at what he was saying, her hand on his cheek just before she left. And Harry, he was like those black children in Africa you see in magazines who are suddenly in the presence of Princess Di, all smiles and bashfulness. Very cute. I have never had that kind of effect on any man. But that doesn't mean I wasn't still trying.

The weekend in New York was wonderful. That first night, dinner in Little Italy, tickets for *Phantom,* drinks in the hotel bar, and sex. Late into the night sex.

Saturday, after a walk around the city during the afternoon, a replay of the day before. Dinner in Chinatown, *Les Miz,* a bottle of vodka for the room, and rounds three and four in bed. I dozed off on the ride home Sunday.

And then, when we got back, a few seconds after Paul kissed me good bye at my door, the doorbell rang. I had smiled, thinking he was looking for one more romp before going home. But when I opened the door, Ben was standing there.

"Who was that?" he asked angrily.

"None of your business," I said, angry that he was there. I stood in the doorway, barring his entrance.

"I'll find out who he is," Ben said. "And it is my business. You're still my wife."

"This marriage is over, Ben. Go back to your apartment."

"Where were you today? Were you with him last night? I called you last night. No one answered."

"Well, I'm answering you now, Benny. Go away."

His foot shot out as I began closing the door. "Are you fucking him?"

"Jesus, Ben, stop. I don't have to answer to you."

His face was getting redder by the second. His fist closed. I thought he might hit me.

"You're a whore, Eileen," Ben hissed at me. "A cheap whore. My mother told me you were. That I was making a mistake marrying you. I should have listened to her."

"Move your foot, Benny," I demanded.

"A two-bit whore."

"Move your fucking foot," I yelled at him, and put my weight into the door.

Ben cursed loudly as the door slammed shut.

"You're still my wife," he said, loud enough for me to hear. Loud enough for the neighbors to hear. "You better start acting like it." Then he was gone. I heard a car start and looked out the side window in time to see his Mercedes pulling away.

I leaned against the door, shaking. The whole ordeal, everything that was going on, had me on edge. Some nights I couldn't even sleep, worried if I was doing the right thing, worried if I'd survive it.

I grabbed my coat and the car keys. I needed to talk and relax. I needed to calm down. I needed to go to him. I drove through the gathering dusk and parked in front of the house. Hurrying up to the door, I pushed hard on the bell, impatient, hoping he was home. And then the door opened.

"Eileen. What are you doing here?"

I stepped past him into the house, then turned and fell into him, my arms clinging to his body.

"Hold me, Ernie. Just fucking hold me."

"SO THAT'S WHERE you were all weekend? With Costa? You told me you were going to visit your mother. Jesus, Eileen. I don't believe you. You slept with him? Are you serious now? How am I suppose to react to that?"

"Not you, too?" I said, shaking my head. Are all men the same? Ernie knew what was at stake. Then he said, "I feel like putting your head through the wall."

"What did you think when I told you what I was doing?" I asked. "Did you think Paul and I would just be friends? Dinner, dancing, drinks, innocent kisses on the cheek at my door and wishes for sweet dreams? How long do you think that would have lasted?"

"I don't know what I thought," Ernie Mancini said as he paced in front of me. "I thought it was a bad idea at best, and, probably, nothing would come from it."

"You never said it was a bad idea," I said. "Not that it matters. And, what? You didn't think I could get a man interested in me?"

"I didn't say that," he said, stopping in front of me, towering over me where I sat.

"I got you interested easy enough," I said.

Ernie Mancini plopped his ass down on the sofa, shaking his head at me and frowning.

"I don't like it," he said. "That's all. I don't like that you're sleeping with him."

I stood, walked to him, slid in between his knees, took his head in my hands and cradled it against my body.

"I know, baby, I know," I said. "I held off as long as I could. I knew you'd be upset. But we're playing a dangerous game here. How long do you think a man like Paul would be with a woman if she wasn't treating him like a man?"

"So, how long do you have to be with him?" Ernie's rough hands circled me, grabbing my ass and pulling me even closer.

I was running the fingers of one hand through his thick black hair, the other hand caressing a cheek in need of a shave.

"The court date is December eighth," I said. "I don't think anything will happen before then. But who knows. I think we wait a little while longer."

He slid up the cushions to the edge of the sofa until his crotch met my knee. I could feel him. I kissed the top of his head. Ernie Mancini was a twenty-six year old hot-headed Italian. But I knew how to handle him.

"I've missed you, baby," I whispered in his ear. "Missed you bad. You going out with the boys tonight, or do you have time to give me what I need?"

Ernie stood, his strong hands lifting me like I was light as a feather. Ernie wasn't much of a talker, or a thinker, but he was a damn good doer.

32

Paul called the following morning, waking me from a deep sleep. His tone was light, but I detected something in it that had me curious. I asked if everything was okay, he said it was. I would find out later that Benny had called him. Ben Landry was not only boring, he was predictable. That would work to my advantage. Paul asked about getting together that night, but I begged off. I was one sore broad and needed a few days to recover. Ernie Mancini could get a little rough in his love making, but after finding out I had spent the weekend with Paul, Ernie was out to prove something. Anyways, I made a date with Paul for Wednesday night for drinks at Harry's.

Wednesday night, while I was getting ready to leave for Harry's, I came out of the bathroom and Ben was sitting at the kitchen table.

"Going out, Eileen?" he asked. "Going to see your boyfriend?"

"What do you want, Ben?"

"A drink would be nice. Some conversation. Ask me how my day was."

I stood staring at him.

"We need to talk," he said. "Get me a drink."

Ben enjoyed seven and seven. It was all he drank after six o'clock. I made one up for him and took a seat across from him.

"I saw the old man today," he said after taking a sip. "Told him you wanted to get a divorce. He wasn't pleased."

"Why'd you bring him into this?" I asked angrily. "It's not his business."

Ben frowned. "Don't be naive, Eileen. He wants to talk to us."

"I see no reason to talk with him. I'm not going to change my mind."

When I had first sued for divorce, I hadn't considered Joseph Glendali would interfere. Or even care. But Ernie must have, because he said the same thing to me at the time. 'Don't be naive, Eileen.' I decided I wasn't going to allow the old man to become a roadblock in my plan, but he could become a speed bump. So plan A was dropped and Plan B was formed. And that was when Paul entered the equation. Naive? No, I don't think so.

"I wouldn't ignore the old man, Eileen," Ben said, a smirk on his face that he liked to show when he thought he held the upper hand. "He has concerns, concerns that you better take seriously. And I told him who your boyfriend is."

He smirked again. "Got his plate number the other night. Called in a favor. Paul Costa. Really? That the best you can do? A private detective who lives in a cheap condo in Saugus? Well, what can you expect from a woman who used to cut hair."

"Finish your drink, Benny, and leave," I said. "You show up again, and I'll get a restraining order. You understand?"

"Drop the divorce, Eileen. Do yourself a favor, and drop it. We'll work things out. I'll forget all of this. Past will be the past. We'll move on."

I frowned at him. He shrugged, and stood. "Think about it, Eileen. Be smart." Then he walked slowly down the stairs and out the door.

Christ, that man could try my patience. But I was planning on having the last laugh.

WHEN I ENTERED Harry's, I saw Paul at the bar and I went straight to a booth. Paul came over carrying a drink for me. He asked if everything was okay, I think I replied it is now. We joked back and forth for a bit, and then he told me Ben had left a message on his phone and he had done a little investigating into Ben Landry. I wasn't surprised by that. It was bound to happen. But I had to act like I was not happy that he was digging into my life. Paul apologized, but I had to finally agree that maybe I should have told him who my husband was.

Then he began explaining to me the danger I might be in with the mob if I went through with the divorce.

"But I don't know anything about his business, Paul," I had said.

He said they wouldn't know that, or believe it. That Glendali couldn't afford to believe it. I acted like it was the first time hearing this. That I had never given it a thought. When I nervously stubbed out a cigarette, I saw that Paul noticed a bruise on my arm. Like I said, those big hands of Ernst Mancini can be rough sometimes. But I had wanted Paul to see the bruise, just like I had wanted him to see the one on my wrist that first night we talked. He didn't say anything about the bruise, but his face colored just a bit, his mouth turned down, and his eyes turned cold. I wasn't surprised. I was still forming opinions about Paul Costa, but one opinion I had formed early on, he would protect me, or any woman, with his life. I had heard about how fierce a man he could be, and I had just seen that fierceness in his face. I was counting on it. But not yet. I made him promise me he would not hurt Benny, or interact with him at all. He said he wouldn't.

That Saturday night, we were back at Harry's. The place was packed, a group was in playing the oldies, and I was looking forward to dancing the night away. Paul was a willing partner, and it was a fun night. At one point, as we walked back to our table, I looked over at the bar and saw Ernie sitting there with Bobby. Bobby was talking, Ernie was looking at me and Paul. If looks could kill. I was nervous the dumb Wop would make a scene and ruin everything, but, thank God, he didn't.

But I can be a royal bitch sometimes, especially after a few drinks. After my third Manhattan, my dancing became a bit risque and I was hugging and kissing Paul as we walked from the dance floor to our table. I glanced over at Ernie. God, I could tell he was pissed. I smiled.

He stood and walked out of the bar, Bobby looking around wondering what the hell had just happened. Bobby had no idea Ernie and I had been screwing around the past year. No one did.

I have to admit, I was a little juiced up from the dancing and the booze and the anticipation of having Paul in my bed later, but when I thought of what Ernie would be like when I saw him again, I was wet and trembling by the time we left the bar.

As soon as we pulled out of the driveway, I reached for Paul's zipper. And then I told him to park. I couldn't wait. Oh, God, what a night that was. I felt real affection for Paul that night. Yeah, really, I did.

PAUL HAD A busy week, or so he said, and I didn't hear from him until Friday night when he asked me if I was free for a dress up party Saturday night. When the words 'dress up' and 'party' are in the same sentence, count me in. It had been a while. Saturday, from my closet, I dug out the shortest, tightest black dress. I worked on my hair and make-up. When Paul picked me up that night, his eyes told me I had made good choices.

My week had been kind of boring. I had talked with my friend about going back to work in her salon, but I really wasn't expecting I would be doing that. I had other ideas. Plans that were much grander.

Something I was expecting, however, but that didn't happen, was a call from Ernie demanding we get together. I would have bet the mortgage jealous Ernie Mancini would have been eager to remind me he was still in the picture. But I guess he decided he would punish me with the silent treatment. He could be such a boy sometimes. I never did ask him if that was what he was doing, deciding to let it pass. Which it did. A few days after the party, he knocked softly on my backdoor. I discouraged him from coming to my house, never knowing when Benny would barge in, and we were both dead if Ernie was there should he do that. But poor Ernie looked so pathetic standing there, I let him come in. A few hours later he left, strutting from my bedroom like he was the biggest, baddest cock in the hen house.

As far as the party in a mansion out on the Neck, what a fantastic night that was. I had gotten used to parties where Italian guys, in shiny expensive suits, talked loud, laughed loud, and swore at decibel levels that rivaled crowds at football games. And their wives, or girlfriends, hung out in separate rooms, the wives talking about their kids, the girlfriends, all dressed like prostitutes on the streets of Rome, talking about their hairdressers and manicurists, and women who weren't there.

But the party at Peter Gladstone's place was top notch. Money. The place, and those in attendance, reeked of it. The dresses, the jewelry, the conversation, the food; wow! Gladstone was very charming. As were most of the men. The women were a bit stand-offish. Understandable. I wasn't put off by their attitude. I was pleased by it. I looked good enough to be considered a threat. And then I ran into Chance.

Chance and I knew each other from before. She was with a woman named Mary Hamilton. The three of us had a great time. Mary talked me into trying this little blue pill. The night became a blur after that. All I know is, my stomach ached from laughing so hard. What fun. And to top it off, I got to spend the rest of the night in Paul's bed, and then spending a Sunday morning like I used to enjoy before marrying Ben Landry.

Speaking of my four-eyed soon to be ex, he stopped by a few days after the party to tell me, again, to call things off with Paul. Then he tells me he went to Paul's office to tell him to stay away from me. That I was a married woman. Then Ben said that Paul threatened him, but didn't have the balls to do anything more than that. Benny the tough guy. I told him I doubted that. That he wasn't man enough to stand up to a guy like Paul. Big talk. No action. Boy, did that piss him off. He got all red and stomped out of the house.

That Friday night, Paul and I had a date. I decided to roil the waters a bit. When he pulled up to my house, I was already outside. I got in the car, not waiting for him to open my door.

"You threatened, Benny?" I said angrily.

Caught off guard, Paul said, "Eileen, he threatened me. He came to my office and threatened me. What would you have me do?"

"Benny would never threaten anyone. I asked you to stay away from him."

"He came to my office," said Paul, and I could see he was frustrated, and getting angry.

"But he would never hurt anyone."

"The bruises on your arm say differently."

"He didn't mean them, Paul. He's just upset that I'm seeing another man. He's not violent."

Then Paul said something that made me say, "You want to call this off?" I said that harshly. He reacted like I had slapped him. It was a question that could have escalated the argument into an ugly thing, or it could have put the brakes on the discussion. Paul took in a deep breath, and then said we should go to dinner and discuss plans he had for the weekend. A leaf-peeping ride to the Berkshires with a night at a B&B. Crisis averted. Groundwork laid. The important thing was to keep Paul away from Ben until it was time.

That weekend was a delight. Leaves still held color, restaurants were good and the B&B was romantic. On the way home, I remember I talked about my marriage and Benny's shortcomings without being too cruel. Then I mentioned that Benny had been stopping by the house more and more recently. But I didn't go on and on about it. Paul listened, but had little to say.

The house was dark when Paul dropped me off. I left my carryall at the top of the stairs and put on the kitchen light, desiring a cup of tea. On the kitchen table was a jewelry case, a lovely diamond necklace inside, along with a note that said, *It can still be good, Eileen. Ben.*

It was now almost a month before the court date and things were progressing slowly but surely. And then Joseph Glendali decided to stick his big Italian nose into our business, throwing a wrench into my plan, a plan that was tenuous at best to begin with. It was a plan that was worth trying before doing what Ernie had said we should do. But Ernie wasn't a thinker. Think bulls and china shops, and that's Ernie. It all may come down to that, but I wanted to try it my way first. And then the old man got involved.

33

Paul and I were sitting in "our" booth at Harry's. I don't even remember what we were talking about, nothing important I'm sure, when Joseph Glendali was suddenly standing beside our table, and it startled me. He remembered my name, which kind of surprised me, and asked if he could join us. I didn't like that idea, but what could I do? It was the man himself.

He talked with Paul. He told him that he knew his father in the old days, which, I could see, surprised Paul. The father ran numbers. These Wops, they all have something going on the side. It wouldn't surprise me if Father Phil, the priest from my old parish, ran numbers for the mob, or took bets on the Sunday football games. It's in their blood, I swear.

Anyways, eventually the talk got around to me and my forthcoming divorce. Then the Don and Paul started talking in Italian, like I wasn't sitting there. And that pissed me off. But it was the old man, so what could I do? I knew Paul would tell me what was said after Glendali left.

Then Glendali spoke to me. He looked tired, his smile was kindly, but his eyes were not.

"Eileen," he said, "your husband loves you very much. Time has a way of healing things. Please, don't rush into anything. Take your time. Make sure you are doing the right thing." Blah, blah, blah.

Stuff like that. But, while he sounded so caring, there was no mistaking the warning in his words. It unsettled me a bit. Paul had warned me that my divorce could be a problem for the Don. Ernie had warned me of the same thing. I couldn't see how, because I knew nothing of Ben's business, or of the affairs of the Glendali family. So I thought their warnings to be mostly unwarranted.

But a few words from the old man, the soft tone in which they were said, his eyes never wavering from mine, I began to realize I may be entering a dangerous situation if I were to go ahead with the divorce.

I was rattled by the time Glendali bid us good evening. I lay awake most of that night working through what it meant to me and what I had planned. I fell asleep without knowing my next steps, only that I had to do something. I had moved from Plan A to Plan B with luck and wiles. It was time to come up with a Plan C.

I have to say my nerves were soothed a little two mornings later by a story I read in the newspaper about a shoot out at a restaurant on Route One, and Paul's phone call telling me about it. I wasn't doubting choosing Paul Costa for my plan, but his part in the gun play only made me feel better.

We were getting together that night, and I decided I wouldn't mention seeing the story in the Globe, and if he didn't bring it up neither would I. But that news story helped me decide on Plan C.

THE SATURDAY AFTER Joseph Glendali had sat with us, Paul and I had a simple date planned. Dinner, a movie, drinks at Harry's. But I had woken up feeling nervous. Feeling that I needed to move things along at a faster pace. And I knew what I had to do.

Stepping into a hot shower, I let the water run over me, relaxing me, allowing my mind to go to a quiet place. Toweling off, I walked naked to the huge five drawer heavy maple dresser than stands five feet tall. The dresser is solid maple, none of that plastic veneer, and cost a fortune. The dresser is almost four feet wide, and the huge drawers curve out with elaborate brass pull rings in their center. I pulled the second drawer from the top out about a foot. This drawer held my under garments. The middle drawer held my nightgowns and I pulled that one out a little further than the one above it.

From the middle drawer, I took a light-blue opaque nightgown and laid it on the bed. From the one above it, I took red thong panties and laid them on the bed beside the nightgown. I then took a deep breath, two quick steps, and hurled myself against the open drawers as hard as I could. The ribs on my left side impacted the top drawer, the middle drawer, pulled out just a little more, caught me in the area between my ribs and my hip bone. I crashed to the floor and cried out in pain.

Using the bed, I pulled myself up. I knew if I laid on the floor more than a few seconds, I would stay there until I lost my nerve. I quickly took a big step and hurled myself into the drawers again with so much force a jewelry box I had on top of the dresser crashed to the floor. As did I.

I laid there sobbing, my breathing labored, the pain incredibly intense. I may have fallen asleep on the floor, curled up like a child, or I had passed out, but I woke up about an hour later, my body throbbing. In the bathroom, looking into a mirror, I took a facecloth and cleaned up some dried blood from a scrape on my hip bone. My side was already a purplish horror. Bile rose in me, but I swallowed it down. I got dressed in the nightgown and robe, brewed coffee in the kitchen, did my best to get comfortable, and waited for Paul to call.

When he called, I begged off our plans, said I wasn't feeling well, suggested he come with a movie and pizza.

I don't know how I made it through the day and the movie, so intense was the pain. I loaded up with aspirin, which did little to help. Paul wasn't going to stay, but I insisted, saying I just wanted to cuddle. I needed him to stay. Sometime during the night, I played with him until he finally woke up. Then, with soft moans, I straddled him in the dark. I lifted my nightgown so his hands could fondle, and teased him until he had had enough of my teasing. When he moved to be on top, I let out a scream.

"What's wrong?" he asked, concerned.

He went for the light switch, I knew he would, and I was making a poor attempt at dropping the nightgown that was above my breasts. When the lights came on, he saw the bruises.

"When was he here?" Paul demanded.

I told Paul I had slipped and fallen down the steps. I played that tune for a minute, but finally confessed that Ben had been here. That he was angry. That I was frightened of him for the very first time. That he had a strange look about him.

I told him Ben was telling me we could work things out. That we shouldn't divorce. That I would have to stop seeing my boyfriend. When I refused, he threw me against the kitchen cabinets. Picked me up and threw me on the floor. Kicked me in the side. Threatened me before he left that I better drop the divorce.

The look on Paul's face frightened the hell out of me. If Benny had been there, Paul would have killed him. I was sure of it. He would have beaten the shit out of him.

I then made a big deal out of saying he couldn't hurt Ben. That this would all be over in another month. That I was a big girl and I could take it. That he wasn't to do anything. I could tell by the way Paul looked, and the words he said to calm me, that if he ever saw Ben Landry he would hurt him bad for what he was doing to me. Maybe even kill him.

But I wouldn't take any chances. I'd make sure of it.

And then the old man stepped in again. Damn that man. But that wasn't until December. First came Thanksgiving, and a trip back to the old neighborhood.

MY SISTER, PATRICIA, lives in a house three streets over from where we had grown up in Brooklyn. She was hosting Thanksgiving dinner this year. I hadn't been back to the neighborhood in five years, and I wasn't crazy about being there, but I did feel the need to get away for a while just to have time to think. Ten minutes after walking into her house, I regretted being there.

Patty, and her husband, Fred, have three kids. Two daughters, seven and nine, and a boy who is six. Right away they warmed to me, and I to them, like a Popsicle stuck in a snowbank. They're good kids, polite and well-mannered, but me and kids operate on different wave lengths. They picked up on that pretty quick, like city kids can, making sure they were always sitting far from me in any room we were in, and keeping conversation to a minimum.

It was obvious the kids were the joy in my sister's life, and she lived for them. I think she enjoys telling me about the stuff they do in school, how smart they are, how well behaved, and I don't think she does it in a mean way, trying to show me how empty my life is because I don't have kids. She's not that type. My younger sister is a loving person.

Me, on the other hand, pops into her home wearing a designer dress, designer coat, designer bag, rock on my ring finger, my new diamond necklace, and shoes that cost more than her weekly food bill. She was showing me one life, I was showing her another. Neither had an affect on the other. Just a waste of our energy and time.

I had spent the night in my old room in the house where I grew up. My mother, having gotten the house in the divorce, still lived there with her second husband, Charlie. They seemed happy enough. Charlie was grossly overweight, collecting disability, and enjoyed watching sports on television and drinking beer. Ma had her neighborhood friends, and they got together most afternoons to play canasta, or 45's, or some card game. I had no idea. And she had taken up crochet. Crochet for Christ's sake. Sitting there in the evenings crocheting, while her fat husband watched the Rangers, drank beer and farted. Yeah. The old neighborhood. If I spent more than two days there, I'd kill myself.

I told her I was getting a divorce. 'Good for you', she said. 'Take him for everything he's got.' That, and a lot more, I thought to myself.

The day after Thanksgiving, I saw my dad. He lived ten blocks away from Patty. We had a nice visit. His third wife, Georgina, a bleach-blonde bundle of energy, is wonderful, and she treats dad great. They seem to get along, and, after two failed marriages, I'm happy to see he has found someone who makes him happy. He had no comments when I told him I was getting divorced, but I could tell by the look he gave me that he was concerned. He knew what Ben did for a living. At his door, when I was getting my coat on after a pleasant visit, dad asked me if I knew what I was doing, divorcing the mob's accountant. I told him not to worry. I'd be fine. That I had it all under control.

And I had thought I did. My plan, if I pulled it off, was solid. Then, like I said, I come back home, wait patiently for the right time, and, boom, Joseph Glendali butts himself into the picture again. The old S.O.B.

34

It was the morning of the first Sunday in December, less than a week before my court date, when the phone rang. I thought it might be Paul calling to say his plans had changed and we could get together later. Instead, it was Mr. Glendali's bodyguard, a man named Vincent, who said the Don wanted to see me at his house in Nahant. There would be a car to pick me up at one. Could I be ready? I don't know anyone alive who has refused a request from Joseph Glendali, so of course I would be ready.

The black Cadillac pulled up in front of my house at exactly one o'clock. My Ernie was driving. I started to get in the front, he told me to get in the back. Which I did.

"What's going on, Ernie?" I asked as soon as he began driving away.

"No idea. They just told me to come and get you. Did you request the meet or did they summon you?"

"They called me," I said. "I'd never call them. What do you think it means?" I was worried, and I know I sounded worried.

"I don't know what it means, baby. You try and figure out what the old man is thinking, your brain could cramp. Know what I mean? Your boyfriend was at the house couple weeks ago. Did he tell you?"

"Don't call him that," I said. "You're my boyfriend."

"That's what I thought, too, Eileen," Ernie said, looking at me through the rearview. "Lately, I'm having doubts."

Like I didn't have enough on my mind. Christ. "I'll come over Tuesday night, baby," I said, smiling sweetly into the mirror, "and take care of those doubts."

His mouth frowned, but his eyes brightened.

"Do you know what Glendali and Paul talked about?" I asked. Those two having conversations wasn't part of my plan. It was after Paul had seen the bruises, so I had a pretty good idea why he went there, but I wasn't happy that he did.

"No idea. I was outside. Vincent said something to him before he left, don't know what. With Vincent, you never know if he's warning someone, or if he's asking if they want to take in a Red Sox game. Know what I mean?"

I've never had a conversation with Vincent. He always walked into parties with the old man, and walked out with him. In between, he stood by himself and watched. I never saw anyone approach him, never saw a drink in his hand. Never saw an expression on his face that gave away the mood he was in. Vincent was a scary mother. He was probably as short as that dispatcher in that funny show *Taxi,* certainly better looking, but even from across a room, there was a vibe about the guy that was quite unpleasant.

"You know, Eileen, I know you think you have this thing figured out," said Ernie, looking in the mirror again, "but you should have let me do this my way. I could have taken care of Ben months ago. We'd be down in Argentina now lying on a beach, soaking up the sun, and living off the money he stole."

Like I've said, bull in a china shop.

"You think? Ben Landry gets killed by a mysterious gunman. A month later, I disappear, as does the Don's personal driver. You don't think the old man is smart enough to figure out what happened. What do you think? Four, five months later, we wake up in bed and Vincent is standing over us. You think it would take him that long to find us?"

"How's he do that, Eileen? It's a big world."

"Not big enough when your enemy is Joseph Glendali," I said. "As long as he knows who pulled the trigger, and then I disappear, he may not come looking.

He'll be happy to have me gone."

"Don't be so sure, Eileen."

Ernie wasn't doing anything for my nerves. When we got on the road to Nahant, I leaned forward and ran my fingers through Ernie's thick hair.

"Baby," I said, "if this was a one way drive, you'd tell me, wouldn't you? I mean, you'd never drive me there if you knew I'd be in danger, right?"

"You're going to his home, Eileen," said Ernie, frowning at me in the mirror. "His home. Marie's there. She'd never allow it. I can't speak about after you leave. Be smart, baby. Say all the right words. Make the man happy. Give us time to figure something out, okay. Just keep that fucking temper of yours, will you please. And watch your mouth."

"What do you mean?"

"You know exactly what I mean, Eileen. Now sit back. We're almost there. And until we're back on this road again, don't give me one look, or a word, that might arouse curiosity in Vincent. Understand? He picks up on everything."

I leaned back as we passed the restaurant at the end of the road, my body a bundle of nerves. When the gate opened onto the Don's property, I was surprised to see Ben's maroon Mercedes parked in the driveway. I suppose I shouldn't have been, but I was. Once inside the house, the surprises kept coming.

Don Glendali greeted me at the door with a kiss on each cheek, placed my arm in his, and escorted me to the living room, thanking me for meeting with him as we took small steps. He was dressed in dark gray wool slacks, a white dress shirt and light gray cardigan, his thin hair brushed straight back. I found his cologne to be pleasant.

Ben was sitting in an over-stuffed chair with a floral design, sipping from a coffee cup. The Don led me to a sofa with the same floral print, and bade me sit. Then he sat in a chair where he could see the both of us at the same time. We were the only people in the room. There was a pot of coffee and pastry on the coffee table, and he asked if I wanted anything. I said no.

The house was quiet. Glendali looked at us for several seconds, then he frowned, waving a finger in front of his face.

"I do not like to place myself into the lives of others," he said. "A man should never involve himself in the affairs between a husband and wife, even if they are family." He shrugged. "But, when those affairs might affect the lives of everyone else in the family, the patriarch may find he has no choice. I look at you both as members of my family. So, of course, I want to help. Do you understand?"

I didn't. I looked at Benny. He was nodding. So I nodded, too, even though I had no idea what the old man was getting at. What could he do?

The Don smiled at us. "Good. I have given your situation much thought. I believe I may have come up with a solution, temporary, perhaps, but worth consideration." He leaned forward, his eyes becoming more intense. "I want you to consider what I say very hard. Will you do that?"

Again, Ben was nodding, so I did, too. I had told Ernie I would not say anything to anger the old man, and I was trying hard not to. But my divorce was none of his business, despite what everyone was telling me. I didn't work for the man. We weren't family, despite what he had claimed.

Leaning back again, his eyes traveling back and forth between Ben and me, the Don said, "I suggest the two of you, instead of divorcing, instead of finalizing things this Friday, put a pause on everything and continue as you have the past few months."

I looked at Ben. He sat quietly, one leg upon the knee of the other, a coffee cup balanced on his leg, his eyes behind those coke bottles staring straight ahead. I was pretty sure this idea had been discussed between the two of them before my arrival. Well, I needed to speak up.

"I'm sorry, to what purpose would I do that, Mr.

Glendali?" I asked. "I don't see me changing my mind."

The old man smiled. "Call me Joseph, Eileen. We are family. If things continue as they have, even if you don't have a change of heart, what is the harm? In the eyes of the church, and of the law, you are married, even if the vows you have taken no longer control your lives." He frowned then. "Unless you have plans of remarrying any time soon?"

"I don't," I said. "I also have no plans to stay married to Ben, Joseph. I have lived in this loveless marriage too long already. I deserve a chance to find someone who loves me."

"I love you, Eileen," said Ben, finally speaking.

"I need more, Ben," I said, looking at him. "I need more."

"Okay," said Joseph Glendali, leaning back into the soft cushions, "you may not change your mind, Eileen, but you are not looking to marry again right now. So, what is the harm in staying married if the two of you can live as if you are not?"

"What does that mean?" I asked.

"You stay in your home. Ben agrees to a monthly income for you, plus he pays the expenses of the house. He agrees not to interfere in your life at all. You two live as if you are not married. I believe this is nothing different than the lives you have lived the past few months."

Ben leaned forward, placing the coffee cup on the table. "With respect, Don Glendali," Ben said, "I agreed to continue as we have since I moved out, paying for the house, giving Eileen money to live, but then I find out she has been seeing this man. Traveling with him." Ben looked around the room as if searching for something. "Obviously, being intimate with him. I can agree to continue supporting her, but she must stop this behavior."

"I will not," I said. "Either we agree that I am free to live my life as I choose, or I go through with the divorce so that I can do whatever I damn well please."

Ben pointed a finger at me. "Do you see, Don, do you

see what I have told you? How can I be expected to pay for all her expenses, let her live in the house I purchased, while she goes whoring around and fucking anyone she chooses in the bed I bought? I can't do that. What man would agree to that?"

"Enough!" Joseph Glendali said, his face flushed enough to show color. From the corner of my eye, I saw Marie Glendali peek into the room from a doorway.

It was his turn to look around the room, as if answers to his problems were written on the walls. He harshly whispered to himself, 'Questi due mi stanno facendo impazzire!' I wasn't sure what that meant, but I was sure he was upset with Ben and me. I decided to take a shot at ending this.

"Joseph," I said calmly, although I wasn't feeling calm. "I have been told that you may feel unease should Ben and I divorce." The old man looked at me through half lidded eyes. "I must tell you, there is no need. I know nothing of the work Ben does for you. Nothing. He has never discussed what he does. I have never asked. It was not my business. Never." I smiled. "I could be tortured, and I would be unable to tell anyone anything."

I said that last part as a joke. I could see the old man saw no humor in it. He leaned towards me and took in a deep breath.

"Mrs. Landry," he said, "it doesn't matter if I believe that or not. Your husband knows the financial history of my family, as well as the history of others. Others who hold even more power and influence than me."

He looked down, brushed at the fabric of his pants. "I have told you both what I expect. I have suggested a way that calms any fears anyone may have. What happens next is for you two to decide."

Glendali then looked at us, and waited.

As nervous as I was, an idea came into my head. I saw an opportunity. An opportunity that I hadn't considered on the drive here, but suddenly seemed like I couldn't have come up with a better plan if I had tried.

"I will do as you ask," I said, smiling at the old man.

"I believe you are a wise man."

His eyes shifted to Ben.

"Don Glendali. Do you understand what you are asking of me? The humiliation I will feel? The mocking of me that will go on behind my back?"

When Glendali said nothing, just continued to stare, Ben finally nodded his head.

"Good," he said. "Molto bene." He didn't smile. "Now, please, you must leave. You have exhausted me. I will never speak of this again. You understand? Now go."

He labored to rise from the cushions. Ben and I stood, too.

"Vincent," Glendali called out. Vincent immediately stepped into the room. "See that Mrs. Landry gets home safely."

Joseph Glendali came to where I stood and gently took my hand in his. "Do you have plans of going home for Christmas?" he asked. I said I did, even though I didn't, and he wished me a Merry Christmas and a Happy New Year. He then took Ben's hand in his, told him to stop by on Wednesday night to discuss something important, and then walked from us. Marie came to his side without a look at me or Ben, and escorted him from the room.

Ben, without a word to me, got into his Mercedes and drove away. Ernie was sitting behind the wheel of the Cadillac as I approached, he gave me a quick glance, then eyes forward. Vincent opened the back door for me, and, without a word, closed it. We got to the road out of Nahant in a few minutes.

"Well, what happened?" asked Ernie.

"The old man gave me an idea," I said.

"What the hell does that mean, Eileen?"

"It means, my Italian stallion, when I come over Tuesday night, after I remind you who my boyfriend is, we have things to talk about."

35

We laid upon the rumpled sheets in the dark, passing a cigarette between us.

"You still have questions?" I whispered.

"With you, I will always have questions," Ernie said, his hand caressing my ass. "You are the devil. Now tell me what plan you have in your beautiful head. How will you now get us both killed?"

I told Ernie of the demands Joseph Glendali had made to Ben and me. How angry the old man had become until Ben finally agreed to them."

"And you agreed to them?" Ernie said.

"You told me not to anger the Don, so I didn't."

"When have you ever listened to anything I've said?" He playfully squeezed me. "I know who you think the brains of this outfit is. So, now what is the plan?"

I told Ernie what Glendali had said about his concerns of a divorce.

"Exactly what I had said," Ernie said. "The old man is not a fool. There are no limits to what he'll do to protect the organization. I've heard the stories of the old days, when he was moving up. Do not underestimate this man, Eileen. He could shake your hand warmly, smile at you, kiss your cheeks three times, and have Vincent put a bullet in your brain without a twinge of guilt. You understand?"

"I do. That's why I think we have to move quickly. When I go to court Friday, Ben will be expecting me to have told my lawyer that I am dropping the suit. Ben will have told his lawyer that is what will happen. Except I won't be."

"Christ," Ernie sighed. "You told Glendali that you would, and now you won't. This isn't a game, Eileen."

"Listen, baby, listen." Men. If only their brains were as active as their dicks. "I have it all figured out. Ben will be livid. I'll talk to him after, explain to him that Paul got so upset about the Don's plan, that he demanded that I not do it. That he screamed and yelled and hit me. That he demanded that I go through with the divorce. I'll tell Ben that he has to come over to the house so we can talk. That I need him to help me. Then, I'll have planned for Paul to come over just a little bit later."

"And then what?" asked Ernie.

"Then, with some luck, and acting on my part, within a month, you and I are lying on that beach in Brazil."

"Argentina," said Ernie.

Brazil, Argentina, Greece, wherever, as long as we weren't lying in a hastily dug patch of land in the woods of New Hampshire. Which is probably where we'd end up if things didn't go as I hoped.

ON WEDNESDAY NIGHT, Paul and I met at Harry's, and the first thing he said to me was why didn't I tell him I met with Glendali. I explained to Paul, tactfully as I always am, that the divorce is really none of his business, but that it was all worked out. The old man seemed happy when I left the house.

Then I decided to get a little flirty with Paul. Move the conversation away from the divorce. I told him how much I liked being with him. Told him we should have some drawer space in each other's home. That we should plan a little get-away after court on Friday. I could see he liked that idea.

While he talked I found myself thinking, I could really be attracted to him if things were different, if circumstances weren't what they were. Manipulating Ernie didn't take much. Getting him to buy into any plan, no matter how dangerous, where he got me and the millions in a bank in the Cayman's, was easy. Realizing the kind of man Paul Costa was, he would never be a part of what I was doing. Never. But if I thought he would, I think I would have preferred him over Ernie to be my partner, even though Ernie was a tiger in bed. Outside of the bedroom, however, Ernie had little to offer. His idea of a Broadway show, was two drunks having a fight in Everett Square.

Before leaving, I made a big deal of us going away, promising to be ready at seven Friday night, promising to make it a great weekend. On the drive home, I went over everything I would do in the next two days, everything I would say. Played it all out as I expected it should go. Before bed, I called Ernie and told him to stop by Thursday night. There was something I needed him to do. I hardly slept that night, my nerves a total mess. I was planning the death of Ben. A horrible thing to be doing. A terrible risk to be taking.

But all that money hidden away. Didn't I deserve that for the years I have suffered being married to Ben? I had told Paul there was a million dollars in a bank in the Cayman's, money ripped off from the mob, which was silly of me for letting that slip out. Foolish, really. Spilled milk. In reality, there wasn't a million dollars. According to the paperwork I had seen, there was over three and a half million down there, and I wanted it. All I needed was a death certificate and some numbers. Three and a half million, Ernie Mancini, and warm sand between my toes. A girl could do a lot worse.

So it was, in court Friday morning, I said nothing to my lawyer about stopping the divorce. When the fireworks started, I thought Ben was going to leap across the tables at me. But then, while the lawyers were talking to the judge, Ben smiled at me and slowly shook his head. It was then I realized I may have blundered badly.

After leaving the courtroom, I huddled with my lawyer in one part of the hall outside the courtroom, Ben huddled with his lawyer in another part. When the lawyers left, Ben came to the bench I was sitting on, so I didn't have to call him over, which I had planned on doing.

"You made a mistake, Eileen," he said as he stood in

front of me. “A big mistake. You and the Don had an agreement, an agreement, by the way, I was not happy with, and you reneged. Joseph Glendali is not a man you renege on. I can't help you, Eileen. You brought this on yourself.”

I reached out and took Ben's hand, but didn't look up at him. “Sit down, Ben. Please.”

Ben hesitated, then sat. I let a few seconds pass, then slowly pushed the sleeves of my coat and blouse up to the elbow of my left arm, revealing a nasty purple bruise.

“Paul was very upset when I told him of our agreement,” I said, still not looking at Ben.

I looked around to see if we were drawing any attention. Several people sat on benches at the other end of the hall not paying any attention to us. I unbuttoned my coat, pulled my blouse up on the side so he could see the remnants of the bruise that was on my side. Fading, but still obvious. I made eye contact with Ben, there were tears in my eyes, then quickly looked away. Buttoning my coat, I pulled the silk scarf I was wearing away from my neck, revealing the bruises I had Ernie inflict the night before.

Looking at Ben, tears now on my cheeks, I said, “I'm so afraid, Ben. I don't know what to do.”

“That son of a bitch,” Ben hissed. “I'll kill him.”

“No, Ben, no,” I said, grabbing his arm and squeezing. “He's a killer, Ben. Listen, come over tonight, okay? Six thirty. We'll talk. We can go to the Don. He'll help us. Can you do that, Ben? Please? Come over tonight?”

Ben reached out and hugged me. “Sure, Sweetheart, sure. I'll call Glendali. Tell him what happened.”

“No, baby, no,” I said. “Let's talk first. Then we'll go to the old man together. I'm scared, Ben.”

“Don't be, Eileen. I'll take care of everything. Don't you worry.”

36

It was a little before six-thirty, I had just gotten off the phone with Paul, telling him that Ben Landry was upset with the way things had gone at court, that I was ready and he should come now, as I watched through the large picture window in the living room as Ben stepped from the Mercedes parked on the other side of the street. Ben hustled across the street, and I stepped further into the room. I heard him trying his keys, which no longer worked because Paul had changed my locks. I could hear Ben cursing, then the doorbell rang. After a few seconds, there came knocking at the door. I went to stand at the top of the stairway. Ben began banging harder and yelled my name. Then he pounded on the door, and the door shook. He must have put a shoulder to it. That was when I went down and opened it.

"Jesus, Eileen," he said. "Couldn't you hear me?"

I stood in front of him with just a short nightgown on.

"I'm sorry, Ben. I was in the bathroom. Come upstairs."

I let him go in front of me, and I left the door open as I followed. He took a seat at the kitchen table, then he looked up at me with those coke bottle eyes when he noticed the .38 on the table.

"What the hell is this?" he demanded, picking up the handgun.

"Protection," I said.

"You know how to use one of these?"

I shrugged. My father had guns in the house. I was shown how to use one at an early age. 'Can't live in Brooklyn and not know how', my father used to say.

"Point and shoot," I said to Ben.

He frowned.

"You know, he accused me of hitting you. Why are you

still with him if he beats you, Eileen? Why didn't you tell Glendali Sunday?"

"I'm afraid he'll kill me, Ben. You don't know him. Paul has a temper. The slightest thing can set him off. The bruises on my side? I got them because I told him you had been in the house. Had left me a necklace. His face turned red. You should have seen him. He pounded the table so hard, I thought he split the wood. I've never been so frightened in my life. I thought he was going to hit me again."

"We go to the Don," said Ben. His fist was beating on his leg, like he does when he's nervous. "We go now. Or, if you want, I make a call. Get Tony over here. Tony will take him out as a favor to me. He owes me. Tony will beat the crap out of him. Put him in the hospital. Hell, in the morgue. He deserves it."

"What are you saying?" I said, my hand going up to my mouth in horror. "Kill him?"

"It's what he deserves, isn't it?"

Ben reached out and took my hand.

"Why didn't you tell me about this sooner, baby?" he asked. There was genuine concern on his face. In his voice. I was touched. Poor Ben.

"I didn't want you to do something crazy, honey," I said. "I didn't want to see you get hurt."

He dropped my hand. "What are you saying, Eileen? I can't take care of my wife? Can't protect her?"

"No, Ben, no. That's not what I meant. But Paul is a killer. You read about what he did in the restaurant parking lot, didn't you? Two guys came after him, and he got them. He's not someone to screw around with. I'm just worried about you, honey. That's all."

"All right, all right," Ben said as he looked around the kitchen. "Why don't you let me do the worrying. Now, go get some clothes on and we'll go see the Don."

I stepped up to Ben and wrapped my arms around his head, gently pulling it towards me until it was nestled against my warm belly. I glanced at the clock on the wall. I still needed to kill some time. Give Paul a chance to get here. I expected him soon, unless traffic was heavy. But I could stall, taking some time to dress, if I had to. I went to the refrigerator and filled a glass with cold water.

"You want anything, baby?" I asked Ben. "A seven and seven?"

"No. Come on, Eileen. Get dressed."

"I'm sorry about court this morning, Ben. I should have warned you. I didn't know what to do."

"It's okay, Eileen."

"I've been afraid for so long. I'm just so confused. This is all my fault. Can you ever forgive me, Ben?"

"Forget it, Eileen," Ben said. He was getting nervous. Upset with my not getting dressed. "We'll work it all out. Don't worry. Now, get dressed will ya, please."

Just then I heard a car brake hard out front. I stepped away from Ben, smiled down at him, and moved toward the opening to the dining room, carrying the water.

In seconds, I heard someone enter downstairs, causing Ben to turn in his seat toward the sound. I let the glass slip from my hand and it shattered on the floor.

"Eileen?" Paul called up the stairs.

"Ben," I whispered. "It's Paul."

I backed away. "No, Paul." I screamed.

Ben grabbed the .38 on the table, stood and fired quickly toward the front door in a panic, then hid behind the wall overlooking the stairway

I took a chance and rushed to Ben. "What are you doing?" I cried out as I grabbed at his arm.

Ben looked confused. And scared. "Stop it!" he said harshly and pushed me away.

It wasn't that hard a push, but I dramatically fell backwards. Slapping at the counter top of the central island before falling onto the kitchen floor behind it. The island afforded me a lot of cover from flying bullets. I also made sure I was in position to grab at a gun that I had in the bottom drawer of the cabinets. Both of the .38's were registered in the name of Ben Landry. Ben fired off two more shots. I opened the drawer. Ben then reached out and shut off the lights.

Ben shot again. I grabbed the .38 and fired towards where I thought Ben was, but from the floor, with the island in front of me, I doubted I hit him. But then I saw his darker shadow. He must have turned to look at me. Then Paul shot and I heard, rather than saw, Ben go down.

I think I screamed. The violence, the tremendous noise of gun fire in such a small space, my nerves, I know I screamed. And I began crying. The months of tension. Was it now over? Was Ben down? Was he dead? Had Paul been shot? What if Ben wasn't dead? The months of planning. What then? I lay on the floor, unable to move, more afraid than I have ever been in my life. What if Ben was still alive?

And then the kitchen lights came on and Paul came into the kitchen.

He stood over Ben, felt for a pulse, then came over to me. He took the gun from my hand and lifted me up, settling me in a chair. He asked if I was hurt.

"I've never seen Ben like this," I said, tears in my eyes. Real tears. I was scared shitless. "He was going to kill me, Paul. I was afraid for my life. Is he, is he dead?"

"Can't hurt you anymore, Eileen," said Paul as he slumped onto a kitchen chair.

Paul told me to call the police. Then we sat and waited.

I looked at Paul, who was looking down at Ben. I had taken a big chance shooting at Ben. If he wasn't killed, things could have gone badly for me. There would have been questions. Ben would have given answers that would have made things difficult. Yeah, I took a big gamble. But what else could I do? Ben had Paul in a bad spot. My entire plan was for Ben to be killed. Anything else was failure. Maybe even my death. So it had to be done. I had to shoot. Why can't anything just go smoothly? Why couldn't Paul have killed Benny before I had to do something? Why do I always have to do everything? Jesus, are all men useless?

PAUL HAD TOLD me to get dressed, so I did, choosing clothes that didn't hide most of the bruises. When the cops arrived, Paul knew one of them. Then a Detective showed up, a rugged looking guy named Hancock, who took me into the dining room to ask me questions, while others were in the kitchen doing stuff. Hancock had Paul sit in the living room. Then he went back and forth between the two of us. He started with me.

"Can you tell me what happened, Mrs. Landry?" Detective Hancock asked.

I sat quietly at the dining room table, deciding that it would be best to seem a bit in shock, and just a bit out of it. I didn't want the drama of tears. I didn't think I could carry it off. I told him everything, from the time the Mercedes pulled up until the shooting stopped. My version of everything.

"So," Hancock said when I shrugged at the end of my recounting of the events, "you're sure Mr. Landry fired the first shot?"

I nodded.

"How long have you been separated?"

"Since June. I started seeing Paul in September."

"You say your husband abused you in the past?"

"Never when we were together. But, yes, the last few months, Ben has been abusive."

The bruise on my arm was obvious, as was the red skin of my neck. I pulled up the fabric of my slacks on my left leg to show a bruise on my calf. I got that when I plunged to the floor, banging it into the corner of the island. Hancock wouldn't know better.

"Why did you let Mr. Landry in tonight?" asked the detective.

"I thought he was going to bash in my door," I said. "I knew he was upset about what happened at court this morning, so I thought we had better talk about it. I mean, he's gotten physical in the past, but I never feared for my life. I guess I didn't realize just how upset he was. Tonight I feared for my life, Detective Hancock. I really did. Like I said, he was threatening to kill me."

"Did you know he had a gun when he came in the house?"

"No. I never knew Ben to carry a weapon, although we had guns in the house."

"Why was there a gun in the bottom drawer of a kitchen cabinet? Seems an unlikely place to have one."

I shrugged. "I asked Benny the same thing when he put it there. He said, 'Can never be too careful'. I had forgotten all about it. Until he pushed me down on the floor. Then I remembered. Crazy how the mind works, huh?"

I could see by the look on the Detective's face that he wasn't entirely buying it, but he could never prove I wasn't being truthful. The .38 that Benny picked up from the table, the one I had placed there, I had used gloves when handling it. The only prints on it would be his. That gun had come from a drawer in a desk in the small third bedroom that Ben had used as his study when he lived here. The same desk where I had come across evidence of money in an off shore account way back last February. The piece of paper that had started this whole thing.

When Hancock went to talk with Paul, in those times I sat quietly, sipping from a water bottle and composing myself. I even surprised myself at how in control I was. I took those opportunities to consider how I should act the next time Hancock came to me. How upset, or in control, I should be. After the third time of him asking me questions, I noticed we were covering old ground, the same questions being asked a different way. Finally, after I knew they had taken Benny away, and the others had left, I asked Hancock if we could continue this in the morning. That I was exhausted and too upset to continue. He said he understood. I thought I would see Paul before he left, but I guess Hancock didn't allow it.

When I was finally alone, I went and sat in the living room. I noticed a few of my neighbors were still milling outside, looking up at my house as they stood in small groups. A police car was parked across the street. I needed a drink.

Entering the kitchen, I looked down at the blood, now drying on my tiled floor. I was surprised to see there wasn't much of it. I wondered if that meant Ben had died quickly, the heart stopping, blood not being pumped out of the wound. I didn't know. Half a tall glass of vodka, mixed into half a glass of orange juice, and I was back in the living room.

I now had more to consider. As soon as I could, I wanted to be on Cayman Island, showing the bank my marriage certificate, Ben's Death certificate, and the number of the account that held what I assumed was stolen mob money. I would then transfer the money out of there, after opening an account somewhere else.

Two things I had not considered in all this time, suddenly hit me in the quiet of my living room while holding a half empty glass. First, where did I want to disappear to? I had to have a bank to send the money to. Where would that be? Second, and more importantly, what if the money wasn't pilfered from the mob? What if they knew it was there? Accounts secretly set up by my deceased husband for them. Could I get the money? If I did, and Glendali knew of the accounts, I was dead. And it wouldn't matter where I went to disappear, I'd be found. Almost a year of planning this, and I had never considered that. I had always figured Ben Landry was just a thief.

Finishing off the screwdriver in the dark, I went to bed. If not for the liquor, I probably would not have fallen asleep.

The lit dial showed the time of 3:12 when the phone on the nightstand began ringing. Even through the cloud of not being fully awake, I knew not to answer the ringing. And yet I did. It's like I have this need for chaos and tension. Maybe laying on a beach in Rio would bore me to tears.

I picked up the phone, but said nothing.

"Eileen? You there?" It was Ernie. He was whispering. No idea why.

"Yeah." I said.

"Can you talk?"

"Why are you whispering, Ernie?"

There was a hesitation, then Ernie said, "I dunno." That's my guy.

"What happened?" he asked in his normal voice. And I told him.

"I thought you were going to tell the police that Ben was trying to protect you from Paul? That Paul was abusing you? That Ben got killed because you asked him to come over and protect you from your abusive boyfriend? How did you screw this up, Eileen?"

"Once I had to pull the trigger," I said testily, "that idea went out the window. I had to think fast, Ernie. Cops would ask why I had shot at my husband if he was there to protect me."

The truth was, I never intended to make any such claim. Paul certainly didn't deserve it, and I didn't really believe I could pull that off. I had only told Ernie I would do it, just to silence all the nagging questions he kept hammering me with after I told him my plan. Like I didn't have enough pressure on me already. Really, all the pressure was on me. Ernie only had to sit back and see how it all played out. And then reap the benefits if I pulled it off. Maybe I'd get the money and never tell him where I was. Did I really need this shit now?

"Did you kill Ben or was it Paul?"

"I don't know, Ernie. It was dark. I might have hit him. I don't know. Which is why I couldn't say Ben was there to protect me. I had to go with the story that Paul was trying to protect me."

Ernie was quiet for a long time. "Now what?" he finally asked.

"We stick with the plan, baby. Nothing has changed. As soon as I can, I go for the money. Then, you join me."

"Where?"

"Not sure yet."

"That's if Glendali let's you live long enough to disappear."

Like I needed reminding.

SATURDAY WAS INCREDIBLY difficult. I was a jumble of nerves. I guess the finality of what I had caused just hit me like a ton of bricks. I had two visits by the detective, Hancock, with the same questions as the night before, only phrased differently. The second time Hancock came to the house, there was a lawyer with me, a Mr. Morris, sent by Paul. I could see Hancock wasn't pleased about that.

In between the visits, I got out the Spic and Span, a bristled brush, and rubber gloves, and scrubbed at the blood stain. When the stain was gone, so was most of my anxiety. My sister called. How she had found out what was going on I didn't know, and I didn't ask. Just got off the phone as quickly as I could, promising I would still be coming for Christmas. Ben's brother called demanding to know what had happened and blaming me for Ben's death. I hung up on him. I received no call from Paul. I could only assume the police were keeping him busy. Also, I received no calls from anyone connected with the Glendali family.

Reporters for the newspapers and television stations were outside my door. I ignored them. That night I curled up on my sofa downstairs and watched a movie, my body trembling uncontrollably. What the hell had I done?

At eleven o'clock the phone rang, waking me from where I had nodded off on the sofa. It was Paul.

"You okay?" he asked.

"Can you come over?"

"Not tonight, Eileen. I'll be there in the morning."

There was concern in his voice. Concern for me. And something else. He sounded tired. I suppose no matter how many people you kill, it still has a sobering effect. Not for the first time, I hoped the bullet that killed Ben came from Paul's gun and not mine.

37

And now, here we are locked in a tight embrace. I don't ever want to let him go. I'm trembling, and it's no act. "It's all right," Paul whispers in my ear. "It's all right." After a while, I slowly release him, then take his hand and lead him up the steps to the kitchen.

Placing a cup of coffee in front of Paul, I tell him about yesterday. The phone calls from my sister and Ben's brother. The questions from Detective Hancock. The advice of my lawyer. Also, Attorney Morris saying I might be called in front of a Grand Jury.

"I spoke with Hancock this morning before coming here," says Paul. "It was my shot that killed Ben. Your bullet was embedded high up on the wall. If they want you in front of a Grand Jury, it will be for other reasons, not for murder."

Immediately, I feel lighter. Like a huge weight has been lifted from me. I feel clear-headed again. I feel in control. This feeling of guilt just being washed away.

Paul talks about Glendali. How I have to be careful. That I need protection. He then suggests I might want to consider Witness Protection. Witness Protection is certainly not in my plans. Besides, I actually don't have anything to tell the Feds that would get me Witness Protection. I really never had a discussion with Ben about his efforts for the crime family. I have been telling Paul and Glendali the truth. I don't know anything.

"You could tell Glendali about the secret account," Paul suddenly says. "The million dollars stolen by Ben. Swing a deal. Give it back, for the guarantee you'll be left alone."

I am trying very hard not to look at him like he is the craziest man on God's Earth. This is why I couldn't have planned this with Paul. Give the money back? Are you fucking crazy?

"Do you think that's a good idea, Paul," I ask innocently. But I'm looking in my coffee cup when I do. I don't want him to see my eyes.

"It might save your life," Paul says.

"I haven't thought about the money," I lie, and I am really good at lying.

I ask if he thinks I should go see Glendali. Paul says that is a bad idea. Which I knew he'd say. He'll do it. He gets up to go, saying he'll be back later. I hug him again, melting into him, my kiss passionate. Needy.

Before shutting the door behind him, I notice that there are now only two reporters out front in the cold, who immediately start yelling questions at him. I close the door before they can ask me anything. And then I begin laughing. Uncontrollably laughing. I can't stop. Give the money back! Oh, my, God, I can't believe it. Give the money back. I'm coughing. I can't catch my breath. Tears are running down my face as I collapse on the stairs. Give the money back. Oh, God, these men in my life. Are they all insane?

"EILEEN, JOSEPH GLENDALI."

My heart is in my throat.

"Mr. Glendali."

"My sincerest condolences for your loss, Eileen. This is very terrible. Like losing a beloved nephew."

I take in a deep breath to steady myself. I've been thinking about what I would say if the old man called.

"Joseph, I swear, on my grandmother's soul, he was like a madman. I've never seen him this way before. I think he came here to kill me."

"And we know why, don't we, Eileen? We know why. I wish I could understand. Help me to understand."

I'm actually smiling. Understand, old man? If I told you the truth, you'd probably have a coronary. But not before ordering a hit on me.

"Joseph,..."

"Not on the telephone, Mrs. Landry, please. I would

like to send Vincent to see you."

I'm not smiling anymore.

"You can tell him what happened. We are all very concerned."

I have to think fast.

"Can this wait, Don Glendali?" I ask with as much respect as I can. "The police come all the time. I am still in shock."

"I'm afraid it cannot, Eileen. Vincent will be there at seven this evening. Please be home."

The line goes dead.

PAUL IS BACK, and while he showers I am making a salad. I took steaks out this morning. I'll do scalloped potatoes. A nice meal. A bottle of red. Not too much wine. Not with Vincent coming. Maybe after he leaves, if things don't get crazy. I told Paul that he was coming at seven. Paul didn't seem nervous about it. Me, I'm scared. I can only think of three reasons he would be coming here. The first is to kill me. But I doubt that's it. The second is to hear my reasons for reneging on the deal proposed by the old man. That seems reasonable. The third is to go through any papers that may be in the house implicating the crime family. The first thing I did after getting off the phone with Glendali, was to go into the study and look at everything still in there. There isn't much, Ben having taken a bunch of stuff with him when he secured an apartment.

I went through everything that was left very slowly, and found nothing that mentioned any off shore accounts. The papers that are left, I care nothing about. I know the bank, account number, and the information needed to withdraw the funds, and that information is safely hidden away in my closet, waiting for me to act on it. And I will do that soon.

"Paul," I say as I'm washing dishes at the sink after dinner, "I'm thinking I should leave for my dad's house Friday. You have work to do, and you can't be baby-sitting me all the time. You really shouldn't anyways. I don't think I'm in any danger. Not really."

"Probably a good idea, babe," Paul says. I notice he didn't touch his wine glass during dinner. "I can drive you down there if you want?"

"No, no," I say. "I'll take the morning shuttle and have dad pick me up. I'll stay a few weeks, but I'll be back in time to spend New Year's Eve with you. Would you like that, Paul?"

His smile tells me he would like that very much. Poor Paul. By New Year's Eve, I'll be out of the country and covering my tracks before reaching my final destination. Drying the plates, with my back to him, I smile. Maybe it won't be my final destination. With almost four million dollars, maybe I will spend years traveling. Italy, Greece, France, Japan. Anywhere I want. Me and Ernie on a romp around the world. At least until I tire of him.

At exactly seven o'clock the doorbell rings. Paul answers it and Vincent comes up the stairs. Vincent apologizes for interrupting my evening. Vincent is five-five, maybe five-six, and slightly built. He's a good looking guy, in a Peter Falk kind of way, and you wouldn't think anything of him if it weren't for his eyes. Those pale blue eyes make your blood run cold. Which mine is doing now. I'm trembling.

Vincent is only in the house about fifteen minutes. He went down to the room Ben used as his study, coming back with a few plastic bags filled with stuff.

"Vincent, tell the Don, Ben came here to kill me." I show him the purple bruises on my neck. "He was out of control when he came here. If Paul hadn't shown up, I'd be dead. I never wanted this, Vincent. Please, tell Mr. Glendali, I never wanted this."

Vincent has no comment to that, just says good night.

When Vincent leaves, I go to Paul. Hug him. Feel the gun inside his coat. Feel the tingling inside of me from the hardness of the gun and from the tension of the last quarter hour. I am trembling, but not from fear.

"Take me to bed, Paul," I whisper into his chest. "Take me to bed now."

PAUL SPENDS TUESDAY and Wednesday with me all day and night. I'm not used to always having someone around, and his constant presence has gotten on my nerves. There's only so much time you can spend in bed. I mean, I have things to plan. But I think what I'm really concerned about, is that Ernie Mancini, my impetuous, immature, hunk of man, will be knocking on my backdoor wanting to know what's going on. And wanting something else, too. No way to explain him to Paul

We've done a good job emptying my freezer. It's Thursday morning. Tomorrow, I'm out of here.

"Paul, you must have things you need to do," I say over coffee and eggs, "and I have some shopping to do for incidentals. I'll be out in public, so I'll be safe. You go do what you have to do, pick up some Chinese for dinner, and we'll make love all night if you want, before I leave in the morning."

We leave the house together. There is no police car parked across the street. No reporters in front of my house. Only my next door neighbor peeking through his kitchen window. That used to piss me off. But it was his testimony to the cops about the night of the shooting that had helped, so I don't flip him the bird.

I watch Paul drive away, then I drive to a drug store to pick up a few things. From there, I drive to Ernie's apartment. No one answers the knocks. I didn't expect him to be home. When I get home, I'll call him and leave a message. I have not booked a flight yet. I didn't want to take the chance Paul would see the tickets. I'll book a flight when I get to the airport in the morning. It won't be to LaGuardia. Where it will be, I don't know. Wherever there is an empty seat. And then from wherever that is, I'll make my way to the money.

I kill some time walking around a mall, think about getting Paul a present, but don't, then, before heading back home, I drive to the bank. I close the checking account, taking all that money in cash. I plan on paying cash for near future purchases. I watch television, so I know enough not to use credit cards. I close out the savings account, taking all of that money, almost ninety thousand dollars, in a cashiers check. I ask if my dear husband, recently departed, may have had other accounts in the bank. I was told he did not.

Back home, I pack light. A single suitcase so Paul doesn't become suspicious. All the important stuff I put in the largest of my designer bags, including my passport. It's still okay. I got it for our honeymoon, mine and Ben's. We flew into Miami with the idea we would take a cruise. Then Ben decided he didn't want to. That was Ben. Don't do something fun if you can do nothing. I call Ernie. When the machine picks up, I leave a quick message. I tell him to stay patient. I'll contact him soon and tell him where to meet me. I tell him how much I'm missing him. I'm telling him what I'm going to do to him when we do meet up again, when the machine shuts off half way through my naughtiness. Probably just as well. I've got so much on my mind, I probably don't sound convincing.

By the time Paul comes through the door carrying Chinese take-out, I'm certain I have everything I will need. And I am ready. Jesus Christ, am I ready.

VERY SLOW, TANTALIZINGLY slow, I push myself up the length of Paul's naked body, kissing his side every few inches. His strong fingers are wrapped around my hair as my head emerges from under the sheet.

"Was that good?" I ask.

Paul laughs. "You're a devil woman."

I've heard that before. "So it was good." I'm kissing his chest.

"Better than that," he says, pulling on my hair until my lips meet his.

"I don't want you to forget about me after I'm gone," I purr after breaking the kiss.

"Not much chance of that," he says. "It's only going to be ten days."

Laying my head on his chest again, I think to myself, 'Sorry, babe. That one was for doing what needed to be done. And to give you something to remember me by.'

Although I'm certain Paul Costa will never forget me for a few other reasons.

Over a cup of coffee, I ask Paul what he'll be doing until I get back. The importance of a lie is to keep the story line going. Simple dialogue to give the lie a foundation. That way, no suspicion. Of course, you need to be careful. One little slip around a guy like Paul, or Vincent, or the old man, and suspicion would grow in their heads like ivy on the walls of Harvard.

"I have this on-going thing with an Insurance Company," Paul says. "And there was a message on the office machine I'll check out today. Looks like I'll be busy for a while. Grab your stuff and I'll take you to the airport."

"No, Paul. Logan on a Friday morning? I'll take a cab. Just give me a kiss to last me two weeks, and check on the house every few days."

Paul looks at me. There is a sadness in his eyes. The poor guy is really going to miss me.

As we part on the sidewalk in front of my house, that I will probably never see again, me into a cab, Paul into his car, I am feeling a pang of remorse. I am forever leaving a man who is probably the best man I have ever been with in my life. I'll have regrets about that, I'm sure. Probably not four million dollars worth of regrets, however.

"Logan," I say to the driver, and then settle back. The great adventure begins. Can I pull it off? Hell, the hard part is done. What could go wrong now?

38

This isn't like any bank I've ever been in before. There is no counter where you fill in a withdrawal or a deposit slip. There are no mousy looking women standing behind a long barrier, dispensing tens and twenties from drawers onto the polished top and sliding them to the customer. There are no customers.

There is a guard at the front door, which is locked, who looks like George Foreman, and where you need to provide identification before he allows you to enter. There are four steps you need to climb before entering the spacious, and sparsely furnished, main room. The floor is white marble, highly polished, and you could dine off of it. High windows allow massive amounts of sunlight to enter, so with the white walls and the white floor there is a feeling of entering heaven when you reach the top step.

God is not waiting for me there, however. Instead, waiting to greet me is a very tall, very thin, man. His sandy colored hair is thinning and cut short. He wears glasses with black frames. Think Clark Kent. His dark blue pin-striped suit is perfectly tailored. The white dress shirt is definitely starched. He greets me with a look that lacks warmth, as does his voice. It's British, so no surprise there. His speech is clipped, business like, and immediate. As he leads me to a desk tucked into the far corner of the large area, we pass five other desks spread about. Four of them have men similarly attired as my escort, all are quietly speaking on a telephone. One desk has no one sitting there. It's early Saturday morning, the street outside is almost empty, but these men are all busy.

After showing him - his name is Oakes, Mr. Simon Oakes - everything he required me to show him, Mr. Oakes asks, “What can I do for you today, Mrs. Landry?”

"I have a check I would like to deposit into the account, Mr. Oakes," I say, smiling. I think one of us should, even if it may be bad business practice here on a British Territory. "And, I need to set the account up so I can have the funds forwarded to another bank."

"Of course," says Oakes. He doesn't appear upset that I am taking my money out of his bank. "Do you have the account where the funds will be transferred?"

"Not yet," I reply. "But I will soon. Is there a way I can contact you, relay the account information, and have the funds transferred, without my coming back here?"

"Of course," he says, and then precedes to explain to me how it can be done, and to create the necessary paperwork.

When all the 'i's are dotted and the 't's are crossed, Mr. Oakes leads me to the front door.

"Please accept the banks sincerest condolences, Mrs. Landry, for your loss. Rest assured, when you are ready, your funds will be transferred, minus our fee of course, without any problem. And we wish you the very best."

I shake his offered hand, noticing that he is now smiling. It is not a very pleasant smile.

My hotel is only a few hundred yards from the bank, and I walk to it in weather that may be as perfect as weather can be. I feel a hundred pounds lighter. The check is no longer in my possession, so there is a relief. But the fear I have had for months that I would be unable to access Ben's account is now gone, and I feel lighter than air.

As I walk along the tree lined street, I think about how easy it was to get here. I've traveled a little, not a lot, so I wasn't confident. I mean, I knew I would eventually get here, I'm just amazed at how easy it was.

On arrival at Logan, I made my way to Delta. I didn't want to fly from Boston to the Cayman's, just in case anyone was checking, or had the ability to check later on, or if I even could. My first thought was to fly to a city in Florida. Miami. Tampa. However, those flights were booked solid. A Friday in December. Big surprise. Then I thought about Atlanta, and checked to see if I could go from Atlanta to Cayman. I could. My luck held out, and with very little wait between flights, I landed on the island at the Owen Roberts International Airport at twilight. I took a cab to a hotel, oceanfront room, a delicious fish and chips dinner from room service eaten on a balcony with a view of the dark ocean, followed by a few nips from the room bar. Below me was the sound of diners enjoying a night out on patios that stretched along the edge of the beach. Music filled the night air.

Don't get me wrong, but after all the bullshit jobs I put up with before marrying Benny, I knew married life with him was a big step up. But this? This is living. I now wanted to do what the people below me were doing on their vacation. Only, I wanted to do it every night. And now I could.

Maybe the islands are the way to go, I thought as I ate. The Bahamas. Aruba. Not Puerto Rico. I needed to think about that. I don't think Ernie has a preference. We actually never talked about it, other than he wants to be on a beach.

It wasn't lost on me that one can live cheaper than two. Would he really tell Glendali about secret accounts off shore if I never called him? Could my guy really be that stupid? It's Ernie, so I know the answer. But I like the big stud, so I called him when I got to the room and I left a message on his machine that I'd let him know which beach he'd be rubbing suntan lotion on me as soon as I decided. And to be home the next time I called.

At a shop near the hotel, on my walk back from the bank, I purchased a bathing suit. Baby blue and very little fabric. Laying by the hotel pool now, I'm noticing the looks I'm getting. As I soak up the sun, ignoring the hungry eyes of other women's husbands, and having a few drinks, I run alphabetically through places where I could disappear, beginning with Aruba. Aruba? I heard it's nice there. Bahamas? Can't go wrong with the Bahamas, I think. Deciding is harder than I imagined it would be.

Maybe I should just throw a dart at a map? Let fate decide my destination? With my luck, I'd probably hit Cleveland. Aruba? I wonder if they speak English there? It would probably be easier going somewhere where English is spoken. But I'm fairly certain, no matter where I go, even if people can't understand me, they'll understand my money. The world knows the dollar. Yeah. The dollar is the universal language, and I now have enough to make people understand. And to jump.

OPENING MY EYES Sunday morning, through open sliders to the balcony, I can see sunlight reflecting off gentle waves in the distance, as a warm breeze caresses my naked body. Paradise is what I'm thinking. There is a song playing in my head. I know the song. I just can't name it. Or who sang it. But I know it. What are the words? *Da, da, da. Da, da, da. Where you want to go.* YES! Who sang it? It's on the tip of my tongue. Think! And then, BAM!

Beach Boys. *Kokomo.* Bermuda. Bahama. Aruba. Jamaica. Key Largo. Montego.

I must have been dreaming about where to go, and now the song is in my head.

Montego? Montego Bay. Where is that? Jamaica? Yeah, Jamaica.

Montego Bay? Why not.

It's eight thirty in the morning as I roll across the king size bed and pick up the hotel room phone and place a call to Ernie's phone two thousand miles away in the frozen Northeast. I'll wake him up. I'll make his day. Tell him to pack a bag and get his hot ass to Jamaica. We were going to wait a month before meeting up, but screw that. I want him with me now. Time to celebrate.

The phone rings until the machine picks up suggesting I leave a message, which surprises me. He never left for Glendali's before nine. Ernie told me the old man doesn't get out of bed before nine thirty. Then I realize it's Sunday. Maybe the old man and his daughter are going to

Mass.

"Where the hell are you, Ernie? Listen. I have news. Be home at eight tonight. I'll call then. Get ready, baby. Mama needs you." And I hang up. Then a bad thought enters my head. Maybe my shit lover had a sleepover with some putanna at her place. Is the son-of-a-bitch cheating on me? While the pussy's away, the mouse will play? Careful, big boy, I think to myself as I stretch and yawn. One can live cheaper than two.

I decide on a change of plans. I'm going to spend another day by the pool. Maybe even a walk along the beach. I was going to leave the island today, but I'll do it tomorrow, I decide, even as I break my first rule of survival. Don't get complacent. Never stop thinking. Rules I must now live by.

But first, after a shower and breakfast, I'll go to the airport. See what I need to do to get to Jamaica, and when I can do it. I'll check out Montego Bay before committing myself. Island hopping. I have to smile. Not for the poor. Or the squeamish. I'm neither. Not anymore.

39

The afternoon flight is a little under one hour, and while we cruise along, I'm enjoying my first class beverage and reading a booklet I picked up at the airport that tells me all about the islands of the Caribbean. I read about them all, but Jamaica is the one I'm interested in.

English is spoken there. Thank God. Jamaica is the third largest island down here, and is under the British Commonwealth. Over seventy percent of the island is black people. No problem for me, but Ernie may have a big problem with that. The biggest problem I see, is that two white people may have a difficult time blending in. More like sticking out. Sort of like two Cadillacs on a Volkswagen sales lot. But, and it's a big but, tourism is huge, millions coming to the island each year, and my guess is most of them are white. Stick to the touristy spots, we should be fine. And no place on the island is more touristy than Montego Bay. Which is where my plane will land in a few minutes at the Sangster International Airport.

I am reading that the economy in Jamaica right now is not good. For me, that is good. Rental property should be cheap. If I decide to stay, I can probably get a nice place for short money. Before reading this pamphlet, I knew two things about Jamaica. Bob Marley and his music came from Jamaica, and Ian Fleming had James Bond do stuff there. I read that in a fan magazine years ago in the salon.

If I find Montego Bay not to be modern enough, or fun enough, we can try the capital, Kingston. If neither excite me, moving on only requires money. I now have money. Lots of it. And if Ernie Mancini doesn't answer his phone pretty soon, he didn't again last night, I may find someone else to spend that money with. I noticed the stares I got in my baby blue swimsuit while I lounged by the pool. I'm thinking excitement won't be too hard to find.

THE LAST BIT of sunlight is fading as the taxi drops me off in front of the hotel. Before coming here, I had the man drive me through the hot spots of Montego. The main boulevards, where I looked for banks and places to shop. It was still a bit early for the night life crowd, but there was a vibe in the air already. Clubs everywhere. Beautiful scenery. A sense of excitement. We passed several banks and high end stores on the main street. Restaurants with outdoor seating in abundance. And the air. Scented and sweet and warm.

To get to this area of higher end, however, we drove through neighborhoods that were run down. There is poverty here, no doubt about that. I have the sense there is a lot of poverty here. I don't think I'm going to like being close to it. Poverty usually means crime. Crime is not something I want to be around. Nothing says we have to stay here if I begin feeling uncomfortable.

The hotel is high end, and my room has an ocean view. Looking down from my third floor balcony to a sandy beach, I can see paved patios running left and right along the edge, filled with tables and diners. Music fills the air, as it did on Grand Cayman, just with a different rhythm. And as darkness settles in, the lights above the patios glow softly. When I was a kid, Coney Island's boardwalk and beach was what I wanted. For a while, Revere Beach was okay in the summer. But this, this is a lot better than okay, and definitely what I want now.

After a long shower and settling in, I order something light from room service. While waiting for it to come, I call Ernie Mancini. He should be waiting for my call. But the machine answers. That son-of-a-bitch.

"Listen to me you stupid Wop," I angrily hiss into the phone. "I don't know what your problem is, but I'm tired of your shit, Ernie. I'll try one more time in the morning. I have the money. Answer your damn phone."

Slamming the receiver down, I'm seething. Who the hell does he think he is? I should have just hung up when the machine picked up. This isn't like it has been the past year, when I needed the only talent that bastard has and I would let him get away with a lot of shit because I did. Things are different now. Big time different. Ernie wants to play his games? He can play by himself.

Christ, I'm trembling. So much has happened in just a few days, the excitement of it all, I should have someone to celebrate it with. I need someone to celebrate it with. I can hear music from outside. People dining, dancing, laughing. I should be out there. Who has more to celebrate than me?

Picking up the phone again, I make the connection for Paul's number. I want to hear his voice. I want to hear him say how much he misses me. I want to hear the concern in his voice, asking if I'm okay. The phone is picked up on the fifth ring. It's his machine. Jesus Christ.

I almost hang up. But, taking a breath, I say, "Hey, baby, sorry I haven't called before this. Been catching up with family. Miss you, Paul. Do you miss me? I bet you do." And I hang up.

THERE ARE SEVERAL banks along the main avenue through the better part of Montego Bay. I spend some time in each of them, getting information on interest rates on saving accounts, ease of transferring funds, finding out who has a free toaster if I make a deposit, stuff like that. After a light lunch of Jamaican patties, which are spicy and delicious, I take a cab back to the hotel. The afternoon is spent by the hotel pool, going over the pamphlets I picked up this morning.

There are many guests lounging, and I pick up on all the languages being spoken. French and English are predominant, but there is an Italian couple not far from where I am. She is young. He is not. She is doing most of the talking. I'm more interested in the language being spoken by the wait staff. It seems to be a blend of English and French, although I'm not sure. The cadence is lovely.

I feel as if I should know what they're saying, but I can't make out half of it. What's funny, when answering a question from a guest, their English is quite good. When conversing among themselves, they go into this mishmash of words. I remember a movie I saw that was set in New Orleans. I think Richard Gere was in it. Anyway, the locals in the movie sounded like this. Creole, was it? I don't know. But I like listening to it.

After a long shower, I take an outdoor seat on a patio along the water in a restaurant within walking distance of my hotel. I am dining on Jerk chicken, a spicy, delightful dish, while a four piece combo is setting up.

"A beautiful woman should never dine alone."

Looking up, there is a man standing by my table smiling down at me. Medium height, full head of dark brown hair, thin mustache. He is dressed casually, dress shirt opened at the collar, tan suit coat, dark brown slacks. Gold bracelet on his right wrist, gold watch on the left, heavy gold ring on his right hand.

Even though this handsome man has caught me off guard, he's getting my best Bette Davis eyes. Coolly, I say, "I don't mind eating alone."

Still smiling, he says, "I'm afraid I do. I hate dining alone. And most of the tables are full. May I join you? My name is Pedro."

"Mexican?" I ask as I take a sip from my drink, making no offer for him to sit.

"Spain. Barcelona. Here on business and seeking conversation."

"Only conversation?"

He shrugs. "May I sit?"

It's funny, I think, as I look up into his smiling face, how the thought process changes when your station in life changes. Several weeks ago, had I found myself dining alone and approached by this man, despite juggling two lovers, I may have invited him to sit to see where the night would take us. I've never been adverse to one night stands.

But today, I had spent the morning in several banks,

discussing the transferring of significant funds into their vaults, and now I am being hit on. I know I look good, so I'm not surprised at his interest, and God knows I could use what comes after conversation, but rule number two must never be ignored. Never stop thinking.

"Someone is joining me shortly," I say, without smiling. "I'm afraid you'll have to dine alone this evening. I'm sorry."

The smile doesn't leave his face, but the eyes lose their amusement. Giving a slight nod of his head, he moves away to an empty table on the other end of the patio.

While I sip at my second Manhattan – two will be my limit tonight – I find I am enjoying the music that the combo makes. Reggae. I like it. I thought I may tire of it after one or two songs, but I haven't. I notice the Spaniard who smiled down at me, now has a woman sitting with him. She looks young in the dim light across the patio. Good for him. Probably good for her, too. I pay my check and head back to the hotel.

Other than a few spots along the road back, there is sufficient lighting, so I'm not nervous about walking alone in a place I don't know. And yet, I'm aware that I'm not. I've never been nervous, or even cautious, about walking alone at night, but now I'm thinking I should be. Is it the poverty of the island that has me thinking like this, or the fact that I now have money, and should anyone be aware of that, I could be targeted? I giggle to myself. Now there's a thought. Poor people don't have to worry about being kidnapped, do they? The rich do. Rule number one. Don't get complacent. Or comfortable. A rich woman in a foreign country should probably have a big Italian bodyguard walking with her. Well, this woman should. I need to take care of that.

It's after nine, and I place a call to my big Italian stud. Five rings and the goddamn machine comes on, pleasantly informing me that I've reached Ernie Mancini. He can't come to the phone right now, but he'll get back to me if I leave a message. My mood sours into anger by the time the message is finished. "Ernie, this is Tuesday night. I'm in Jamaica. I've called you four times already. This is my last call. Pack a bag and fly into Sangster Airport in Montego on Thursday. I'll be at the airport all day waiting for you. You aren't here on Thursday, Ernie, go fuck yourself." I hang up. The son-of-a-bitch.

I HAD A hard time getting to sleep. Something was bothering me, and I just couldn't put my finger on it. Besides not wanting to be alone, there was something else. And now, waking early, looking at the clock on the nightstand showing 5:32, I feel like I'm having a complete meltdown. I'm breathing deeply, trying to control my nerves. My heart is about to pound out of my chest. The dark room is beginning to spin.

Sitting up, I lower my head between my legs and take deep breaths. I used to have what they call anxiety attacks when I was a kid, especially before cheerleader try-outs. My mother told me to do this when I had them. Usually, it worked. By the time I get to where I feel in control, where the room has stopped spinning, it's 5:47.

Reaching for the phone, I dial Ernie's number. Again the machine answers. I hang up.

40

PAUL

After watching the two cabs turn right at the corner, I slowly look around the street to see if anyone else is watching. The street is quiet except for four kids walking to school together. As I turn to go back inside, I see her neighbor looking out the side window. He is a nosy little ass, thank God. I take a hot shower, lock the house up securely, and I'm off to the office to await a phone call.

There is a fax waiting for me from my researcher, and I study it while I devour the two powdered doughnuts. If what I suspect comes to be fact, I'll have decisions to make. His research may help me after the decision is made.

"Costa Detective Agency," I say, picking up the phone on the second ring.

"She didn't go to the Eastern counter for the shuttle, Paul."

"You sure it was her, Sal?"

"I have the picture, Paul. It's her. My cab was a little behind hers, but I caught up to her pretty quick."

"Which airline did she go to?" Damn.

"Delta."

"They have a shuttle?" I ask.

"I was in line behind her at the counter. I heard her ask about a flight to Atlanta. If she could connect to someplace called Cayman, or Gayman, I'm not sure, from there."

"Did she buy a ticket?" Cayman Islands. Top of the list I got from the researcher.

"Paid cash," says Sal.

"Sal, you notice anyone taking particular interest in her? Anyone following her when she left the counter?"

"You mean besides me? No."

"Okay, Sal. Good work. You okay?"

"Yeah, I feel good. Airport is busy, Paul. Where do you think everyone's going?"

"If I had to take a guess, Sal, I'd say Florida. Get the hell out of this cold. Maybe Arizona. Go on back home. You did good."

I called Billy Shute. "You packed?"

"Like the fluted cups at Richie's Slush when the pretty girl uses the scoop to push it down," says my best friend Billy. "Where am I going?"

"You have your passport?"

"This gets better every minute. Yeah, in the suitcase."

"You ever hear of the Cayman Islands?" I ask.

"Didn't the Queen of England just bomb the shit out of them a few years ago? Must have been her time of the month."

With Billy, you never know when he's kidding.

"Those were the Falklands. Not so far south," I say. "This is what you need to do." I read off the list. "Get to the airport. American Airlines. Get a flight to Texas. Dallas if you can. Houston or San Antonio if you have to. There are a few airlines that can get you to the Cayman's from there. Call me when you get to Texas. Let me know what's going on."

"You sure she's going there?"

"As sure as I am about any of this," I say. Which is to say, not very much.

"Don't forget the picture," I tell Billy.

"I got it, Paul. But I have to tell you, this beauty is imprinted on my brain. I'll have dreams about her. She a client, or a client's worst nightmare?"

"Call me from Texas, Billy," and I hang up.

Leaning back in my chair, I find I'm not surprised by what Eileen is doing. I had this premonition while standing on the sand of Nahant in the cold and the wind.

It's the money. It's always the money. Sixteen years doing what I do, seeing every kind of human behavior, more even than psychiatrists I bet, and it usually boils down to the money. It must have slipped out of her that night at the Kowloon when she mentioned an off shore account. She's down played it since then. Like telling me the other day she hadn't thought about the money, when I could tell she had. A million dollars. Eileen is playing a dangerous game for a million dollars. Not that a million dollars is anything to sneeze at.

I would like to think she's taking my advice. That she'll come back with a check and hand it to Joe Glendali in exchange for her safety. Win his favor by returning the money her husband stole from him. As grand a gesture as anyone could make. But I don't believe that's what she's going to do. She'll come back here. Try to convince me we can be very happy. That I should be happy for her. But I think she knows better. If she didn't, she would have asked me to go with her.

That's if she comes back. Even with inflation, you can live pretty good on a million bucks. Go somewhere far away from Glendali and his threats. She probably believes that is possible. I know better.

Picking up the phone, I push the buttons.

"Yeah?"

"Billy," I say.

"Paul. What is it? The cab is beeping for me."

"Send him away and unpack your bag. Forget about it."

"What? You don't want me to go now?"

"Que sera, sera, Billy. Just like the old days when you drove your Corvette like a maniac along the Parkway and I knew my life was in the hands of the Gods. In my whole life, nothing has changed. We'll let the Fates decide what happens next."

BEFORE LOCKING UP the office and heading to Sears in the Saugus Mall to do Christmas shopping, just to get my mind off of everything else, I had called the woman I was playing phone tag with. She had left a message again last night.

She wanted to hire me to investigate her twenty-four year old unmarried son who she suspected of being a homosexual. She impressed upon me that she was only being a caring mother. With all the talk about AIDS in the newspapers and on television, she was only doing what any loving mother would do, she said. I told her I was not taking on any more clients at the moment.

After spending several hundred dollars on gifts, I drove out to Wakefield again and parked down the street from the house I was watching. Six hours there, sitting in a cold car, trying to keep my brain from overload, and nothing happened.

Porter Tufts, and the insurance company he works for, are concerned about the couple who live in the big house and the activity they fear is going on inside it. The house, the cars, the couple, all have policies with Tufts company. Hefty life insurance policies. Tufts believes there may be illegal things being done inside the house. Drugs, to be specific. Maybe worse. There is no evidence there is. Only speculation. My job is to keep a surveillance that could lead to a search warrant.

At six o'clock, I leave and drive into Revere. Harry's is quiet. In a few hours it won't be. There's a young guy over on the stage setting up speakers.

"Solo act tonight?" I ask as Harry places a beer in front of me.

"This guy is fantastic," says Harry. "He sings a Billy Joel song, he sounds like Joel. That guy who sang about the shipwreck, can't think of his name now, he can sing like him. The Italian guys? They love him. Sinatra, Martin, even Al Martino. They yell out sing this or that, and the kid sits at the piano and sings the song and sounds just like Sinatra or Martin or whoever."

"What's his name?"

"Al Williams. Bills himself as the man with a thousand songs."

"He looks Italian," I say.

"He is. Stage name, I guess. You should hang around. He goes on at eight-thirty."

"I have to get some food," I say.

"Hit Kelly's and come back. Bring Eileen. She'll love it."

"Eileen went to the airport this morning."

Harry raised his eyebrows.

"Suppose to be visiting her family in Brooklyn," I say.

"Suppose to be?"

"Can you ever believe what they tell you?" I ask, raising my eyebrows.

"I think, in a relationship, it's important that you can."

"You watching Dr. Ruth again, Harry? How many women have you been honest with? Round number."

Harry smiles. "Not even my mother."

"You think all these women have been honest with you?"

"You made your point, Paul. But I've seen the way she looks at you. She's with family."

And that's why you're a bartender and I'm the Private Dick, I thought to myself.

Finishing the beer, I say, "Kelly's sounds like a plan. It's been a long day. But I'll be in before Christmas."

"You got me something?" asks Harry, smiling.

"A tie."

"I don't wear ties."

I leave a Lincoln on the counter as I slip from the stool.

"Then I'll give it to my brother-in-law."

As I open the door, Rose is standing there. I hold it open for her.

"You leaving?" she asks.

"Been a long day, Rose."

"We could share a long night," Rose says, smiling. She looks to be in a good mood.

I wink at her and leave.

I pick up a clam plate at Kelly's after standing in the cold for fifteen minutes. I eat in the car while watching the the lights of Nahant across the water reflecting on the

Atlantic. These clams have the bellies. None of those sissy strips. Belly clams are best eaten while they're warm. Same with the fries. Cole slaw was the only part of the meal that could have waited for me to get home.

As soon as I enter my condo, I hit the remote. Bruins are on a five game road trip and this game is just beginning the second period. Grabbing a cold one from the fridge, I plop onto my recliner just as the puck is dropped.

Friday night, and I'm home alone watching a game and taking it easy. This is just what my Friday nights have been like for years. Three months ago, that changed. As of right now, I'm not sure what my Friday nights will be like in the future.

41

The weekend passed without any excitement. Saturday I did food shopping, needing things after not being here for a week. Yesterday, I went to Judy's house in Malden. Sal and I watched the Patriots. Judy made a magnificent chicken parm dinner.

Sal wants to get back to work. Judy wants him to take another month. I offered no opinion.

Now I'm at the office, it's Monday morning, and the messages on the machine total four. None of them are from Eileen. Two of them are seeking my services. Before the newspapers reported a gunfight where I killed a man in self defense, the phone rang sporadically. Suddenly, my dance card is filling up quickly.

The first call I make is to Detective Hancock. His was the third message, with a request to call him this morning.

"Detective Hancock," I say when he picks up, "this is Paul Costa."

"Mr. Costa, thanks for calling back. I wanted to speak with Mrs. Landry, stopped over there Friday and Saturday, but found no one home. No one answers my calls."

"She flew to be with her family for the holidays. Is there anything I can help you with?"

"I was just checking to see if she's okay. Any problems with her husband's employer?"

"None. At least not yet. Listen, I appreciate the extra attention to the area. Eileen has plans to be away until New Years."

"Well, when she returns, should you have any problems, let us know. We like to be aware of things that are going on before they escalate."

Couldn't help himself, I guess. "Sure. Merry Christmas," I say before hanging up.

My next three calls were to answer the three calls of those wanting to hire me. The first was to the lady who called last week. We set a three o'clock meeting at her home in Revere for today. The other two, we agreed on times tomorrow.

Leaning back in my chair, sipping at a coffee that's quickly cooling, I think about Eileen. If she has gone to the Cayman's, as I assume she has, she could have gotten the money on Saturday if the bank was open on Saturday. If not, then she would probably go today. What would she do? Close the account with a check for the amount and then deposit up here? Transfer the funds to her bank? She certainly won't be carrying a million dollars on a plane. That was if she was coming back. If she was taking a runner, where would she go? Brooklyn, where her family is? We had never talked about places she would like to visit. Never talked about taking a vacation together. A vacation together was probably something a couple might discuss after they've been together more than three months. So if she took a runner, I had no idea where she would think to go.

That leaves me to second guess my decision with Billy. I had considered sending him to the airport she would be flying into, if Sal told me she wasn't going to LaGuardia. He'd hang out at the airport she had flown into, waiting to hopefully notice her when she left the country and try to find where she was going, the same way Sal had at Logan on Friday. Immediately after hanging up with Billy the first time, I had realized that was a bad idea. It could have been days before she decided to leave. Not knowing how sprawling the airport might be, it could have been an impossible task for Billy. But the determining factor came down to, what did it matter. Either she was coming back, or she wasn't. I'll know soon enough. And I would never interfere in the decision. People have the right to determine the road they take. For good or ill, we all have to decide on our own way.

What if she doesn't run? She comes back here after the holidays. Puts the million in the bank. Anyone questions the money, it's her dead husbands insurance policy, which, she shared with me, he didn't have one. Does she have the patience not to change her way of life? The sense not to draw unwanted attention to herself with extravagant purchases? Not to tweak the interest of the Glendali family who, no doubt, will be watching Eileen with great interest for quite a while? Providing they don't eliminate the problem altogether, can she not draw attention, and the questions such attention would bring.

Eileen seems level-headed, so I'm sure she'll be smart about things. But when it comes to new found wealth, who knows what she'll do. Who knows what any of us would do. It's like hitting the lottery. Complete strangers who live on your street notice that either a rich relative died, or you hit the lottery. They notice. The Chevy becomes a Lincoln. The steps aren't shoveled after a storm, because the owner is on another vacation. A Jordan's Furniture delivery truck makes three deliveries in two months. These things get noticed. Especially if someone is looking for signs.

I SPEND FIVE hours in Wakefield watching the house until the kids come home from school. Both the husband and wife drove off during that time, separately, returning within an hour. The wife carried shopping bags into the house. The husband was empty handed. No one visited. Neither the wife, nor the husband, seem to have a job that takes them away from their home during the day for hours at a time. Big house. Nice cars. Fancy neighborhood. Maybe they hit the lottery.

After leaving Wakefield, I meet with the woman who I have the appointment with in Revere. She lives on a quiet street off of Park, in a tiny ranch in desperate need of painting and upkeep. She appears to be in her late seventies, barely five feet tall, with a pleasant wrinkled face and a plate full of oat meal cookies on her kitchen table, where we are sitting. Her first name is Florence.

Florence Hale.

"Whenever I leave the house, Mr. Costa," Florence says, as she places a glass of milk in front of me, "there is someone following me. For some reason, I have a stalker interested in me. I can't imagine why."

Florence is maybe five or six years older than my mother. In her kindly face, I see mine and my sister's future. Hopefully. The alternative is not something I have often considered. Just one more fact of life most people would rather not think about. "Do you leave the house often?" I ask. The milk and cookies are untouched.

"I do try to get out at least once a week," Florence says. "But, of course, it's harder in the winter."

"Do you have relatives or friends who visit?" I ask.

"My son lives in Connecticut. He works there, you see." Florence is smiling. "And I have a daughter in New York. I was hoping she could make it here for Christmas, but she's very busy. She works for a big bank in the city. Very important job."

A shadow darkens her face. "And friends? Well, they are no longer with us, I'm afraid."

I can see into the living room from where I'm sitting. It appears Mrs. Hale enjoys collecting things, all kinds of things, and seems reluctant to part with any of it.

"Have you seen the person who you believe is following you, Florence? Can you describe them?"

"I'm afraid I can't." Florence is smiling again.

"Male or female? Young or old? Perhaps an old admirer?"

Averting her eyes, she shakes her head. "Oh, my goodness, no. I don't think so. But, of course, it is winter, so with a hat and heavy coat, I wouldn't be able to tell anything about them."

"They are wearing a heavy coat?"

"Well, they must be, Mr. Costa. It is winter. You should have a cookie. They're really very good. I baked them myself." She colors a bit. "Actually, I bought them at the store. But they are very good."

"Have you called the police?" I ask.

"No. No, what would I say? I only have a feeling someone is stalking me. I don't have proof."

"So, you would like me to be around when you go out, to see if you are being followed?" I say. "Just to make sure someone is following you? Is that correct?"

"Oh, someone is stalking me, Mr. Costa. I'm sure of that. But, yes, I want you to watch and catch the person who is stalking me. Can you do that?"

"When do you think you'll be leaving the house again?" I ask.

Florence perks up. "So you'll help me?"

There is no one following Mrs. Florence Hale. She may believe there is. She may imagine there is. Imagination can be just as frightening as reality.

"This is what I can do, Florence" I say. "You call me and tell me when you are leaving the house. If I can, I'll come and watch your back. I'm very busy right now, but I could do this once or twice. Okay? Either I catch the person doing this, or we find out no one is following you. Either way, you can rest easy. Does that sound good?"

"Mr. Costa, that would make me feel so much better. Yes." She fidgets a bit. "We haven't discussed your fee. Are you very expensive? I live on a fixed income, and social security barely gives me enough to survive."

Smiling as I rise, placing a business card on her table that has my business and home phone on it, I say, "We can discuss my fees later, Florence. Not for you to worry. My rate is very affordable"

She places a few cookies in a small, seal-able baggie and places them in my hand at her door. She watches until I turn the corner at the end of her street.

I grab a pizza and head home. A message on the machine reminds me there is a card game tonight. Last one of the year. A bunch of old Saugus cops who get together and still invite me, even though I only had three years on the force. They like having me at their games. I'm usually a sure bet to drop sixty bucks before the night is done.

TONIGHT I ONLY lost forty-seven dollars. But the conversation was good and the laughs never stopped. Worth every penny just to give me a break from thinking about Eileen. As I enter the condo at eleven thirty, I see the light blinking on the machine. One message. Hitting the button, I hear 'Monday, December 18th, 8:12 PM. "Hey, baby, sorry I haven't called before this. Been catching up with family. Miss you, Paul. Do you miss me? I bet you do."

TUESDAY I HAD meetings with the other two messages. Both were women. Both believed their husbands were being unfaithful. I agreed to investigate. Driving back to the office, I stopped at my favorite sub shop and picked up an Italian with everything on it.

While taking on cases so I can pay my bills is something I have to do, I am feeling like what I really need is a vacation. The killing of Ben Landry is weighing heavy on me. Really heavy. I can feel myself slipping into a dark place, a place I have been before, and I'm not sure if keeping busy or taking a break is the best way to keep from sliding further. As far as I know, welders don't have to shoot anyone.

There are two messages on the office phone as I unwrap the sub. They can wait. But the phone rings before I can even take a bite.

"Costa Investigative Agency."

"Mr. Costa, this is Viola Mansfield."

"Yes, Ms. Mansfield." A vivid picture flashes in my head of a very attractive Viola Mansfield. And the memory of a drink refused is remembered.

"I've heard about the trouble Peter is in," she says. Her voice is soft over the line. "Did you have anything to do with him being caught?"

"The insurance company decided to check further. I had nothing to do with it."

"Am I a terrible person for hoping he'll rot in jail?" she asks.

"Is that really what you want, Ms. Mansfield?"

Long seconds of silence.

"Ms. Mansfield?"

"No. No, I suppose not. But I do want him to suffer, Mr. Costa." Again, silence. Then, "I was thinking about what we talked about when you were here, Mr. Costa. I have some other things I can tell you about Peter Gladstone. Things that he told me about people he didn't like. Things he bragged about after...after...when we were alone. If you care to come to my home, Paul, I would share them with you. You could come for dinner."

Before I have a chance to refuse her invitation, Viola Mansfield says, "I saw in the newspaper you had some trouble in Winthrop. You didn't get hurt, did you? I'm sure you don't want to talk about it? But if you do, I'm a good listener."

"You're correct, Ms. Mansfield. I don't want to discuss it. And as far as Peter Gladstone is concerned, I am no longer working for him."

"I see. Well, the invitation for dinner still stands."

"I'm no longer accepting dinner invitations from attractive women, either."

"That's too bad, Paul," Viola Mansfield purrs. "I think you would have enjoyed the menu I was planning. Especially the dessert."

"I have no doubt," I say. "Goodbye, Ms. Mansfield."

Hanging up, I stare at the phone. I can't remember the last time I refused an invitation from a beautiful woman. Probably because it has never happened. Except for a refused drink with the same woman.

I'm feeling edgy, and attack the sub with something akin to anger. I've noticed when I'm agitated about something, food doesn't taste as good as when I'm not. The only thing lacking in the sub was my enjoyment of it. This is the first time I realize I have something more than curiosity going on with this situation with Eileen. I haven't allowed myself to have any feeling since Friday, other than curiosity. Now, I am suddenly aware I am feeling anger. Not boiling, erupting anger, but I am feeling an undercurrent of it. And I don't understand why.

Whatever Eileen decides to do, it is her right to decide it. If that means I am no longer in her life, then that's the way it'll be. I would miss her, but, being real about it all, I have three months invested in a woman I hardly know. Do I have a right to be angry if she decides that three months doesn't require a life time commitment from her? I wouldn't think so. But I've killed a man, so my rationalization of emotions and sense may be skewed just a bit.

It should have never come to that. To the death of Ben Landry.

Did he deserve a beating for the bruises he inflicted on his wife? In my estimation, certainly. Did he deserve to die? No.

I push the button on the answering machine.

"Hello, Paul Costa," begins the first message. "Do you know who this is? Of course you do. Just want to wish you a merry Christmas and a happy new year. And to thank you again for helping me. Things are okay. Just want you to know that. Things are okay. Thanks again."

Dani Gallagher.

Some people figure things out before they turn twenty-one, while others are still searching for answers on their death bed.

That's not to say Dani has all the answers, I don't think any of us do, what with the curve balls life can throw at you, but I do think she might not swing and miss at every curve ball thrown her way.

The second message was a Christmas greeting from the car dealer where I purchased the 300. They leave one every year. On my birthday, I get a message from them offering me a sweet trade in on a new 300.

After creating files on my new clients, I lock the door and head out to join the crowds at the mall to do more Christmas shopping. And to buy a sweater. Every Christmas I purchase a sweater for myself. I don't place it in a box and wrap it, but I do wear it on Christmas day. I have two drawers full of sweaters. Most have been worn once.

FRIDAY AFTERNOON, THREE days before Christmas, I'm tidying things up in the office before leaving. I won't be back until Tuesday the twenty-sixth. There has been no message from Eileen since the one she left Monday night. The only message that's been left on either machine was left by my mother reminding me she is going to my sisters tomorrow, so I don't have to pick her up Monday morning.

There's a quick rap on the door to the outer office, and then it opens. Vincent walks in. He's alone. I'm standing in front of my desk. The Beretta is not within reach. Vincent has something in his hand. It's not a gun.

"Got a minute?" Vincent asks.

I nod and take my seat behind the desk. Vincent sits in one of the chairs in front of me. I can see he's holding a telephone answering machine. I look at it, then at him, with an inquiring look. As usual, his face gives nothing away as to his mood, but there is something in his eyes I haven't seen before and I don't think it bodes well for me.

"Do you know where Mrs. Landry is?" Vincent asks.

"What makes you think she's not at home?" I ask. A question for a question. I hate when people do that, but I'm not adverse to doing it.

Vincent stares at me. His eyes are telling me something, but I can't understand what they're saying.

"Were you expecting her to fly to New York last week?" he asks.

I see no reason to continue being coy. I have the feeling Vincent knows a lot more than I do. I might as well try to find out just what that is.

"Eileen was going to her father's for the holidays," I say.

"She didn't," says Vincent. "I think you may know that."

"What makes you think she didn't?"

Vincent holds up the cord to the machine. I nod to the side wall where there is an outlet. He puts the plug in, then sets the machine on my desk. He stares at me again, his finger hovering above a button. Very dramatic. He pushes in the button.

"Friday, December fifteenth, seven forty-five PM. 'Hey, baby, I'm here. I'll let you know where I'm going when I decide where you'll be rubbing suntan lotion on me. Try to be home when I call, will you please, Ernie. I want to hear your voice.'"

The message stops. It was Eileen's voice. I'm staring at the machine, but I can feel Vincent's eyes on me.

Ernie? Who the hell is Ernie? My face must be asking the same question my mind just did.

"I didn't think you knew," Vincent says, "but I had to be sure."

He pushes the button again.

"Sunday, December seventeenth, eight twenty-seven AM. 'Where the hell are you, Ernie? Listen, I have news. Be home at eight tonight. I'll call you then. Get ready, baby. Mama needs you.'"

Looking up at Vincent, I say, "Ernie?"

"Mr. Glendali's driver."

The kid with the big hair. The kid who was watching me and Eileen dancing at Harry's.

"They been screwing around for about a year," says Vincent. I detect no derision in his voice, no disgust or pity at my unawareness, no elation at my stupidity.

"You knew?"

Vincent sits and shakes his head.

"Like you, no clue. The boss would not have been happy."

I look at the answering machine, then back at Vincent.

"That Sunday Ben and Mrs. Landry were at the house," Vincent says, "I noticed a look pass between Ernie and Eileen as she was leaving. It was a look I didn't understand, because she was seeing you. But it was also a look that couldn't be ignored. So, I put them both under watch. See if anything was going on. Mr. Glendali had made a deal with the Landry's. I didn't want Ernie mucking it up. I'd have a serious talk with the kid if I found out they were fooling around, but first I had to know if they were.

"Two nights later, a Tuesday, Eileen shows up at Ernie's place. Spends a few hours in the dark. Two nights later, the night before court, Ernie is knocking at her backdoor. Leaves after an hour and a half. Then, Friday, the shit storm in court, and eight hours later Ben is dead."

Vincent casually crosses his knee. "So, Mr. Costa, you're the detective. What would you think if you were me?"

I can't make eye contact with Vincent, so I'm staring at the small gray machine that may hold more secrets. I'm thinking about that cold day standing on the sand of Nahant Beach, the thoughts I worried about then, the thoughts I'm having now so much worse.

To answer the shooter, I say, "I'd be wondering why I was in the picture."

"I did wonder about that," says Vincent. "Couldn't understand it. So I decided to ask Ernest Mancini. It wasn't easy getting him to talk. But he eventually admitted that he had been seeing Mrs. Landry for almost a year and that he wasn't happy that she was seeing you. That was on the Friday after Landry's death. Last Friday. I talked to Ernie at Mr. Glendali's house before he left for the night.

"Something felt off," Vincent continued. "So I had Ernie taken to a place in Revere where I had a few of the boys keeping an eye on him. At this point, I still didn't know Mrs. Landry had left town. I had someone go over to Ernie's place to see if she showed up there again. It got cold Sunday night, and he went into the house to warm up and get some sleep. The phone woke him."

Vincent pushes the button again,

"Monday, December eighteenth, eight-fifteen AM," the mechanical voice says. Then Eileen's voice, loud and irritated. "What the fuck, Ernie!" The message ends.

"My guy calls me," says Vincent, "and tells me a woman just left a message on the machine. And he tells me what she said. I tell him to make himself some breakfast and hang out there. I want to know if any more messages come in."

I'm looking at Vincent now. His face gives nothing away. The eyes have changed, though. Harder. Perhaps angry.

"A little after eight that night, he calls me. Says I have to come over. I need to hear the message. Insists that I come. So I do."

Once again, Vincent hits play.

"Monday, December eighteenth, eight oh seven PM. 'Listen to me, you stupid Wop. I don't know what your problem is, but I'm tired of your shit, Ernie. I'll try one more time in the morning. I have the money. Answer your damn phone!'"

Vincent asks, "You know about the money?"

I see no sense in playing stupid. Vincent is obviously way ahead of me.

"She let it slip out one night. Almost a million dollars off shore. Money she thought Ben may have skimmed from the Family."

"And?"

"I suggested she inform Mr. Glendali about the money. That she knew nothing about it, only that she had seen information about it while cleaning the study. That she would return it to him. A show of good faith. He would then see that she was loyal, could be trusted, and there would be no reason for the old man to consider her a threat."

"When she went to Logan last Friday, did you know she was going for the money?"

"I thought she was heading to her family for the holidays. But to satisfy myself, I had her tailed and found out she was going for the money. Nothing I could do at that point except wait for her to return."

"You really thought she'd be coming back here?" Vincent almost smirked. He did know more than I did.

"What do you know?" I ask him.

After staring at me for a long few seconds, Vincent shrugs. "After listening to that message, I went to where we had Ernie. I asked him what Eileen meant by 'she had the money'. He swore he didn't know anything about the money. I impressed upon him that I didn't believe him. It took a while, but eventually he told me about money in a bank in the Cayman's. Money Ben had stolen from the Family. I asked him where Eileen was going with the money. He swore he didn't know. The plan was she would call him when she had the money and a place to move it to. He would then meet her."

"Did you believe him?"

"If he did know where she was going, he took that bit of information to his grave. But we found out."

Vincent pushes the play button once more.

"Tuesday, December nineteenth, nine twenty-two PM. 'Ernie, this is Tuesday night. I'm in Jamaica. I've called you four times already. This is my last call. Pack a bag and fly into Sangster Airport in Montego on Thursday. I'll be at the airport all day waiting for you. You aren't here on Thursday, Ernie, go fuck yourself.'"

"Do you have her?" I ask.

"If she was there, we missed her. I don't think she showed."

"She could be coming back to return the money," I say. "Especially now that Ernie won't be joining her."

"She won't know about Ernie. I think she's on the run. We're making inquiries at hotels in Montego, but I don't think she's on the island anymore. Maybe I'm wrong. I do believe you don't know anything about that."

"A million is a lot of money," I say, "but not enough that a person can run forever. Eileen is smart enough to know that."

Vincent is staring at me without a change of expression, yet I pick up his vibe.

"Ernie give you a different number?" I ask.

"Let's just say the lady could live a very comfortable life for a very long time," Vincent says. "Has she called you?"

"Once, to tell me she's catching up with family."

"Is it too much to expect you might tell us if she calls you again?"

I frown and shake my head. I'm in no mood to play games. "The only thing I'll guarantee you is, should she call me, I'll not be traveling to where she is."

I can't tell if my answer upsets the shooter, or if he expected it.

"There was one more message," he says, and pushes the play button.

"Wednesday, December twentieth, five forty-seven AM."

Nothing.

Vincent stands, unplugs the machine, and turns to go.

"Where do I stand with the old man and the killing of Ben Landry," I ask. I'm now feeling like it was an assassination, and not a matter of self defense.

Vincent stands in the doorway looking down at me.

"Mr. Glendali has told me that all debts are now paid in full," he says.

Vincent ignores my look of confusion and leaves the office.

42

EILEEN

I can't come to the phone right....'

I hang up. I close my eyes, getting my breathing under control, clearing my mind. Looking at the clock again, only a few minutes have passed. 5:51. What to do? Where to go? Exit one plan, begin another. One without Ernie. How the hell did the old man know?

By 6:05, I'm packed and out of the room. At the front desk, I request a cab. I wasn't planning on going to the airport until tomorrow, but that's the thing about plans, isn't it? While the cab driver speeds along city streets like we're out in the country, my mind is racing, too. Where to go next? And should I stay there? If I get there?

At the airport, I'm looking at flight departures. Three destinations catch my attention. The flight I really want isn't until one-thirty. I'm not about to sit in this airport until one-thirty. For all I know, there are men here who have been waiting for me. Or they are on their way. There's a nine-fifteen plane to Miami that isn't full. Benny and I had honeymooned in Miami. It's not like I'm familiar with the city, but at least I've been there. Taking my bag, and the ticket, I find I seat behind a pillar. Two hours. Can I stay safe for two more hours?

There is no way Ernie told Glendali about our plans. No way. Not without being forced to. Thank God we didn't have a set destination. I should have known something was wrong when Ernie wasn't answering his phone. Should have known. I never should have said where I was on his machine. God, that was stupid. Don't get complacent. Never stop thinking. I forgot that rule pretty quick. Think, Eileen, think. Or you're a dead woman.

Sangster Airport is fairly busy. Not like Logan, but busy. I'm acting as casual as I can, but my eyes are everywhere. Every time I shift my gaze from one spot to another, I expect to see Vincent staring back at me. These two hours will be the longest two hours of my life, I do believe.

BY THE TIME the plane lands in Miami, it's a little before noon. While sitting at my window seat, looking down at cloud cover as we flew, I had come up with a plan, and as soon as I entered the airport I got started on it. I was hungry, but food could wait.

At the Hertz counter, I rent a car and grab a map. Leaving the airport, I drive west, picking up route 41 after several rights and lefts in heavy traffic. Traffic thins out quickly as I start the long drive across the state. It's an easy drive, few cars, just keeping an eye out for animals and gators. I have a few hours of peace and for the first time today, I feel myself relaxing. The plan is a simple one. I'm going to drive to Naples and drop off the car. From Naples, I will pay a cab driver whatever he wants to take me to Fort Myers. I've heard people I know talk about vacationing in Fort Myers. I think I will find it to be a place I can blend in. Rent a place in the city center so I won't need a car. Have the money transferred to a bank there. Do nothing to attract attention. Just exist. That's not the life I was expecting I'd be living with almost four million in cash, but it is the one I now must live. I have to believe Joe Glendali knows about the money now. I have to believe that. My life depends on me not trying to convince myself he doesn't.

I had thought about going to the Keys, but I realized the Keys were no different than Jamaica. Being on an island when it's time to boogie, is no place to be. Transportation out is what's important, and the more options you have, the better. I'm not even sure Fort Myers is the best place to be. On the plane, I thought it might be best to get to California. Los Angeles area. People. Lots of people. Lots of options. I have a million things going on in my head right now. I need to relax. Need to rest. Figure things out. Never stop thinking, is the rule, but decisions under duress are not always the best decisions. I'll be all right. Just need to rest.

Ernie. Poor Ernie. How the hell did Glendali know? What about Paul? They'll go after him. With almost four million dollars at stake, they'll go after him. God, they might go after my family. Shit. How does the old man know?

Hey, I didn't steal it. Ben Landry stole it. Glendali wants revenge? Let him go after Ben's brother. Jesus Christ, Glendali was never suppose to know about the money. I should have never mentioned the money to Ernie. Or to Paul. Me and my big mouth. A few drinks, and I'm Little Miss Gabby. This is what always happens. You involve men in your plans, and they screw everything up. Everything.

Maybe I should call Paul. Tell him what's going on. Tell him how much the money really is. Tell him I need him. Need his help. Tell him we could be really happy. I don't know. Just let me get to Fort Myers. Just let me get somewhere where I can rest. Where I can think.

God damn the old man.

43

PAUL

There are moments in everyone's life when they can look back into the past and wonder why they had done something a certain way, or not seen something differently than how they had. Don't we all have regrets at how things had gone at a particular time? I think in retrospect it's easy to see the obvious, but not so easy in the present. Maybe humans are just good at fooling themselves. Better if we were more like animals, sensing when something is wrong. Instinctively knowing when to take a step back, survey the situation, proceed with caution and eyes wide open.

But I'm a forty-seven year old private investigator, working for a hundred and a quarter a day plus, when I have work, so what the hell do I know.

I'm sitting on a bench painted dark green, under an old pavilion along the sidewalk of Revere Beach Boulevard. In front of me, on that patch of sand that extends to the water, is the place where I hung out with my friends thirty years ago, tossing a football around, puffing out our chests and showing off for the babes in the two piece swimsuits who pretended not to notice us.

Across the Boulevard, the Cyclone stood. The white rickety old wooden roller coaster that we all defied death on. Like my youth, it's gone now. All the amusements are gone, the land they occupied too valuable to be just a place for families to enjoy a summer day. Or night. Back in the day, I don't think any of us ever considered that we wouldn't have the opportunity to take our kids on that coaster. Or the Wild Mouse, Ferris Wheel, Tilt-A-Whirl. How could we have known it would all disappear?

Should I have known that Eileen was playing me? In retrospect, maybe. Not at the beginning, I don't think. All innocent enough. She played it cool. Led me to believe we had to move slow. Smart to keep me from going after Ben Landry. Letting the anger build towards him until the third act. I now doubt he ever laid a hand on her. The scene in the courtroom must have been a major blow to Ben. And then what? Did she place the blame on me, beg him to come over to her place knowing I'd be coming, too? The whole scene coordinated like Hitchcock had set it up. And me the easy mark.

It was when Rose had told me that Eileen had been asking about me during the summer, that warning signals should have gone off immediately. But they hadn't. It wasn't until I was standing on the sand of Nahant, after being denied access to Joe Glendali, that that tiny worm began boring into my brain. Too late. The horrible deed was done.

There are flurries swirling around me now, and a cold wind blowing in from the water. The cold matches my mood. It's Christmas tomorrow, I'll spend it with family, and I can't bring this funk into my sister's house. I'll watch my nieces and nephews open the gifts I got them, and I will smile as they thank me. My mother will tell me how much she loves the scarf and glove set, and we will kiss cheeks. My younger sister, Donna, and her husband will thank me for the five bottles of red wine I'll carry into their house, and I'll shake Roger's hand, smile, and kiss Donna. I will do my best to hide this pain, and my best will be enough. It always has been before.

The cold is eating through my coat as I look out over the Atlantic through light that is quickly darkening. A sliver of a moon is appearing over the water. There are no boats out there now. No freighters coming or going on the horizon. It's Christmas Eve. Time for work to cease. Time for those who are fortunate, to thank their God for their blessings. Time for those who are feeling guilt, to seek forgiveness. It is a time for reflection, and self absolution. Were it only that simple.

As darkness descends, I leave the solitude of the pavilion, and walk along the street. No one else is out here walking, and only a few cars drive by. It's a long walk from where I was to where the 300 is parked in Harry's parking lot. The energy spent to cover the distance did little to warm me up as I enter the bar.

There are two groups occupying several tables and they are in a festive mood judging by the laughter that comes from them. At the bar, a man and a woman sit at the far end, they are holding hands and whispering to each other. Rose is sitting alone in her usual spot. Harry is closing early tonight, so Rose must have come in early because of that. Harry is also alone at the far end of the counter.

"What's in the box?" I ask him as I lean against the bar in front of him.

Harry opens the box, which is not much larger than a box that would hold a watch. Inside is a very nice man's wallet.

"From Rose," Harry says. He hands it to me. It is a great wallet. Smells like leather. Black and soft.

I look over at Rose who is looking at us. I mouth a big 'WOW', and she beams.

"I had a visit on Friday from the Don's man, Vincent," I say, as Harry is putting the wallet back in the box. He looks up at me.

"And you're still able to come in here for a beer. Nice to see you two are getting along."

"Yeah. We're besties. He told me, as far as Joe Glendali is concerned, all debts are paid. What did you do?"

"What did I do?" asked Harry. "I paid my debt."

"Your debt?"

"Yeah. My debt. The one I owed you for saving my life that night. And I paid it by collecting a debt that Mr. Glendali believed he owed me, even though I told him a thousand times he owed me nothing."

"I never felt as if you owed me anything, Harry. I don't even understand why you would think that."

"Why, Paul? What's to understand? You gave me my life, that night. I could have been killed, probably would have been killed. Every day since that night is a gift. Given to me by you. I owed you something for that. My life is worth something. Not enough money in the world to repay you. I have nothing of value to give you, that would repay what you gave me. And Mr. Glendali felt the same way. There was nothing he could ever give me that could come close to repaying what I did for him and Marie that night. I certainly never required anything. Just seeing Marie occasionally over these years has been reward enough for me. And even though Mr. Glendali would tell anyone who listened that he was fine being in a debt he felt he owed me, when an opportunity came up where he could grant me something of real value, he made the offer.

"Wednesday night he came in. We spoke. He explained that you had put him in a terrible position. What you had done, killing Ben, regardless of who shot first, was not something to be overlooked. Then he asked, if there was no reprisal against you, would I consider his debt to me paid in full? I was about to remind him that I asked nothing of him. But I looked at this man I have known now for almost twenty years, this man who probably saved my business and has only ever shown me kindness and respect, this man whose body is now shrunken by age and sickness, and I could see that it was very important to him that I accept his offer. So I agreed. And I thanked him, because now I had a chance to pay the debt I felt I owed you. He smiled at that and nodded. What man could understand my need more than him?

"I asked if the reprieve extended to Eileen. He placed his hand on mine and told me not to worry about Eileen. All debts are paid, Paul. No thanks are needed, no more need be said."

Harry is not yet aware that Eileen will not be back. In time, soon, I'll tell him.

Harry took a sip from the coffee he was drinking. "The old man is dying, Paul. Docs say he has maybe two months left. I'm going to miss him. I know the kind of man he was. Know what he did. But he has always been a friend to me."

One of the tables calls out for Harry. He smiles at me, we shake hands, and off he goes. I walk over and sit next to Rose.

"That is a very nice wallet, Rose. I can see Harry loves it." I notice the drink in front of her looks like a cola.

"You think so?" she asks. "Sometimes, with Harry, I can't tell. He's very good at making me think he's happy."

"Well, I can tell, Rose. He's crazy about it."

I know Rose doesn't have plans for Christmas, so I don't ask if she does. She always spends Christmas alone. The accident that took her husband, the truck that crushed their car, killing him and the fetus that she carried, the baby she was going to tell him about on Christmas morning, happened on Christmas Eve, and Rose prefers not to celebrate Christmas.

"Where's Eileen, Paul?"

"Home for the holidays, Rose. New York." She didn't have to know the details.

"You going to your sister's tomorrow?"

"I am," I say.

"What about tonight?" she asks, but without the usual playfulness, without the devilish smile. I look at her. She looks sober.

"Rose..," I begin to say.

"Haven't had a drink all day, Paul. Not one. Never do on Christmas Eve. I'm going to watch *It's a Wonderful Life* when I go home. I wouldn't mind company, Paul. Someone to sit with and watch the movie. Someone who won't expect anything more and who'll leave when the movie is over. Someone who won't ask any questions."

Rose is looking at me. Smiling. Her smile almost breaks my heart. Loneliness is such a terrible thing. It can consume you as you suffer in silence. Little chunks taken from your soul, bit by bit, as time passes. Maybe loneliness is the reason, in some circumstances, that the mind doesn't recognize the truth. Makes a person blind to the plans of others. Leaves a person vulnerable. Rose doesn't want to be alone tonight. I can understand that.

Neither do I.

"What are you drinking, Rose?" I ask.

"Coca-Cola," she says, the smile fading as if I thought she was lying to me.

"Barkeep," I say, tapping on the bar as Harry comes in front of us, "I'll have what this fine lady is having. And make it snappy, sir. The lady and I have a movie to watch."

EPILOGUE

Sal and I are sitting in my living room watching the final game of the first round of the play-offs. The Knicks have fought back from two games down and the series is tied in the best of five showdown. On a lovely Spring day, this game is being played in the Garden. Boston, not Madison Square.

The Celtics have finished second in the Division, one game behind the Sixers, and fifth in the Conference, but New York is giving them all they can handle. And then the unthinkable happens. With time running out, Patrick Ewing, who played his high school ball locally, nails a three pointer, giving the Knicks a 113-101 lead.

"That's it, Sal," I say, standing and stretching, disgusted by what I just witnessed.

"There's still time, Paul."

"Not enough, Sal. Not enough. It's the end of an era, kid. The era of the Big Three is over."

"What are you talking about, Paul? It's not over."

"Over for Boston," I say, "and over for the Lakers, too, I think. The nineties will belong to other teams. Detroit, maybe. Chicago. Maybe Portland. Our run is definitely over. Probably be years before Boston puts another banner in the rafters."

"You're crazy, Paul. Don't talk like that."

I have to smile. It's easy getting Sal worked up. He's watched five banners being raised in the Garden, not to mention the ones the Bruins have won, in his young life, and he refuses to believe that won't continue.

"You want another beer?" I ask as I head towards the kitchen.

In answer, Sal says, "The Celtics will be back on top next year, Paul. You'll see." But there isn't a lot of bravado in his voice. The young always have a hard time watching the end of an era. They have a difficult time understanding that even athletes grow older, their heroes unable to do what they have always been able to do, and do better than everyone else on the planet. It is a life lesson the young all learn.

Athletes, just like everyone else, lose their edge, their quickness, the thing that made them great. Not one pro has ever managed to defeat time. Not one. It must be a bitter pill to swallow, the lessening of their skills, the inability of the body to do what it always could, with the power and speed that it could do it at. With absolutely no choice, the warrior must gracefully, perhaps reluctantly, concede to the passage of time. And then what?

With my hands on the counter, I lean over the sink and stare through the window into the land behind my condo, with a lovely view of a similar building forty feet away. Sometimes when I do this, I see someone in a window just like mine looking out to the back of their property. I don't know their name, even though I've lived here for a dozen years. I know my neighbor next to me, and no one else in the forty units. Isn't that strange?

I've done a lot of staring out of this window the last five months. I've watched the snow melt away and the weeds and grass slowly turn green. I've watched a rabbit nibbling on those weeds and children kicking a ball. Occasionally, I've searched for answers to questions that linger, but find no peace in what I see. There are no answers out there to any of my questions. Maybe tomorrow I will stop pausing here to look out this window, hoping each time to find something different from what I have known since last Christmas.

I'm thankful I've had the case Porter Tufts has had me on. It's kept me going, gotten me out of the house most days and allowed me to not take on more cases. But it will end soon, a warrant will be issued, and the unsuspecting husband and wife will be facing serious jail time. They'll be heading to prison. I'm hoping to escape my self-induced confinement. It's been a struggle.

Reaching for a beer in the fridge, the phone rings on the wall. Sal moans in the living room. Some Celtic player has missed a shot.

"This is Paul Costa," I say as I pop the tab.

No response.

"Hello?" I say.

"Paul. Paul, it's Eileen."

Just when I thought my day couldn't get any worse. Celtics lose, I lose fifty bucks to the bookie, Eileen calls. Seems I hit the Trifecta.

"Paul, I know you must be very upset with me. I'm sorry. I just wanted to hear your voice. Know that you're okay. I miss you, Paul. I really..."

I don't hear the rest of what she has to say as I hang up the phone. I don't want to hear what she has to say. Five months, and not a single day I haven't thought of Eileen. And not a single day that I wanted to talk with her. I've worked it out in my head what she did, and it has taken a toll on me. But I'll get past it. I will. Like a bad disease that ravages you, but you beat it. You never want to go through it again, because you can never forget the pain and suffering it caused you. You will never forget it. Never. And even though you survived it, the memory of what it did to you will always be with you. Always. But you move on, because you must, it's what you do, it's what you have always done, with a prayer to God for the strength you'll need.

"Paul, the game's over," Sal cries out from the living room. "They lost."

There's a lot of that going around, I think to myself. But there will be another season. There always is.

THE END

www.ingramcontent.com/pod-product-compliance
Lightning Source LLC
LaVergne TN
LVHW040222110826
845146LV00004B/1251

9798990804449